DUNGEON

MW00413648

By William D. Arand

Dedicated:
To my wife, Kristin, who encouraged me in all things.
To my son, Harrison, who now lets me type, but only when he isn't yelling at me that he needs to go peepee under the door.
To my family, who always told me I could write a book if I sat down and tried. I've now written quite a few.

Special Thanks to:
Niusha Gutierrez
Caleb Shortcliffe
Michael Haglund
Eric Leaf

Thanks to my Beta Readers:
Robert Hammack
Zach Johnson
Caleb Morris
Bill Brush
Brian Walker

I appreciate you reading through an unedited nightmare

Chapter 1 - Reliving It -

Ryker woke up slowly. He hurt. Hurt all over. Every part of his body seemed to at least have an ache.

And some had more than just an ache.

Groaning, he began to slowly stretch himself out where he lay. His body refused his commands at first, screeching at him and his attempts.

Telling him to stop.

Especially his side where Claire had stabbed him. That was an especially tender point for him right now. For reasons not entirely focused on the wound and the pain itself.

He squeezed his eyes shut, really not wanting to think on the fact that Claire was pregnant with his child on top of everything else.

Except, shying away from Claire and all she represented only brought him closer to the other gargantuan problems he had.

They were named Adele and Diane. They were also both aware of the full extent of what Dungeon, the county, and the dungeon were for him.

They hadn't spoken to him since yesterday when he'd given them the whole rundown. Sparing them absolutely no part of the story he had to tell them.

Part of why they didn't talk to me was that they fell asleep afterward though, right? Then I was working, and then I fell asleep, too.

They're not avoiding me… right?

I guess we'll find out today.

Opening his eyes, Ryker saw that he was going to have to deal with a different problem already, though.

With the fall of Dungeon the city and its rebuilding as Dungeon the dungeon-city, Ryker had been forced to accept some changes.

And a slew of things that had happened at the same time.

The first was that the Dark Lord of the North wanted to speak with him.

Him personally.

Ryker would have to do everything in his power to absolutely avoid ever having that meeting.

Second was that the Queendom of Dale was in a spot where it didn't seem possible for them to survive or make it through intact.

Except Ryker had formally thrown in his lot with Lauren, the rightful queen.

Third, Wynne had clearly been hiding some things from him. Rules for the dungeon that were clearly much more important than she'd made them out to be. They'd almost lost the dungeon core itself for that lack of information. Now, he needed to run her down and find out what that meant, and what had been hidden.

On top of that, the trio of Fairies he trusted the most hadn't checked in with him for a while.

And the last new problem was a big, naked minotaur in his bed. She'd been tasked with being his personal guard. Somewhat of a surprise at the moment, though, was her joining him in his bed. Last he remembered, she had been standing watch over him.

Lifting his head up, he looked around his private bedroom. No one else was here. Looking back at the Minotaur, he laid his head back down on the pillow.

She was as big as ever. Probably close to seven feet tall, if he had to guess. Her chest was massive, both outside her armor and in it. Her black horns pointed upward and away from her head. Very fine, short fur covered her entirely, as she was more a monster than humanoid. Even her face was much more creature like than most people would be comfortable with.

To Ryker, though, she was cute. Like a puppy.

He'd just never tell her that again.

Not to mention her personality was growing on him.

And her boobs are bigger than Marybelle's. Damn.

"I'm awake, and on duty," Meino said, her voice a soft rumble. "I grew tired, and you looked cold."

Her eyelids slid open and she looked at him with her pale, almost colorless eyes.

Then he realized he was actually rather warm. Comfortable.

Normally the room felt cold. Going with it, he pushed up into Meino and stuck his head under her chin.

In all the insanity and with everyone running around in every direction, Meino had stood by him. Stood by him and was prepared to remain.

"You make an amazing body pillow, Meino. Hell of a heater too," Ryker said, snuggling into her.

"That… tickles," said the Minotaur, one big hand coming to rest on the back of his head. "I'm glad you seem more cheerful this morning. You were very sad yesterday."

"Yeah. Long day. Lost a city. The mother of my unborn child tried to kill me and I told two women I'm in love with I've been sleeping with Fairies the entire time, my queen Fairy has been lying to me as far back as I think we've known each other, and I revealed that I am essentially the dungeon to the Dark Lord of the North, and probably both pantheons," Ryker said in a rush.

"Mm. I'll groom you now. It's a bit before dawn. I'll finish before the sun rises. Your Fairies have come to the door throughout the night, but none knocked or entered.

"Your enemy wife also stood outside your door for ten minutes," Meino said. Then she eased Ryker deeper into the bed and moved closer to him, one of her arms draped across his naked middle.

Grooming him seemed to be something she wanted to do constantly. Especially when he showed any distress at all.

In some strange way, though, he'd started to enjoy it.

"Thanks, Meino," Ryker said, closing his eyes and laying a hand on the side of her big head.

At this moment in time, he could use some attention. He was feeling pretty mentally weak right now.

***

When the sun had officially risen, Ryker headed to what he considered his "throne room" to start the day.

He still felt a little funny from being given a bath from head to toe by Meino, but he did seem rather clean for it.

Clean and feeling better.

There'd only been a little bit of awkwardness for about ten minutes when she'd refused to skip a certain area.

Yanking his mind back from that weird encounter, he sat down on the chair Meino had brought for him from his old study. Sitting in front of it was his old work table.

Then he felt Meino practically materialize next to his chair.

A single finger pushed through his hair, as if moving a stray lock around.

"There," said the Minotaur. "I smell your enemy wife and your ally wife. They're waiting in the other room."

Ryker nodded at that. He was glad they wanted to talk to him, but also slightly nervous that they hadn't told him so.

Then again, Arria the will-o'-the-wisp Fairy wasn't working out as a personal secretary. Wynne had already said she was replacing her.

Maybe this was a transition period?

Before he could call up his dungeon and set to work for the day, the doors from the common areas opened. Adele and Diane walked in unannounced, the doors closing on their own behind them.

Adele was dressed in what looked like riding gear mixed with leather armor. It reminded him of when he'd seen her the first time.

Her black ringlets were a bit longer now, though they were arranged prettily. Her bright blue eyes were locked on him even as she approached.

Pretty, self-aware, and with an athletic grace that gave her some serious sexual appeal. Which clashed whenever Ryker caught her picking her nose.

Walking next to her was Diane, the daughter of the pretender queen. Who'd given Adele and Claire to Ryker as toys practically so he wouldn't pitch a fit about Dungeon being taken over.

Diane was beautifully put together again today. Dressed in a sleek black dress that hung perfectly on her. Her dark-brown hair that bordered on black was gathered behind her head in a braid. With dark-brown eyes and a face that had won the genetic lottery, she looked like what any noblewoman would strive to look like. On top of that, she was young, not even twenty yet, and had a full figure in an hourglass to boot.

Immediately getting up, Ryker walked over to stand before them.

They both looked upset and tired.

Hurt.

Knowing he was the cause, Ryker felt true remorse and regret.

Rather than apologize, argue, or say anything, he fell to his knees in front of them.

"I can't say anything more that I haven't already said yesterday," he said honestly. He'd wrung himself out to them already. Told them the truth in all things and laid it all bare. "I love you both. I love Lauren, the queen. I'm pretty sure I love those four silly Fairies as well.

"I betrayed both of you in different ways. And I... don't know what to do. I know I want to work through this, though, and somehow fix... all of this. I just don't know how, or if you'll let me even try to do so."

Adele looked confused. Though also happy at the same time. Of the two of them, he'd done significantly less damage to her. He imagined she would be likely to forgive him, and rather quickly. So long as she didn't take too much umbrage at the fact that he'd been dallying with his Fairies.

Diane on the other hand looked angry, hurt, and confused. There was no warmth in her at all.

"Give me your soul card," she said suddenly.

Ryker blinked once at that, considering her demand.

His soul card was the quick and easy way to his deepest, darkest secrets. It was the cheat sheet for everything about him.

Soul cards weren't given up lightly, or to just anyone.

Often, even husbands and wives didn't share them. It was simply too much information. It might be shared perhaps once in a lifetime.

Truth be told, he couldn't even view his own card. If he was willing to give it to her, she'd be able to read everything about him at any level of detail she wanted.

Looking to his wrist, he casually peeled his soul card out and sent it to Diane.

"Of course," he said simply.

There was a moment of shock on Diane's face, followed by a twitch of a smile, and then she was reading his card. She held it in one hand, using the other to make more information appear as she went.

Thirty seconds in, Adele sighed and came over to Ryker.

She got down on one knee in front of him, staring into his eyes.

"Do you love me?" Adele asked.

Ryker snorted at that and nodded.

"I do, Adele. For all your nose picking, ass scratching, masturbating in public, farting, burping, cursing, and general lack of courtesies. I love you," Ryker said with a smirk.

"I only did that... that in front of you at the inn because you were watching," Adele said, her cheeks turning red. "It was a fun thought, and I wanted to see what you would do."

"Really? That was before we were wed, though. Were you trying to get my attention?" Ryker asked, curious.

"A little. Maybe I'm more adventurous than you thought," she said with a grin, which then faded slowly. "The Fairies... were you sleeping with them before me?"

"Yes. I was. Before I even went to the capital," Ryker admitted.

"Alright. A bit better that they were before me. And if you admitted you'd been sleeping with them, you'd have had to admit to a whole lot more about the dungeon," Adele said.

"Yeah. It would have all come apart. You were already the most knowledgeable about it all there at the end," Ryker said.

"More than Lauren?" she asked suddenly.

"Yeah. You knew more about it all in the end than Lauren," Ryker said.

Adele nodded slowly.

Then she slapped him with what seemed like all the strength she could put into it. The smack of her hand on his face was loud like a whip-crack. Ryker felt like his head was ringing, and his entire body hurt with that hit.

"I'm sorry," Adele said, both of her hands holding his face gently. "But you deserved that. Don't ever lie to me again. We're going to talk more about the Fairies. It's just Tris, Marybelle, Charlotte, and Wynne, right?"

Ryker nodded.

"Good. I like all of them. I'm going to start talking to them about proper etiquette and how to be in a royal marriage, though," Adele said, stroking the cheek she had struck with gentle fingertips. "Lie to me again and I'll leave you. Sleep with anyone else at all and I'll kill you. Do you understand?"

Ryker nodded his head. "Yes. I understand."

"Good," Adele said, and then she sighed. She gave him a warm smile and kissed him quickly. Then she looked up to Diane standing next to her. The woman was still engrossed in Ryker's soul card.

Leaning in close to him, Adele hugged Ryker tightly.

"Be honest with her. Tell her everything, hold nothing back. She loves you far more deeply than you think," whispered the royal cousin in his ear. "Now kiss and make up. The quicker you do that, the quicker I can jump your bones. I just had my monthly time pass by, and I'm kinda feeling needy."

Getting up to her feet, Adele patted Diane on the shoulder and then just left.

I... ok? Ok. Adele and I am... ok. We're ok.

Almost right where we were? Yeah.

Wait, did she just say she wanted sex?

Feeling his heart unclench somewhat, Ryker looked up to Diane and waited. He dared not move or say anything. He would give her all the time she needed, and then more if that was what she wanted.

The very idea of her possibly leaving him caused him considerable distress. She'd done nothing but good by him, and he'd betrayed her.

Finally, after perhaps ten minutes, Diane looked up from his soul card, but she didn't let it go.

"Everything you said yesterday was the truth," she said.

"Yes."

"The Fairies came first," she said.

"Yes."

Diane brushed her thumb back and forth across his card. While she held it, any answer he gave her or thought would reveal everything of himself to her at the same time.

"I want to ask you questions," Diane said. "I want to ask them while holding your card. I'm hurting... Ryker. I love you.

"I love you, I'm hurting, and I'm angry. I'm so angry that I need to understand. I don't know what's going on anymore.

"Can I ask you questions and hold your card?"

"Of course, Diane," Ryker said. "I said I want to make this work. I do. I—"

Ryker paused and looked away, then back up to Diane. "I love you. I truly do. I don't know... how it hap—No, I do know how it happened. It was when a young woman who'd just become a wife decided she wanted to learn how to farm with her husband. That was the moment it changed for me."

Diane couldn't seem to fight the smile that blossomed on her face. Then her eyes dipped down to the soul card in her hand, and her smile grew wider.

"Did you ever consider killing me?" Diane asked, her eyes going back to his.

"Of course. Just as you probably considered killing me. But that was before your mother married us," he said.

"Did you intercept communications from my mother to me, and vice versa?" she asked.

"Often. I never removed any of the personal messages from her to you, but I did remove all the terrible things she said about me. It was mostly to find out information about where her troops were so I could help close out the war faster," Ryker said.

Diane's eyes were still glued to the card, and she nodded her head a bit.

"You killed Robyn? The paladin?" she asked.

"I was responsible for her death, but I didn't kill her. I accidentally trapped her soul in a core and then released her into the dungeon after a while," Ryker admitted easily. "I couldn't let her kill Lauren."

"Do you... love Lauren?" Diane asked.

"I do. She's treated me like a person from the very start. She always asked me permission to do things and treated me like an equal. Never anything less. We... connected," Ryker said.

There was a strange smirk on Diane's face at that, her eyes reading his card.

"What are your plans going forward?" she asked.

"I'm going to... I don't know, actually. I know I want to help Lauren. I want to crush the church of light and the dark. I want to put the Queendom of Dale back on the right path," Ryker said.

That was all the truth. He would do what he had to do to preserve Lauren and her kingdom. If only for her.

"Beyond that... I want to kill a number of people who wronged me. Punish the adventurer's guild. That's... about it, really.

"Oh. Find Claire. I need to talk to her and figure things out if possible."

"What? She tried to kill you. Why?" Diane asked, looking up from his card.

"She's pregnant," Ryker said with a small shrug. "Call me an idiot but I can't overlook that."

Diane glanced down at his card, her mouth a frown. Then she shook her head almost sadly.

"I understand... in the same way that you couldn't overlook Claire... I must pose this question to you.

"Ryker, if I asked you to spare my mother, my family, my home... to grant them mercy, clemency, and let them have things they have no right to... would you let me do that?" Diane asked.

Ryker had to stop from immediately responding. He wanted to carefully consider her words before answering. It wasn't a simple question.

She was supposing her mother would lose the war. Lose it, and terribly so. Would Ryker fight Lauren directly to help out Diane's family?

He didn't want to. Didn't want to do a damn thing for them. If it was up to him, he'd rather see them swing by their necks on a short rope.

But for Diane...?

If it's for you, Diane. I'd do anything I could to help you preserve your family.

Smiling up at her, he nodded his head slowly.

"For you, I would do all that you asked. If only to make sure you were happy," Ryker said. "I don't think for a minute they deserve anything other than a swift death for what's happened. But for you, I would go against Lauren herself on their behalf."

"Did you even consider for a moment letting me die to that assassin?" Diane asked.

"No," Ryker said immediately.

Diane's eyes went to the card. Finally, she looked back up and released it.

It fluttered in the air, then vanished.

Once it was gone, she slowly knelt down in front of Ryker, her knees pressed to the same stones as his own.

She gave him a small, tight smile.

"I love you, Ryker. I'm not as sure as you are when it happened for me, but it did. My family is going to be torn apart by this, but I'm going to trust in you to help me save them.

"I don't like that you were sleeping with the Fairies while married to me and Adele, but... they were first, so I can forgive it to a degree. I am still hurt by it, though. You'll need to work to make me feel better."

Ryker nodded quickly to all of that.

"I'll ask Adele if she doesn't mind me being there when she talks to the Fairies. It'll be good for us all to start a dialogue now," Diane said, and then she sighed. "I want to slap you. Slap you harder than Adele, even — but I don't think I can. Instead I'll say this: you genuinely hurt my heart. You wounded me, husband. Terribly."

Ryker grimaced at her words. Half wishing she'd slapped him instead.

"But as I love you, and I do want this to work, we'll get through this. But... I have to know," Diane said, then leaned in close to him. Pressing her forehead to his. She snuck in a quick kiss and then smiled at him. "Did you really let Meino... groom... your privates with her tongue?"

Ryker blushed a deep, dark crimson. Apparently that had been on his soul card.

"Goodness. And you liked it too, or so the card said," Diane said with a strange little chuckle. "Was it rough? I've never seen a Minotaur tongue before."

Well. At least she's forgiven me.

And she's laughing.

That's... good... right?

Chapter 2 - Rules -

Diane had set off back for her own private room. Looking far more settled than he thought she would.

I don't think I would've taken it as well if I were in her position.

Then again, she has a very different mindset than I do. I'm a trained wizard become farmer turned Dungeon. She's been raised her whole life to be a duchess. One just like her mom.

That'd put a different strain than the normal load on anyone, wouldn't it?

Shaking his head and clearing his thoughts, Ryker considered what to do next. He'd briefly checked in with the city of Dungeon and found that almost all of its citizens had remained. It was functioning much more closely to how it had before the church of light or Veronica had brought ruin to the county.

That wouldn't last.

Couldn't last. At some point, Ryker would have to reopen the dungeon to the public. Especially if he wanted to succeed in his goal of punishing Chadwick, Veronica, and everyone else who'd raised a hand to Dungeon and Dale.

And then his personal revenge.

Ryker leaned forward in his seat, looking at the magical construct of Dungeon in front of him. It had everything laid out, including current monster routes, people who didn't belong, and citizens.

Everything was as it should be.

Even the emissary of the Dark Lord of the North and her two guards were outside dungeon boundaries.

He had no idea where they'd gone, though, or if they'd actually left.

Chadwick and his forces had hightailed it to the south, putting them outside the borders of dungeon but also much further away from Queen Lauren.

What about walls? That'd work, wouldn't it? Make a wall seed... expand and expand and expand... but first...

First... Wynne.

Getting up out of his seat, Ryker pushed a hand to his neck and bent it to the side. With an audible pop, he felt some of the tension bleed away.

"Are we leaving?" Meino asked.

"Yeah, I need to go see the Fairies," Ryker said.

"Ah. Alright. I'm glad you made up with your enemy wife and your ally wife," Meino said.

"Why do you call them that?" Ryker asked, looking at the Minotaur.

"Because that's what they were," Meino said with a shrug of her big shoulders.

"Use their names, Meino. They use your name," Ryker said.

The Minotaur's face twitched and then she let her shoulders sag slightly, her head bowing.

"You're right," said the Minotaur. "I'm sorry, my lord king. I will use their names. It's hard sometimes. I feel like... I'm many different people. I hate... your wives... and at the same time I think they're beautiful."

"I often find myself confused. I hear... voices. Saying different things."

Ryker considered her words. They made sense of course, given how he'd made her. Meino was a living amalgamation of many memories.

Opening himself up to the spells he had used to make her, he carefully took hold of her pattern.

What made her Meino.

He could see there was a change. Parts of the pattern he'd laid down were being shoved out by new bits he hadn't put in himself.

Looking at them closely, they felt organic to him. They were growing in curves and swirls rather than the rigid interlocking bits he built with. Stroking a single channel of one with his senses, he got the impression of what it was.

An overwhelming need to groom. To groom the one she loved and protected. To groom him constantly.

Ah. This is all part of her forming a soul. Her pattern is shifting because of that. She's… becoming alive.

"Meino, I can fix it. Would you like me to? You might feel a bit funny for a while. Might even feel like you lost a piece of yourself. But it's the piece that's causing you problems," Ryker said, still peering at her pattern.

"Do you want to fix me?" Meino asked.

"I want you to be happy. I can see what's causing you distress, and I can fix it. It's up to you, though."

"Then… yes. Fix me," said the Minotaur.

With a thought, Ryker snipped away all the old bits of the pattern she no longer used, though he was careful to confirm each piece before he did it.

When he was done, her pattern looked much cleaner and seemed to flow better within itself. Its energy had no bottlenecks any longer.

Disconnecting himself from his magical hold over Meino, he looked to her.

She was staring down at him, her eyes wide.

"They're gone," she said. "The other voices."

"Yep. All gone. Now you're just Meino. Ok. Off to the Fairies!" Ryker said, moving quickly. He was just barely starting to be able to identify when a grooming session was coming.

This would feel like an opportune time to her, he imagined.

Slipping out of his throne room and into the adjacent hallway, Ryker moved fast. He could hear Meino's heavy steps behind him, and they were getting closer.

She's too damn fast!

Turning the corner, he made his way to Wynne's home. Reaching her door, he kept going, having at the last minute decided to see if Marybelle was free first.

She'd been his hidey hole and confidant. Sometimes he'd slip away from everything just to be with her, tell her his worries, and seek solace in her. Sometimes in her bed, sometimes just in her presence.

Today he'd take either. Or both.

Knocking gently on her door, he waited.

"She's inside," Meino said softly. "She wasn't expecting you, and she's panicking."

"One minute!" Marybelle called through the door.

Smiling, Ryker looked up to Meino. She was staring at the door, her head tilted to one side.

"So, can you smell her? Is she talking? How do you know this?" Ryker asked.

"Scent, mostly." Then she turned her head to look at him. "Thank you, Ryker. My head feels much more mine, now."

"Course, Meino," Ryker said, patting her on the side of her hip.

"I want to groom you," she said suddenly. "Now."

"Later," Ryker said.

Meino nodded, then suddenly took a step to the side.

The door opened, and Ryker was staring into Marybelle's face.

Her curly brown hair had been styled and was bound with small blue ribbons. Black eyes regarded him, her lips a wide smile.

He'd once thought of her as one beer away from being a cute human. Now he only thought of her as a beautiful Hobgoblin that he tried to bed whenever he had the chance. Though her racial heritage only really showed itself in her nose and cheekbones.

It didn't hurt that she had an impressive bust and a wicked figure that could overwhelm her clothes if she wasn't careful.

Wearing a white dress that wrapped tight to her body, she stepped to one side and gestured inside.

"Come in, dear. I'm so happy to see you," Marybelle said.

"Thanks," Ryker said, walking into her home. "I was hoping to get you alone. I needed to run some things by you, see what you thought."

Closing the door, Marybelle caught up to him and then guided him to her living room. She sat him down in a rather tasteful love seat.

"Of course. I'm always happy to entertain you, especially alone. Can I get you anything?"

"Water would be nice. You sure I'm not bothering you?"

"Not at all, dear. I'm genuinely excited and pleased that you came to see me. I'm flattered, in fact," Marybelle said, stepping out into the attached kitchen. "You haven't even seen Wynne, Tris, or Charlotte yet. You came to me."

"That's true. What can I say, I'm a Hob addict," Ryker said, settling into the love seat.

The clink of glasses and then a liquid being poured was all he got back in response. He got a definitive strange feeling from her in the dungeon sense, though. As if his comment had hit something sensitive.

Coming back out, she handed him a glass and then sat down next to him. Practically in his lap. Then laid her head on his shoulder.

"Talk to me," she said, taking a small sip from her own glass.

Chuckling, Ryker laid an arm around Marybelle's shoulders and pulled her closer, taking a sip from his glass.

"I'm not going to ask you to tell me the rules, but I want to know why Wynne didn't want to tell me about them," Ryker asked simply.

"Because it's her fault. That's all," Marybelle said. "She's just afraid you'll not be able to forgive her."

"Is that... is that all?" he asked.

"Yeah. That's all it is. It just got harder and harder for her to tell you. Too much to unpack and explain, with her being the center of it all. I'll leave the details to her, but that's all it is," Marybelle said.

"Oh. I guess that's... all I needed then," Ryker said, laying his cheek on the top of Marybelle's head. "You're an amazing woman."

"I'm not a woman," Marybelle said.

"Huh? Pretty sure you are."

"I'm not, though. I'm not a woman. I'm not a Hobgoblin. I'm a Fairy," Marybelle said, her tone becoming a touch brittle.

"I haven't... I haven't been in my body in a very long time now. I can't even imagine being in my body anymore. This feels like me now," Marybelle said, one hand pressing into her chest. "I'm very me in this body. I breathe, I eat, I drink, I use the bathroom, I feel lust, I have sex, I sleep."

Her hand dropped from her chest and landed on Ryker's knee. Gently, she began to massage it with her fingers. "I love. I feel jealousy when you sleep with Charlotte or Tris. It pains me. But then I'm overjoyed when you come and get into my bed with me and love me.

"And none of this is me."

Getting up, Marybelle set her glass down on the coffee table. She walked over to a cabinet off to one side. Opening it, she took out a four-foot-long, elaborately decorated box. It was covered in ribbons, bows, and fluttering fabric.

Setting it down on the table, Marybelle undid the locking mechanism and opened it.

Inside was a three-foot-tall Fairy laid in a very comfortable-looking bed. To Ryker it almost had the feel of a coffin.

"This is me, and I couldn't feel any further removed from it," Marybelle said, scooping her own limp form from the box. "This is me, Ryker. And I know I'm not alone in this feeling. All of the Fairies feel this way. Those of us who have been with you longer, more so. The Imps are starting to feel the same.

"There's an actual side business that sells pretty 'Fairy Boxes' just like this, where we store our... our bodies."

Ryker held his hands out to her, as if to take her body. Marybelle hesitated, then gave herself to him, gently laying her body in his arms.

Cradling the small body, Ryker peered at her face.

There was no resemblance at all. It was a very pretty Fairy—they all were—but it didn't look like Marybelle.

"I'm a Fairy. I'm not a woman, or a Hob," Marybelle said. "And I'm terrified that if I go back into that body, I'll lose who I am. Because I'm not a Fairy anymore. I realized it when I died at the temple battle. I lost my body. I refused to let my soul go back into my Fairy body. I... hovered around in the dungeon sense instead while I recreated my avatar. My real body."

Gently smoothing the Fairy's hair back, Ryker laid her back into her Fairy Box, as Marybelle had called it.

He adjusted her clothes and made sure she looked comfortable. Then he closed the lid, locked it shut, and put it back into the cabinet for her.

"My personal suggestion," Ryker said, closing the cabinet doors. "Lock your Fairy body down deep in the dungeon. Deep where no one can ever get to it. Treat it as if it were your core. Your soul."

Marybelle nodded her head slightly after a second.

"As far as who you are—Hob, woman, Fairy, whatever. You're Marybelle. You are you. Your flesh changes nothing of that," Ryker said. "Right now, you're just a woman with a Fairy as her heart, and the body of a beautiful Hob. That's it.

"Honestly, I'm a little jealous. I'd love to be able to remake my own self, instead of One-Pump the wizard," Ryker said with a grimace. "Oh, and as to loving me. I love you, too."

Marybelle was staring at him, her face looking confused and disbelieving.

"You do?" she asked.

"I do."

"Even though I'm not real?"

"I love you as you are, both Fairy and Hob."

"Show me?" she asked, slipping out of her dress and letting it fall to the floor.

"Gladly," Ryker said with a grin.

***

Stepping out of Marybelle's home and closing the door, Ryker adjusted his collar. Marybelle had been very needy today in bed.

The after-sex cuddling and pillow talk had been intense, focused on her Fairy body again.

As he had reassured her and over and over, she'd finally seemed to settle down.

"She sounds happy," Meino said from the side of the doorway. "She's giggling right now."

"Yes, well. We had a good talk," Ryker said, turning and marching off toward Wynne's door.

"Are you going to have a good talk with Wynne, too?" Meino asked, a hint of amusement in her voice.

"Don't know, but... let's hope not. I don't think I'm ready for that," Ryker said, a hint of concern in his voice.

"Stamina potion. Helps fix that," Meino said, moving to the side of Wynne's door. "One of those... memories I don't know how I know, but I know."

Really? Huh. Never heard that.

Can't hurt.

Creating a stamina potion from nothing but the dungeon mana, Ryker downed it quickly and then had the dungeon take back the glass it had come in.

Squaring his shoulders, he lifted his hand and knocked twice on Wynne's door.

"Ahhh? One second," Wynne called from inside. "Ryker!?"

"Yep. It's me."

"Why...? You didn't even... just... ah. Ok," Wynne said, right on the other side of the door. It was obvious she was flustered, even without him seeing her.

The door opened slowly. Wynne appeared in the gap, her home dark and unlit behind her.

She was dressed in what looked like a very simple black nightgown. There were faint rings around her eyes, and she looked very tired.

"Good morning, my lord king," Wynne said, inclining her head to him but not making eye contact.

"Good morning, my darling queen. May I come in?"

"Of course," she said, and shoved the door a bit, stepping behind it.

Moving into Wynne's home, he looked around.

Her home was clean, but utterly dark. It was as if she'd only just woken up, but Ryker would swear it was much closer to noon by now.

"Wynne, go sit down," Ryker said, pointing to her living room couch. Then he generated a small globe of mage fire and sent it toward the middle of the room. Everything was lit with a gentle blue glow.

"Ryker... could we do this later? I'm—"

"Sit," Ryker said, interrupting the very tall and very lovely Fairy. Trooping by him, she sat down, folding her hands in her lap and looking quite down-spirited.

Wynne was the single biggest Fairy he'd ever heard of. Standing at five foot one, she was life sized now. Her wings were equally as large, fluttering behind her slowly almost all the time.

Black hair hung around her dream-like features, unbrushed and somewhat tangled. Her nightgown did nothing for her, but the sheer size of her bust and hip made it look wonderful. She was comparatively on par with Marybelle, if not a hint bigger.

Coming around behind her, Ryker eased her wings out of the way, brushed her hair away from her shoulders, and then began to gently rub her back.

"Wynne, you're the queen of my dungeon. Lauren is my sovereign, but you're my queen here," he said. He'd had a lot of time to think about how to handle this. There was no denying he was angry at Wynne. Upset. Hurt.

He felt betrayed by her.

Much in the same way Adele and Diane had probably felt with him.

If this had happened before today, before he'd become the lord of a dungeon, before he'd gotten married. He'd have probably written her off in his "to kill" list and moved on.

Diane had forgiven him. Adele had forgiven him.

How could he not forgive his partner? If even the rest of the entire world burned down, he and Wynne would forever be bound.

"Wynne," Ryker said, his fingers pressing and rubbing along her shoulders and neck.

"Yes?" she asked, melting into his hands and her seat. Her voice sounded nervous.

"Tell me what's wrong with the rules. You said they were much lesser than this. We seem to be getting crushed by them," Ryker said.

Wynne moaned as Ryker eased her head to one side, rubbing into the base of her skull.

"The rules are the same," Wynne said, her shoulders slowly drooping. "It's just... we're being held to them very strictly."

"Why?" Ryker asked, slowly easing Wynne's head the other way, all the while massaging her neck.

"Because of me. Because of all the Fairies," Wynne muttered. "With so many Fairies in one dungeon, all tied to the same core, the rules matter. All of them. I tried playing with their bindings—" She stopped talking, moaning softly as Ryker worked her neck out. "And how many we actively had in the dungeon. The moment I took us past nine, the stipulations hit us. There's... nothing I can do."

"Alright. So, we have to be very careful of the rules at every level. Is that about it?" Ryker asked, easing her head straight back till she was looking up at him.

Pressing into the hinge of her jaw with his thumbs, he continued to rub at the back of her head.

"Yes," Wynne said, staring up at him. He swore her eyes were actually tearing up. "I'm sorry. I almost cost us everything. I saw the chance to get my revenge and I took it. I took it all.

"I probably control over nine-tenths of the dungeon Fairies in all of existence. And I've already captured half of the dungeon Imps. Out of their entire race. I've wiped out entire villages and claimed them. And... I can't stop."

Ryker thought on that as he moved his fingers carefully back and forth.

"Why?" he asked.

- 15 -

"Why? Why can't I stop?" she asked, to which he nodded. "I still feel... empty. Nothing's changed. Nothing... I want to burn their villages down and take them all, but... there's nothing left. I'm Queen of the Fairies, and I still want them all to suffer."

"Do you, though? Do you want Tris, Charlotte, Marybelle—Arria, Sierra, and all the hundreds of others I can't even name—to suffer?" Ryker asked.

Wynne frowned at that, her eyes clouding as she gazed up at him.

"No," she said softly.

"I still want to desperately murder Rob," Ryker said. "But I find my need to actually kill... considerably lessened. I regret... I regret killing Gavin and Nikki. I regret it not for just harming Lauren, but because despite being shitty to me, they didn't deserve what I did. All I had afterward was an empty feeling. Like being hungry after eating a feast."

Wynne nodded her head a bit. "That's exactly it."

"Then you should begin to consider the same I have. That revenge isn't what you really wanted," Ryker said with a smirk. It was something he'd only come to realize after almost losing Diane and Adele. He'd really only wanted to be included and cared for. It sounded patently saccharine and naive, but it was true.

Wynne's face turned into a classic example of a pout, tears leaking from the corners of her eyes. He'd never heard of a Fairy actually crying.

"Forgive me, my king?" Wynne asked.

Ryker gently patted her cheek once.

"Of course, my queen. Just... confide in me. Much as my wives told me this morning, no more secrets. Ok?" he asked.

"Ok," Wynne mumbled.

Then Ryker leaned down and kissed her. Her lips were soft and warm.

After a few seconds, though, he forced himself to pull back from her.

"Let's go clean you up a bit and put you back to bed. You look like you could use some more rest, my poor tired queen," Ryker said.

Wynne nodded, but then her hand came up, clamped to the back of his head, and pulled him down into another kiss.

Chapter 3 - Orders and Promotions -

Ryker was on his way back to his throne room again.

In the end, Wynne had wanted more from him, but had been too tired to do anything. For which he was secretly grateful. He didn't want to test out the stamina potion Meino had suggested.

If it ended up failing, it had the potential to just make Wynne feel worse.

The Fairy queen had practically chapped his lips, though, with how much she'd kissed him. Right up until he tucked her into her bed and she immediately passed out.

"That was sweet," Meino said, clomping along beside him.

"You know it's a little weird that you can hear that well through doors, let alone apparently smell through them," Ryker said.

"Tris can almost hear as well as I do. Her sense of smell is terrible though," Meino said, not really responding.

"Speaking of Tris," Ryker muttered.

Ryker opened himself to the dungeon sense that was the massive spiderweb of connections to and from the core. He could feel and sense everything and everyone throughout all of Dungeon.

From Robyn in her temple, praying to deities that wouldn't respond, to Arria processing new Dungeon Imps who had just been captured.

Everything immediately stopped for several seconds as he arrived, however. He'd once been told that everyone knew whenever he was fully present in the dungeon.

"Tris, Charlotte, Marybelle," Ryker said gently into the dungeon sense. "Come see me in person. Bring your lieutenants with you, or those you would make so. You'll need a total of six for each of you."

He received three magical acknowledgments.

After entering his throne room, he went and sat on his not very throne-like throne. Right before he actually disconnected his dungeon sense, he realized there was something he should do first.

He could generally sense what Robyn was doing at the moment. She was kneeling in the unbuilt temple of light.

Praying.

"Robyn," Ryker said, sending it directly through the connection she shared with him. He decided to be a bit more formal with her today. "I greet you on this day. I wish you well and thank you for your assistance yesterday. Have you made any progress in your quest?"

Her head lifted, and he could practically see the smile on her face.

"None at this time, my dungeon lord. I am... tranquil and unperturbed. I have slain many of the false one's religion. I could feel the taint of him in their souls," Robyn said. He could feel the fiery vengeance burning inside her. If he were to give her a designation, it'd be a spirit of retribution. "...ot responding to me. But I shall continue to try. The faith and magic given to the priesthood remains a powerful tool and ally. I must only catch their attention. Then I can begin to build."

"I'm glad to hear things are working out. Is there anything else you need, Robyn?" Ryker asked. At the same time he'd been speaking with her, he'd been inspecting her core as gently as he could.

Everything appeared as it should. Energy was flowing freely from her core to her avatar and back. Though there was one notable change he noticed. The link she had to the core had gone dark, though the one she shared directly to Ryker had doubled in size.

I'll need to ask Wynne about that.

"No, my dungeon lord. I am well cared for. I appreciate the soldiers you've given me to rebuild with. They are dedicated and faithful to you, and therefore to me," Robyn said.

Taking a second, Ryker checked those around Robyn.

They were dungeon imps. One and all. The magic coming from them to the core and then to Ryker was also different. It felt like fanaticism. Towards Ryker himself.

"Of course, Robyn. You're my champion, and the only paladin in the entirety of the dungeon. Only ask, and it shall be yours," Ryker said. "Though, I must go for now. I'll visit you in person later."

"Yes, my dungeon lord," Robyn said, lowering her head again in prayer.

Coming back to himself, Ryker opened his eyes just in time to find Meino leaning over him.

"Meino, please, not right now? I'm going to have the girls show up in a second," Ryker said, reaching up to put both hands to the sides of her mouth. "You can groom me all you want later. I promise."

Pale blue eyes watched him, weighing his words. "You don't dislike it?"

"What, being groomed? It's not so bad. Your tongue is a bit more muscular than a human's, certainly bigger, but it's just as soft. You've never left any bits of anything on me afterward, either. And your breath never smells, which is a plus," Ryker said, pushing her head backward. "I just need to be ready for them is all. Promise."

Nodding her head, Meino backed up and took her place on his right as his guard.

"My breath doesn't smell because I brush after I eat. Just in case I get a chance to groom you," said the Minotaur.

Oh. Huh.

Looking to his table, Ryker began to make small corrections to the dungeon. Fixing broken things from the battles, adding patterns, and building paths for those who would dare to enter.

Slowly, he was beginning to section off the parts of the city where his citizens dwelled and the parts where adventurers, soldiers, and treasure seekers would travel.

It'd take time, but he planned on having a city for his people, and the dungeon city for those he wanted to kill or train.

The doors opened to admit Charlotte, Tris, and Marybelle. Then, swinging back on their own, the doors clicked shut.

Closing the pattern for the mini-boss over the inn he was working on, Ryker stood up and walked over to stand in front of them.

Marybelle looked unchanged from when he'd last seen her, though she was wearing thick leather armor.

Standing between Tris and Marybelle was Charlotte.

Dark midnight-black hair, and eyes the same color. With a skin tone that one would call a step or two above pale at best.

Charlotte was also incredibly pretty, athletic, and proportioned in a fun way. She was no Marybelle, but she wasn't lacking either. The light leather armor she wore hid a lot of that, unfortunately.

She was Ryker's assassin, rogue, and thief all in one. Somehow, she'd also become the center of this trio of Fairies.

To her right was Tris.

Standing tall in her Elven self, she was the picturesque alien beauty Elf women tended to be. Light skin, lovely green eyes, and short white hair, wrapped up in a personality as straightforward as the longsword always on her hip.

Adventurous, to the point, and loyal.

"Thank you for coming, but… where are your lieutenants?" Ryker asked, looking past them.

"They're outside," Charlotte said, her brow furrowing.

"We thought you'd want to tell us whatever it is privately first," Tris said, jumping straight to what Charlotte was trying to work around. "You met with Adele and Diane this morning. We think they're going to tell you to stop… to stop… being with us."

Charlotte looked pained, and for the first time in his memory, Tris was wearing a neutral mask that she clearly forced on herself.

Marybelle had a small smirk and seemed undisturbed.

Considering I just gave her a solid tumble, she clearly knows better.

"I met with Diane and Adele. They're well aware of all three of you now, and that I'm sleeping with you. Chances are, they're going to start beating manners into you. Probably try to get you to behave as if you were in a royal marriage," Ryker said. "This is your opportunity to get out if you want out. Otherwise they're probably going to consider you as my wives."

"Oh?" Marybelle said, her interest suddenly brought right back to the conversation. "Then I'll be the first to say I'm going to happily keep welcoming you back into my bed."

"Me too," Tris said, looking annoyed that she hadn't been the first to say it.

Charlotte was smiling while staring at Ryker, her head tilted to one side.

"Can I ask you a question, Ryker?" she asked. It was the first time in a long time she'd said his name directly like that.

"Of course."

"Did you tell them about us, or did they find out on their own?" she asked.

"I told them. Told them I'd been lying with you three before I'd even married them. That you were in my life before they were," Ryker said.

Charlotte's eyebrows went up at that, but she didn't say anything to it.

"Then I accept my position as your wife. I look forward to speaking with Diane as an equal. I have many questions I'd like to ask her about you," Charlotte said.

"Great. Fuck if I care," Ryker said. "I asked you here because I have plans. First, I need to change your bond spells."

Each Fairy looked a bit nervous at that statement.

"I'm going to pull you out of going from the core to Wynne to me. Instead, to me directly," Ryker said. "And through me, to the core."

"You're... making us equal to Wynne?" Marybelle asked.

"She'll still be your queen, and you will defer to her wishes, but... yes, on a binding level. You'll be her equal. She's already aware of this. Concerns?" Ryker asked.

All three women shook their heads.

"Great," Ryker said, then plucked their bonded spells from the core. All three women flinched, and Marybelle fell to her hands and knees. Tying their bonds to himself took only a single second, and only a second more after that to lash them into his connection to the main dungeon core.

"That wasn't... fun," Marybelle said, panting.

"Sorry. But it's done. And it was needed," Ryker said, then turned to Meino. "Can you go get their lieutenants?"

"Yes," said the Minotaur, heading for the doors.

Ryker went over to the Fairy women, offering Marybelle his hand. "Would you like seats? A drink?"

"Yes, Dear. Thank you," Marybelle said. She grabbed hold of his hand and pulled herself upright.

With a thought, four chairs, a table, and four glasses of water appeared in front of them. All provided by the dungeon.

Marybelle immediate flopped into her seat, Charlotte and Tris only a second behind her. They looked in better condition than Marybelle, but only marginally so.

Taking his own seat between the women, Ryker continued.

"I'm going to have two of you building walls. Walls to seal off the Queendom of Dale from the outside world. The two on wall duty will be in charge of building to the north and west. The third of you will be helping me construct a massive dungeon behind the city. Your lieutenants will be responsible for manning sections of your walls. You'll each be receiving enough cores to bring your number of lieutenants up to four in total.

"Each of you will receive an additional two cores beyond that for your captains. You will give those captains each two of your lieutenants."

"I understand," Tris said, trying to sit up straight in her chair and only managing to get to a partial lean.

Charlotte was slouching low in her own chair, her eyes lidded.

Marybelle looked wasted, almost slumped over one arm but sitting upright. Barely.

"You're putting a lot of trust in us, my lord king," Charlotte said.

"Considering I sleep next to you at times, I think we're past that," Ryker muttered.

Tris snorted. "My turn today," she said, changing the subject. "And I'm collecting."

Meino came back into the room, leading the candidates that had been brought along.

Surprisingly, there were even a few Dungeon Imps among their number. Though the only reason Ryker could tell them apart from the Fairies at all was that their sense in the dungeon felt different.

Stopping ten feet in front of Ryker, they all fell to one knee in unison.

Didn't Wynne put a stop to this type of thing happening? It's tiring and doesn't really do anything.

"Please rise and welcome, one and all. I recognize a few of you, though many I don't think I've ever met before," Ryker said. "You've been brought here because you're part of my plan to take back Dale. I'm tired of being passive. Tired of letting our enemies do what they want."

He could feel a charge coming from the women he was speaking to. It was the same strange type of feeling he got when a lightning storm was coming.

"We're going to turn the entirety of Dungeon into a wall. A defense against anyone who would dare to raise their hand to us, or our country.

"We'll start today and block out everyone. Or as many people as I can manage. First we have to seal in our territory here in the city.

"After that, we'll seal up all of Dale. What is ours, and what will be ours. Behind dungeon walls manned with dungeon creatures, overseen by dungeon Fairies and Imps."

Ryker turned to Charlotte and Tris on his left.

"Charlotte, name your two captains," Ryker said. Those present seemed shocked at that statement. Not that he was surprised at their reaction. A captaincy had never been brought up before this point.

Looking to the crowd, Charlotte's dark eyes went from person to person.

"Hana and Penny," she said.

Ryker nodded, then went to the back of the room and retrieved a large sack he'd set to one side.

"Step forward, Hana and Penny," he said, standing in front of the group of women. Charlotte had levered herself up from her seat and was standing to Ryker's right.

Taking out two dungeon cores, he handed them to Charlotte. With a single thought, he tied them to her directly.

Two women came up and received their cores directly from Charlotte, and Ryker bound them to those cores while it happened.

"Charlotte, name their lieutenants — two each," Ryker said, looking to the Fairy. "Each lieutenant will be responsible for ten Fairies or Imps."

Quickly as he could manage it, Ryker led the three Fairies through their regime change. Once all the captains were named, their subordinates matched, and plans made to each recruit their ten people, Ryker went and sat back down in his chair.

"Congratulations to one and all. Captains, please remain; the rest of you, go prepare. You'll likely be leaving Dungeon as your walls build further and further away. We'll never be far from each other though, as you'll all leave your true bodies here with me. I shall guard them. And should you have a need, the dungeon sense is always open to all," Ryker said. "Good day."

The newly minted and existing lieutenants filed out the door, looking spooked and proud in equal measure.

As Ryker focused a single thought, six chairs were summoned in front of the original four, facing them across the small table. Taking a moment, he made the table fit the size of the seating arrangement, and six more glasses of water appeared.

Not needing to be told, the six captains sat themselves down quickly.

"Now, for more detailed work," Ryker said. "Tris, I'm giving you the western wall. Charlotte, the north. The mana you'll be given to work with will match the land you've already taken as you go, plus a stipend from me.

"I expect you'll need to build small encampments on our side of the wall for response units, as I do not doubt we'll have people attacking it."

Charlotte and Tris both nodded at that.

"I have no rules to limit you, other than follow the dungeon rules, and build. Lock us in," Ryker said.

"Can we build mini dungeons? With entrances to let people try their luck?" Charlotte asked.

Ryker thought on that, then nodded.

"Yes, that's fine. Just make sure the risk is extreme for any dungeon that lets them out on the other side of the wall—with a warning to that effect, of course. We're trying to prevent people from getting through. Make it obscene.

"Anything that takes them back to the same side of the wall they came in can be less," Ryker said. Then he smiled. "Just make sure it's an interesting dungeon. Nothing boring. Our goal is to murder them all, but we have to do it with a little bit of style if it's a dungeon."

"Can we field armies?" Tris asked.

"If you have the budget for it, I don't care what you do. So long as you maintain the wall and keep anyone from crossing," Ryker said. "If you want to build an army, Tris, then do so."

"Understood," said the Elven warrior.

"Questions on the walls?" Ryker asked.

Tris and Charlotte shook their heads.

"Ok. Marybelle," Ryker said, turning to the Hob.

"Yes, dear?" asked the woman, leaning closer to him.

Chuckling, Ryker poked her in the forehead with a fingertip.

"You're going to be my partner. We're going to build the ugliest, meanest, most fatal dungeon there ever was behind Dungeon," Ryker said. "If they want into the Queensland, they're going to go through hell to do it.

"Your job is to help me do that, while minding the rules and laws of a dungeon."

"Isn't... that Wynne's job?" Marybelle asked, suddenly sounding unsure.

"Wynne will be managing all the other Fairies, Imps, and the city of Dungeon. Eventually we'll be turning over the one we're building to her as well," Ryker said. "Again, she's well aware of all this. I had a good talk with her about it."

"Alright," Marybelle said with a smile. "I have no questions then."

Ryker smiled and then held his hands apart with his palms up. "I have nothing else then. We'll start building tomorrow. You're all dismissed to go start your new jobs."

His personal generals and their captains got up and left his throne room, talking amongst themselves.

Dismissing all the chairs, table, and glasses, Ryker went back to his own chair in front of his table.

"Your voice doesn't match you," Meino said, moving to stand in front of him.

Ah... another grooming session is coming, isn't it? I think I'm going to need to curb this behavior soon. It's starting to get in the way.

"What do you mean?" Ryker asked as Meino got down on her knees next to his chair.

"You're a dungeon lord. A hero. You have multiple wives, a harem. Your voice should be... different," Meino said, her large fingers coming up to try and undo the buttons of Ryker's tunic.

"What, were you expecting something deeper? Manlier? Sorry to spoil it for you, but I'm a petty wizard with a mean streak," Ryker said. Then he sighed and reached up to help Meino with the buttons. There didn't seem to be a way out of this right now.

"Yes, but you're Ryker, the only dungeon lord ever. Can't you change your voice with a spell?" Meino said, grabbing hold of the top of his tunic and then pulling it up over his shoulders and off his body.

Thinking on it, it didn't seem like a terrible idea.

She's not wrong. I'm sure there's a bunch of people that would expect me to sound different than I do. Strange, though. It isn't as if my voice would dictate who I am.

Whatever.

Ryker started with a simple wind and earth spell built to the smallest degree he could manage.

Suddenly he was much more thankful for the anatomy classes he'd taken. It had originally been so he could correctly identify critical areas, but he'd taken it further. He actually knew what vocal chords were.

But not how they worked, exactly.

First he tried compressing them a bit, which produced a voice that sounded a lot like what he imagined a squirrel would use.

Flattening them out, lengthening them, and adding a bit of tissue with earth magic, he sounded deeper than Meino the next time he tried.

Carefully, he edged it back until he found a range he felt like worked for him.

Looking to Meino, who was licking at his shoulder, he tested out his latest change.

"How about this?" he asked, his voice sounding deeper with a touch more breath to it. It felt commanding to him.

Meino's eyes flicked to him as her tongue slid up his neck.

She paused for a second in her grooming.

"Again?" she asked.

"Meino, you really need to find a better outlet than grooming me," Ryker said. "You can't do it as often as you have been."

Meino's nose flexed, her ears swiveling toward him.

"I like it. It made me want to groom you more," she said, then ducked her head back down to his shoulder.

Hm. Seems petty to me to change my voice, but… whatever.

Chapter 4 - From Outside -

The rest of the day went without issue. Nor was it eventful for Ryker.

Tris called on him later and gave him an exuberant go of it.

Later, he had dinner with Adele and Diane, both of whom seemed to be recovering faster than he thought possible. They were both also acting as if they'd been on the best of terms for a long time.

More surprising was when Diane wished them goodnight, giving Adele a kiss on the cheek, Ryker an actual kiss, and then going to her own room.

Which had magically been moved by Arria to directly connect to his own bedroom on the right-hand side. Adele's being on the other side.

For her part, Adele attacked him as soon as the door closed. She rode him till he gave out, apparently determined to get what she wanted from him.

Now she was snoring away next to him while he lay in bed staring up at the ceiling. He knew it was morning, because he could sense it through the dungeon.

But he didn't want to leave Adele's side either.

Diane had gotten up a short while ago, left her room and gone to see Wynne.

Hard not to spy on people when I know where everyone is at all times.

Adele snorted, coughed, and then rolled over one way. Her hands felt out around herself. Realizing where she was, in whatever state of sleep she was in, she promptly scooted across the covers till her hand found his chest. Her fingers stuck to him and she snuggled up into his side, her face pressed to the side of his arm.

And promptly resumed snoring, though a bit softer than previously. Diane would keep her title as Queen of the sleeping lumberjack saws.

Wrapping an arm around Adele, he drew her in closer, closed his eyes, and sank himself into the dungeon.

He could still work from here.

Tracking down Marybelle, he subsumed her dungeon presence in his own. He didn't want others to hear their talk today.

"Oh! My king? What are you doing?" she said, her voice coming from within his own head. "This is different. Feels warm."

"You're bonded to me, so I can more or less enter you or pull you into me. I've done it to Wynne a few times," Ryker said. "Anyways. I wanted to discuss where we are with Dungeon and the dungeon."

"My lord king…" Marybelle started. "I'm… flattered at all this attention, but is this good? Shouldn't this be Wynne's position?"

"Not for the moment. She's working on other projects," Ryker said. "Now, let's get started."

"Wait, since we're doing this, why not use a bond space?" Marybelle said. Then, before he could ask what that was, he found himself standing in Marybelle's living room. She was there with him, and wearing a perfectly tailored blue dress that fit her amazingly. "Ah! That was incredibly easy. And thank you, by the way. I never thought you'd trust me so much as to let me into your own soul like this."

Into my soul? I guess that's accurate. Never really considered it.

Then again, even if I had, I'd still do this.

"Right," Ryker said. Marybelle walked over to the table in the middle and waved a hand over it. Immediately it became a much larger table, and an impressive, perfectly laid-out map of Dungeon appeared, as well as the surrounding lands of Dale. "Handy, nicely done."

"What now?" Marybelle asked, standing next to the map. He could tell she was excited, nervous, and happy all at the same time.

"We need to secure Dungeon. As far as I can tell, I've separated the entire city into two parts. One for citizens, one for everyone else," Ryker said, gesturing to the table. "Can you see anything I missed?"

Marybelle was staring at him now, her eyes narrowed.

"You changed your voice," she said.

"I did. Meino said it didn't fit my 'presence' or something," Ryker said with a shrug. "I'm still a whiny wizard at heart, but I figure this'll appeal to all those finicky little ninnies."

"I like it. Makes me want to test out how much we can play in the bond space," Marybelle said, then looked down to the map. She began to make small finger movements, and small bits of blue energy traveled through the city one after another.

Several minutes passed by in silence as she did whatever she was doing. Long enough that Ryker took a moment to check on Adele, who was sleeping the morning away.

She'd now practically crawled atop him, with one leg over his hips and her head up under his chin.

"There," Marybelle said, standing upright and catching his eyes with hers. "I only found one gap, but everything else you had sealed. Well done, my lord king."

"It's Ryker, not king or whatever," he said, looking at the change she'd made. It was two buildings that were side by side. Between them there'd been a wide enough gap for someone small to squeeze through.

"Okay, dear," Marybelle said. "Now what?"

"Next, we need to prevent portals from dropping into Dungeon. In fact, I want to prevent them from going behind Dungeon as well. So if any spell tries to cross Dungeon in any place, it'll fail," Ryker said.

"That's a good idea," Marybelle said, then held her hands out around the display. A golden sphere formed in the middle of Dungeon and then began to rapidly expand out from there.

Slowly, the display of Dungeon continued to grow smaller and smaller as the golden ball grew.

"There!" Marybelle said and then let out a quick breath. "That didn't cost very much at all since it's all our territory. I haven't done that much magical heavy lifting in a while."

Ryker leaned in and began to spin the display around, looking at it from every angle. There was nothing that would pass through Dungeon spell wise. It was a literal wall of rebound magic. It also seemed to stretch all the way to encompass Dale in either direction. Much the same route the walls would take.

"Tell me more about yourself, Marybelle," Ryker said, sliding the view toward the camp that Charlotte would be building out of. "What was your life like as a dungeon Fairy waiting for a dungeon?"

Zooming in slowly to Charlotte's camp, he could see a small battalion of avatars and presences buzzing around.

"I sat around teaching spell-work and spell theory, mostly," Marybelle said, watching what he was doing. "Whenever a new Fairy was created, I'd take them in and begin working with them. It was a very boring life. It was unlikely I'd ever get a dungeon of my own."

"Ah... you were someone Wynne wanted to capture very much then, I imagine," Ryker said.

Construction on the wall wasn't starting immediately on Charlotte's side. Plans and blueprints were being made while her captains, lieutenants, and soldiers went about their orders diligently.

"I always encouraged Wynne. She has a lot of talent, just little patience," Marybelle said. "As for being captured... actually, that was Tris. She brought Charlotte, myself, and another Fairy. You only met her briefly when we saved Robyn from the church.

"After that you kept throwing us three together, so we just... grew into one another."

Spotting Charlotte, Ryker turned the entire viewpoint around until he had her perfectly centered in it. Then he zoomed in until it was her staring off toward her people.

Her brow twitched, and her head slowly turned toward the dungeon view Ryker was peering through. Her eyes slowly focused on it. It was as if she were peering back at him.

Then she smiled, and visibly chuckled to herself. After giving him a wave with her fingers that she tried to hide, she made a small shooing motion with her hand.

Feeling mischievous, Ryker deliberately zoomed in on Charlotte's chest until that was all he could see.

Several seconds passed before a blushing Charlotte's face appeared in the view, her mouth a flat line.

Alright. Game over for now.

Ryker pulled the feed away and sent it buzzing toward Tris's camp.

"You fluster her. It bothers her, but she loves your attention," Marybelle said.

"Tell me about her and Tris," Ryker asked, looking over Tris's wall.

"Charlotte was a teacher with me. She was much the same then as she is now. Dark, unhappy, moody. She'd been with two dungeons that had failed in her lifetime, and she'd somehow survived both," Marybelle said. Then she clicked her tongue. "She used to be dark, unhappy, and moody, I suppose I should say. She's quite different now, when I put a thought to it."

He found Tris almost immediately, standing in the open with her hands on her hips. Managing her people by force of will and direct orders. Her form of leadership was very different than Charlotte's.

"Tris is young. She knew me because I'd just taught her spell-work. Charlotte was her teacher for dungeon basics," Marybelle said, then laughed as the view circled Tris. "She's a strong-hearted and willful young woman, but she's as afraid of you as she is in love with you. You terrify her because of what you make her feel.

"I'm personally quite happy that she's here. I don't think she would have done well as a dungeon Fairy. Extremely talented, but too direct. She would have died very young."

Dropping the viewing window right in front of Tris, he put her in frame in the same way he'd done to Charlotte.

Tris's reaction was much faster, her eyes locking to the window and instantly piercing through the spell-work.

Her cheeks immediately turned a deep, dark red, her eyes clearly fastened to Ryker. Smiling, he raised a hand and waved at her.

Tris's eyes darted away as if pretending she couldn't see him, only to come back to him.

Waiting, unwilling to move away. He kept waving at her, smiling.

Realizing his intent, Tris begrudgingly brought a hand up and waved at him. The smallest of smiles on her lips.

Ryker blew her a kiss and then winked right before he stood up, forcing the view to be centered right on his belt buckle.

"Think this'll make her lose it?" Ryker asked, looking to Marybelle.

There was a pop, and the projection in its entirety turned off.

"Ah... yes," Marybelle said, then brought the whole project back up with a small hand wave. "You enjoy teasing them. And me, at times. Why?"

"Because you're all so interesting. You're much more honest with your feelings, even when you try to hide them," Ryker said, sitting down on the couch in front of the table. "You're so new to much of this that it's... refreshing."

Marybelle came over and sat down next to him, one hand lifted to the table. It tilted sideways and floated over to them, hovering in the air.

"What now, dear?" she asked.

"Probably start planning out all the different mazes, zones, and dungeon encounters for the fatal area beyond the original city dungeon. All those wings and things like that will remain," Ryker said. "They'll generate mana for us and fill our needs while still providing a valuable resource to anyone willing to come."

"That's a very smart and logical move," Marybelle said, then laid her head down onto his shoulder. "What do you want to do with Robyn? You can't leave her in the city dungeon."

"Heavens no," Ryker said with a chuckle. Reaching down, he slipped his hand into Marybelle's. "I'm going to put her as the entry boss. I watched her deal with others before all hell broke loose. She tended to verbally challenge people to duels, usually while insulting their religion.

"She didn't actually attack people immediately. Which works, as far as I'm understanding the rules. A duel to the death is very different than a dungeon monster fighting an adventurer."

"Especially since Robyn can't die," Marybelle said with a snort. "That'll work nicely."

Lifting her free hand up, she put together a pattern around Robyn's temple and set the destination for it at the exit to Dungeon. Which would make her the entry to the new Death Dungeon, and its first encounter.

A soft white hum penetrated his mind, and Ryker had to focus into the dungeon sense to see what it was.

It was Arria attempting to get his attention. Focusing in on her, he gave her a mental prod.

"Ah! My lord king!" Arria said. "There's multiple messengers here to see you! They're all standing at the front gate of Dungeon!"

"Oh?" Ryker asked. "Alright, I'll make an avatar and go see what they want. Did you happen to hear where they're from?"

"Both the church of light, dark, Trevail, and Adelona," Arria said.

"That'll be fun. Maybe I'll get a chance to kill one of 'em," Ryker said and disconnected himself from Arria, fleeing back to Marybelle.

"I heard. Go," she said, dismissing the entire imagined space and sending Ryker back to his body.

Adele had stopped snoring, and her fingers were lightly tickling back and forth across his chest.

Giving her a gentle squeeze with the arm around her shoulders, he cleared his throat. "You awake, dear?"

"Yeah," Adele said, a fingertip trailing along one of his ribs.

"Messengers arrived. They want to talk to me," he said, not letting go of her.

"Ah. I figured they would. What just happened is beyond expectations. Both churches kicked out, champions being killed, and the Dark Lord of the North arriving. On top of that, the count of Dungeon vanishes into the dungeon itself," Adele said.

"I'm going to make an avatar that looks just like me and send it to talk to them," Ryker said. "Would… would you be interested in making an avatar of yourself and joining me?"

Adele lifted her head up and looked at him, a faint smile on her lips.

"I could do that?" she asked.

"I'd have to put a small contract or bond between your soul and mine. But that's it. You could easily separate it after, or whenever you wanted," Ryker said.

"And I could… play in the dungeon after that? Make avatars, go fight monsters, do what I want?" Adele asked, her excitement becoming very obvious. "If I wanted to go help Charlotte, I could?"

"Yeah," Ryker said, wondering what she was planning.

"Can Diane do it, too?" she asked.

"Of course."

Adele lifted her head and looked around the room.

"Little white fairy? Ahh… what was her name… Aris?" Adele said, chewing at her lower lip.

Ryker chuckled softly.

"What are you doing?"

"I want the little glowing fairy that sometimes follows you to go get Diane," Adele said. "She'll want to do this, too."

Smiling, Ryker wrapped both arms around Adele and pulled her close to kiss her. At the same time, he prodded Aria with a mental command to ask Diane to come see him.

Letting the princess go, he smiled at her.

"Then we should get dressed. Diane is on her way," Ryker said.

Thirty minutes, two minor soul bonds, and three avatars later, Ryker, Adele, and Diane were standing just inside the gate to Dungeon.

"This is so exciting," Diane said from Ryker's right.

"Isn't it?" Adele said. "We can go fight monsters without a worry."

"Or learn fist fighting!" Diane immediately added, her voice changing pitch entirely. "Remember? Husband said everything is stored in cores. We can learn whatever we want."

Huh. They're not wrong. I guess being part of the dungeon is the ultimate training tool. Isn't it?

The benefit of learning anything and everything, and experiencing it without fear of harm.

"Ryker," Adele hissed, one of her hands pressing to his back. "Are there any sword-master cores?"

"Several," Ryker said. He knew that off the top of his head because people with those skill sets were very rare. Two had died in the fall of Dungeon, the third at Robyn's hand.

"Here they come," Diane said, taking a step forward and leaving Adele a step behind Ryker. Diane's left hand came up and slipped into Ryker's hand, giving it a squeeze. "Sorry, Adele."

"It's alright. I don't mind it at all. I kinda like not being in politics anymore," Adele said. "I'm just a housewife now."

Chadwick, a woman Ryker didn't know, and two men were all walking up the path to Dungeon.

"Wynne," Ryker cast out with his sense.

"Yes?" came the immediate and warm response.

"If you get a chance, drop a rock on Chadwick. If the rules permit. Please?" Ryker pleaded.

Wynne's soft, chime-like laughter rang in Ryker's ears.

"If I can, I will – if only to hear you beg me for something again later," Wynne said. Ryker detected a somewhat hungry undertone there. He couldn't deny he was curious about exploring Wynne. They'd been as close to each other as they would be living in one another's pockets since this whole ordeal started.

It'd be strange and interesting, he was sure.

"Greetings," called the woman. She was standing next to a man who looked like he belonged to the church of the dark. Both of them were wearing richer than normal clothes, and both appeared to be in their middle age. "You're the count of Dungeon?"

"I am. May I have the pleasure of knowing whom I'm addressing?"

"Yes, of course. I'm the duchess of Western Trevail. My brother foolishly launched a campaign against your city, and you crushed him, deservedly, under your boot heel," said the woman. "The man next to me is Vicar Anthony, from the church of the dark."

The man standing next to Chadwick cleared his throat, sensing his chance to step into the conversation.

"I'm the heir to the throne of Adelona, Prince Kesley," said the man. "With me is the prestigious—"

"Murdering shit-heel of filth who will be killed if he sets a single foot into Dungeon, Vicar Dickless," Ryker said, interrupting the prince. "To you other three, I greet you and acknowledge you formally as the count of Dungeon. What can I do for you?"

The three seemed completely at a loss on what to do with how Ryker had addressed Chadwick. Then the duchess and Anthony began laughing.

"We would like to discuss the terms of the surrender of Dungeon," Anthony said. "If you give in to us willingly, we'll be very kind to you and your populace."

"Dungeon won't be surrendering. To anyone, or anything," Ryker said. "If that was the full intent of your discussion, you can just run along home now."

"I think we should ask what the young mistress Chas thinks," Chadwick said. "Last I heard, Queen Chas ruled in Dungeon."

Diane smiled at the Vicar, then sighed dramatically.

"I'm afraid, Vicar, that when you and my mother plotted to widow me of my husband, I decided I no longer needed anyone else. I'm formally in support of the queen of Dale, Lauren the Second," Diane said. "I formally decry my mother as a usurper and will do what I can to restore the throne."

"Perfect," said Anthony. "Then let my army pass, and we'll be happy to assist her."

"That won't be happening either," Ryker said. "Unfortunately, the only people allowed into Dale are Dale-landers. We'll solve our problems on our own, thank you very much."

The entire goal of preventing everyone from getting through was to give Lauren's army a chance to not just win against Veronica, but beat the church allies as well. The more soldiers she had to deal with, the worse off she would be.

"Now, I think—" Anthony started to say, but stopped.

Off to one side, a blue portal opened out of the thin air. A massive knight in full black plate mail stepped out of it. Wielding a massive double-bladed axed, the knight scanned the area and then stepped to one side of the portal.

Coming out behind the knight was a Lion beastkin dressed in partial black plate mail. A hatchet was belted on one side of its waist, and a hand axe to the other.

Last, a familiar and beautiful face stepped through the portal.

Bright gold eyes, hair as black as pitch, and a form-fitting robe came to stand between the two knights. In her hand was a stave, and on her collar rested a golden medallion depicting a triangle. Each corner of it seemed to have a different image, but Ryker couldn't make it out.

"Greetings," said the woman, smiling at Ryker. "I wish to speak with you. I am afraid the last time we met, it was under difficult circumstances."

.

Chapter 5 - Devil's Deal -

How in the world did they open a portal? Didn't we just remove the possibility from everywhere in our zone of control?

Does that mean they could have portaled straight into the dungeon if they'd wanted to?

Are they just toying with me?

The vicars of both churches were already working at casting spells.

The golden-eyed woman turned to look at them.

"I do not think it is wise for you to do that. At this point in time, I'm under orders to not kill you unless attacked," said the woman. "You can stop this before it begins."

Ignoring her, both men finished their spells. Dual simultaneous thunderclaps sounded in the air, and a very strange feeling of powerful magic washed over Ryker. Magic the like of which he'd never felt before.

A man appeared next to Anthony, and a woman next to Chadwick. They were wreathed in faith-magic. The air around them crackled with divine authority.

Light and dark champions. But... the champions both died the other day.

The big axe-wielding black knight took a step forward, hefting the axe up easily.

"The emissary has warned you to not attack. This is your second and last warning," called the knight, voice echoing hollowly in the helmet. In the dead center of the axe head, a red cylinder was slowly growing brighter and brighter.

"They'll not listen," growled the Lion, stepping up next to the big knight. "They never do. Did I?"

The black knight's head turned to the Lion, then back to the other two. They looked as if they were preparing for a fight.

"No. In his infinite wisdom, he spared you, however. They will not receive such a blessing from me," said the knight.

"Nor I," said the Lion.

Then the champions dashed forward. The man tried to go around the black knight toward the emissary. The woman went straight at the Lion.

Faster than Ryker thought possible, the black knight appeared in front of the man, a large gauntleted fist striking out.

In an explosion of violence, the champion went tumbling away as if thrown by a monster. Bouncing and spinning, he rolled and bumped along the ground.

The champion of the light reached the Lion. Her weapon was already launching forward to skewer it.

The blade fell out of her hand at the same as her head dropped off her neck.

Standing where they'd been before, the Lion remained, bloody axe in one hand, in a direct line with where the champion's neck had been.

"With the one from the other day," said the Lion, leaning down to wipe the bloody blade on the corpse of the champion. "That makes sixteen."

"Nineteen, including last week," said the black knight, helmet turned toward where the champion of the dark had stopped moving.

"You are both being very rude," the emissary said.

Both the knight and lion immediately stopped talking, their heads dipping fractionally. Coming to stand next to the beastkin, they looked chastised.

Now that Ryker was really looking at her, though, he realized the emissary wasn't a cat tribesman but an actual fox.

"You are the count?" asked the emissary, staring back at Ryker.

"I am," he said. "Ryker's the name."

"Ah, wonderful. I am here to discuss a proposition from my lord," said the emissary. "Would you prefer to speak of it here, or at a location of your choosing with this company?"

Both of the vicars looked shocked and frightened. They had clearly not expected the champions of their faith to be sent to their gods so quickly.

And easily.

Diane saved Ryker from having to answer, as she bowed her head deeply to the Fox. "On behalf of my husband and I, I would welcome you into Dungeon formally. Would you care to have a meal with us in our home? Your retainers are welcome to join us."

"That would be quite acceptable and appreciated. I shall attend to this matter by myself, however. My retainers, as you called them, would like to explore the dungeon," the emissary said, bowing her head to Diane in return.

"Please forgive us," Diane said, looking to the four other diplomats. "We'll be entertaining the emissary of the North for a time. If you'd wish to discuss further items with us, please don't hesitate to send a messenger."

Diane gave Ryker's hand a gentle tug, guiding him back into Dungeon. Adele immediately fell in beside Ryker on his other side. Behind him, he could hear the trod and crunch of heavy boots.

The emissary dropped in next to Diane, her hands folded into themselves.

"Wynne," Ryker started.

"Working on it. I have a nice route planned for them so they can test out the dungeon to their hearts' contents.

"Arria is already putting together a very nice late breakfast for you all in your home," Wynne said.

"Thank you, Wynne. You're a beautiful, intelligent, amazing woman," Ryker sent her way, full of devotion to her planning ahead for him.

"I know I am. I have to be, to be your queen. You're hard to keep up with," Wynne said.

"Any chance I can convince you to have dinner with me tonight or tomorrow?" Ryker asked suddenly.

Wynne's presence faded away for a second and then came back, though slowly.

"Yes. I'd like that. Tomorrow? I want to plan a little for it."

"Done," Ryker sent back.

As he led the emissary through the dungeon part of Dungeon, all the spawns and monsters ignored them completely.

"The layout of your city is very symmetrical," the emissary said. "I like it very much."

"I'm glad to hear that, ah, Emissary," Ryker said, glancing over his shoulder.

"My apologies. My name is Satomi," said the woman with a smile.

"I'm Diane Chas, heir presumptive to the duchy of Chas once the queen clears the field," Diane said, then gestured to Adele. "This is another of Ryker's wives. Princess Adele, cousin to the queen."

Adele looked shocked at how Diane had addressed her, but smiled and bowed her head to Satomi all the same.

Ryker turned past the inn and motioned to it with one hand. "The entry to the dungeon is right in there."

"Ah. This is where I lost you last time," said the black knight.

"Still can't believe he outran you," the Lion said, leaving the group and heading toward the dungeon with the knight.

Turning toward the mansion that had served as his office and home for so long, Ryker felt odd. Most obviously so since he was technically in an avatar of himself right now.

Ryker was on auto-pilot right up until he sat down at the table in the dining room. Fairies in all different types of avatars came in and began laying out a full breakfast course.

"Goodness, I feel as if you are treating me," Satomi said, smiling at her three hosts.

She doesn't feel like an emissary to a lord of death and ruin.

"While they are going about their duties, I will begin to broach the subject my husband sent me here for," Satomi said, looking to Ryker.

Her husband? Fuck me with a damn potato.

"I am one of his many wives, much as you have more than one," Satomi said with a delicate wave of her hand, dismissing the fact. "He would like to know about the new life form you created."

"Life form?" Diane asked, her head tilting slightly to one side.

"You mean Meino," Adele said, her brows drawing toward one another.

"Meino?" Satomi asked, looking from Adele to Ryker. "Do I?"

"Meino the Minotaur," Ryker said, wishing for a brief split second he'd never made so many changes without consulting Wynne.

But in this case, his regret lasted only a moment. He enjoyed Meino's company. Her personality was fun, and he was just starting to figure out her humor.

"How much do you know about me, Satomi?" Ryker asked.

"You are a dungeon lord by enslaving a dungeon core. Your partner has enslaved every Dungeon Fairy she can find and is currently doing the same to the Imps," Satomi said. "Would you like me to say more?"

"No, that's… quite scary as it is," Ryker said honestly. "Meino is… I took a bunch of different cores with human memories in them and fused them into a new core. Like a mishmash of personalities and memories. Then I bound it into a pattern, made it loyal to me, and let it go. I didn't bind it to the dungeon."

"Ah. I see. Thank you for the information," Satomi said, her golden eyes peering at Ryker.

It's like she can tell I told her the truth.

"Would it be possible to inspect this Minotaur? I have been authorized to trade. As you have been generous with information, I already plan on rewarding you in exchange," Satomi said.

"Can I just say you don't seem anything like what everyone says?" Adele said, cutting into the conversation.

Satomi blinked, then smiled at Adele, showing her white sparkling teeth.

"That we of the North are evil? That my husband is the Dark Lord himself? That we enslave the dead, destroy souls, eat children, and bring ruin to all?" Satomi asked.

"Yeah, some of that," Adele said, nodding.

"We do not enslave the dead. My husband has indeed torn the souls out of thousands, has brought back the dead, and battles the pantheon of the light and the dark. Though he does bring war everywhere he goes, he does not bring ruin," Satomi said with a smile. "Does that answer your question?"

Adele nodded quickly. Ryker and Diane did the same.

Casually admitting her husband had ripped out souls and brought back the dead was frightening enough.

"Uhm, you can see Meino, but you can't hurt her or take her with you," Ryker said. "She's a living, breathing person now. With a soul."

"That would be fine. I only need to see her for but a moment," Satomi said. "Yet you made no requests upon me for what it would be worth to you. I am now left in an uncomfortable position."

Ryker didn't know what to say, so he said nothing.

"What is it you need at this time?" Satomi asked.

He was about to respond with nothing when he realized he did have needs.

"Would it be possible to have as many cores, mana crystals, and mana potions as possible?" Ryker asked.

"Ah, that would be acceptable and easy to handle. Your request is granted," Satomi said, looking to her three hosts, one at a time. Then she smiled at them, flashing her teeth. "Please, eat your meal. I do not eat food in the same way you do. I shall have a meal later.

"I do have to tell you, however, that after today I will not be returning for a time. Should I and my friends remain longer, the pantheons of your continent would send a force even we could not repel."

Awkwardly, and feeling like he was dealing with a giant who had come down to play in his tiny sandbox, Ryker began to quietly eat his breakfast as he'd been told.

***

- 31 -

Dropping down into one of the chairs in his bedroom in the dungeon, Ryker sighed. He'd been on edge all day dealing with Satomi. She'd been kind enough, but she'd also said things that had terrified him outright.

She was a strange person representing an entity that was well known to commit evil deeds. Apparently, the Dark Lord had plowed under an entire country to the last person because they had risen up against him.

"You look tired."

Looking up to the voice, Ryker found Diane standing in the doorway to her room. She was dressed in a black nightgown that didn't hide much but definitely made Ryker interested.

"Not that tired," Ryker said immediately.

Diane smiled at that and held her arms out at her sides, looking down at herself.

"I take it you approve?" she said, turning partially to one side.

"Very much."

"Thank you," said Diane, coming over to sit next to him. "Speak to me, husband. What drives you to such a sad evening?"

"Just… everything, I guess. I'm wondering if they'll band together to try and raze Dungeon, or if they'll fight first and the winner will come at us.

"Lauren is running around in the heartland of Dale trying to battle an army that at last report was one and a half times the size of her own army. I've just more or less told her reinforcements to go fuck themselves, and now we're holding our own defensive line," Ryker said. "Against two armies? Three? Four?"

"Four, husband," Diane said, patting his hand gently. "But we knew this. This was a choice we all made before we went into this."

Dark Church, Light Church, Trevail, Adelona.

"I wanted to discuss that with you as well," Diane said, her fingers slipping into his hand. "I think it might be best if Adele and I traveled up north to join up with Lauren.

"It would do very well to report what Dungeon is doing, who it supports, and who I support," Diane said, giving him a small sad smile. "And honestly, husband, there is little for me to do here for you. The politics and maneuvering I'm suited for are worthless here."

Ryker didn't like this talk. At all.

"I'm not going to vanish. You don't have to squeeze my hand so hard," Diane said with a soft laugh.

"I don't want you to leave," Ryker said simply and honestly.

"I know you don't. Adele doesn't want to leave either, but she admitted that it would be the best thing for Lauren if we did," Diane said. "And you wish to support your third wife, do you not?"

He winced at the memory that Lauren had officially engaged herself to him.

"You love her," Diane said. "There's no reason you would do so much for her otherwise."

"Yeah. I do," Ryker said. "Alright. Joining Lauren would… would be a wise idea. You're right. You could easily leverage what you know Dungeon has to help her plan accordingly while updating her about what's going on here. And as you said, that doesn't even count to the fact that you'd officially be supporting her against your mother, with Adele no less."

"And don't forget you and Dungeon," Diane said, her other hand coming up to put the back of his hand in hers. "You and your city count for much, husband.

"And while I'm away, you'll firm up our county, build our walls, and repel the enemy," Diane murmured softly. "We'll get this war ended, I'll come back to you, and we'll settle down. You get to be my duke."

Grinning at him, Diane flicked one of his knuckles. "You can just be arm candy if you like, or help me run the duchy. I'll treat you just as you did for your county."

"Thanks… wife," Ryker said, then leaned across to kiss her for several seconds before pulling away again. "I just really don't want you to leave is all. I worry for you."

"I know, which is why I won't say no when you inevitably detach a host of avatars to come with us. I'm sure Wynne already has a contingency plan for such an event. She's a clever one," Diane said.

"I hate to disappoint her, but I didn't have a plan. I'm already making one, though," Wynne said. "I like Diane. She never had a harsh word for me, always greeted me and treated me kindly. She even came to talk to me yesterday about our... our marriage."

"I'm glad to hear it. We're all in this together," Ryker sent back.

Nodding, he gave Diane's hands a squeeze. "When do you plan on leaving?"

"Tomorrow," she said with a shrug. "It'd be ideal. We'll take fast mounts, leave with almost no luggage, and just ride straight for Lauren."

"Alright. That all makes sense. If that's the case then, I'd suggest you let me carry you to our bed right now, my beloved wife. My Diane," Ryker said, getting out of his chair and crossing over to hers. "I'll not waste another minute of time with you. Though I wonder if that's why you made sure Adele and I were alone last night."

"It was. We'd already planned this after you fell on our collective mercy," Diane said, looking up at him. "It was very romantic by the way, the way you just... gave me your soul card without a thought. That you pitched yourself out, told me everything, laid yourself bare to me.

"I loved it. I love you."

The next morning's dawn ambushed Ryker. For him, the night had ended far too quickly.

Diane and Adele left with a contingent of twenty-three dungeon Imps and twenty-three dungeon Fairies. Collectively they had enough strength in their avatars to easily destroy a force five times their number.

Ryker had even gone so far as to turn over two captaincy cores and four lieutenant cores to the leaders of each group. All to make sure his wives were protected.

And then they were gone, leaving Ryker alone with a city on the edge of a war and a dungeon to build.

Truth be told, though, he figured he had the easier job between them. They had to march through enemy territory, cross a front line, and get in front of Lauren. Dungeon was more or less behind enemy lines at this point.

Especially since Duchess Chas wasn't that far away to the northwest.

And now I'm alone with my dungeon.

Which is what I wanted at the start... but not anymore.

Wish I could see Lauren's face when she reads my letter.

Ryker chuckled.

Or when they give her my "back taxes." Those church troops sure had a lot of money.

Chapter 6 - Work, Work, Work -

Ryker settled into his chair and called up his map of Dungeon, then his dungeon sense.

"Hello dear, is it time to get to work?" Marybelle said, practically from inside his head.

Was she waiting for me? I swear I didn't even feel the dungeon yet.

"Yeah. You want to join me?" Ryker asked.

"Of course, but why bother to work there at all, dear?" Marybelle asked. His dungeon sense transformed rapidly into Marybelle's living room. The table was once again a display table, and sitting on it was the entirety of Dungeon and the dungeon.

Just like last time, except he'd done none of it.

"Huh," Ryker said, turning his head to look at Marybelle.

She was sitting on the couch in front of the table, one leg crossed over the other, and wearing a black dress that was practically painted on her.

Smiling in a way that promised and invited too much, she patted the spot next to her.

"You invited me into the bond, dear. I never left. The moment you were in the dungeon sense, I knew, and I could pick up what you were thinking," Marybelle said. "Has anyone ever told you that the way you think is amazing? Impressive?

"Your thoughts just never stop. They're always so fast, too."

Ryker was immediately out of sorts and mortified.

Wait, does this mean Wynne really could read my mind after all?

"No. Not unless you pull her into you the same way you did me," Marybelle said with a lovely smile. "And I'm glad you like the dress. I had it made a few days ago but haven't had a chance to wear it for you yet. This seemed like a good occasion to at least show it off a bit, even if it's just an imitation."

Running his hand along his jaw, Ryker didn't know what to do or say.

"I'll make sure to not read your thoughts going forward," Marybelle said, holding up her hand. "I already sense and know your unease, dear. Though… you could always read mine just as easily, if you wanted."

Even though it felt like a trap, Ryker tried to peek into her mind.

And was flooded with an overwhelming sea of loving lust that threatened to drown him. Closing the door on her thoughts quickly, Ryker tried to hide that anything had happened at all.

Moving over to her side, he sat down next to her and gave her a thoughtful look.

"You don't seem as perturbed today about doing this work," Ryker said.

"Oh, I spoke with Wynne. She gave me an entire rundown of everything she's doing and working on. I suddenly felt like I wasn't doing enough for her, even with taking over this duty," Marybelle said. "My little student has become such a grownup now. She may have become our queen by force, but she's a very good queen to us."

Ryker clucked his tongue at that and looked to the table and its display.

"I wanted to get to work on the dungeon. We need to get it reconfigured for people coming through it as if it were a city, and a fatal entrance to the Queendom," Ryker said.

"Ah, yes, that'd be a wise move," Marybelle said.

"Most especially considering the four armies out there are avoiding one another and sending messengers back and forth," Ryker muttered. "It seems they've forgotten they hate each other entirely. I'm beginning to worry they might be considering Dungeon as a mutual enemy."

Marybelle's delicate brows came together, her head turning toward the map.

While she was investigating what he'd just said, Ryker evaluated his dungeon.

The human encampment, minus all its spawns, was outside of Dungeon and on the wrong side of the Queendom.

Going to need to pull that to this side of the walls and get those NPCs going again. Get them training our soldiers, guards, and blades with skills.

Except he wasn't quite sure how he was going to manage to bring an entire wing of the dungeon over, except piece by piece.

Setting that problem aside for now, Ryker let his mind slide through the dungeon part of the city.

It was an almost exact replica of the original city area it was meant to be. From the entrance gate to the inn, the mayor's mansion, an unfinished royal palace, the failed light temple, and the exit of the city.

The biggest difference was that one couldn't get to the original city, or Ryker's farm. Anyone who had been in Dungeon before now would probably notice the hill and its farm were much further away than they remembered.

Otherwise, it was the same and would serve his needs perfectly.

Moving into the false inn, Ryker slipped down into the original dungeon.

The dueling wing and the two story wings were still there. Of everything, those three had been the least impacted by the ongoing problems above ground.

Even now adventurers, citizens, and blades were grinding away. Working to improve both their skills and their lot in life.

"I see," Marybelle said with a profound sigh. "I think you're right, dear. It's rather clear they're willing to put their hatred aside to deal with us right now. Though I don't think it's based on us. I think it's… more based on the fact that the Lord of the North's emissary was here.

"I would almost think they're terrified he's sending something to help you."

Ryker shrugged his shoulders at that.

"Technically, I suppose he did. The number of cores, mana potions, and crystals they left is… staggering," Ryker said bemusedly. "All just to talk to Meino for little less than five minutes."

"Wynne mentioned she was handling the distribution of all that," Marybelle said. "You're dividing it up equally and sending it to Charlotte and Tris?"

"Yeah, it'll help speed the construction of the wall along," Ryker confirmed. "Rather than having to build, wait, store mana, and build more, they can rapidly deploy massive sections of their respective walls."

"That's very true. If one focuses all those gains to putting the wall up, it should go very quickly," Marybelle said, nodding. Leaning toward him, she wriggled around until she got her shoulder up under his arm. Then she scooted over completely and pressed her side to his. "You wouldn't do such a thing unless you were nervous or paranoid about something."

Unable to deny that, Ryker nodded his head slightly. "I am indeed. If they decide to go around Dungeon with part of their force rather than keep everything here to claim it, Lauren will be drowned in soldiers she can't hope to stop.

"My goal is the same as I stated previously. Walls up, keep everyone out, force them to grind through the dungeon to make it."

"Then we actually have several goals that are interconnected," Marybelle said, holding up a finger on her left hand. "The first is simple: prevent, reduce, and weaken anyone who would seek to enter the Queensland that isn't part of the loyal forces of Dale.

"That includes both churches, and both countries."

Mentally, Ryker threw that goal up to the top of his checklist.

"Second, to encompass and 'fence in' all of the Queensland. This is part of our first goal, but it is a goal all in itself. The faster it is accomplished, the better the results of goal one," Marybelle said, holding up a second finger.

"Third, to build Dungeon in such a way as to train the soldiers, mercenaries, and blades so they can be used to help reclaim all of the Queensland," Marybelle said, holding up a third finger.

"That's right. You're absolutely right. It isn't just one goal, but three smaller ones," Ryker said, adjusting his view on the whole thing based on her words alone.

"The first goal is connected to the other two but is itself separate as well," Ryker muttered. "Then… it comes down to which path to pursue first. Assist Charlotte and Tris with the walls or continue with the dungeon."

"I would suggest the dungeon, dear," Marybelle said, letting her left hand drop onto Ryker's thigh. "It's what you want to work on, and would be the best use of your abilities as our dungeon lord.

Charlotte and Tris, while they'd be happy to entertain you and receive your assistance, are very capable women. They don't need your help."

Blinking several times, Ryker laughed, tightening his arm around Marybelle's shoulders.

"You're absolutely right. There isn't even a question, is there? Alright. First things first, then—Robyn, and her temple," Ryker said.

"I spoke with her yesterday," Marybelle said, watching as Ryker summoned a top-down view of Robyn. "She's very interested in you right now. She seems to think you're perhaps some guardian spirit watching over her.

"The fact that you're the one who had her killed is obviously known but means nothing to her. She views her afterlife as a mere continuation of her life."

That's rather odd, isn't it?

"Not sure how that really works in her head," Ryker said, setting down small boundary markers around the temple that Robyn inhabited. "As you said, I had her killed. I stole her soul. I stuck her into a prison."

"And freed her from everything. I would say it's a lot like how the vast majority of us Fairies feel about our imprisonment. The Imps even more so," Marybelle said. Lifting her right hand, she began to spin intricate and tightly wound spell forms around the areas Ryker had marked. "We were all forced into servitude. Bound, conquered, and dominated. Yet now we're an organized force. Our numbers are increasing. We have a presence and a dungeon lord who can support however many of us he can catch. He can also make more dungeon cores."

Finishing up his marker placement, Ryker let out a quick breath.

"What are you working on there? Something to make this easier for me, I hope?" Ryker asked.

"That's exactly right. I've put in a spell form that will pull everything inside that boundary you made and treat it as one. You can effectively scoop out her entire temple and put it somewhere else," Marybelle said. "Though I'd recommend being careful about it. You could blow the whole thing up if you go too quickly."

Ryker delicately slid down over Robyn and enfolded her into his personal dungeon sense. He took special precautions to lock her out from going further, though, considering what had happened with Marybelle.

He immediately felt her mind become rigid, defensive, and hostile. Like a raised sword pointed at someone.

All that lethal force and hostility melted away in an instant when she discovered it was him.

Just as quickly as it vanished, it was replaced with a golden warmth that was unmistakably Robyn. Especially with how it reacted to him.

It smashed into the edge of his dungeon sense like a battering ram. Cracking into it with the second hit. He felt a strange moment of apprehension from her as the edge crumbled away.

Then that bright, glowing glory that was Robyn filled his dungeon sense completely, taking over every inch. Looking through his eyes, his senses, she assessed everything he'd been looking at.

With as much care as was humanly possible, Ryker reached into Robyn's temple. He sliced into the patterns laid into the ground itself that tied it to the dungeon, then lifted it free from its anchor points.

Robyn was getting a front-row seat to him making her the gate guard to the new dungeon. The Death Dungeon.

Setting the temple, Robyn's pattern, and all her followers down against the entrance to the new dungeon, he hooked everything back into the patterns.

After spending some time to make sure it was right, Ryker connected it all up, built in some new ones, and then gated her temple off. Anyone who wanted to enter the Death Dungeon had to cross Robyn and her temple.

Releasing his hold over the temple, Ryker let it begin siphoning mana and energy back from the dungeon. Slowly, the bits and pieces of it began to light up, turning back on and pulling energy in to feed the patterns.

Putting down a simple sign at the front of the Death Dungeon, Ryker let out a mental sigh. The first step had been taken.

The golden spirit of vengeance that was Robyn spun itself through Ryker's dungeon sense several times before slowly leaving. Drip by drip, she fell back into her pattern and avatar.

With a crackle, her avatar pattern exploded into nothing and reformed itself before Ryker had a chance to panic. Then the pattern for the temple did the same, and then all the avatars who reported up to Robyn.

Standing in the middle of her temple, the seat of her power and her pattern, was Robyn.

Bright golden luminescent wings spread out from her back. Her eyes glowed with an unearthly light, and her blade seemed to be fashioned from fire.

"I think she took your sign very literally and is more than willing to act the part," Marybelle said. "It also fits the rules quite well. Wynne will approve, as I do. You made it a choice, and a promise."

Smirking, Ryker checked the sign one more time to make sure it got his point across.

All who cross this point shall be judged at the highest levels and inspected with utmost scrutiny. The likelihood of death is almost a guarantee.

Rewards will be minimal, except for the gift of knowing your own strength and the promise of learning new skills and abilities.

Those who enter will suffer the wrath of Dungeon for the attempt to exterminate it.

Do not enter.

"Did you notice how she tried to fill your entire presence with her own?" Marybelle asked.

"Yeah, and she did, too. I don't think there was a single bit she missed," Ryker said. He was moving his view back to the human dungeon encampment now. He had to figure out how to move that next, and he was hoping Marybelle could help him again.

"You might be right. Once she'd stretched herself to your own boundaries, she settled in like you were a warm blanket on a cold night," Marybelle said. "It was like watching a puppy snuggle itself into someone."

"Whatever you're trying to say, spit it out," Ryker said. "And while you're doing that, any chance you could do those nifty spells for me as I lay out markers again?"

"Of course, dear. And yes, I'll get to my point presently," Marybelle said. "Robyn is treating you as a savior figure, for all intents and purposes. It makes me nervous. Her faith is dangerous. You might want to curb that when you can.

"That or redirect it into something else. She might be amenable to getting in your bed if you do it right."

"Hah, no—my bed is sealed up nice and tight. Diane and Adele would both take a turn killing me, and beyond that, I'd hurt them," Ryker said with a shake of his head. "I'd rather hurt myself than hurt them, or you for that matter."

Charting out the boundaries for the human encampment, Ryker went through and placed a marker for each shift of the border or change in its pattern.

Marybelle was there as soon as he finished every single one, weaving a complex pattern Ryker didn't even want to try picking apart.

Given time, he could, but it was clear Marybelle was just as accomplished a wizard in her own right as he was.

"Your ability is splendid," Ryker said.

"Comes with time," Marybelle said casually, tying up another pattern atop a marker. "I'm two hundred years old, after all. If I wasn't as good as you, I think I'd have to give up my confidence in my status as a teacher."

"No matter how impressive you are for your young age."

Ryker felt a momentary stutter in his thought process with that revelation.

"I had no idea. You're amazingly young and beautiful in your Fairy body."

"Why thank you, dear," Marybelle said, tying up another point. "Wynne is only a few years younger than you. Tris is perhaps half your age. Charlotte is one hundred and seventy, I think."

Ryker took a breath, then grabbed the entirety of the area they'd bound and tagged, and pulled.

With a shuddering crack, the massive sprawling fort and compound came loose from the earth. Then it floated over Dungeon and landed on the opposite side of the town. Putting it squarely on the interior side of the expanding walls.

"There," Ryker said. "Now we just have to add some new skill teachers, enchanted-item vendors, and tie it all to blade points," Ryker said, immediately calling up old blueprints he'd had stored away for a long time. "And once we're done, activate all the blades, give them orders, and let them do as they please."

"To be sure, the way you're utilizing the willing mercenaries is interesting. I would never have considered doing something like that," Marybelle said, laying her head back down on his shoulder.

"You're a warm-hearted instructor who got dragged into a war. If you were anything else, you wouldn't be you," Ryker said. "And for who you are, I'm grateful."

"You say lovely things at times," Marybelle murmured. "Oh, and we should probably establish this now before our next dungeon-building session."

"Establish what?" Ryker asked, starting to tie in all the patterns once again. He needed to make sure it all matched and flowed correctly. A lack of mana would kill a wing faster than an army attacking it.

"Whether you're getting into my bed before we work or after we work," Marybelle said, her hand on his thigh giving him a gentle squeeze.

"Oh, that's an easy answer," Ryker said, putting in a sword master trainer and tying all the skills he knew to token rewards. "Both. Before and after. Which means I think I should stop working for an hour. Need to make sure we adhere to the rules after all."

"That's a very good idea. I like it. Did you want to play in here… or in my actual home?"

That's an interesting thought. I still have my contracts with Diane and Adele, don't I? And they have cores, establishing the area as Dungeon territory… I wonder.

Chapter 7 - Can You Hear Me Now? -

Spinning his view further out on the four armies, Ryker really wasn't quite sure what to think about it.

"It's rather... hm... I was going to say depressing, but that just doesn't feel right to say," Wynne said over his shoulder, staring at the same thing as him.

They were seated in her living room after having a private dinner together.

Wynne was playing it close to the chest, and she hadn't kissed, hugged, or flirted with him very much. For all intents and purposes, he got the impression she wanted to take it very slow.

And he didn't have any reason not to let her.

"How about... overwhelming?" Ryker said, pulling the view back further. Between the four armies, there must have been at least two hundred thousand soldiers.

All of whom wanted a piece of the Queensland, and Dungeon. The major problem was that it seemed like they were starting to mend their differences. At least for long enough to get through or around Dungeon.

"They don't even have more than a handful of sentries," Ryker muttered. "Are they going to come together and have a gods-damned orgy in the middle of the field?"

Wynne chortled at that and laid a cool hand to his jaw, tapping at his cheekbone.

"You're always so quick to anger," she murmured next to his ear.

She was hovering over his shoulder, standing behind the couch while he sat in it and looking at the table.

"I'm sure you already even have a plan for how to change this," Wynne said confidently.

Unfortunately for him, she was right. He did have a plan. Or at least, an idea to try and see if it'd work.

"You're my rule keeper," Ryker said. "Would it cost us to kill a few sentries and then fire arrows blindly into the center of the church armies?"

Making a humming noise, Wynne seemed to be considering.

"No, not much at all. They're more or less engaged in a war with the dungeon. Killing a few sentries could walk the line if you killed enough directly. But firing indiscriminately into their camps? That'll be fine, so long as you're not targeting someone specifically," Wynne said.

"Nope, I just want to sow a bunch of random chaos, then have both sets of archers run at each other when the enemy inevitably engages," Ryker said. He was laying down a very simple pattern for a human. It could march, run, fire an arrow, and turn around. Otherwise, it could do nothing else.

"Oh, that's rather evil and fun. You think they'll chase the archers right into the other group chasing their own set of archers?" Wynne asked.

"I have no idea. But it's worth trying. Best case, I get a lot of people killed, feed the dungeon, and get those two armies killing one another," Ryker said. "Worse case... I just kill a lot of people with arrows. Wait, can I use flaming arrows?"

"That'd be perfectly fine. I can't see a problem with it. The fire is far less direct than the arrows. As I said earlier, indiscriminate," Wynne said.

"Great. Alright, I'll just put together a thousand of these on each side and get them ready to go," Ryker said, using a quick pattern to copy patterns and paste them elsewhere. He'd seen Marybelle use something similar and liked the idea.

He went from one archer to two to four to eight in seconds. They were all facing the church of the light.

"You've been playing with Marybelle," Wynne said, watching. "She's a wonderful teacher. She was very kind to me. I was annoyed when Tris brought her and Charlotte in. But now I'm rather glad."

"She talks well of you behind your back," Ryker said, tying off a group of five hundred archers and then duplicating them.

"Who, Tris?" Wynne asked, her arms tightening around Ryker's shoulders.

"No. Marybelle. She said you have a lot of talent. You just don't have the patience for it," Ryker said. Pulling the group of a thousand archers together, he duplicated the whole lot of them. The second group was placed on the opposite side of the field, facing the dark church.

"I'm glad to hear that. I don't talk with her as much as I should. I fear she doesn't much care for me anymore," Wynne said softly.

"Actually, she said you were a good queen. I get the general impression from your subjects that they're not entirely upset with how everything turned out. She even said your numbers were increasing," Ryker said. "I took that to mean they were going up naturally, without you capturing people."

Giving the archers their orders, he started them marching toward their respective targets. He'd chosen the locations specifically to give them some room to walk. Leave footprints. Make it seem like something actually walked.

Rather than appeared.

"Amazingly enough, they are. They just... pop right up here in Dungeon. They get captured and converted instantly, then sent to class. Just like they would if this were a normal Fairy village," Wynne said, then pointed to the map. "Now what?"

"Now I'm going to put together an avatar and go kill any messengers that try to go from one camp to the other. Then make it look like something else," Ryker said before letting out a short sigh. "Care to join me? You don't have to do anything with your avatar. Just keep me company, maybe?"

"I can do that," Wynne said. "I suppose I can keep a view on where your archers are at the same time. That way I can update you on how it's going and make changes."

"That'd be great. Alright. Time to go into an avatar, then," Ryker said, lying down on the couch right there. "You go lie down in your bed."

Watching him with a strange look and a small smile, Wynne finally nodded. "Alright. Any preference on my avatar?"

"Make it you. You're beautiful," Ryker said, then closed his eyes.

In moments he'd made his arcane-monk avatar, just with his own face, hair, and eyes.

Though this time he had given himself a crossbow with an entire quiver of quarrels, a simple steel dagger, and several healing potions. Just in case.

If he didn't have to remake an avatar, he wouldn't. He didn't have the mana to waste, but he did have a surplus of healing potions he could simply transfer and conjure.

As he stood in the wide, open field, there wasn't much to do. He could see distant campfires for both camps, though neither one was very close.

They might be playing nice for the moment, but they're still mortal enemies after all.

Ryker lowered the faceplate of the crossbow down to the ground and put his boot tip into it. Grabbing the string, he cranked it back and locked it into place. Then he pulled a quarrel free, dropped it into place, and lifted the crossbow back up.

Several seconds after that, Wynne appeared. Looking exactly as she did in real life.

Her avatar was a mirrored image of everything, except that she'd chosen to remove her wings.

"That wasn't so bad," Wynne said, looking down at herself. "And it feels as if I'm in my body exactly as I should be."

"That's right, you never really made an avatar, did you?" Ryker asked.

"No, I never felt the need to. Though for this, it seems prudent," Wynne said. She held her hands apart, and a small magical construct appeared between her fingers.

There in the middle was an overhead map with dots representing the archers in both camps, as well as enemies. In the middle of it all were two bright white dots.

"The sentries fell easily enough. Since we knew right where they were," Wynne said. "No problems from the core."

"I was wondering... can we expand the core? Make it bigger? Stronger? Or is it permanently that and nothing else?" Ryker said.

"It's a spirit core. It's not like it can just... make itself bigger or grow. The size is what it will always be. That's why some dungeons end up very strong, and some very weak," Wynne said.

Ryker nodded at that. It made sense. The idea of a core or a crystal somehow growing itself seemed far-fetched to begin with.

"They're firing," Wynne said. "Both sides."

Lifting his eyes to the sky, Ryker watched where he thought the archers firing on the dark church would be.

Pinpricks of light fluttered through the air. Soaring above, they looked like a swarm of fireflies.

Seconds later, they landed. Small fires popped up all over, and a second wave of flaming arrows went flying into the camp.

Glancing over his shoulder, Ryker looked at the church of light camp. The same was happening there, but the fire was much larger.

With any luck, they'll hit an oil depot. Hah. Maybe it'll all go up.

Feeling a strange emotion well up from deep in his guts, Ryker tried to fight against a thought that was struggling to break free.

I wonder where Claire is? She's not over there… is she?

With a soft whump, a big flame went up about thirty feet into the air.

"That was the command tent," Wynne said. "Did they soak it in oil or something? It just went up instantly."

"Some fabrics burn much easier than others," Ryker said in an offhand voice. "If you're a wizard specializing in fire, it's worth knowing which does which so you can buy a robe accordingly."

"And what did you specialize in?" Wynne asked. "I'm pulling the archers back towards each other now. Both camps are starting to send out people to fight the enemy."

"I specialized in everything, honestly. My control, talent, and mind are that good," Ryker said without any braggadocio or humility. It was a simple fact for him. A short whisper of anger blew across his soul and vanished instantly.

As if that matters. I'm the dungeon lord. I'm the husband to Diane, Adele, and Lauren.

I'm so much more than I could have been.

Nodding, Ryker looked from one camp to the other.

"Care to bet on who will send out the first messenger?" he asked.

"No. Human gambling still escapes me. I've watched it often enough. Adventurers risking the dungeon is a gamble itself, yet it makes no sense to me. Almost all gambling is a risk and almost always guaranteed to lose if given enough time," Wynne said.

"You're not wrong, of course. Maybe I was just looking for an opportunity to get you to wager something to me. Like eating dinner naked tomorrow," Ryker said.

Keeping her eyes glued to her small window into the dungeon sense, Wynne didn't seem to have heard him.

Not pressing his luck, Ryker waited. He knew this was going to be boring, so he was thankful for Wynne's presence. Even if she wasn't talking, it was better than him standing here alone.

"I'm scared," Wynne said.

"Of what, dying in your avatar? It's not that big a deal. You just… fly away," Ryker said with a vague hand gesture. "It's kinda weird."

"Not that. I'm scared of you. Of how you make me feel," Wynne said. Lifting one hand, she shifted the view she was on towards the church of light. "Messenger coming from the light. We should be right in his path, but I'll keep an eye on it."

"Scared? Of me? Pretty sure I've been fairly direct and there's no surprises," Ryker said.

"That's why I'm scared. I like your directness, but suddenly when I'm in your crosshairs I don't like it at all," Wynne said. "I still don't care if you sleep with the other Fairies, or your wives, but I get a strange fluttery feeling at the idea of you being with anyone else.

"And I ache for you. I ache in my body so bad it almost hurts."

Sticking his tongue out between his teeth, Ryker bit it gently as he thought.

"Sounds like Fairies really do experience all the emotions of normal humanoids then. You were just never given the chance to have 'em," Ryker said. "As for the fluttery feeling, that'd be jealousy, I imagine. And the aching sounds a lot like, uh… being horny. Or randy. Wanton?"

"I know what horny is. I've watched more than enough of the guards go through the brothels every night," Wynne said. "We need to shift north. He's going fast. We can catch him easily at a fast walk."

"Got it," Ryker said, bringing up his crossbow and moving northward.

"That's south," Wynne said.

"I knew that," Ryker said, turning around and heading the other way.

Wynne was giggling when he went by her. He could hear her even as they moved, her trailing behind him.

"You're a brilliant wizard, but you have no sense of direction," Wynne said.

"I'm aware. It's not like there's a sense-heading skill or something, ya know?"

"There he is," Wynne said, pointing to a fast-moving shadow not as dark as the sky heading their way.

Ryker lifted his crossbow and pulled the trigger the moment he sighted the rider.

A hard thump echoed in the night as the bolt shot across.

There was a pop, followed by the crash of the rider falling from the saddle and tumbling through the dirt.

Running over to the fallen messenger, Ryker pulled the steel dagger loose from his belt.

A young woman was lying on the ground, wheezing, her hands pressed to her chest. The bolt was sticking straight out from her, blood welling up from between her hands.

Grimacing, Ryker moved in to finish her.

She looked like Lauren. Black curly hair, good figure, wide blue eyes.

Falling down to a knee next to the woman, he stuffed his knee up under her armpit. Then he grabbed the top of her hair with his left hand, pulling the dagger up under her neck.

And couldn't do it.

Rasping, the woman stared up at him.

Ryker grit his teeth and jammed the blade up into her throat. Bringing the blade around to sever everything and make it quick for her.

Or trying to.

His arm was locked in place. Ryker found he was unwilling to kill the woman.

"Fucking damn me for my stupid sappy heart," he cursed, looking up from the woman laid out in front of him. "Is another messenger coming, Wynne?"

"Yes, from the dark church, but he hasn't even gotten on a horse yet," Wynne said.

Looking back to the woman, Ryker didn't know what to do.

"Hey, are you related to the queen?" Ryker asked.

The woman blinked, blood frothing on her lips as she struggled for breath. Then she bobbed her head fractionally.

"Distant cousin?" Ryker asked.

Again, the woman nodded.

"She know you?" Ryker asked.

Another nod.

"And you're trying to get her killed by serving the church of light? You're not a very good relative," Ryker said.

The woman slowly shook her head at that. It only made Ryker confused as to what she was shaking her head to. Being a bad relative or trying to get Lauren killed.

Grumbling, Ryker pressed his left hand to his temple.

"Name?" he asked, trying to figure out what to do.

"Shir-lee," wheezed the woman.

Grabbing her tunic with his right hand, he yanked it roughly to one side. Tearing it away and exposing Shirley's bare chest to the moonlight. If her eyes could have gone any wider, they did when she realized he'd just stripped her.

Leaning in close, Ryker peered at the entry point. Blood was oozing up from the wound, with bubbles.

"Probably hit your damn lung. What the fuck are you doing as a messenger for those zealots? Stupid. Stupid, stupid," Ryker grumbled. He wrapped his hand around the bolt and jerked it out. Flicking it aside, he looked into the wound.

It wasn't good.

With his left hand, he pulled a healing potion out of his belt and stuffed it into her mouth. Straight up to the base of the flask. He didn't have time to coddle her.

Using his right hand, he pinched her nose shut.

"That's right, swallow it all," Ryker said.

"You sound like some of the worst guards at the brothel," Wynne muttered from behind him. "I'll handle the dark church messenger. Get ready, though — the two counter-attacks are about to crash into each other. I imagine more messengers will be coming then."

Staring down into Shirley's panicking eyes as she choked and swallowed the health potion, Ryker sighed and nodded.

"For what it's worth, I'm Lauren's husband. Count Ryker of Dungeon," Ryker said. "That makes you my cousin-in-law, I guess, Shirley."

When the glass vial was empty, Ryker grabbed it and tossed it off to the side.

Pressing his hand to her chest, he looked into the wound. It was slowly closing up already. Using both hands, he began to gently feel around her chest to see if any of the ribs were broken.

A healing potion could right many things, but if a bone was crooked, it would still need to get shoved back into place.

"Lucky for you," Ryker said, his fingers trailing along her rib bones. "Everything seems to be intact.

"Alright. You're a prisoner of war now. I'm going to take you back to Dungeon and lock you away until Lauren can deal with you."

"*Arria!*" Ryker shouted into the dungeon sense.

As if she had already been there, the wisp avatar popped into being.

"My lord king?" Arria asked.

"I need you to make a normal avatar, or a life-sized version of yourself, and carry her back to my personal chambers. Make sure she's healthy and cared for," Ryker said, pointing down at Shirley. "Questions?"

"No," Arria said.

"Good," Ryker said, then looked back at Shirley. Giving her a grin, he patted her cheek a touch roughly. "See you soon, cousin."

Shirley stared up at him, completely lost in her own world.

Then he got up and took off at a run to get back to Wynne.

They had work to do.

Chapter 8 - Return to Sender -

With the coming of the dawn, Ryker and Wynne had retreated back into their bodies.

Both sides had clashed the entire night, and slowly, more and more forces had been brought up. Lines were drawn in the dark as spells, faith magic, and champions brutally fought one another.

And through it all, Wynne and Ryker slaughtered any and every messenger that came their way. Other than Shirley, who was tied to a chair in Ryker's bedroom right now.

"Arria?" Ryker asked, staring at the freakishly similar-to-Lauren, half-naked woman in his bedroom.

Shirley was staring back at him while sitting limply in her chair, her eyes wide.

"Yes, my lord king?" Arria said, flying in from the wall.

"Is there a reason she's tied up and still partially nude?" Ryker asked.

"She tried to cast spells when she was left alone, before I could deliver clothes," Arria said. "I asked Marybelle for advice, and she suggested I tie her up as comfortably as possible until you could decide."

Shirley's eyes dropped to the ground, looking somewhat embarrassed.

"What kind of spells?" Ryker asked.

"I don't know. They all failed as soon as they encountered the protective wards in your room," Arria said. "They were all from items on her person, and they're all depleted of energy now."

Nodding, he walked over to Shirley and bent down next to her. Leaning in toward her chest, he pressed his fingers to her ribs and pushed gently against them. They felt better now, didn't seem to give as much.

Pressing his hand to her chest more firmly, he pushed on her ribcage. Shirley made no move and seemingly felt no pain. Her eyes were locked on him all the while.

Ryker nodded again, then looked at the wound itself.

It was now a massive and ugly scab. Huge, red, and ruinous, it was disturbing.

"Sorry, Shirley, but I kinda need to see it. I'll do what I can to get it patched up after," Ryker said. "Actually, Arria, could you get me a nice clean bandage? Or have Meino bring it in?"

The Minotaur was napping in her bedroom, which was now just behind his bed on the other side of the wall.

"Of course!" Arria said, and she shot away like a bolt of lightning.

Reaching up, Ryker began to unwind the gag around Shirley's mouth.

"Sorry about that. They're overprotective. Most of them have a good head on their shoulders, but they're inexperienced with—" Ryker paused in his statement to consider. "Well, pretty much everything."

Pulling the wad of cloth stuffed in her mouth out, he sighed and dropped it to one side. He was sure he was about to get reamed out by another noblewoman.

If there were a profession involving being yelled at by noblewomen, I'd be the best in the business.

Shirley opened and closed her mouth several times, working some moisture into it. She coughed once, then closed her mouth and looked at him.

"What, not going to yell at me?" Ryker asked.

"No," Shirley said. Her voice was soft, light. But it still fell right in the same range as the rest of her family.

"Huh. Great," Ryker said, still looking at Shirley's chest.

It's pretty dark red. That's usually a good sign so long as it doesn't go black. Won't know till I peel it off. Going to suck for her, though.

"You're married to Lauren?" Shirley asked.

"Engaged, technically. But I'm officially married to Adele, Claire, and Diane Chas," Ryker said, running a finger along the edge of the scab. He was hoping it'd have a lip to it so he wouldn't have to go scooping at it with his fingernails. "Lauren will be wed to me as soon as this war is over."

"Adele, Lauren, and… Claire?" Shirley asked.

"Yep. Claire tried to kill me, though. She ran off with the church of light vicar. Haven't seen her since. Couldn't care less either," Ryker grumbled, not mentioning the fact that she was pregnant.

"And Diane Chas, the… the pretender queen's daughter," Shirley said.

"Yeah, her. You know, the one you were riding dispatches for."

Shirley didn't respond to that, and instead fell silent.

Ryker was getting impatient now. There was no reason for Arria to not have returned by now with the bandage he'd asked for.

The door opened, and Marybelle walked in. She had bandages, a suture kit, water, and several small potions all laid out on a large tray.

"Hey there," Ryker said, grinning at her. "I'd be glad just to see you as you are, but you brought everything I needed, too."

"Arria came to me in a panic, acting as if you were threatening to eat her," Marybelle said with a shake of her head and a smile as she walked over to him. "She's such a mess when it comes to you. After she explained what was going on, I figured it'd be best if I came."

"Wise woman. Marybelle, Shirley — Shirley, Marybelle," Ryker said, looking back to the wound. "I was just about to pull this off and see how it's looking in there. When I shot her, the bolt went right in and hit her lung."

"Goodness. I can see why you'd want to check it," Marybelle murmured, setting the tray down next to him. "A moment."

Marybelle got down closer to Shirley and froze.

"Isn't that a surprise. She's almost a mirror image of Claire, isn't she?" Marybelle said, staring at Shirley.

"She is?" Ryker said, then looked at Shirley's face again. Then he leaned back and looked at her in full.

She had the right build, bust, hip size, hair, and face to be a near body double and match to Claire.

It'd just take a haircut and maybe a bit of product.

"Huh, she really is. Even her boobs are pretty close. Actually, she might be a bit bigger than Claire," Ryker said. "Which side of Lauren's family are you on?"

Shirley grimaced, looking away, her face turning red.

"I'm Claire's younger sister. By a year," Shirley said. "Our family was rounded up by Queen Chas and told to serve or die. So… I served. The rest of my family was exterminated. I've been looking for a chance to escape, and you caught me on my way out after I had disguised myself as a messenger."

"Great, give me your soul card so I can confirm that," Ryker said, staring at her.

"My… my soul card?" Shirley squeaked. Then she looked at Ryker and the flat stare he was giving her. "I… ok. Sure. Don't hurt me. Here."

With a tap, she cast her soul card to Ryker.

Reading it over, it only took him a few seconds to confirm exactly what she'd said.

"Well alright then," Ryker mumbled.

Can certainly understand surrendering under threats of violence. I more or less coaxed Adele into a similar situation to become my wife.

Interesting claim about escaping. Definitely possible.

Marybelle looked to him after a few seconds.

"I can't sense anything wrong internally, outside of this area being… bad. Obviously," Marybelle said, indicating the wound. "My arts don't tell me more than that, though."

"Goodie. I get to play battlefield surgeon and go digging. Sorry, Shirley. I'll be as gentle as I can," Ryker said. "But we kind of need to know if there's anything in there, and if it's healing right. You can't use another potion for quite a while. And we can't risk using magic to do it until we need to.

"This is what happens when you're brought to death's door in one go. Why weren't you in armor?"

Before she could respond, Ryker slipped a fingernail under the scab and peeled it back with a quick flick of his fingers.

Shirley hissed, flexing the bindings around her hands and quivering in the chair.

"Nothing in the wound. No bits of arrow or clothing. Seems… clear," Ryker said, pushing a finger against the area. It was bleeding slowly, but not a concerning amount of blood. "That's always the worst part about this stuff. When things get in a wound. Cloth and fabric are the worst offenders."

"More of your youth spent in an adventurer classroom?" Marybelle asked, holding out a bandage to him.

"Indeed," Ryker said and took the bandage. Looking at the wound, though, he was sure it wouldn't do. "No. I'm going to sew it up. That'll be a helluva pucker scar otherwise. There's enough skin here that I should be able to make it fairly clean. If I keep the stitches close and tight; it'll be a teeny tiny scar."

Ryker got to work.

Shirley passed out.

***

Ryker sat on his throne, looking down at the tabletop. It was centered entirely on the enemy forces outside of Dungeon.

Marybelle and Wynne were with him, each of them owning a part of the current situation.

"All in all, it seems close to thirty thousand soldiers died last night," Wynne said. All the cores that the… the Dark Lord left us have been filled.

"We effectively cut down ten to fifteen percent of each army in a single go."

"I have a few of my girls reading cores. They started with all the messengers, though," Marybelle said. "It would seem both sides distrust the other as mortal enemies, but they're trying to get in touch if only to break Dungeon."

"In other words, it's quite possible they'll be back to plotting our demise by tomorrow," Ryker said.

"That's quite possible. So far, they've only sent a few messengers back and forth, and I've had them all killed," Wynne said with a shrug of her delicate shoulders. "I'm employing a couple blades. They're doing it simply for coin and a few points. They're happy to do it. I'm having their orders sent by Ratfolk. They're mostly ignored by everyone."

"Blades killing people for trade in points," Ryker said. The moment the blueprints went live for the vendors and skill masters, everyone had been in a mad panic to figure out the cost to learn such things.

The blades knew, of course. The vendors were there for them. They were getting powerful, and quickly. And far more reliant on the dungeon every day. A number of them had challenged high-ranked enemies for the right to live in a dueling box.

"Our willing blades," Ryker muttered. "Let's double down on our tricks tonight. Let's have the blades firing random arrow shots into the camp. Pay them per hit on a living person.

"On top of that, let's do another arrow attack tonight. It probably won't work, but I still want to try. Worst case scenario we kill some, best case they end up attacking one another again."

"I'll take care of that portion," Wynne said.

"Next… I want a king of the hill–style battle put down out in front of Dungeon. Just like we did for the temple battle," Ryker said. "Let's put down a giant platform large enough to fit a fifty-versus-fifty battle. Army that walks away gets riches based on how many of their team survive, and weapons they can use on one another. Like a scorpion."

"Scorpion?" Marybelle asked.

"It's like a smaller ballista. Easier to move but pretty nasty."

"Ok, I can do that," Marybelle said. "Do we want our own people on the platform at all?"

"Only to talk about the rewards, nothing else. Remind them it's to the death, of course, and it doesn't have to be the enemy army they're fighting. If they want to kill each other for wealth, who am I to disagree?" Ryker said.

"Got it," Marybelle said, smiling at him and then Wynne. "This is rather enjoyable. Do you two often plan like this?"

"Often enough that Arria takes notes," Wynne said, indicating the wisp avatar fluttering in the corner. "What else?"

"Not really sure. I mean, let's make sure we put a massive bounty on the two vicars. Would love to see them go down," Ryker said. "Let's also put one on Veronica Chas, but to have her captured without harm. In any way, shape or form."

Wynne nodded.

"And... and one for Claire," Ryker said, gnawing at his lower lip. "Same thing. Unharmed and unhurt in any way."

"I'll handle it," Wynne said softly. "And speaking of Claire... what do we want to do with her sister? She's sitting quietly in her cell for the time being. Not making a ruckus or a problem of herself."

"I don't know. I want to cut her head off and boot it out of the city, but in the same breath... that's anger directed at Claire and Veronica," Ryker said. "Shirley did nothing to deserve anything like that. So far as I can tell, she was dragged along. Just like Adele was."

"And Claire," Wynne said.

"Yes, and her," Ryker growled out.

"Can we use her?" Marybelle asked.

"How? I mean, I wouldn't even know what use she is," Ryker said. "Whatever. I'll leave it be for now. You think Adele and Diane made it up to Lauren already?"

"They did," Wynne said. "The two captains you put under me checked in this morning."

"Great. I'm going to go bother them. They already set up the cores, right? Wherever Lauren is, it's an impromptu dungeon, right?" Ryker asked.

"Yes, it is," Wynne said, nodding.

"Great. Meino, let's hit the bedroom. I need to send a letter," Ryker said, hopping to his feet and practically skipping out of the room.

He'd never admit it, but he was looking forward to talking to Diane, Adele... and if he could manage it... Lauren.

***

Zooming across the open expanse of dark fields, Ryker headed towards the Fairies. They knew he was coming. They'd clearly sensed him the moment he dropped into the dungeon sense.

And their reaction had been immediate when he'd started heading their way.

It was as if someone had kicked over an ant hill. The avatars went scurrying in every direction, preparing things for his arrival.

During his flight so far, he'd realized he could probably summon up an avatar to speak with them in person. But it'd drain the amount of mana the Fairies had on hand considerably.

Punishing them for the sake of seeing who he wanted in person rather than in a private dungeon sense, a bond space, was foolish. Not to mention incredibly selfish.

Suddenly, he popped out of the single line of power from the dungeon to the captains, into their temporary dungeon area.

All the Fairies had arranged themselves in a strange semi-circular fashion. It felt like they were receiving him more than anything else.

"My lord king," they said in unison.

"Yeah, no. None of that. Where's Diane, Adele, and Lauren?" he asked.

An Imp floated over to his own sense, and he felt a gentle prod come from it. It pointed him deeper.

Following the direction she indicated, he zipped over.

Diane, Adele, and Lauren were sitting around a small table. It was obvious they were just finishing a private dinner.

"...push out from the south?" Adele asked.

"We could, but it's always a question of how far I can go before they start hitting my supply lines," Lauren said with a sigh. "They're constantly working around behind me to make our advances fail."

"No, I mean launch from Dungeon. Ryker seemed dead set on letting no one get through to you. Friend or foe," Adele said.

Lauren's eyes dropped to the table, her face becoming a strange and complicated mask.

She looked the same as he remembered her. The strong and sad queen. Not as womanly in figure as her cousin Claire, not as athletic looking as Adele, and not as pretty as either. She ran the middle line.

To Ryker, she looked lovely.

"He's yours," Diane said, putting an elbow down on the arm of her chair and resting her chin on it. "As much as I turned him to me, and Adele herself, he never lost sight of helping you. Or being there for you.

"I even learned to swear in my wooing of him. I had his Fairies help me."

Tar nodded its head in Diane's lap.

The fuck? Since when did my damn familiar go with her? I didn't even realize he'd left.

Fuck.

"I cannot doubt you, given how much he sent with you to support me. And the fact that you two are actually here," Lauren said. "And the very… interesting… women who came with you."

"Don't let their looks cheat your thoughts. They're all extremely deadly," Diane said. "As well as I can determine, he utilized a very large amount of rare resources to get us here, and to provide you with that protection in addition to our arrival."

"I couldn't land a hit on any of them," Adele grumbled. "They just… dodged me. Then pushed me to the ground. Like a child.

"They wouldn't even fight me at all. They're terrified of harming me and how Ryker would react."

Diane nodded her head. "They are a bit protective of us three, aren't they?"

Lauren started to laugh softly, then leaned back in her chair, pressing her hands to her face.

She let out a groan, and her fingernails dug into her skin.

"What the hell is wrong with me?" she said. "I have a war going on and all I can think of is that dumb farmer saying awful things to me. He always makes me laugh."

"I miss talking to him as well," Diane said. "He always has interesting things to say."

Adele chuckled, her face turning a slow and deep red.

"Oh, he's fun to talk to. But why talk? I can't stop thinking about what he does in bed and how I need it right now," Adele said, fanning her face lightly with a hand and turning a deep, dark red.

"Yes," Diane said, lifting her chin slightly, her cheeks flushing as well. "Yes, indeed."

Lauren pulled her hands away to look at her cousin, then Diane.

"Really?" she asked.

"I mean, coming from a place of no experience at all, it's all I know," Adele said. "But it's… very fun."

"Likewise, and similar sentiments," Diane said. "Especially —"

Ryker chose that moment to push on the bonds he held with Diane and Adele. They'd never canceled them, after all.

Both women froze up, their eyes staring into nothing.

"Ah… are you two alright?" Lauren asked.

"Ryker's calling me," Adele said.

"I can feel him pulling at me as well," Diane added.

Sliding out of the room and hurrying back to where he'd entered the dungeon sense, and the Fairies, Ryker pulled on the two contracts a bit harder. Drawing them up into his dungeon sense and then the bond space the same way he'd done with Marybelle.

At the same time, he dropped a bond contract to Lauren, exactly the same as Adele's and Diane's. Though he did add a small hook that when she accepted it, if she did, it would draw her straight into his bond sense.

He also put an actual limit to it all so that the three of them couldn't read his mind or emotions.

Slowly, Diane and Adele materialized from nothing. A muted burst of magic happened as each of them formed fully.

"Ryker?" Diane said, looking at him with a small smile on her lips.

"Hi," Ryker said, waving at the two women.

Adele bolted across the middle distance wordlessly. Her face a giant smile, she looked very much completely unlike herself. She slammed into him, her arms wrapping around him tightly.

"You big stupid idiot," Adele said into his chest. "If you could do this all along, why didn't you come sooner?"

"Because you needed to be stationary," Ryker said, hugging Adele back tightly.

"Now, who wants to go ask Lauren to join us? She just needs to make a tiny contract to me, just like you two did," Ryker said. "I already set it up for her."

Squeezing him tighter for a second, Adele pulled back and kissed him quickly.

"I'll go," she said, and then vanished, her face bright red.

Diane laughed softly after Adele left and walked over to Ryker, her arms out.

"Hello beloved," Diane said. Reaching him, she hugged him tightly. Even perhaps more so than Adele. "It's good to see you. Very good. Adele has been in poor spirits since we left, and it was obvious she was quite depressed without you."

Her greeting of him was a study in contrast to Adele. But she radiated warmth and absolute love of him.

"I love you," Ryker blurted out, holding to Diane.

Making a small noise that sounded almost like panic to Ryker, Diane turned her face in and pressed it to his neck.

"I love you, too," she said against his skin.

Everything is so very different now.

Diane took two steps away from him and adjusted her dress.

"Look at me, acting like a little school girl in love," Diane said. "I'm a married and full-grown woman. I'm the heir presumptive to the duchy of Chas."

"I dunno. When you're cute like that, it makes me want to just shower you in more attention," Ryker said.

Diane looked at him and quirked a brow with a smile.

"Then maybe I shouldn't be reserved in private, and that's something for later. For now, Lauren is coming. And I don't want to get in the way of her reunion with you. In fact, if this is anything like the avatars…" Diane said, then disappeared.

Two seconds later, Lauren appeared with Adele.

The latter took a look for where Diane should be, saw her missing, and then popped right back out of existence.

They left me here with Lauren? They left me with Lauren.

Chapter 9 - Royal Orders -

Lauren had arrived in a royal dress, much like what she wore with everyone else.

As soon as she realized Ryker was standing in front of her, though, her dress flew away in an instant and was replaced with far more casual clothes. Clothes he knew for a fact he'd seen Adele wear. Even Lauren's hair went from a coiled mass to a single ponytail.

"Ryker?" she asked, her head tilting partially to one side. Then she looked around. "Where did Adele go? And where's Diane? She said they'd both be here. And where are we?"

Grinning, Ryker let out a short breath.

"They both left. Can't imagine why," he said. "As to where we are... we're in my dungeon, so to speak. A special place inside my soul, I guess."

"How is that possible? I can still feel myself. I feel quite keenly where I stubbed my toe this morning," Lauren said, pointing down at her foot. Then she froze.

"Why am I wearing boots? Actually, how did I get in these clothes?" she asked, looking at herself.

"No idea. That's just how you showed up," Ryker said.

Lauren reached up and pinched her own cheek. "Ow. I still feel pain. I'm also breathing. Is this real or not?"

"It's real. And you'll feel everything, it just... won't be felt with your body, I guess? Though I suppose if you really wanted, you could turn off feeling, breathing, and blinking."

"Sorry, this is all new to me. I'm not really an expert; I'd need Wynne or Marybelle here."

Lauren looked at him again, her eyes seeming to take him in piece by piece.

"Are you well?" she asked finally, walking over to him slowly.

"I mean, I guess I am. The stab wound is healing up. Gonna be a great scar," Ryker said with a shrug. "Otherwise, it's what Diane and Adele probably told you. Holding back four big armies with my little county. All for the sake of the beautiful queen I'm madly in love with."

Ryker bowed at the waist with a flourish.

"All in a day's work, I guess," he said, standing up with a grin.

Lauren was directly in front of him now. Her hands came up and grabbed the sides of his face, her fingers cupping his jaw.

"Do you honestly love me? You barely know me. We've barely had any interaction at all," Lauren said, staring into his eyes.

With a soft huff, Ryker nodded.

"Yeah. The dirty farming dungeon wizard loves you. I mean, let's call it what it is. I could have easily squatted in my dungeon like a beetle, contacted no one, built up a power base, and made my own country," Ryker said. "I could have done that still after I met you.

"Instead... instead I met an intelligent young woman, hounded by trials and tribulations that made my own difficulties look petty, who still hadn't given up on the world. Or those around her."

Ryker set his hands on her hips and gave her a small pull, moving her closer to him.

"I'm in love with who you are as much as what you are. You're everything I know I should be, and you make me strive to be that," Ryker said. "And that you're great looking isn't terrible. I mean, I know Claire fills things out better, but you really own the sexy-queen thing in a great way."

Lauren's brow creased, her entire face a frown.

"That's not romantic at all," Lauren said.

"Uh... sorry? I'm not really good at that stuff. If I were, I wouldn't be sending you love notes about candelabras," Ryker said honestly.

Letting out a short burst of a laugh, Lauren shook her head and then began to laugh in earnest.

"I do suppose, for you, that was incredibly romantic," Lauren said, her hands sliding down his face to rest behind his neck and shoulders. "So... this place is private, won't reflect in the real world, but feels like the real world."

Lauren paused and leaned in close to him, planting a warm and tender kiss on his lips. She smelled of cinnamon.

"Do you think Diane and Adele plan on returning soon?" she asked him.

Ryker built a construct of his mind around the bond space and set it firmly in place.

Lauren jumped in his arms, her eyes widening. As if she'd actually felt the sudden and drastic change.

"Did you just... slam and lock the door, so to speak?" Lauren asked, grinning at him. "I'm flattered, and I like where your mind is going. But I must put my country's needs above my own for the time. Just... just know that I'm eternally grateful for all you've done for me, Ryker. As both a woman and a queen. And I'll make it up to you. Go ahead, open the door and invite them in?"

Giving him a quick peck on the lips, Lauren took a handful of steps away from him and folded her hands in front of her.

"Yeah, yeah. Tease the dumb farmer," Ryker muttered, and opened everything up again. Gently, he gave Adele and Diane a pull on their contracts.

Both women appeared. Casually, they both looked to Lauren, then Ryker, and back to Lauren. It was obvious they were wondering why they were back so soon.

"Count, would you pl—"

"Lauren, really? Look at yourself," Adele said, grinning.

Lauren looked down at her clothes and then sighed, pressing a hand to her head.

"Fine. Fine. I... ok. Ryker. What's going on? Why are you here?" Lauren asked. Adele shot Diane a grin and Diane winked back at her, both of them turning to Ryker.

"Check in, say hi, make sure you three know that I can do this," Ryker said, shrugging. "See you three."

"Good. I was worried for a minute," Diane said, a relieved smile on her face.

"Yeah, no, everything is fine. I got the churches to fight one another the other day. They took some serious casualties," Ryker said. "Though something interesting happened during the fight. I was laid up in the middle between the two armies killing messengers as they tried to talk to one another."

Adele nodded at that, Diane looked a little disturbed, and Lauren's face was blank.

"I knocked one off their horse and went to go finish them. It was a woman," Ryker said. "A woman who looked like she'd fallen out of the royal family tree."

Lauren and Adele looked interested suddenly, and Diane had a grimace on her face.

"Apparently she's a cousin. Branch family. One Shirley. Sister to Claire. Apparently her family was wiped out by Veronica to the last, minus her and her sister. She and Claire are all that's left," Ryker said.

"I'm not surprised by that. My mother has demonstrated nothing but absolute disregard for everything," Diane said, sighing.

"I remember Shirley," Lauren said, turning to Adele. "She was only a year or two younger than Claire, right?"

"Yeah, we played with her. She was quiet and mousey. Never stood up to anyone and always looked for a quiet way out," Adele said. "I always got her confused with Claire when we were little."

"Apparently that similarity didn't stop in their youth. Didn't realize it till I got her in some light, but she's a damn double of Claire," Ryker said. "I've got her in a prison cell right now."

"She is?" Lauren asked. "A double, that is."

"Yeah. If you put them side by side you could probably figure it out, but you'd have to know what Claire looked like first," Ryker confirmed.

Lauren lifted a hand to her chin and tapped a finger to it thoughtfully.

"Can you show me a likeness of her, and of Claire?" Lauren asked.

Ryker winced at that, looking off to one side.

"I'm so sorry, Ryker. I didn't even think—"

Before Lauren could finish what she was saying, or how Ryker could think to do what she asked, two lifelike images of Claire and Shirley appeared.

Claire was completely naked, standing there without a smile. Next to her was Shirley, naked from the chest up, also standing without a smile. They were posed in very similar ways, and it seemed as if someone had worked to make sure they were relevant to one another in that pose.

A tiny poke from Marybelle with the mental image of a smile gave him his answer.

"Oh, my," Lauren said, walking over to the perfect recreations of her cousins.

Ryker looked down to one side again, not wanting to look at Claire at all. His ball of feelings involving her was still wound up tight.

"Is she really…?" Lauren asked.

"Yeah, she is. Shirley's bigger, it seems," Adele said. "Damn, she really does look a lot like her sister. You got a sneaky plan in that queenie head of yours?"

"Same one I'm thinking of, probably," Diane said. "Make Shirley be Claire. The rest of her family is dead. If Shirley takes the role, she keeps her head and that branch family can live on. She claims the real Claire is a fake, dolled up to help give Mother some credibility.

"If not… send her this way under guard. Probably a single Imp, and Shirley tied to a saddle. Lauren can use her one way or another."

"Well said," Lauren commented, nodding her head. Then she turned to Ryker. "Would you do that for me, Ryker?"

Ryker shrugged; he didn't care.

"Just give me the terms you want to tell her, and I'll have it done," Ryker said.

"Thank you, I'll have them for you tonight," Lauren said, giving him a wide smile. "Without Dungeon — without you — I don't think I'd still have my head, or my crown."

"You wouldn't," Adele said, scratching at her ass.

Lauren rolled her eyes.

"Anything else to report?" she asked, giving Ryker a warm smile.

"No," he said. "Do you want me to check back in…?"

"Yes. Come back tomorrow with Shirley's reply. We'll go from there," Lauren said. "For now, nothing else."

"Great, you two leave. I need some me time with my husband. Just give me the terms to give him later," Adele said, making shooing motions at both of them. "Unless you two wanna watch this happen."

Diane and Lauren vanished, and Adele gave Ryker a predatory grin.

Pretty far from the alcoholic rough rider now.

***

Popping back into himself, Ryker gave his body a shake. Everything felt a little strange, but not wrong.

Like he'd fallen asleep on something, and everything was a little tingly.

"Welcome back, dear," Marybelle said, setting down a teacup she'd had in her hand. "I already prepped everything for you that I saw coming through your mind back to your body. I had Shirley fed and given a fresh set of clothes as well, courtesy of you."

Blinking several times, Ryker looked at Marybelle and let out a bark of laughter.

"That's how you knew… ah. You really enjoy just lounging around in my head, don't you?" Ryker asked, walking over to her.

"I do," Marybelle said, looking up at him standing over her. "Going to kick me out?"

"No, but I might lock you in. Do be careful what you wish for. You said you had it prepared for me?" he asked.

Marybelle arched an eyebrow at him, then picked up a scroll and held it up to him. "Don't tempt me."

Ryker took the scroll, thinking about bothering the Hob some more. Then he changed his mind. Leaning down, he hugged her tightly.

She's doing a lot for me. Need to make sure I say thank you.

"Thanks," Ryker said, then released her and went to Shirley's cell without looking back.

Not bothering to knock or even announce his presence, Ryker just opened the door and walked in.

Shirley was perched on her bed, legs pulled up in front of her. Her wide eyes locked on him, fear evident on her face.

"Lauren has put her name to you, and I've received your judgment," Ryker said, then flicked the scroll to her.

"What…?" Shirley asked, picking up the paper.

Ryker walked to the only chair in the room, then dropped down into it and waited.

Shirley's eyes moved from one side of the paper to the other, her face showing clear fear and distaste.

At least she's nothing like Claire. But in the same breath, she'll have to work on that.

"I'm to be… Claire?" Shirley asked, looking at Ryker.

"That or I tie you to a horse and send you to Lauren. I imagine she'll just lock you away until she figures out Claire," Ryker said. "I'll… I'll ask her to spare you if only for my sake. You don't seem like a bad person. Just stuck in a bad position."

"You would?" Shirley asked, her mouth forming a pout.

"Yeah, I would. Want to think on it? Lauren wants to know by tomorrow night," Ryker said.

"No. Not really. Her demand is pretty straightforward. Become Claire, become your wife in her place, live the role," Shirley said, shaking her head. "You want me to be the one thing I despised more than my mom."

"Up to you. You can be Claire, or you can be Shirley," Ryker said. "Either way, I'll do what I can to help you. Promise."

"Why?" Shirley asked, still pouting, and looking rather upset.

"Because I believe you really were escaping. Read the truth of that on your soul card. You weren't even wearing armor," Ryker said with a chuckle. "No weapon, no armor—you didn't even have boots on. You bowed your head, waited for a chance, and then ran."

"How do you know I won't run again?" Shirley asked.

Ryker shrugged with a smile. "I don't. But if you promise me, I'll believe you. Because you're not Claire, and I'm not forcing you to make a decision. I'll even help you if you decline."

Shirley turned her head to one side, looking at him out of the corner of her eyes.

"You seem awfully sure of yourself. You're hiding something," Shirley said, then turned her head in the other direction, looking at him from a different angle. "You survived Queen Chas, the churches, and managed to help Lauren gain ground down here.

"People are saying you got help from the Dark Lord of the North… but that didn't happen, did it? You're… the dungeon itself, aren't you?"

Chuckling, Ryker raised his eyebrows at her. "And how'd you figure that all out?"

Shirley shrugged, looking down to her bedsheets. "Just because I'm not Claire doesn't mean I'm an idiot. I'm probably smarter than her. I didn't want to be anybody, though. I just wanted to be left alone.

"And you being the dungeon makes sense for anyone who pays attention. Wizard, powerful, ex-adventurer, dungeon pops up under your inn, strange women around you. You survive battles, assassination attempts, a pretender queen, and a tug-of-war in a civil war. Then you somehow dodge champions, and the Dark Lord of the North. The only answer that fits is you're one with the dungeon."

"Smart. Well, about being left alone, I hear ya there. I just want to tend to my farm and kill a few people who made me angry," Ryker said. "Well. I wanted to kill a few people. I'm somehow mostly over my rage.

"Now that I think about it, I don't think I've had a temper tantrum, as my dungeon queen would call it, in a while."

"And the dungeon?" Shirley asked, pressing her chin to her knees.

"Yes. I'm the dungeon. Point to you for logical deduction," Ryker said.

"I'll become Claire, be your wife, and be loyal to you in all ways, but I won't sleep with you," Shirley said.

"That's fine. Diane and Adele wouldn't like me sleeping with you anyways," Ryker said with a shrug and stood up. "I'll take your promise now."

"I promise to be your wife, to be loyal to you, and serve the rightful queen Lauren," Shirley said.

"Great, let's go get dinner together and get you situated in a room. And a haircut. Tomorrow you'll need to do your best Claire impression and see our citizens," Ryker said.

"Okay," Shirley said, getting out of her bed.

She was dressed in much nicer clothes now than when he'd first met her. She'd also cleaned up, and she looked fresh. She was beautiful and, eerily, almost a clone of Claire.

"I guess after this moment, Shirley no longer exists, and you're just Claire," Ryker said. "You sure about this?"

"Yes," Shirley said, straightening her shoulders and letting out a short breath. Her face blanked out to a neutral, polite mask. Turning her head to Ryker, she gave him the cold, dead Claire smile.

"If you would escort me to my room, husband?" Shirley asked in a spot-on match to Claire's tone.

"Yeah… don't do that in private," Ryker said with a wince. "Claire tried to kill me just before she ran away with the vicar. Kinda… bad feelings… there. Though I'm surprised she didn't try to free you after she joined the church."

Then again, maybe I'm not surprised. Maybe she views her direct family as poorly as her extended family.

Shirley's mask fell away and she shook her head, looking at the ground. The mousey woman coming back.

"I managed to get to see her once. She greeted me. Said hello. Then just… went back to work," Shirley said. "As if I didn't exist."

"Too bad for her. You're going to be an amazing problem for her going forward, and get all the rewards she would have gotten," Ryker said, wrapping an arm around Shirley's shoulders. "Come, dinner awaits and I'm starving. I think we should get to know each other as well as possible since… technically… you're my wife now. And Lauren, Adele, Diane, and I will be the only ones who know the real you. A haircut, too. Then we'll have to dig out Claire's wardrobe and have you pick through it."

Shirley gave Ryker a small smile and nodded her head, leaving the cell with him.

Chapter 10 - Misdirection -

Marybelle, Wynne, Charlotte, and Tris were all sitting around a table in a room offset from Ryker's throne room.

Shirley was sitting quietly next to Ryker, in full "Claire" mode, busily taking down notes as the four fairies and Ryker talked.

For the first ten minutes, the Fairies had all stared at Shirley in turns, clearly unnerved and unwilling to ask the question they all shared.

Even Ryker had a hard time looking at Shirley without only seeing Claire. Wearing the clothes Claire had left behind, and with her hair now cut to the same fashion, she was a strange mirror likeness of her older sister.

"And that brings us up to today," Ryker said, looking at Shirley. "Any questions?"

"Nothing at this time, husband," Shirley said, making small notations to the right of her previous notes. "Though I'm sure I'll have some at a later time. Especially about our finances since I was here last. Even from just our casual conversation so far, it sounds like there's been some serious gaps in its management."

Fuck me, she really is Claire.

Or... is she actually a lot like Claire, just without the awful personality?

Lifting her head up, she found Ryker watching her.

The mask slipped away for a moment as she gave him a small awkward smile. Then it was back in an instant as she set her notes to one side.

"Alright, I'm tired of seeing Claire part two," Ryker said, looking to his Fairies. "This is Shirley, if you haven't figured it out already. I'm sure you already knew, but... there we are. What do you think?"

"Truthfully?" Wynne asked, looking at Shirley. "I was positive it was Claire. That she'd somehow come back and wormed her way into your good graces. You really know how to put on a perfect Claire disguise, Shirley."

Shirley shrugged, the Claire persona melting away. Leaving only a mousy version of the woman in its place.

"I just... act like a bitch and pretend no one matters to me but me," Shirley said.

"I was fooled," Marybelle said. "And I actually met you before this."

"What's the plan? Why are you doing this?" Tris asked, looking at Ryker. "You only get tricky like this when you have a plan."

"Shirley is going to pose as Claire. Become Claire. It'll discredit Claire, make Veronica Chas look bad for faking her allegiance, and then cause her to be accused of murdering her family. Which she did," Ryker said. "It'll force the Church and Veronica to abandon Claire and take a black eye for their part in it.

"We'll need to make an announcement today about Claire coming 'home' to me, and that she escaped captivity. Beyond that, she'll end up having to be visible today. She'll need guards."

Wynne nodded her head with a smile. "I can handle that."

"Great. How'd it go last night with the churches? We get anyone to bite?" Ryker asked.

"A little. Not nearly as much as the other day. They didn't send any messengers this time, either. They just... backed away from each other after a while," Wynne said.

"Sounds like they figured it out. Time to move to the next piece, I suppose. Let's do the same thing to Trevail and Adelona. I think they're far more likely to go all out on one another," Ryker said.

"They are," Shirley said, taking notes again. "They're much more hostile to each other than the churches are. That's part of the problem with their politics."

"Could you elaborate on that?" Marybelle said, giving Shirley her best 'I'm your friend' smile.

Shirley smiled tentatively back at the Hob, nodding her head minutely.

"Trevail and Adelona are much more willing to kill one another than the churches are. They've blamed one another for everything that's wrong with their countries for so long that their populace no longer sees anything but an enemy anymore," Shirley said. "There's really no going back for them. They're held in check by the churches right now."

"Perfect," Ryker said, gesturing at Shirley. "Thank you, Shirley. That's wonderful. Do you have any suggestions on how best to set that grudge match to a full-on 'death to the last man' type of battle?"

Shirley's mouth became a pensive frown, her eyebrows coming down.

"What are the limitations on you as the dungeon?" Shirley asked. "Can you actually make people who look like they're from Trevail or Adelona?"

"We can make people from Adelona quite easily. We massacred an army of theirs and have all the appropriate standards and the like," Wynne said.

Shirley opened her mouth, then closed it before nodding her head once.

"Ok. Do the same thing you did last time, but actually let a few of your dungeon… creatures… get pulled down and killed in the initial chase," Shirley said. "In full Adelona colors. It sounds like part of the problem last time around was that neither of the churches ever saw confirmation that it was the other one shooting on them.

"Did they even find a single corpse of the archers?"

Wynne looked like she was thinking on that question. Finally, she shook her head. "No. They all escaped from both sides."

"They never got confirmation of what was shooting at them," Shirley said. "It might actually work to have those Adelona archers take a pot shot at the church of light, and let them fall there, too."

Ryker nodded his head. Shirley was right. If there was nothing to confirm who was shooting, it was more than likely they would get suspicious.

I mean, I would. I'd be sitting there wondering. And then… and then probably start running detect life. Ah.

Sighing, Ryker shook his head with a grin.

"They're using detect life. That's why they didn't really respond last night. Let's just make it worth attacking them outright for the churches," Ryker said, leaning forward. "Make catapults, archers, crossbowmen, mages, and just have them all lobbed into the camps of both churches. They're not going to follow us anyways.

"For Adelona and Trevail, carry out Shirley's plan."

"Ryker, I could use some of your time," Charlotte said before anyone else could jump in.

"Oh. Alright. How about now? I didn't have anything else to discuss, other than to tell you all to please treat Shirley as my wife," Ryker said, then got up.

"That is… yes, right now is fine," Charlotte said, getting up quickly to follow Ryker as he left.

Meino lumbered along behind them, her heavy footsteps plodding along.

"I wanted to discuss the wall," Charlotte said, catching up to him and matching his pace.

His goal was his farm. He was tired of being underground. Tired of hiding.

On top of that, he'd already worked out a deal with the Dark Lord of the North. He had no interest in him anymore.

Turning toward the exit ramp, Ryker started going up the stairs quickly.

"Ryker… the wall… I can't talk to you… like this," Charlotte said, bouncing up the steps behind him.

"Don't worry, just heading to the farm. I'm sure it's sprouting weeds. I just need my hoe and my trowel," Ryker said.

"Your farm?" Charlotte asked incredulously behind him.

"Yes, my farm. It's not just my… job. It's—well, it's my hobby. It helps me center myself. It's been like a week," Ryker said, exiting the dungeon into the inn.

Adventurers and citizens alike stared at him as he exited.

"Hey," Ryker said nonchalantly, holding up a hand.

A number of people waved back at him, and the rest of the inn went back to what they were doing.

Everyone in Dungeon knew the dungeon protected Ryker. Him coming out of it was normal.

I should track down Edwin and see how he's doing later.

Getting out onto the street, Ryker made a beeline for his farmhouse at the top of the hill.

Meino and Charlotte were right on his heels.

"This isn't advisable," Charlotte said. "That Fox woman might still be around."

"I don't think she is. And even if I'm wrong, she's not interested in us anymore," Ryker countered. Reaching the front door to his home, Ryker grabbed his hoe, bucket, and garden trowel. They were all where he remembered leaving them against the front wall.

Moving to the first row, Ryker spotted a small weed immediately.

"Fine. Fine, ok, the wall," Charlotte said, standing over him. "I've been watching what's happening with the camps and the soldiers. They're starting to make scouting runs at the walls to see what's going on."

"Uh huh. We figured that'd happen. And?" Ryker asked.

"We killed as many as we could, but they got curious after we started repelling them. The enemy is well aware of the walls that are going up now," Charlotte said. "They're starting to break down their camps and get ready. It started with the simple stuff, but now they're loading wagons and carts. I think they'll be ready to go by tomorrow or the day after. I can't tell."

Ryker paused, his hand trowel buried up to the handle in the dirt.

"Alright," Ryker said, shaking his head. "We're nowhere near done. At all. Are we?"

"No. A month away, even at the rate were capturing and converting mana," Charlotte said. "It's a long way to the ocean for me, and the mountains for Tris."

"I gave all the resources from the Dark Lord to Wynne. Did she redistribute it all back to you and Tris?" Ryker asked.

"Yes, but neither of us have used any of it. In total, if you include both stockpiles, it's enough to put one side to the target, and the other most of the way there," Charlotte said. "But not both of us."

Thinking, Ryker levered the weed up and pulled it out with his other hand. After dropping it into his pail, Ryker started moving down the row in a crouch. Looking for another weed.

He didn't have far to go to find another. Looking further down, he saw several. Letting his eyes move one row over, he saw it was just as bad. If not worse.

There was no way he could solve both. Which meant he needed to minimize the damage now. Weeds were weeds, after all.

"Alright," Ryker said. "Let's see what they do. We could raise the wall as part of their army crosses and strand them, right?"

"Maybe have some of our forces waiting to welcome them into the Queensland and bury them right there."

"We can try that. It might delay them," Charlotte said.

"If we do it a couple times, they might stop trying to cross entirely. That'd be nice," Ryker grumbled.

"If they did, you'd have to have the Death Dungeon ready to go. How's that looking?" Charlotte asked, standing over him.

"About as well as peeking on you when you're bathing and not expecting me," Ryker said with a smirk.

"In other words... lots of attempts and no actual payoff?" Charlotte said with a chuckle. "You could always just join me. I wouldn't turn you away."

"It's more fun peeking," Ryker said.

Charlotte began to gently scratch at the top of his head with her fingernails.

"Maybe we use that to our advantage. What if we do it in a way that makes the wall look unstable," Charlotte said. "Unstable, and that they need to push hard up against it so we can grind them down."

Ryker lifted his head up a bit, no longer weeding, trying to get her to keep touching him.

Charlotte began to curl her fingers through his hair, her leg pressing up to his shoulder.

"Then later after that... maybe that bit of the wall collapses. We have some dungeon spawn scramble as if they're trying to rebuild it," Charlotte said. "Think they'd rush the gap?"

"Probably. I'd rush your gap," Ryker said.

Charlotte choked, then laughed softly, rapping him on top of the head with a knuckle.

"You're so dumb. Just come see me tonight," Charlotte said, sounding incredibly awkward while petting him on the head now. "I'm going to go set up my trap. I'll keep you updated. See you tonight?"

Ryker reached back into the earth again.

"Yeah, I'll see you tonight," Ryker said. "Be ready for me to rush your gap."

Meino's shadow fell over him as he kept working.

"It's very good watching you lately," she said. "You're very happy. Very… warm. You smile a lot now."

Pausing for a second, Ryker nodded and flicked a weed toward the bucket.

"Yeah. I'm happy. Of course, it makes me scared that I'm in danger of losing it all, but… I'm happy," Ryker said.

"Don't worry. If all else fails and the world falls down around you, I'll be there," Meino said.

Ryker grinned to himself.

"Thanks, Meino. I love you, too."

***

Ryker watched from above as the battlefield he'd asked for was completed.

It was a massive structure made of stone that went nine hundred feet in either direction. It took up a massive amount of space in the front of Dungeon, and it was something you couldn't miss.

"You think they'll actually come try it out?" Ryker asked.

"I think so," Shirley said, sharing the bond space with him. "You did send that lovely little note."

"My note? You wrote it, not me," Ryker said.

"Your note," Shirley said.

"How can it be my note? I had nothing to do with it other than sending it."

"Your note. And did you like my performance today? I made sure everyone saw me who could," Shirley said calmly.

Shirley had become infuriating. Talking to her was like conversing with a brick wall at times.

Except it was also somewhat amusing to fight with her. There was something about the give and take in banter that never failed to bring a smile to his lips.

"It was very lovely. Everyone was remarking about how well you looked," Ryker said.

"Ah, see? Here comes some now. Your note was perfect. If I'd written it, I'd be proud of it," Shirley said, her presence shifting slightly.

"You did write it. I saw it. It was just a long, expletive-filled piece of paper. That's all it was," Ryker said. "Curse words."

"Yes. You really made a work of art," Shirley said. "A noblewoman like myself would never do such a thing. A dirty little grub farmer like you? You'd do that."

"I swear to the heavens I'm going to watch you go to the bathroom and put the memory of it into a core and share it with everyone in Dungeon," Ryker said.

"That'd be interesting to see," Shirley said. "Especially with you trying to push my credibility up."

"You're horrible," Ryker grumbled.

"I like her. Very much," Wynne sent into his mind.

"She's great," Marybelle added in a different message to him.

Because she antagonizes me. She's great because she… whatever. Definitely going to peek on her.

A group of a hundred or so soldiers from each of the churches marched up to their side of the stone battlefield.

The church of the dark immediately took the field. When the fiftieth soldier crossed the line, no more were allowed in, and a loud trumpet blew across the open fields.

"The church of everlasting darkness has challenged the church of the goat-fucking choir boys!" declared a neutral voice.

"Oh, that's a nice add. When did you put that in?" Shirley said.

"I didn't add anything! You did it. Why do you keep saying I did this?" Ryker asked.

A second trumpet blasted back in the other direction.

"The church of the true light has accepted the challenge of the virginal church of dickless losers!" shouted the voice a second time.

"Well, that's uncalled for, Ryker," Shirley said.

Nope. Not responding. Nope. Nope.

There were no officers in either group; they were all line soldiers. There was no leadership at all. Each side just ran at the other, screaming in absolute fury.

When the two forces came together, it was a massive crash of arms and armor that made the air quake with its volume.

The dying began almost immediately, people falling as each group stabbed and flailed at one another.

Even as they died, more and more front-line soldiers kept showing up, arranging themselves in groups and getting ready to fight the enemy for glory and prizes.

"Huh…" Ryker said. "For what it's worth, good job Shirley. I honestly thought you were being a little lazy with the note but… I can't argue with results. I'm impressed."

"They're little more than angry peasants with a grudge, looking for coin," Shirley said, her voice sounding a touch embarrassed. "It wasn't hard to manipulate them."

When the first groups finished, the church of the dark had won. They had twenty survivors in their group. Which was significant given that both groups had started with even numbers.

"Reward them well," Ryker sent to Marybelle.

Almost immediately, a massive chest of gold dropped down in front of the survivors with a boom. As well as gear, equipment, and a keg of beer.

Cheering, the dark church soldiers dragged their winnings off to one side and off the platform. They began to patch themselves up without fear of reprisal.

Anyone within three thousand feet around the battlefield would be protected by the dungeon with extreme prejudice. Fights outside the battle arena were disallowed.

"Peasants or not, good job Shirley. Good job," Ryker said.

The second groups of each army were already sprinting up onto the battlefield as fast as possible, even as the corpses and gear of the last group vanished into the stone. Only their service tags were spared, piled into two offering plates at the middle point of the battlefield, though outside the arena.

One for each side to access as they liked.

"The blessed church of light has challenged the church of the sheep-sucking idiots of the dark!" shouted the battlefield announcer.

"Your vocabulary is interesting," Ryker said.

"Thank you," Shirley said. "Oh! Look! Officers."

Men on horses were galloping toward the battlefield, their fancy helmets marking them clearly as anything but line soldiers.

"Think they'll get them to leave?" Shirley asked.

"No. Did you see how they all looked when the chest dropped down? Their greed will keep them here. And we'll bleed them of troops," Ryker said. "Bleeds, poisons, and diseases suck in a dungeon. This is just a giant bleed. That's all.

"And we'll bleed them dry."

Chapter 11 - Inevitability -

Ryker popped out of the transfer chute and came to right in front of the Fairy and Imp company.

"Welcome back," said an Imp presence. He noticed it was the same one who had greeted him last time, once he put some attention to her.

"Name?" Ryker asked, peering at the glowing presence.

"Benni," said the Imp.

"Benni, please go announce me to the queen, Diane, and Adele—that I've just arrived and I'm available at their pleasure," Ryker said.

He had happily crashed into them without giving them any notice the other day. Hadn't bothered with any etiquette in any way or fashion. He couldn't do it every time, not without expecting them to eventually get upset and angry at him.

They did deserve the respect of at him least giving them the opportunity to decide how to respond to his arrival. He equated it to knocking on a door and waiting to be invited in.

Rather than just exploding through the door and screaming, "Hey!"

"Of course, my lord king," Benni said, and her presence faded significantly.

Waiting quietly, Ryker idly started to look around into the temporary dungeon presence here.

The Fairies and Imps had started to dig into the ground, hollowing out spaces to hide in, store things, and move through. There were also several patterns he couldn't identify set off to one side in a small room.

"They're patterns for you to generate an avatar," Benni said, coming back to him. "I put them together based on the avatar you use, and... and what you look like and can do. I only made a few changes here and there to them that I thought beneficial."

Grinning, Ryker turned back to Benni.

"You made avatars for me?"

"Yes," Benni confirmed.

"Well aren't you an industrious one. You're a captain?"

"I am."

"Hm. I'll bring your name up to Wynne when I get back. Good work, Benni," Ryker said. "Any response from my wives?"

"They were all happy to hear the news that you were back, and they are working to finish up the meeting they were having," Benni said.

"Meeting? What kind of meeting?" Ryker asked.

"The local vicar of the dark church is pushing demands on the queen right now," Benni said. "He has since stopped trying to force Lauren into marrying him, and now has been working on having more temples built."

Ok. Don't like that fellow.

"If you get the chance to kill the vicar, kill him," Ryker said immediately. Then shook his head and grimaced. "Actually, let Lauren decide that. Just make sure she understands how versatile you are."

"I will do so, my lord king," Benni said.

"Anyone else bothering the queen?" Ryker asked.

"There was a poor attempt at an assassination yesterday. I crushed the fool's head," Benni said.

"Oooh? And what's your avatar, Benni?"

"I'm an Orc warrior. Very pretty, very human-like. I matched my sizes to your preferences as well," Benni said.

Ryker chuckled.

"Consider me flattered and interested. Be sure to remember I'm taking no one else to bed unless Lauren, Diane, and Adele approve it. You missed that boat by a week or two," Ryker said.

"I've already been working closely with all three of them, and Adele has already said I could try for you. I need only two more approvals," Benni said.

Uh... alright. I wasn't expecting that.

Then Ryker felt a small tug on his presence. Following it back, he saw all three of his wives had already transferred into the dungeon space and were waiting for him to pull them into a bond space.

"Until later," Ryker said, and moved over to where the three ladies were. Rather than pulling them into the bond space, he knocked them out of the dungeon sense. Then pulled the avatar Benni had made for him into the room where they were standing.

There was a soft pop in his ears, and then Ryker was standing in front of Diane, Adele, and Lauren in what looked like a private study.

Diane and Lauren were dressed to their station, and Adele in little better than riding clothes.

"Ryker?" Lauren asked.

"It is indeed I," Ryker said, then bowed at the waist with a chuckle. "In the flesh, but... not flesh. It's an avatar to look just like me. Benni made it."

Lauren stared at him, her eyes curious but a touch cold.

"Oh, uh..." Ryker said, realizing she had no reason to trust him. "I can drag you off and shut the door and lock it, if you like?"

Sighing, Lauren closed her eyes and pressed a hand to her head.

"Yes. Welcome back," Lauren said, not lifting her head up. She looked disappointed. "I really don't know what I expect each time, but it's never what you actually do."

Adele and Diane were all smiles, though. They'd already figured out how to use avatars themselves, and they'd peeked into the dungeon sense to see it was him.

"Do me a favor and teach Lauren how to make an avatar and look into the dungeon?" he asked. "Otherwise I'll have to do equally silly things to assure her it's me in the future."

Adele snorted at that.

"I mean, I can think of a few ways for you to prove to me you're my husband," Adele said, lifting a delicate eyebrow.

"Good gracious, when did you become such a flirt and a sex fiend?" Lauren said, glaring at Adele.

"When I realized I got what I wanted, and now I can enjoy it. I even made it back home here to help you out," Adele said with a laugh. "I got everything. So why the hell shouldn't I enjoy it?"

"Anyways," Ryker said, butting in. "Shirley agreed and is already acting the part of Claire. Haven't had any problems with it so far, other than she likes to antagonize me.

"Everything else is—"

A memory slammed into him at high speed. It was Charlotte talking to Marybelle, but the memory was from Marybelle's point of view.

"I need Ryker, now," Charlotte had said. "The church of light is already on the move. They're trying to slip through with a force even as we speak."

"I'll do what I can," Marybelle said, her voice sounding odd in her own ears to Ryker.

"Thanks," Charlotte said after that, and ran off.

"Ah, looks like I spoke too soon," Ryker said with a sigh. "The church of light is trying to move around our wall at the current moment. I need to go and see what I can do to turn them back.

"Oh, if you had to pick a force to deal with, would you want to deal with church of light soldiers, or church of dark?"

"Dark," Lauren said immediately. "They're technically friendlies, but no one in the Queendom worships them. They'd have a much harder time doing anything."

"Alright," Ryker said, then waved his hand. "See ya later. I'll try to come back as soon as possible."

Dropping the avatar and cutting his sense completely, Ryker flew back to his real body.

Hopefully with time to spare and nothing going absolutely wrong.

***

Sprinting into the field, Ryker felt weird. It was nighttime, and a battle was being fought in limited moonlight.

He hadn't made his arcane-monk avatar this time. Instead, he'd gone with something he understood perfectly and could wield without issue.

A representation of himself, without the mana problems he lived with every day. A version of himself with a massive well of mana that refilled quickly.

Out ahead of him, the vanguard was engaged with enemy foot soldiers. All around them were the crumbled remains of a half-built wall that had collapsed inward.

Charlotte had filled him in quickly when he'd arrived earlier.

The church of light had rushed the gap as expected after she'd cut off a large chunk of enemy forces, and the wall had collapsed.

Now it was a brutal slug-fest in the gap. She couldn't rebuild until it was clear, and the church kept pouring more and more soldiers into the space.

He could see where the Fairies and Imps were holding the line in the wall. They weren't very deep in their numbers, but they were holding. One side did have a bit more room for the enemy to move around and flank, however.

Getting close, Ryker flipped his hand to one side and instantly created a framework of lightning. Giving it a spin and throwing a touch of air magic to it, Ryker flung it forward.

With a crackle and a boom, the spell hit the enemy flank and branched out rapidly to those behind the target, then those behind that, and then those behind that.

Love chain lightning.

Dropping his left hand, Ryker brought it back up with a solidified blade of air and chucked it out in an underhanded toss.

After splattering the first several soldiers it hit, it began to curve upward and blasted out through the heads of six more, then went into the air.

Ryker let out a quick breath and came to a stop. Folding together a latticework of earth, air, and energy, he began to form a shield. He tied it to a spot two feet in front of him and gave it a steep slant upward, then popped it into being.

Pulling his hands down, Ryker began drawing in all the heat from the surrounding area. He piled it all in one spot, and a ball of bright purple flame sprang up between his palms.

Compressing it as it came to life, Ryker fed more and more heat into it while also pushing a thin, steady stream of air through it.

There was a whump in his hand as the fire collapsed on itself and became something altogether different.

Once it reached this point, Ryker started feeding it energy directly. Letting the mana flow into the artificial construct.

Several arrows slammed into the shield in front of him, sliding off to the sides.

Then a blast of pure magical energy hit the center point of his shield and blew off all around him. Ryker could actually feel his skin crisp up a bit just from the heat the magical spell put out as a byproduct. Through the heat shielding he'd made.

The compacted ball of roiling death in his hands was starting to become unwieldy. It was jittering slightly around between his fingers and would shortly break free of his control.

Encasing the ball in a small energy shield that would break apart the moment it hit something, Ryker was done.

He threw a spinning air spell behind it and launched the whole thing forward.

Sailing over the clash and scrum of battle, it went right over the front lines and vanished into the back rows of the church of light's forces.

Then it detonated, and a wave of bright blue fire with a white center blew out across the enemy lines. Sweeping them up in a raging inferno of flame.

Ryker clapped his hands together and then swept his hands out in a line. A construct of stone and earth flowed out behind his hands.

Once more clapping his hands together, Ryker then moved his hands forward, and a flat plane of magic slid out in front of the first construct.

As he cast it forward, the rectangular magical pattern stopped above the enemy position. Latching onto it with his mind, he began to rapidly build upon the whole of it. Expanding it in every direction.

Once it was large enough to cover almost the entire front line, Ryker began dumping massive amounts of mana into it. The spell pattern began to rapidly convert all that energy into stone and rock, exactly as Ryker had set it up to do.

In a flash, it finished its task and transformed into a hulk of stone.

Then promptly fell to the earth, crushing everyone beneath it.

Between the lightning attack, the fire attack, and this stone attack, the front line and back line were separated. Those at the front were now trying to push to the back, and those in the back were pressed between stone and those trying to go through them.

Grabbing the magical shield with his left hand, Ryker began to move forward. Creating small magical missiles with his right hand, he attached them to the shield. They were constantly pulling in small bits of free-floating mana and adding it to the spell weave they were made of.

By the time he reached the turning flank of enemies, he'd created forty of the balls.

Summoning a lance of lightning, Ryker held it in his right hand and stabbed out with it. He slipped it between two avatars in chain mail and into a church of light soldier. It caught him right in the belly.

The spell inlaid in the spear fired, smashed through the soldier, stole the life from his body, and used it to explode backwards in an arcing dance of lightning.

Grabbing one of the missiles attached to his shield as he retrieved his spear, Ryker fed it a burst of mana and lobbed it over the front line into the rear ranks.

It detonated and magical energies rushed out to devour soldiers.

Grabbing another, Ryker tossed it further down towards the other end of the line. Another explosion of lights and lethal magic rushed out in every direction.

Picking up several of the missiles, Ryker threw them toward the back middle.

The massive detonation of magical energy made everything shake.

Slowly, the vanguard front line began to grind the enemy soldiers down to nothing. Ryker found himself stepping over the dead and dying as he pushed on with his people.

Taking the entire shield in hand, Ryker tossed it forward into the enemy.

The light of the spells breaking apart and releasing everything was blinding, flashing wildly. It was as if the night had been replaced by the midday sun for several seconds.

The vanguard reached the point where the wall was missing and stopped. Retreating backward, the enemy tripped over themselves, crushed their wounded, and trampled anything in their way.

No sooner had the gap cleared of anyone standing, a massive segment of wall appeared. As if it had been there the entire time.

Staring up at it, Ryker was confused. He hadn't remembered that this was the ultimate goal of the attack. To push the enemy back so Charlotte could throw up a wall and lock this section down.

All the while costing the enemy soldiers. Bleeding them of their resources. With any luck, they'd also capture a good chunk of mana from their deaths.

Taking a number of steps backwards so he wasn't practically hanging off the women in front of him, Ryker let out a slow breath.

Then he cut his avatar free and went back up to the dungeon sense itself.

"Charlotte?" he asked into the empty space.

"Here. Using all that spent mana to build—one second," Charlotte said.

Floating over to where she was working, Ryker watched. People were dying, using spells, drinking potions, activating items and treasures.

All of that, everything, was bleeding mana out all over the place. Charlotte was funneling it all rapidly into a pattern set where her wall branched out from Dungeon.

As she loaded more and more into it, the end of her wall kept expanding. Growing longer brick by brick.

Minutes ticked by. Minutes became an hour, and Ryker began working on other projects while waiting for Charlotte.

"And that's it," Charlotte said, her presence turning to face him.

"Oh? All done?" Ryker asked, putting down the patterns he'd been toying with. He was always trying to think up new enchanted items to make. If he could somehow make a bulk of them, drop them into Lauren's army, and have no problems for it, he'd do it in a heartbeat.

"Yes. I've converted everything possible and squeezed everything out of it," Charlotte said. She sounded tired and spent. "Honestly, it only gained perhaps a day or two for the walls, but even that much gain isn't going to help. They'll just go to the end and pass us by. We were lucky they were willing to run a gap for no other reason than they saw weakness in it."

"Yes," Ryker said, sighing. He was rapidly coming to the conclusion he was going to have to treat the situation no differently than his farm.

He only had two hands, and the time in a single day to get the job done. Rather than leave two tasks half done and let the weeds spread wildly, he'd clear a row entirely. And do what he could for the next one.

It limited the amount the weeds could grow and maximized his effect on the farm.

He'd do the same here.

"Alright. Start using the cores and crystals. Burn 'em up until your wall hits the ocean. I don't want them to even have the chance of getting through.

"I'm going to tell Tris to use her resources more sparingly, to keep her walls two days ahead of the enemy main body at all times," Ryker said.

"I can do that," Charlotte said. "I'll try to minimize my usage of the resources so Tris can build her wall further."

"Good. Thanks, Charlotte. And what happened, by the way? I thought we weren't expecting them to move till tomorrow or the day after?" Ryker asked.

"They didn't stop at evening. They kept packing, putting things together, and just started marching. Before they were even truly done," Charlotte said. Their baggage train isn't just lagging behind, it doesn't exist yet."

"That's odd. I wonder if making Shirley become Claire spurned them into action. I can't imagine Queen Chas is very happy at that turn of events. Did any of their messengers slip through, I wonder?" Ryker mused.

"I would assume so. A lone messenger on a horse riding well beyond the wall wouldn't be stopped," Charlotte said with a shrug. "Just too much ground to cover."

That made too much sense. To believe they'd catch every messenger traveling into and out of the Queensland of Dale right now was silly.

"I suppose that's it for the night then," Ryker said, shaking his head. "Come on, Charlotte. Let's go cuddle in your bed. I could use your warmth tonight, and that bedroom smile of yours."

Charlotte's presence grew bright for a second.

"I love you," she said. The words sounded confused, but heartfelt.

"Yeah, I love you too. Come on then," Ryker said. He was beat.

Chapter 12 - Mitigation -

Ryker had retired for the night with Charlotte, spent from his brief and ugly fight with the Church. Using magic was just as draining as swinging a sword, it just taxed the body in different ways.

Unfortunately, the mental gymnastics Ryker had to use to get the right spells had no bearing on the avatar he'd been using.

Now, he stared at the absolute graveyard that existed between the two armies of Adelona and Trevail.

It looked like there were at least forty thousand dead between the two armies.

"I take it they took the bait?" Ryker asked.

Shirley's presence was hovering next to him.

"And then some," she said. "Once Trevail ran a few of those archers down, it became an all-out brawl. It didn't help them at all that the church of light was indisposed to offer help or consultation.

"And honestly, the church of the dark feeds off death. They really don't care if their allies are bled a bit in this one. It only empowers them."

Unsure of how to respond, Ryker continued to float along the field of corpses. It had all taken place within the confines of the dungeon, which meant a vast portion of their energy in dying had been transferred over.

There was no doubt in his mind Charlotte was already channeling everything she could siphon away from the dungeon without an issue to finish her section.

"I... I knew this would be the outcome, but I don't think I was ready for it," Shirley said.

"Ever seen someone die? Kill someone?" Ryker asked.

"No. I've never even seen a corpse," Shirley said. "I feel sick."

Huh. I'll need to keep that in mind, I suppose. She's got a good brain in her head, but her heart is soft.

Maybe toughen her up a bit.

Then again, maybe that's why she's tolerable compared to Claire.

"You should go take a bath," Ryker said. "Soak in some hot water. It helps. As far as this goes, they did it all by themselves, and only too happily. All we did was provide an ignition event."

"Yeah... I'm—I'm going to go take that bath. Going to cancel any plans that had me going outside today as well. I'm sorry," Shirley said, then fled before he could respond.

She really is soft. But... that's not a bad thing right now.

Though this might be the last of that softness.

Mentally shrugging, there wasn't much Ryker could say. He understood her problem perfectly, he just didn't identify with it. Life had a lot of death in it.

This was no different.

Moving over to Tris's section of the wall, Ryker dropped down right next to where she was overseeing the work.

"Hey," he said to her presence.

Tris's presence brightened, and her avatar's head dipped.

"Greetings, my lord king," she said. "I spoke with Charlotte this morning. I understand my task as you've given it."

"That's good," Ryker said. "Honestly, it really is the best course of action given the situation. It just... kinda sucks to let them get around us and into the Queensland."

"It does. One cannot parry every attack, but one can always do their best to lessen every blow. That's all we can do," Tris said.

"Hm. Yes," Ryker said.

Starting with a plan to simply murder and burn everything down that was in his way on his path to revenge, Ryker was feeling decidedly strange now.

He'd become what was essentially the protector of Dale. He was the drawbridge and the gate to the outside world.

And Rob still lived. Worse yet, he was a valuable member of Lauren's intelligence-gathering services. If Ryker had any hope of being able to kill the man, it would be after the war ended.

"Is there anything else you need? Moving along as the best you can?" Ryker asked.

"I'm currently staying what I believe is a day or a day and a half in front of the dark church," Tris said. "That way they can't push through, but I'm not wasting resources.

"I fear they may eventually push faster and simply try to outrun my building speed. At that point I'll be forced to utilize resources to counter them."

"In other words, hurry my ass up, I'm slowing you down and I'm risking everything," Ryker said. It was probably the first time he'd ever heard Tris not get straight to the point she wanted to make.

"Ah… yes," she said after a moment. "That's the truth of it."

"Got it. In the future just tell me your thoughts, like you always do," Ryker said.

Tris's presence dimmed and then vanished outright.

Strange. Something going on there.

Off to Charlotte.

Taking Tris's concern to heart, Ryker sped off to Charlotte. She was locked into a building loop again. Pulling everything she could in and expanding the wall as fast as she could with what was available.

"Hi Charlotte," Ryker said, deliberately interrupting her. Previously he'd let her work till she was finished. Except this time Tris was right. He needed to get this taken care of now and get Tris the resources she needed.

"Ryker?" Charlotte asked, her attention on the pattern clearly fading.

"I think we need to just… burn up the resources needed to finish your wall," Ryker said.

"What? I thought we were aiming toward conservation?" Charlotte asked, pulling her focus away from the pattern entirely.

"We're doing a lot. We're pushing everything and doing it well. The problem, though, is that we're still stuck in the same problem. We're still working both sides rather than closing one off entirely and then moving to the second," Ryker said. "We made a plan that would do what we wanted, but we didn't actually change the action."

Charlotte's presence in the dungeon sense glowed brighter, but she seemed to be thinking on what he'd just said.

"You're right," she said after ten seconds passed. "We made a plan to do what we said, but we didn't actually change what we were doing. I'll finish the wall right now and channel any excess mana I have to Tris's work."

"Sounds like a good idea. Thanks, Charlotte," Ryker said, then disconnected himself from the dungeon sense.

Coming back to himself in his own body, Ryker shifted to one side in his throne. Things were rapidly coming to a head. One way or the other, everything was going to be happening in the next day or so.

He'd failed to keep them here, failed to cut the numbers of the church forces down, and failed to keep them out.

Everything was now about recovery. Recovery and mitigation.

"It's not so bad," Marybelle said, sitting in a chair next to his projection table. "Nothing has actually changed from where we started, except that we've taken a blood toll out of everyone."

Unable to counter that statement, Ryker could only nod. She was right, of course. They really had done everything they could to help move the situation toward Lauren's favor.

All things considered, they'd had accomplishments beyond what a reasonable person could expect for success.

"Now, should we focus our efforts on the break in the wall we'll be forced to make?" Marybelle asked.

She was right. They'd end up with a gap an army could pass through. There was no denying that. It would be ideal to turn his attention to it.

"Yeah, let's... do that. I'd like to turn the whole thing into a kill zone and do what we can to really cull their numbers," Ryker said. "If you were to extrapolate how far Tris's wall would go based on current resources, where would you put the end point at?"

Marybelle grabbed his projection with two fingers and sent it flying down and away from Dungeon. Deep to the north and towards the mountains.

She controls my constructs far too easily. It's unnerving.

"Regardless of resources, I'm sure we could make it happen in such a way that we could force an enemy through this," Marybelle said, pausing the view on a valley. "I'm no tactician, but I do pay attention to you and your actions. This is where you would want them to go through, yes?"

With both hands, Ryker began to turn and shift the viewpoint around the valley she'd selected.

Reaching out across a wide range, the mouth of it could easily bring in an entire army. There wouldn't be any funneling here, and it sloped quite gently into the basin.

The highest points on the sides didn't look that high from the outside point of entry, either. Once Ryker got down to the floor of the valley, the rise on either side looked almost impossible to climb up and out of.

Moving to the far end of the valley, Ryker could see it actually narrowed considerably as it came up and out of the basin.

Unfortunately, that was also its biggest drawback. The way out was such a gentle slope that one could probably take it at a run the entire way up.

"It's... probably the best we'll find," Ryker said, already thinking up what resources he could deploy to cut people down. "And if we present it in such a way that would entice them into the valley, perhaps similar to the gap Charlotte made, then it would be all the easier."

There was a massive explosion of mana, and what felt like a boom resounded in Ryker's head.

There was so much free-floating magic that the projection on the table flickered wildly before coming back to a normal viewing.

"What in the heavens...?" Marybelle said, looking around.

Ryker didn't have to even look to know what it was.

"Charlotte just built her wall," Ryker said.

Even before he could think of telling someone to do it, all the mana that was floating around went rushing toward Tris's wall.

"That was... a lot of mana," Marybelle said, looking very uncomfortable.

"Was a lot of wall to build in one go. I'm sure there's a massive chunk of those lovely gifts from the Dark Lord that are now simply missing," Ryker said. "Easy come, easy go. So... let's plan for the valley then. This is going to be where we fail. Let's fail within reason."

***

Wynne was quietly going through all the patterns that had been put down. From the spawns to the gear to the attached skills, and the levels of each. She was in a full audit to make sure everything lined up with the rules and how it'd affect the core.

She was the Queen Fairy, which meant she was the only one who truly knew the condition of the dungeon core itself.

It'd been left where it had always been, and everyone still thought it was visible in the exit of the original fallen city layout. No one ever tried to get close to it anymore, though. It was more of a looksie, and a notable thing to look at on the way out.

"This one is too strong," Wynne said, indicating a Minotaur with a bow that was more like an axe with a small metal rod for a string. Marybelle was there in an instant, modifying the pattern and bringing it down a few levels of power.

"That'll work," Wynne said, moving to the next one.

Ryker had already been watching this process for the better part of two hours. It was into the midnight hour, and Tris and Charlotte were struggling to put down as much wall as they could. They had to reach the valley, skip it, and build beyond it.

Easing himself away from the two Fairies, Ryker looked over the whole of the canyon.

All along the canyon were patterns for simple archers to fire mindlessly into the center of the basin. They were equipped with longbows, quivers full of arrows, and certain areas they would just fire into unceasingly.

Set throughout all those archers were scorpion launchers. Manned in the same way as the archer spawns, they were also low cost, high volume, untargeted fire.

The problem wasn't mana at this point, however. It was space.

They'd filled all the possible spots that could hold an archer, a scorpion, a rock slide, or people throwing fire bombs. There simply was no more room to fit anything else.

That very reason was why they'd tried experimenting with a massive Minotaur archer. It took up almost the same space, but might have accomplished more.

So went the entire valley. It was covered at almost every angle, approach, and section with indirect and constant fire.

On top of that, the basin itself was liberally dotted with spell patterns that would indiscriminately trigger, as well as go off if stepped on.

It was a death trap.

Need to remember this. So long as things like this are documented and stated clearly, they're legal.

"Can we add casters to the back? Have them lob things in at an angle above forty-five degrees?" Shirley asked, suddenly floating there beside him. "They should be able to fire further than archers, yes?"

Startling slightly at her sudden presence, Ryker didn't respond immediately.

"Couldn't we?" she pressed.

"Yes, and we considered it. It's a mana cost thing. To cast the spell, the dungeon would have to foot the outlay. Arrows are much simpler to create," Ryker said. "It's why almost everything out there is based on simple materials."

"Ah. Yes, that'd make sense," Shirley said. "Wynne mentioned something about 'blades' being enlisted. Can you explain that?"

"The blades… are people who have willingly killed other adventurers, soldiers, or officers for rewards from the dungeon. They're effectively agents in the employ of the dungeon," Ryker said. "They can receive gear, items, skills, or spells from vendors we provide and maintain. Their payment is in points, or kills."

"Interesting. They'll be on this field today?" Shirley asked, indicating the valley.

"Yeah. They'll be wandering the edges of the valley and firing in, casting in, or something along those lines. I'm sure some of them will get inventive," Ryker said. "Human ingenuity fueled by greed is a truly frightening thing."

"Yes. Yes, it is," Shirley said, moving over to the exit of the valley. "I assume we have to leave this open for it to be fair, according to dungeon rules?"

"Yes… you've really been paying attention, haven't you?" Ryker asked.

"This is my life now, after all. Your dedicated wife. Claire. I'd be foolish to think putting my head in the sand would make it all pass me by," Shirley said, floating past a clump of archers.

"That's quite fair. Honestly, though… I think we're done here," Ryker said, watching Wynne and Marybelle move through the spawns. "We've spent all the mana we had, filled in almost every space possible, and any mana upkeep we get is going into having the trap patterns reset.

"I'm going to bed. See you tomorrow, Shirley. Should be an interesting day, one way or the other."

Checking out, Ryker slid back into his body. He was lying in his bed, staring up at the ceiling. He doubted very much he'd be able to sleep, but it would be easier than waiting.

At some point in between worrying, random thoughts, and not knowing what he could do, Ryker heard the door open.

Lifting his head, he watched Wynne close the door to his bedroom and start heading his way.

"I can't sleep either," she said.

"Yeah," Ryker said, laying his head back down. "Kind of hard to sleep when it feels like the fate of Dungeon could be determined tomorrow."

"Of Dungeon?" Wynne asked as she pulled back the covers to his bed and crawled in.

"If we have an army behind us and one in front of us, we'll effectively be under siege," Ryker said. "It'll be rather difficult to get anything done at all. It may sound truly selfish, but… if we kill enough of them tomorrow, they might just take their whole army to Lauren rather than trying to split it."

"In other words, you're hoping we kill as much of them as possible," Wynne said, turning to face him in the bed. "So they go become Lauren's problem."

"It sounds awful, doesn't it? I want to support Lauren, but if we get locked into position, there's not much we can do other than hunker down," Ryker said.

"Awful… yes. Reasonable? Very. Personally, I think you've made amazing progress. Not long ago you were a little petty raging ball of flame that blew up when things went wrong," Wynne said, smiling at him. "Now you're in actual healthy relationships, you have a couple people you trust, and your every moment isn't thinking about killing Rob."

Ryker lay there, staring at Wynne and considering her words.

She was right, of course. She tended to be.

He wasn't really the same person anymore. He cared and wanted to help people other than himself.

"Yeah," Ryker said, smiling at Wynne. She'd kept their relationship to cuddling, kissing, and little more. And he wasn't about to risk it by pushing for more. "Thanks, Wynne. You're an intelligent beauty I can't imagine doing this without."

Wynne sniffed once and grinned at him.

"I know," she said, reaching out to pat his cheek. "And we'll get through tomorrow, one way or the other. And I won't even tell you we should focus on the dungeon because… I agree with you. Lauren is a good person, and I also want to help her out. Not just burrow into the dungeon and hide."

Wow. That's more surprising than me not murdering Rob.

"I'm going to try and get some sleep… Goodnight, Ryker," Wynne said and closed her eyes, snuggling into his bed a bit more deeply.

Yeah… that's worth trying for I suppose.
I just don't think I'll fall asleep.

Chapter 13 - Losing for Winning -

A heavy hand shook Ryker's shoulder, knocking him out of a fun dream he'd been having.

Blinking, and feeling like he was drugged, Ryker rolled over to look up. Up into the face of Meino, who was inches from him.

Her big tongue came out and went from his jaw up into his hairline.

"Time to wake up," she said, her face hovering over his.

"Guuuh," Ryker said, reaching up and putting his hands over Meino's mouth. "Not right now. I've got a raging hard-on and the last thing I need right now is a tongue."

"I could groom your c—"

"No! Nope. Not gonna," Ryker said, pinching Meino's mouth shut with his fingers. "Keep your tongue in your head. Are you waking me cause it's morning or something else?"

Meino mumbled something through her closed lips.

Sighing, Ryker relaxed his death grip on her mouth just a little.

"The enemy army has reached the valley. They're sending scouts further up to see if they can get through a different way," Meino said.

Ryker nodded, and clamped his fingers shut on her mouth again.

"Got it. I'm going to go take a bath, and then we're going to go to the throne room and settle in for the day. I imagine this is going to be... well, an all-day thing. Got everything you need for an all-day session?" Ryker asked, loosening his fingers again.

"Yes. I have a bag of oats behind your throne just in case. I also had Arria make me a tiny outhouse to one side—that way I don't have to leave for long," Meino said.

"Great," Ryker said, pinching her mouth shut once more. "Alright, please go wake Shirley and let her know what's going on. I don't think anyone else will bother her."

Meino nodded, but didn't leave. She mumbled something again.

Ryker cautiously let go of her lips.

"You sure you don't want me to groom your—"

Ryker clamped his hands down again, glaring at her.

***

Dropping into his dungeon sense, Ryker quickly slid toward the valley. Appearing almost immediately due to the presence of the wall, he found himself hovering directly above the church of the dark.

Rank upon endless rank of soldiers were all standing far from the wall, outside of arrow range. It was obvious they were getting ready to run the valley itself to get to the other side.

"They scouted and scouted and scouted," Tris grumbled, floating next to him.

Casting his awareness around himself, he found Charlotte, Tris, Wynne, Marybelle, and Shirley had lined up with him.

"They finally hit the end of the wall, then just went back," Tris said. "Far as we can tell, they're just getting ready to make the rush."

"That's what I'd bet on," Wynne said. "Their ranks are forming for the cavalry to go first, followed by the infantry. I imagine they're hoping to get as much of their horse soldiers through before the way becomes choked with corpses."

"Yes, one can never assume their enemy is a fool," Shirley said. "And when the key people start marching in, I completely expect them to be in a shielded square from one side to the other. That or riding horses in a square. Something like that.

"They're going to do the best they can to get through with as few losses as possible. They are very determined."

"Huh," Ryker said, thinking on that one. "We should have someone keep an eye on officers and give some blades key target orders. Have a mob spawn with instructions for them. Like a wisp."

"Got it, dear," Marybelle said. "As soon as you started to ask, I thought it might be something like that."

"Thanks. Especially for preempting it," Ryker said.

There was a weird flutter from Charlotte and Tris at that. But it was gone before he could concentrate on it.

"Here they come," Wynne said, pulling Ryker's attention away from asking the other two about what he'd just sensed.

Cavalry soldiers began walking out from their formations, their lines becoming loose but staying together for the most part.

"Great," Ryker said. "Grand. Lovely. Perfect. Because this is exactly what I wanted. To end up having a brawl to the death with four armies, all for the sake of a damn pretty smile."

"Pretty smile?" Shirley asked.

"Ryker is in love with the queen. She gave him attention, treated him like an equal, and opened up to him. He fell for her instantly," Tris said, sparing no one involved.

"Thanks, Tris. Remind me to bend you over something tonight and see if I can't break your spine," Ryker muttered.

Tris's presence turned a faint pink, then a deep red.

"I had no idea," Shirley said. "I thought it was a convenience marriage. Everyone did."

"It wasn't," Marybelle said, her tone shaded with a bit of whimsy. "He truly did fall for her. They had an amazingly frank and deep connection. She loves him just as much, but mostly because he says awful things to her and tells her everything without a filter."

"Ok, great, thanks. Enough about me," Ryker said. "How about the fact that people are dying over there."

"Not much to say," Charlotte said. "They're dying, and the infantry is a bit further away than would be useful for us to do anything with."

Growling, and not wanting to be surrounded right now as he was, Ryker created an avatar.

He stomped down to the edge of the valley and looked out at the horsemen as they raced across.

After clapping his hands together, he pushed his left hand out and his right hand backward. Using the motion to help focus his pattern, Ryker dropped down a six-foot-tall, three-foot-wide stone wall.

It was unfocused, unset, and unbound. The whole thing hit the ground with a crash and then shattered. Rocks and stones began spilling out in every direction from the impact point.

The lead horses hit the rocks in the valley and started to trip and tumble all over themselves. Riders landed on the other side of the mess more often than not, then went running for the end of the valley.

This wasn't the goal, though. Ryker really was looking for the second and third ranks to hit that roadblock.

They were the ones who would end up getting crushed in the mad horse crush. Adding their broken bodies to the mess.

"That was impressive."

Looking to his side, Ryker found an avatar version of Shirley.

"Thanks," Ryker muttered, looking down at his handiwork.

"I'd heard your control was impressive, but that was... almost instantaneous. Even the amount of mana used was minimal," Shirley continued.

"Yeah, great, grand, thanks," Ryker said, shaking his head.

"Don't be mad," Shirley said softly. "I'm genuinely complimenting you. I mean nothing of it. I would wish for even half your talent, ability, and control. I have none of... anything."

Ryker frowned, looking over to her. Then he looked back at the valley below.

I complain about those who have more, yet there are those who would complain about me having more.

"I could teach you," Ryker said. "You're not too old to learn magic. You might have the talent for it. Won't know till you try."

"Really?" Shirley asked, her tone sounding excited for the first time in days.

"Yeah. I don't mind," Ryker said, trying not to sound like an asshole. Shirley was an ally now, and she'd been working to help Dungeon.

"You won't make me do anything for it?" she asked suspiciously.

Chuckling, Ryker looked at her.

"Shirley, you're a beautiful woman, but I've got more than I can handle. Ya know? And if I really wanted to, I—"

"Ryker! The champion of the dark church is coming!" Wynne said in his mind.

"Ryker?" Shirley asked, looking at him.

"Uh, sorry. Apparently the dark champion is coming this way," Ryker said, looking toward the valley entrance. "Think you can make an avatar and try to fight him with me? You don't count towards the dungeon the same way fairies would."

"That'd work, but I don't think she can do much," Wynne said.

Shirley blinked, watching Ryker. Then she nodded her head and vanished.

"Which way am I going, Wynne?" Ryker asked.

"He's heading straight towards you. I don't think you need to move," Wynne said.

"Great, okay, yeah. Anything wrong if I die or lose?" Ryker asked.

"No. Just some mana loss. Same for Shirley," Wynne said.

Shirley popped back into the world in the same spot she'd left. She also looked unchanged.

"Shirley? Didn't you—"

There was a boom that made the ground beneath Ryker's boots tremble.

"There you are!" someone shouted from behind him.

Turning on his heel, Ryker found himself looking into the twisted face of a man who looked like he'd dunked his head into a tub of acid.

The dark has had three different champions in a week. This guy looks like chewed-up beef, though.

"Time to die, Count," said the man.

"He doesn't know you're an avatar. If you die, it's likely they'll find out you're one with the dungeon," Wynne said.

Great, so… try not to die if I can avoid it.

"Uh huh," Ryker said, then flipped out a hand that was shaped to a spear. Building a stone pattern with an edge made of air, Ryker flung it toward the champion.

The spell working whistled through the air with the intensity of the construct. Blindingly swift, it clipped the man's arm off at the elbow when he stepped to the side to dodge.

Screaming at the top of his lungs, the champion sped forward toward Ryker.

With an explosion of fiery red light and black shadow, a cloud of magic formed around Ryker when the champion got within ten feet.

Diving out of the way, Ryker winced when he felt part of his leg become blazing hot, then cold a second later.

He scrambled to his feet and then tumbled back to the ground.

Looking down, he found that his leg was gone from the calf down. It hadn't been hacked off or cut free, but looked more as if it'd melted away.

"Haha," said the champion, marching toward Ryker. "Pity, that first spell of yours was good."

"Pity, I've got more to give ya," Ryker said, and popped an air blast spell off beneath himself. At the same time, he conjured a large working of stone and lashed fire into it.

Launching the whole spell once he was in the air, Ryker was propelled backward even as the massive boulder came out.

After striking the champion dead center, it rolled away with him and bounced along.

Landing with a thump and going head over heels, Ryker managed to come up on his hands and knees. When he could get his one good leg under him, he moved to a kneeling position.

Looking to where he'd last seen the champion, Ryker had almost no time to react.

A constructed spell of black mana and stone was tearing through the air toward him.

Rather than deflecting it, Ryker pulled out the central rune in the pattern. He'd identified it as the point that was holding everything together.

In a detonation, and a scream of what sounded like agony, the strange spell became a torrent of purple flame shooting to the sky. A thin white image of a woman twisted up out of the smoke and then exploded in a purple fireball.

Soul sacrifice!

Gritting his teeth, Ryker suddenly felt like maybe he was completely outmatched here. Champions did indeed have access to all the spells of their god or goddess.

I'm fucking fighting Rannulf himself, to a degree!

Panting, and feeling rather sick, Ryker glanced down at his leg.

The black edge to his calf was slowly creeping upward. The spell hadn't ended. He was on a time limit now.

"Impressive, Count!" shouted the champion. "Very, very, impressive. Your control is beyond exceptional. I would be terrified of you if you weren't just a human."

Drifting away, the black haze of the soul sacrifice vanished. Revealing the champion of Rannulf holding Shirley in front of him.

"You know, your wife is rather pretty," said the champion, one of his hands around Shirley's middle. "It's a pity I don't have more time. Or that I don't have time to waste on taking her home."

"No," Shirley said, and then simply exploded. Her entire body became a living torrent of fire and energy.

"What the fuck – did he just blow her up?" Ryker asked, throwing up a shield to protect himself.

"No! She blew herself up," Wynne called back.

What?

As the massive explosion of fire washed past him, Ryker could see the spot where Shirley and the champion had been standing. Both were gone, and there was only a crater there.

Ryker was pretty sure there was part of an arm at the lip of the pockmark in the terrain.

"He's dead," Wynne said. *"I collected all the mana he had, as well as the mana Shirley's avatar had in it when she did whatever she did."*

With a strange pop-like noise, Shirley simply reformed out of nowhere.

"Oh, that was interesting," she said, putting her hands to her head, then her chest, and finally her hips. "It worked, but being blown apart was a strange sensation."

"You... what'd you do?" Ryker asked, feeling very confused.

"I just put as much mana in my avatar as I could, and waited. I figured he'd make a move on me. Either he'd kill me or grab me. In either case, I'm more useful doing that than trying to fight him. I mean, really, Ryker. I'm not a fighter," Shirley said, smiling at him.

No. You're not. But you're certainly just as dangerous.

Ryker turned back to the valley, then hobbled and hopped over to it. There was still a job to do, and he needed to do it. Or help to do it.

"You'll teach me spell-work? That was quite impressive to watch. I'd really like to try my hand at it," Shirley said, as if the fact that she'd just killed her avatar, killed someone, and then come back was nothing.

The softness he'd previously seen seemed to have vanished.

"Yeah. Sure," Ryker grumbled, dropping down to one knee at the edge of the valley.

Infantry moved through the valley as quickly as they could. Arrows, catapult stones, large scorpion quarrels, and spells rained down on them constantly.

The place where Ryker had dropped his makeshift pile to slow people down was lost in a sea of people. He'd hoped to keep building into that spot to slowly make it an insurmountable breaker.

Now he'd just have to make do with what he could and drop it right on top of them. Even if it would cost a ridiculous amount more of mana.

Building the pattern and starting to flesh it out, Ryker felt the moment when it started to fade away into nothing.

"I'm sorry. We're out of spendable mana. And you draw from it directly for your avatar," Wynne said.

Great. The fight with the champion sucked everything out of us. But Shirley did manage to kill him. So that's a plus, and nothing was revealed.

"I guess we just sit and watch then," Ryker grumbled. The whole thing felt wrong. Anticlimactic.

Like losing.

"That was always the end result, Ryker," Shirley said, folding her hands behind her back. "We were never going to stop them. The honest question we all had was how many of them we could kill before they broke through."

"I would wager we're doing a very good job of killing them."

Ryker nodded his head.

It still felt like a loss to him. Even if it wasn't.

***

Watching the blades pick off wounded stragglers as they hobbled their way to the end of the valley, Ryker was annoyed.

They'd failed to stop the army dead in its tracks, and now a new group of people Lauren would ultimately have to deal with was in the Queensland.

"Fifty thousand."

Turning his awareness toward the voice, Ryker found Marybelle there.

"We killed about fifty thousand, dear," said the Hob, wandering over next to him in the dungeon presence. "Given all their reinforcements, and that they crossed over with so many, that's amazing."

He'd given up his avatar a while ago to put some mana back for the archers to keep firing with.

"Ah. Out of how many that came through?" Ryker asked.

"Something like a hundred thousand entered the pass. We took a half of their number," Marybelle said. "And none of their supplies will make it through. Tris shored up the wall as soon as the last real soldier crossed the gap."

"Huh. It'll be interesting to see what happens," Ryker said. "Though I fear Lauren will end up having to feed or clothe them in some way. Let's hope she's able to fend off that problem."

"I've already instructed the Blades to continue to harass and hound the army as long as they're willing," Marybelle said. "At the same time, I've created a pattern that will summon as many archers as possible to all fire into the enemy ranks.

"With any luck, they'll stop for the night within our territories and I can give them one more parting gift."

"You're rather ruthless when you want to be," Ryker said.

"They've shown no consideration to anyone they've caught in the field. Man, woman, wounded or not—and I've watched it," Marybelle said. "I would happily scour them from the field. But that's all we can do for the time."

Ryker couldn't help but agree. They'd walled off the Queensland and only allowed a single army through.

Now the next problem began, though. Keeping out the armies of the church of light, Trevail, and Adelona.

Though… maybe we can have the church of light go for the throat of Adelona. With their partners gone, they might be a fun and easy target for the enemy.

Tie up their numbers a bit more and get a few more killed.

"Yes. Though that means it's time for you and I to get back to work on the Death Dungeon. Lots to do, and many lives to plan on taking."

"I had some thoughts on how to go about it in an effective way, too," Ryker said.

"Oh, good. Would you like to retreat to our private space to begin working? After our normal ritual, of course, dear," Marybelle said sweetly.

Chapter 14 - A New Day -

Watching the armies out in front of Dungeon, Ryker felt a strange and perverse glee. The soldiers of the church of light and Trevail were working at slaughtering the Adelonians.

The entire time these three armies clashed, Charlotte and Tris were constantly using archer patterns to harass and take lives from the church and Trevail.

And when it seemed as if they might completely forget that they themselves were vulnerable, Tris personally led a charge of the vanguard straight into the command structure of the church of light.

"I saw Claire with the vicar himself," Tris reported, her presence floating next to him.

"Oh?" Ryker asked, unsure what to say to that. He really didn't want to be thinking about her right now.

So instantly disinterested was he, and wanting to avoid it, that he immediately turned away from the battle and started heading back toward Dungeon.

"Yes. She was helping direct the enemy forces. It doesn't make sense," Tris said, following him.

"Great," Ryker said.

"If she was truly all about getting what was best for herself, why would she align herself at this junction with a force that was clearly losing?" Tris said. "Unless she believes they'll win in the end."

Ryker paused at that statement. If Claire was confident the church would win later on, she would indeed stay with them. The question became *why* she was confident.

"Good thoughts," Ryker said, moving on toward Dungeon again. "Keep hitting him, kill everyone you can. Every death helps us, and why not benefit? They so graciously have camped out in our own territory."

Heading straight into the Death Dungeon, Ryker sat there. Contemplating nothing much more than his own thoughts.

Claire was ever the sore spot for him, and he knew it. He'd have to eventually get over it, but it was still far too fresh for him.

The Death Dungeon was also a bit of an open-ended question right now. He wanted to build into it, but it didn't interest him. There was no story to it. No reason beyond killing. Everything he'd done up to this point in his dungeon had a story and was building up to something.

"You seem a touch lost."

Checking the source, Ryker found Shirley in front of him. He'd frequently been seeing more and more of her as time went on. She almost seemed to hunt him down at times, and then get stuck with him till he escaped.

It felt strange. And painful at the same time. He couldn't quite separate Claire from Shirley yet. Most especially because when he went out in public with her, he had to address her as Claire.

Lost.

Maybe I am a bit lost. Maybe I can't seem to find my way because I no longer know the way.

"When was the last time you spoke to the queen? Would that help?" Shirley asked.

"Uh… not in a few days. And maybe? I don't know. It's hard to talk to her right now. Adele and Diane both want attention from me when I visit, so it becomes a multi-hour ordeal. Which isn't terrible, I know, but in the same breath… there's a lot of work to do here," Ryker said. "Then I feel guilty for not working, and—"

"Yes. Lost," Shirley said, interrupting him. "And something I can definitely identify with."

She came a little closer, invading his personal space in the dungeon sense.

"I've spoken with a number of your people. The Fairies, Imps, citizens. The consensus I've gotten from them is you're a man driven by whatever conviction he holds to," Shirley said. "Up until recently, your conviction was revenge. Then it became defense of the Queensland. And now it's still that, but your direct confrontation is over. Now you need to hunker in and become the bulwark. The rock the enemy shall crash on."

Ryker was paying attention to her now. Her words were hitting all the right notes for him, and he felt like she understood him.

"To that end, we must instill your conviction again," Shirley said. "Ryker, do you love your wives?"

"Deeply," he said immediately.

"Your Fairies?"

"Also as deeply," he confirmed without a pause.

"Your citizens, who by and large have remained loyal, and to this day live in Dungeon?" Shirley continued.

"Yes, of course. They stayed with me when it all went to a literal hellscape."

"Then that's your conviction. If you don't build the most lethal Death Dungeon there is, you can guess what will happen to your wives. Your Fairies. Your citizens," Shirley said. "We both know what happens to a conquered nation."

A violent and evil image flashed in Ryker's mind, almost making him gag at the thought. Yes, he knew what would happen to any nation that fell. There'd been several soldiers in these armies present for the fall of a few minor nations. He'd seen their memories and cores.

He knew what would happen to Lauren, Diane, Adele, and Shirley.

"So there it is," Shirley said, gesturing to Ryker. "Your conviction. You must murder, kill, and destroy anyone who wishes to pass through your city. You are the gatekeeper and waystation to everyone else."

In the dungeon sense, one could usually only see a person as a floating ball of energy. Usually emotions would flicker across as colors or hints.

Right now, though, Ryker could practically see the determination and resolve coloring Shirley. It was like steel. Hardened steel.

Except Ryker couldn't figure it out. Shirley was a giant question mark to him that made no sense.

"You're not wrong," Ryker said. "Where are you right now?"

"Me?" Shirley asked, her demeanor changing completely. In fact, she sounded almost embarrassed. "I'm in the throne room. On your throne."

Really? Heh.

"I'll have a throne made for you and matched to mine," Ryker said. "Stay there, I'm coming to you."

"Ryker wa—"

Canceling his dungeon sense, Ryker sat up in his bed.

"Oh? You're up?" Meino asked.

"Yeah, throne room. Shirley is there. I want to talk to her in person," Ryker said, getting out of bed.

"She's a crafty one," Meino said. "I can't get a read on her."

"Really? You're usually so good about that—you losing your touch?" Ryker asked, slapping her on the hip as he walked by.

Even though he'd hit her as hard as he could, it was little more than a friendly pat to the Minotaur.

Chuffing to herself, Meino lumbered after him.

"No, she's just good at hiding herself," Meino said. "Not everyone is as easy to read as you are."

"Uh huh. Says the Minotaur who can't stop grooming me and doesn't seem to understand herself," Ryker said, exiting his room.

"Mmmm, that's a good point. I should look inward later. Maybe when I groom you tonight. It's grooming night," Meino said.

"No, it isn't. You did it last night," Ryker said.

"It is. Last night you passed out while in the dungeon sense. You can't even tell me how you got back in your bed," Meino said.

"What? Are you saying you didn't groom me?"

"I'm saying you can't prove I did, which means tonight is grooming night," Meino insisted.

Grumbling, Ryker opened the door to the throne room and stepped inside.

Peeking around the side of his throne was Shirley, her dark hair framing her lovely face.

"Hey. Stay seated. I'm going to ask Wynne and Marybelle to join us. We need to figure out the limits I can make on the Death Dungeon. We're also going to use this opportunity to start training you in magic," Ryker said.

"Oh? Wonderful. I'm looking forward to it. How should I begin?" Shirley asked.

Chuckling, Ryker looked at the table in front of her.

That'll work nicely. And I can have Marybelle help me teach her. She was a teacher, after all.

"Marybelle, Wynne," Ryker sent into the dungeon sense without entering. "Could you join me in the throne room?"

He received two positive affirmations. One right after the other.

"Your first lesson is actually the hardest," Ryker said. "Sensing the mana in and around yourself. "Hold out your hand. And fair warning, this is going to hurt."

Shirley frowned at him, but slowly held out her hand.

Slipping his fingers into hers, he gently built a tiny ball of mana inside the flesh of her palm, the size of a bean.

"Oh gods, that stings," Shirley hissed.

"Yes. Yes, it does. But… it also tells you two things in the space of about an hour," Ryker said. "The first is if you can sense it, the second is if you have the mentality for magic.

"Because honestly, the number of times I've hurt myself in some way is already incalculable. If you can't handle the mana bean, you're not going to make it."

"It burns terribly now," Shirley said, staring at her hand in his.

"Yes, and it'll get worse. But it also won't harm you permanently. Nor will it last longer than an hour," Ryker said, releasing her hand. "Be thankful I told you all this in advance. My father just did it to me and left me there in my bedroom."

"Focus on the mana and try to feel it. Sense it."

Shirley groaned, grabbing her wrist with her other hand. She was staring into her palm as if it were the complete focus of her life.

What Ryker had failed to mention was his father had done it to both of his hands, and with twice the amount Ryker had put in her.

You really were an asshole, Dad.

Waiting for only a minute before Marybelle and Wynne showed up together, Ryker gave them both a smile.

"Oh my word, what's wrong with her?" Marybelle asked, moving over quickly to Shirley's side.

"Nothing. She's trying to sense the mana I implanted in her hand. If she can sense it, she'll be able to draw it out and spare herself the pain. If she can't, she'll know she really shouldn't try at being a mage," Ryker said with a shrug. "My father did the same to me when I was a five-year-old."

Wynne and Marybelle both stared at him without comprehension. They'd had neither fathers nor childhoods. To them, everything he'd just said was a non-existence. Or so Ryker thought.

"That sounds awful," Marybelle said. "Mana sensing can begin immediately for Fairies, as we're born fully grown. Don't humans take at least eight years before they can sense it?"

"Normally, yes. But if you introduce mana to the body, such as with the bean, it can come much quicker," Ryker said with a shrug. "Anyways. I wanted to discuss my Death Dungeon with you two.

"How lethal can I make this? If I promise them a hundred pounds of gold if they finish, can I literally make it absolutely lethal, but still passable?"

Wynne frowned, lifting a hand to her mouth and touching her lip with a finger.

"Technically… if you put a sign out at the front specifically telling them the risk and the reward, it would be more of a known contract than a risk. If they were to enter the Death Dungeon, as you're calling it, after reading the message, it would be mostly on them," Wynne said. "Though if they did manage to get through, you'd have to reward them heavily."

Ryker had been expecting that to a degree; he'd even thought on a few ways to get around it.

"What if… I gave them the ability to learn any skill they wanted from any class?" Ryker said. "One or two or three skills. Or something like that, however many I needed to put down. Would that work?"

Wynne licked her lips, looking down and to the side. "Yes, I think it would. It'd be costly, though, wouldn't it? We'd be strengthening our enemy."

"Yes, we would, so next question. As far as I know, dungeons only allow one-way movement. You don't go in through the exit and you don't exit from the entrance unless it's designed that way, right?" Ryker asked.

"That's true. That you can't enter through the exit is a fairly well-established expectation," Wynne admitted.

"Once they make it to the other side of the dungeon, they'll never be coming back this way," Ryker said. "There is no way back through without trying their hand at the city of Dungeon. And since they've all formally declared war on Dungeon, I do believe defending it is well within our purvey. Even going so far as to kill anyone sneaking in from an opposing army. No?"

Wynne hadn't lifted her eyes from the ground. She was still contemplating everything he'd said so far.

"Yes. That'd be accurate as well," Wynne said, finally looking back to Ryker. There was a curious glint in her eyes, and a partial smirk on her face. "You're going to put them on the other side, aren't you?"

"Yep! That's exactly it. We give them the ability to have any skill they want. Lots of them, if they manage to complete the dungeon. Then we put the teacher of said skills on the other side of the dungeon. So that it truly is a one-way street, and there is no way for them to get the skills.

"But they're still rewarded correctly, and they can still get their rewards," Ryker said. "Think that'd work? It's some obvious legal tap-dancing, I'd say, but it feels valid to me at all points."

Wynne sniffed and shrugged her shoulders.

"Honestly, it's one of those things that's so gray, there's no way of knowing. Personally, I think it fits all the rules given to dungeons appropriately. It lists out the prize, warns people away, has a single entry and exit, and offers a significant reward plus a valid way to get it. They just can't be an enemy of Dungeon and still get it," Wynne said.

Marybelle clapped one hand to the other and bounced lightly in place.

"Oh, I like all this. This is certainly much more fun than I thought it'd be. So far all the dungeon stuff we've been doing up to this point has just been an excuse to get in bed together," Marybelle said, smiling happily at Ryker and then Wynne.

Rolling her eyes, Wynne smiled.

"Sometimes it can be. Though it's been a while since we really got into some serious dungeon building," Wynne said. "It's… been an eventful few months. Very eventful."

"Ok, so, assuming we can do all that, now we just have to settle in and start building the most evil, lethal, fatal Death Dungeon we can," Ryker said. "And no big deal, but… I imagine the Adelonians aren't going to survive beyond tomorrow night. Which means we'll need to have this all done by the day after tomorrow in the morning."

"That's a very good point," Wynne said, lightly dragging her fingers back and forth across her cheek and chin. "It's going to be a bit bumpy to get it all done, but… I imagine it'll take some time before people start to figure out the early things. So we'll still be able to tweak the middle and later stages even as they progress through the early ones."

"Yes," Marybelle said, then lifted a pointed finger. "Can we have the blades kill people who attempt to leave the dungeon? Have them waiting at certain points in a different 'dungeon' section, so to speak?'

"We could," Wynne said. "Though it'll have to be practically disconnected from the Death Dungeon. Maybe set it up like the dueling cubes? A blade per tunnel, each tunnel coming out over a portion of the Death Dungeon. Reward them based on kills."

"Where did the blades originate from, by the way?" Marybelle asked, looking to Ryker and then Wynne. "They just showed up one day."

"Ryker did it. Originally it was just going to be a death match between two mercenary companies," Wynne said. "Then he gave them the tokens at the end and spoke to them. He did it every time after that. I think most of the blades realized the dungeon was very different after that."

"So far, if they survive their second contract, they don't typically fall. We already have over a hundred of them."

"Ryker," Shirley said from behind him.

Turning to look at her, he was momentarily stunned.

Shirley had pulled the mana bean from her hand, and now it was floating above her palm. She was actively forcing it to change itself into different shapes and sizes.

"Well," Ryker said with a chuckle.

Walking over to her, he held his hand out to the side of hers. With the utmost care, he began to carefully pull on the mana bean with his own ability and control.

He could feel her resistance to his pull. That she was actively fighting to keep it where it was.

Second by second, Ryker began to add more and more of his pressure to her control. Watching Shirley, he couldn't help but be impressed. She was showing a great amount of skill for someone who'd never touched magic before.

Sweat began to bead on her forehead. Her eyes were deeply focused on the mana in her palm.

There was a sudden pop when Ryker's control overcame Shirley's, and the mana bean shifted three inches toward Ryker's hand.

"Shirley," Ryker said, letting the mana fade and looking into her eyes.

Panting, she looked at him, nervous and curious at the same time.

"That was extremely impressive," Ryker said. "It looks like you'll be starting your magical education immediately. And beyond that... how would you like to constantly run avatars through the Death Dungeon? Would be a great way to get you combat experience quickly. That or go fight enemy soldiers at their camp.

"You'd end up eating a whole lot of pain, though, and — "

"Yes," Shirley said, a determined smile on her face. "Yes. Teach me everything and send me into the Death Dungeon, or against our enemies."

"Alright. I hadn't expected to ever be a master to someone given my problems, but I'll be happy to take that role with you," Ryker said. "For now... go get some sleep, and practice harnessing that feeling you had when you controlled the mana."

Chapter 15 - Death and Rebirth -

Ryker and Marybelle retreated to the private space they shared. Wynne went off to keep track of what was going on with the church of the dark as they went further into the Queensland. Shirley practically passed out before she made it back to her room.

"Surprising," Marybelle said, even as she called up the space they'd set aside for the Death Dungeon.

"What is? Shirley?" Ryker asked.

"Yes. Her ability seemed good. Then again, she's much older than most humans are when they start," Marybelle said. "No?"

"Well, yes. But I think she'll do well. The question will be how fast she can catch up. Alright. Now. Death Dungeon," Ryker said and sat down on the couch. "Starting with the simple reality that... well... our original dungeon is... defunct. The people going in there are adventurers and people who are doing their best to not be tied into the Queensland, or the war."

"That is a fair assessment," Marybelle said, dropping down into the seat next to him.

"With that said, our mana intake is... unlikely to be any higher than it is today, not including the deaths. Which means we have to work on a budget, right?" Ryker asked.

Marybelle nodded once and turned partially toward him, putting her arm over the top of the couch. "Right."

"Triggered things like traps, indirect attacks from creatures, nature attacks, and random occurrences are all ideal," Ryker summed up. "Anything else?"

"That's the majority of it," Marybelle confirmed. The arm she put on the top of the couch creeped forward until her hand was behind Ryker's head. Her fingers began to lightly toy with his hair.

"Alright, so, we have Robyn at the gate. She's literally going to be a stop gap and probably murder the vast majority of them on the way in. On top of that, she gets another shot at them on the way out," Ryker said. "Mostly because she'll happily ignore anyone who renounces the church of light. That and actually mean it. After that, though... they'd really have to turn around and leave.

"Otherwise, I think she'll murder them."

"I would agree. It also all fits within the rules," Marybelle said. "Though I would suggest having those who renounce the church do so by stating their name. Then you have that... herald voice you set up... announce it to the army.

"It would only take someone doing it once before the church would send minders in."

"Ah, yes. I'll leave that bit to you. I'm sure you can copy the pattern as easily as I could," Ryker said. Then he focused on the area just after the new temple of the light that Robyn had constructed.

Her area was open to the sky and more geared toward being part of Dungeon the city than the Death Dungeon.

Just beyond her, he set down a massive cave mouth that was the only exit from the temple. It dove straight down into the earth itself for fifty feet.

After that, he leveled the floor out. There, Ryker started to put down traps. Spears that came up from the ground, arrows that fired from the sides, pits that fell out from below, poison clouds stored in vials, and a number of other terrible, horrible things.

Except they were everywhere. There wasn't an inch of ground that wasn't a trap. There were traps within traps on top of traps.

For the triggers, Ryker made them very direct, but also so that only one third of them would be active at any time.

The first pass through might be more heavily to one side, the second almost all the middle. It was random. Indirect, unplanned.

"Least amount of mana, completely indirect," Ryker said.

"Indeed. It's excellently put together," Marybelle said. "I've copied the pattern over for the herald and explained it to Robyn. She would like to see you later."

"Yeah, no. She's a bit like a puppy dog right now," Ryker said.

He added in a few more ugly traps that used spells.

The first type he added only at the front of the hallway. A complete magic nullification toxin. It'd make it impossible for anyone to manipulate mana once affected by it for a few hours.

After that, he randomly added in sleep, disease, paralysis, confusion, and poison spells. All of which would make it hard to escape, move forward, or recover from the hallway.

Pulling the patterns forward, he elongated the whole thing down along Tris's wall for nine hundred feet.

"That's rather gruesome," Marybelle said. "I can tweak some of the trap placements for a touch more lethality, but it's well done. Very efficient on mana as well. Doubly so when you realize they have to come back through it to leave."

"Thanks," Ryker said, setting his hand on Marybelle's knee. "I appreciate you doing the detail work. It'll make all of this much easier."

In the next section, Ryker began to lay down a maze-work of tunnels. Ramps that led up into a blank ceiling, tunnels that fell off and away into nothing, and an endless catacomb that spiraled in a multitude of directions and pointless trails.

Endlessly downward, backtracking looping paths that ended in little more than dead ends. Each and every section was made out of only a few predetermined patterns. Everything had the same look, and nothing was unique.

Amongst everything else, Ryker made sure there were no straight passages. They all curved to some degree, either to the left or the right.

There was no lethality at all in these tunnels. No death waiting.

It was empty. Empty, barren, and dark. There were no sounds, no light, and Ryker had spent a little extra effort to make all the walls have a coating of thick, springy moss. Moss that constantly and always regrew.

There would be no shouting for others, no calling for help, no marking of tunnels, nothing.

Moving to the start, Ryker put in a wind spell. One that would circulate air throughout the entire complex that dove down into the deep depths.

Then he went to the exit, the only single path that led out amongst the thousands he'd made, and set up another wind spell. Blowing in the opposite direction of the first. Creating a flow from one side to the other. Then he made it so they would randomly reverse directions in sync.

There would be no determining which way one was going by fresh air. Ever.

Everything his teachers had taught him about dungeon diving in tunnels, he was using to twist their way.

"They'll chart it, of course," Ryker said. "At which point... I'll just randomize the whole thing. Since it's non-lethal, I figure this is all perfectly valid."

"I'm afraid it's dangerously lethal," Marybelle murmured. "Just not in a direct way. Even then, I don't think this'll be something we can leave in."

"No? Hm. What if I we changed the maximum number of people allowed in this section?" Ryker said. "What if... what if the cave section could support up to a thousand people. Providing that many could make it through Robyn and the trap hallway."

"Oh... that could work. I imagine Robyn would be locked to five at a time, and the trap hallway... ten at a time?" Marybelle asked.

"That works for me. Would that make it valid?" Ryker asked, turning to look at the Hob woman.

"Yes... it should," Marybelle said after looking up and to one side.

"How do you know?" Ryker asked. "What makes it so that you know that?"

"It's... a connection with the dungeon. And something else that I can't even begin to explain. But I know what you proposed would work," Marybelle said.

"Right," Ryker said, not really wanting to push her further. Things were lining up for him, though.

He'd seen champions, religious magic, dungeon magic, and magic that shouldn't exist—and he had experienced far more than he wanted to admit to now.

Things weren't adding up for him anymore. What he had believed he'd known, what he'd been taught, didn't make sense.

Except every time he started to really think about it, he got incredibly light-headed. Light-headed and dizzy, to the point that he wanted to lie down.

Feeling a bout of vertigo rushing toward him, Ryker backed his thoughts off from the whole thing. He was beginning to suspect a god or goddess was behind the dungeons, and that it really didn't want anyone to know about it.

Or for Ryker to know that it actually existed.

An amazing blast of vertigo washed through Ryker and sent his thoughts screeching away from where they'd been.

Focusing back on his dungeon, Ryker let out a slow breath.

"Dear, it's morning," Marybelle said, interrupting his thoughts.

"What? No it isn't. We've only just started," Ryker said, shaking his head.

"No. You were working on those tunnels for a very long time," Marybelle said. "In fact, Shirley is awake and would like to begin her training."

"Ugh, it doesn't even feel like it was that long," Ryker said, rubbing at his eyes. "What... what happened with the church army?"

"I'm not sure. I can check on that if you like while you either talk to Shirley or Robyn. Both of them are waiting for you," Marybelle said, smiling at him.

"Eh, yeah, please. Thank you for staying with me the whole time. I appreciate it," Ryker said. "I'm sure that was rather boring."

"Not at all. I've been happily entertained listening to your thoughts as you work," Marybelle said. "Go on. Pick one and go chat them up. I'm going to stay here and see what happened with the battle last night and yesterday."

Groaning, Ryker decided on Shirley. Robyn wasn't someone he wanted to deal with right now.

Breaking out of his dungeon sense, he felt an extreme sense of fatigue settle on him. To the point that he just wanted to sleep. He really had just been up for something like twenty-four hours already.

Slumping forward in his throne, Ryker slowly toppled out of it.

Two hands grabbed him by the shoulders and eased him backward.

"Ryker, are you ok?" Shirley asked.

Focusing on her, Ryker gave her a tired smile.

"Hey. Yeah, I'm alright, just really tired. I'll be fine once I stand up and give myself a pop," he said.

"Really?" Shirley asked.

"Yeah. It'll be a good lesson for you as well," Ryker said. Patting at one of her hands, he waited for her to step away.

Giving her a once-over, he saw that she'd dressed in what he could only describe as casual clothes. She'd also pinned her hair back, and she looked incredibly excited.

Hah. Maybe I underestimated her desire to be a wizard.

Getting to his feet, Ryker gave himself a firm shake, as if to knock the very sleep out of him.

Holding up his left hand, he put together a potion he knew most adventurers carried with them. It was just called "wake up" and it did exactly what it said.

Though it also had the tendency to turn your piss bright yellow and your shit to liquid acid, and your body would give out after about fourteen hours.

Downing the potion, Ryker closed his eyes and waited.

"What... was that?" Shirley asked.

"Oh... just a potion. It'll get me moving but it's going to suck. And honestly... chances are you're going to be living on these for a while during your training.

"I'm not sure which you'll hate more. The potion, or dying in the dungeon as you test everything out for m—" Ryker froze in place, turning his head to one side as his stomach reacted violently.

Half the trick to drinking one of these was keeping it down.

A minute passed like that, as Ryker literally clenched his teeth and kept himself from breathing. He managed to only gag once, which felt like a new best record for him.

Finally, Ryker let out a breath and looked back to Shirley.

"Doesn't get any easier years later, it seems," he mumbled. "Ready for your next lesson?"

"Yes," Shirley said, all worry for him gone in a flash. Replaced with absolute eager anticipation.

So very much unlike Claire, for being a Claire look-a-like.

"Patterns," Ryker said, then held up his hands in front of him. He began to build out a simple and very easy-to-understand pattern visibly in the air. It was the first spell most students learned. Something Ryker had learned as a kid. "This is a pattern. This is what constructs the mana into the shape and form you want. Patterns are composed of simple shape constructs and runes that designate what you're trying to do. This is a light spell."

Ryker activated the pattern and let the visible aspect of it fade to the naked eye. It'd be visible for those who could utilize mana, though.

A dim light appeared above the pattern, right at the exit point of the energy flow.

"What about all that... spellcasting with words, fingers, gestures, and all that?" Shirley asked.

"Different magics, different focuses. You can use them if it helps you, but they're not required," Ryker said. "I have a tendency to use my hands, as you've seen. Helps me."

Even after Dad tied my hands down. I mean, I ended up learning how to cast without my hands, which is nice, but I still use them.

"You mean... I might not be what you are?" Shirley asked, reaching out with a finger toward the pattern.

"No. You might be something entirely different. All we've established so far is you can see a pattern, harness mana, and feel it," Ryker said as she pushed a finger through the rune at the center.

"People can't always see this?" she asked.

"No. It's part of sensing mana," Ryker said, and dismissed the pattern. "I have a children's book on patterns and runes. It should help you get started. That's my first lesson to you, simply because it's a question of memorizing runes at this juncture.

"It's in my room next to—"

There was a boom that shook everything. It made the very walls tremble and the ground under Ryker's feet quake.

Lying down on the ground right there, Ryker closed his eyes and jumped into the dungeon sense.

Casting about through the city of Dungeon, he saw nothing wrong. When he jumped across to the dungeon itself, he saw the problem.

A champion of the light was casually walking through the reconstructed dungeon version of the city. As if it were the city itself. Killing anyone he came across.

The detonation he'd felt was the champion killing a mini-boss that had been put into the middle of the street itself.

Suddenly, he was very glad to have disguised the entire city as nothing more than ruins. The old husk of what had been Dungeon, instead of actual Dungeon.

Stamping through people, mobs, and things alike, the champion cared little for anything that was in his way. He casually murdered and blew up anything and everything.

He was also shouting at the top of his lungs.

"...op me! Lambart has blessed me!" shouted the champion. "And I shall cleanse this city of its filth and ilk, and let it be reborn anew!"

Goodie.

Ryker concentrated and then pushed a spell through the dungeon.

"You're declaring war on the dungeon?" Ryker asked to the champion directly.

"Yes! A thousand times, yes. The entirety of the church of light has declared war on you. All of Trevail, all of the church's members, everyone. Has declared war on you," shouted the champion at nothing. "Surrender and he shall be merciful."

Uh huh. Right.

Ryker said nothing to the champion. Instead, he made sure to begin pumping more energy and mana into Robyn's temple. It was a battery for her and her people. A place for her to charge and refuel.

It was her holy ground.

Robyn raced up the power flow that Ryker had been using to fill her temple and blasted into his sense again. Just like the previous time.

She viewed the entirety of dungeon through his senses. Filling him utterly and leaving no room for himself.

It's like having a puppy.

Ryker watched as the champion kept moving toward Robyn's temple. A bastion of energy and her belief in the "true church of light" and what it meant.

Though he was starting to suspect her religious views were changing. And he didn't like where it was going.

He was getting more and more of a general feeling that Robyn was actually making contact with a god or goddess out there that was able to take the pantheon of light's place.

Or she was making Ryker her god.

In either case, it made him more than nervous. That conversation with Robyn was going to have to happen much sooner than he wanted it to.

Kneeling in the middle of her temple to the non-existent deity of light, Robyn's avatar was motionless. Even as the champion entered the grounds and marched his way up to the cathedral doors, blowing them inward off their hinges and sending them careening into pews and bouncing around.

"I've come for you, whore!" shouted the champion. "You who betrayed all of us! I'll tear your head off and stuff it into a latrine."

Ryker noticed a strange feeling in himself as Robyn carved part of her awareness away and dropped it into her avatar. But she didn't leave his dungeon sense.

Robyn stood up, dust falling from her shoulders as she did so. She'd apparently been quite motionless for a very long time there.

"You dare defile my rest," she said, turning to face the champion. "Here in the place where I rule. Even if you do strike me down, I'll simply return, and stronger than previously. I am not what you expect."

The champion charged forward, bright white plate mail glistening splendidly.

Robyn didn't move. She stood her ground, staring down the champion as if he were nothing at all.

He swung his massive two-hander around and it crashed into Robyn's full helmet, sending it clattering and spinning away to one side.

Ryker felt a breath of panic in him, then realized Robyn still stood exactly where she had. Untouched and unmoved.

Her long black hair fell down around her head. Her eyes still staring intently into the champion.

"In my own temple, you dare," she said.

Two bright white wings burst out of her back and lifted up above her head. A dazzling golden aura enveloped her completely. Her entirely functional and very bland plate mail morphed and became bright white, clearly more for form now. Her pauldrons vanished completely.

Lifting her hands above her head, she summoned a silver and gold longsword into her hand and held it aloft.

"I shall end you, here and now. Die," Robyn commanded, and her body bent to the strike she was already bringing around to the champion.

Then it came down, and the tip seemed to pass through the champion's helmeted head and come out the other side near Robyn's ankle.

Slowly, the top of the champion's helmet fell away from the bottom part, and then he collapsed to the ground. Everything above the man's jaw remained in the top part of the helmet, while the bottom part of the helmet rested around his neck like a choker.

"Do not send your minions who do not belong into my place of power," Robyn said. "I shall abide by the laws of the dungeon and deter those who do not."

Falling back to her knees in the mirrorlike pose she'd been in before, Robyn returned from her avatar. The wings slid into her back once more, her armor morphing to that which it had once been, and the golden aura departing. Even her helmet simply rematerialized on her head.

Her avatar was as it had been.

And the golden cloud that was Robyn latched tighter to Ryker's dungeon sense. To the point that he wasn't sure he could shake her loose without using force.

Like a puppy in a lap.

Chapter 16 - The Talk -

Rather than pull Robyn further into his personal sense and risk her never leaving, Ryker moved into her core. The core that sat deep below the dungeon with all the other cores.

With the bodies of most of the Fairies and the Imps laid out in protective rooms, prettily stored in formal arrangements in their Fairy Boxes.

Protected, hidden, safe.

Robyn's temple popped into being around him at the same time that Robyn did.

"Oh!" said the paladin, turning around. "Ah!"

Grinning, she marched toward him, the armor vanishing from her body as if it had never been there. Her control over herself as an avatar, and what the dungeon could do for her, grew stronger by the day.

Reaching Ryker, she wrapped him up in a tight embrace and crushed him to herself. Being slightly taller than him, when she pulled his head in, it tucked right up under her chin.

"Hello, Ryker," murmured the paladin against the top of his head.

"Hey... Robyn," Ryker said, giving her a hug back.

"I'm so glad you came to see me. Inside of me, no less," Robyn said, and she took a step back to look down at him.

His normal daily clothes, which were fairly muted and worn in by now, were blown off his body. They were replaced with clothes far more closely set to a count's station.

"There, that looks more correct," Robyn said, nodding her head firmly. "You're a member of the peerage, consort of the true queen, and the only dungeon lord in existence. You should dress better."

Ok. Shit. She has full control over her environment now. Maybe it was a bad idea to 'go visit' her, as it were.

"Did Marybelle tell you I wished to speak with you, or did you just come to visit on your own?" Robyn asked.

"Marybelle told me, but I had been planning to see you for a bit," Ryker said. He wasn't about to lie to her in her own core.

With a finger flick of her hand, Robyn replaced her temple with the interior of Ryker's bedroom. Walking over to the table set to one side, she sat down and smiled up at him.

"Well, I'm thankful either way that you came as quickly as you did. It shows you care," Robyn said. She politely didn't suggest he take the seat across from her, but it was obvious that was the correct response.

Grinning at Robyn, who so far was being exactly in death as she'd been in life, Ryker sat down across from her.

She reached out, grabbed the seat of his chair and pulled it closer to her own.

"There," she said. "Now, I wished to formally discuss my standing with you and your relation to me."

Hiding his surprise at being yanked closer, Ryker nodded.

"Uh huh. That sounds like a good thing to make sure is well understood. So, what part? Or piece? Something in particular?" Ryker asked.

"Yes, actually. First is my allegiance to you," Robyn said, smiling widely at him. "I can safely say that I will be relinquishing any rights I had to be dismissed from your service. My only caveat will be that I will still need to re-establish the church when the time comes. I may no longer be among the living, but I can give those who are a chance to worship truly."

"Oh. That's interesting," Ryker said. "I'm flattered, honestly."

"Yes, well. Once I saw how you interacted with your people, then what happened to Dungeon and how you handled it, I knew this was my place. Knew it as clearly as I know that the church will be reborn," Robyn said. Then she licked her lips and leaned towards him. "I've heard a voice, you know."

"A voice?" Ryker asked, not really sure where this was going. He had a momentary flashback to when Robyn had been literally losing her mind.

"Yes. I heard it. For just a moment," Robyn said. "I was praying for mercy. Mercy, resolution of my wrongs, and atonement. And I heard it. It was a whisper.

"A ghostly whisper that promised me what I prayed for. That all I had to do was continue the path I was on and it would lead to a destination now ordained."

"Right. You're saying... a god or goddess... heard you?" Ryker asked.

"Yes, that's exactly what I'm saying. And they spoke to me directly. They were so weak, though," Robyn said, shaking her head. "But I know what tenets I must follow. I must have a patient heart to heal others, and to give myself warmly and lovingly to those who would receive me. Light, true light, is that which we find in others."

She's cracked, or she really did find something.

"And so, I wished to speak with you. I'll begin holding services immediately in Dungeon to my new deity, unnamed though they may be. I shall preach what I now know," Robyn said, gifting Ryker with one of the most beautiful smiles he'd seen. "And you, my savior. Who pulled me from a darkness I knew not and flung me into the cold light of the truth. You I would ask to attend at my side. I will give you my warmth and love."

Ryker nodded once, slowly.

"Alright. I can do that, but you're going to have to promise me that you keep it to twice a week. And no longer than an hour," Ryker said. He didn't want to flat out refuse her, but he didn't want to spend every single day in a church either.

"Of course. Your time is extremely precious, I'll not waste it," Robyn said. Then she reached out and grabbed Ryker's chair pulling it closer still. "Now. What shall we discuss?"

Feeling completely at a loss and struggling to catch up, Ryker went with the only thing on his mind.

"I need you to slaughter anyone who comes into the dungeon who worships the false church of light," Ryker said. "Unless they forswear the church, that is."

Robyn's chin lifted, and there was a faint flutter as wings appeared behind her back. They slowly spread out, trembling.

"I shall do this, and gladly so," she said with heat. "I rejoice that you've given me this duty and bound me to be your first challenge and test."

"And again as they leave, if they try," Ryker said. "You'll get a second chance at them if they defeat you the first time."

Chuckling darkly, Robyn nodded at that. "Yes. I see it. I had not looked into what you were building that closely, but I see it now. It will be done by your command."

Folding back into her, the wings vanished, but the strange golden aura didn't leave.

"For those who rescind, I shall welcome them into the flock and escort them into Dungeon," Robyn said. "There they will remain a time to ascertain the veracity of their devotion."

Good luck to whoever that may be.

"What else did you wish to discuss?" Robyn asked, her eyes locking back on Ryker's.

"You, in general," Ryker said, looking for anything. "Have you considered a second avatar to walk about the city? Or simply spend time with the Fairies or Imps?"

"Or spend time with you," Robyn said, nodding. "I shall make another avatar immediately and be at your side forever forward, if I can."

There was a faint tickle at the base of Ryker's mind as something disconnected from his sense and reformed itself in the grander dungeon sense.

Then it connected back to his dungeon sense and settled in once more.

"Ah, Shirley is waiting for you," Robyn said. "I told her you would be back later, and that it was likely I would keep you occupied till tomorrow. She said she memorized all the useful runes but would go learn more for now."

Oh. That was quick. I wonder if she just went through and picked out all combat ones.

It's what I'd do, but... in teaching, one must allow growth on its own as well.

"Tell me more of your plans," Robyn said, gazing into Ryker's face.

"Not much more than you haven't already heard, I'm afraid. Survive this, crush the church, and rebuild," Ryker said, smiling with a shake of his head. "It's really that straightforward. Originally, I wanted to... to... You know what? It doesn't even matter what I wanted to do."

"That's like you talking about your life beforehand. It's pointless and without merit. Now I'm just looking forward to when this is all over and maybe I can get back to my farm."

"Did I ever tell you how encouraging it was to see you raise a farm after what happened?" Robyn said. "It truly was a test of character, and you came out the other side in one piece."

Not... really. But I suppose I did in the end.

***

Dropping into a chair at Edwin's table, Ryker gave the other man a grin and a hand wave.

"Hey there," Ryker said. "Thought I'd drop in and see how things are going. Haven't seen you in like a week or three, or... something like that."

"About three weeks," Edwin said with a smirk. He looked much as he had when Ryker had met him. A solid man in his mid-forties, brown hair cut quite short, and cold blue eyes. He had the stamp of a life spent in the military, from his haircut to the way he held himself.

"Oh. That's not too bad," Ryker said, nodding. "I was honestly afraid you were going to say something like a month or two."

"Three weeks... so, find a wife yet?"

Edwin rolled his eyes and waved over the waitress.

Ryker had tracked the man down to a small outdoor cafe in the middle of Dungeon.

It'd been a day since the champion of light had been slaughtered outright. Now the enemy was starting to form up outside the gates. Getting themselves into position to settle in for an attack or a siege—or just settling in.

"I'm a bit old to be trying to marry the ladies round here, Ryker, you twat," Edwin groused. "Old enough to be their daddy."

Ryker shrugged. "You forget you're the mayor now. And that's a hereditary title here in Dungeon, so... maybe you'll need to find the one with some underlying issues?"

The waitress came over and gave Ryker a smile. She was cute, young, and looked like she was probably unwed. She also seemed to have an eye for the older man when she came over.

"Hello Count, what can I get you?" she asked.

"Whatever he's having," Ryker said. "Unless it's you. At that point, he can have you all by himself."

The waitress' face turned a flaming red and she spun on her heel, marching away.

"Ryker!" hissed Edwin, glaring at him now. "What in the fuck are you doing?"

"Giving her the go ahead to make a pass at you, if she fancies it," Ryker said with a snicker. "I mean, you can hurry up and find your own lady, or I can marry you off myself if you like. I could see if Lauren has any cousins that are available.

"Did you fancy Adele or Claire in the looks, because seems like her family can run in either direction."

"Do you know... how... infuriating it is to talk to you?" Edwin asked.

"Yeah. I hear about it often enough. Anyways, Adele or Claire?" Ryker asked.

Edwin shook his head slowly, then blew out a breath.

"Adele. Something... like that. She was feisty and didn't tolerate much," Edwin said.

"Right, I'll keep it in mind. So! On to actual business then," Ryker said. "First of all, there are only two armies out in front of Dungeon now."

"Oh? Where'd the other two go?" Edwin asked, his brows coming together.

"Church of dark escaped through a gap. We mauled them as they went. Church of light and Trevail murdered the Adelonians. They're gone," Ryker said.

Edwin nodded at that, then waited.

"Blades are probably gonna move out of the city. Going to put together an inn specifically for them inside the dungeon," Ryker said.

"Fine. They're kinda bloodthirsty as of late anyways. Keep to themselves and seem to be just… waiting," Edwin said with a shake of his head. "Soldiering is one thing, killing for money or rewards is another."

"Eh, I get it. It's a lot like adventuring. Just killing others instead of monsters for similar loot and valuables," Ryker said with a flick of his fingers. "It's all the same in the end anyways when it comes down to motive for an adventurer."

Edwin quirked a brow at that comment.

"What?" Ryker said. "I've killed people for no reason other than I wanted to. What you're saying is literally something I've done myself. Would you rather I pretend it was different?"

Edwin gave a shake of his head and lifted a hand. "Continue, please."

"Uh, that might be everything, honestly. I mean, that's the super condensed version and all that," Ryker said.

"Talking with you is always an examination of extremes. It's a wonder that I actually stopped in thought a week ago, missing our conversations," Edwin said. "I now remember why each one was always like dealing with a tree stump."

"What do you want me to say? There's really not that much going on. We're fighting the churchies, one got through, we flogged it hard. It's heading north to help Lauren in her fight against Veronica. Adele and Diane are up that way, Claire is here with me," Ryker said. "Beyond that it's really all the same. How's the town doing?"

"Good, actually. After pulling together the defenders and soldiers I could, we started killing everything and everyone who stood in our way," Edwin said. "It'd been a while since I held a sword in anger. Felt like I'd failed though, all things considered."

"At what, fighting off two champions, the Dark Lord of the North's envoy, two dark knights, and an army?" Ryker said and scoffed. "Yeah, real failure there. I couldn't hold them off any better, you'll remember. I stumbled off into the way go downs and hid in a hole."

"Way go downs," Edwin repeated.

"Dungeon thing. What? I don't have to filter myself with you; I can just say what I want," Ryker said. "And sometimes what I want to say doesn't make any sense."

"Most of what you say doesn't make any sense. Honestly, I sometimes wonder what's going on in your head," Edwin said.

"What isn't?" Ryker said with a grin.

The waitress came back, set down two platters and two drinks, then scurried off without a word.

"See? Now you've scared her off," Edwin said, looking back at the waitress as she ran away.

"Eh… if that scared her off, she probably wouldn't have been good to ask out anyways. Wouldn't have worked out," Ryker said. Turning to the plate, he found it was a solid-looking sandwich.

"Ugh. As for the town, we're doing well. We keep getting more people traveling overland now. The uh… dungeon… has been escorting people from the front into the city proper," Edwin said.

"Oh, yeah. Marybelle is keeping an eye on that," Ryker said around a mouthful of food. "How many people are coming in a week?"

"Something like thirty or forty. We're already at the population size we were at previously, and rapidly scaling past it," Edwin said, taking a much more subdued bite of his own food.

"Damn. I had no idea," Ryker said, frowning. He was concerned about that now. The fact that people were coming here wasn't something he'd been expecting. It was outside of his plan because it meant something was going wrong.

If people were fleeing from somewhere else, then they knew something he didn't.

Need to check in with Lauren tonight if I can manage it somehow.

"They're mostly saying they're coming for safety and security," Edwin said, apparently going to the same conclusion Ryker had. "No refugees yet, but… I don't know. I get the impression it's going to start one way or the other soon. Either from Veronica's lands or Lauren's."

Ryker nodded at that. It made sense. People fleeing before things really got bad would be a precursor.

Damn. If we're the exit point for those who would flee the Queensland entirely, we'll need to create some type of post-gate. Let people back out into the mainland.

"Economy is going up. Prices seem steady and constant for us," Edwin said.

"That's rather unexpected," Ryker said.

"Yes, and no? The adventurers are clearing the dead as fast as you make 'em, it seems. Then all that ends up going to your little store and gets sold back out cheap," Edwin said. "It's becoming a leveling effect for everything else in the city. Doesn't hurt that you can summon up food to be slaughtered as well at the inn. I get the impression the adventurers are just butchering everything they can in some of the stranger wings, then bringing it all back up and reselling it."

Ryker couldn't argue any of Edwin's points. He hadn't intended for any of it to happen that way, but it was working out exactly as he stated.

The original dungeon was a massive leveling force for Dungeon and keeping it balanced. Far more than it should be for a country at war.

Alright, well. We just… keep going, I guess.

"You going to be making more regularly scheduled trips up now?" Edwin asked, pointing a finger at Ryker. "You're a crazy little fucker, but you're entertaining."

"Yeah. I might even bring Claire around. She's starting to loosen up some, you know," Ryker said.

He'd been spreading that rumor around as much as he could. The further he could get Claire's "personality" to change, the easier it would be for Shirley to take Claire's heritage over and make it her own.

"Claire…? Ugh… I'd rather you not," Edwin said, shaking his head.

"No, no. Really. She's getting much easier to handle," Ryker said. "A lot easier."

Chapter 17 - Apprentice -

Shirley stumbled as she dodged to the left, tripping over herself.

Recovering from the missed attack, the soldier pulled his spear around and then thrust out with it again.

The spear tip tore through Shirley's simple leather armor. The sound of her ribs breaking was loud even as the spear sank to the shaft in her chest.

Ripping the weapon out of Shirley, the soldier drew back and stabbed her again, then again.

Groaning, and curling up on herself in the fetal position, Shirley died.

Her avatar popped out of existence.

"That went... better," Ryker said. He'd been watching from his throne room, sitting in his chair. Shirley was seated in the throne he'd had made specifically for her, next to his own.

Panting, she pressed a hand to her breast.

"That hurt so bad," she whined, massaging herself. "And it went through my boob."

"Considering your bust size, it'd be impressive if he missed your boobs," Ryker said. "It did go better, though. You managed to kill one before the second got you."

"Ow..." Shirley moaned, pushing at her chest.

"It's phantom pain. Your body thinks you're still feeling it even though you're not. It'll go away shortly. Now... what spell were you trying to use?"

"Lightning. You said you could make it bounce from target to target," Shirley said, slowly sitting upright.

"Yeah. And it can. It takes a bit more than a straight lightning spell, though. Show me your pattern," Ryker said, leaning over toward Shirley.

Shirley looked at him, frowned, and then eased herself over the arm of her throne and closer to Ryker. As she held up her left hand, a rune began to draw itself in her palm.

Watching, Ryker was impressed. For someone who had only begun to barely learn how to do such things a short while ago, she was doing incredibly well.

Finishing up, Shirley pointed at it with her free hand.

"I used lightning, air, and pushed it," she said.

"I see. Let's pick it apart," Ryker said, then enfolded her hand in his own. Injecting a small touch of mana into her construct, he made the pattern larger and brightened the whole thing up so it would be easier to see.

"First, your lightning rune is very well put together. Good job," Ryker said, indicating the small squiggly glyph in the middle. "It's very clean, and much of the force of it will transmit properly. Your air rune is a little soft, but it's still good. The exit point is clean, but your entry point is a bit weak."

Each time he made a point, Ryker pointed to the corresponding part of the pattern.

"The overall layout and channeling, as well as the amplifier, is all done well. The spell itself is good. There's nothing wrong with it as a whole," Ryker said, turning his head to Shirley.

She looked from him to the rune, and back to him.

"Really?" she asked, her tone cautious and quiet.

"Very. I'm impressed. Good job, Shirley," Ryker said, grinning at her.

"Then why'd it fail?" she asked, her shoulders slowly coming down as if she no longer expected to be attacked in his critique.

Ryker could empathize. He remembered long, agonizing "this is why you're an idiot and will fail" sessions with his father.

"Because it just isn't the right spell to do what you wanted," Ryker said. "Now... if you wanted it to jump and arc into what I call chain lightning, then you need to add Earth and a seeking spell to it."

Ryker lifted his hand and began adding the pieces he'd just mentioned to Shirley's pattern. It took him a minute to do it, but he wanted her to see the way it unfolded. If he was in a rush, he could build the whole spell in less than a second.

"Oh. Oh! I see it now. Ok. I understand. The Earth spell is just there to designate the original point so it doesn't come back, is that it?" she asked.

"Yeah. I learned that one the hard way. It will come back if you don't put that Earth spell in. You're the point of least resistance. The bolt is still active," Ryker said. "Then again, if you skip the Earth part, the spell will be much more powerful, and more mana efficient. If I'm not too concerned, I skip the Earth."

"Got it. I'm going to go again then, is that ok?" Shirley asked.

"Of course. Don't need to ask me permission. Just make sure to bust your avatar before they take you prisoner or anything like that," Ryker said.

"I understand," Shirley said, then squeezed his hand with hers. It reminded him that he was holding her hand, and he let go.

"I'm off," she said, settling back into her personal throne. She closed her eyes and was gone. Another avatar that looked nothing like her appeared at the edge of the church of light's camp. Striding toward the closest sentry, she started to build a spell.

"She's taking to war quickly," Meino said, her big head lumbering out from the side of his throne.

"Very," Ryker said. "Almost too quickly. She also doesn't seem too bothered anymore by death and blood."

"She is. She hides it well. She has a much harder time around you with it, though. She smells of fear in your presence," Meino said.

"Fear? Huh. I thought she was over being afraid of me," Ryker said and then sighed. "Oh well. Not something I can really put time and effort into right now. At least her training is presenting us with a way to also whittle down a few of the enemy's numbers."

Ryker started to move the view on his desk away from the army and back to dungeon.

Then paused when he went over the battle-rectangle. No one used it anymore, since the enemy army had perished. No one seemed to want to kill their allies.

He had a sudden flash of an idea.

Skewing his focus on the battle arena, he rapidly began to throw up walls all the way around it. Everywhere — walls and walls and walls.

"What are you doing?" Meino asked.

"Going to make another dueling arena. The entirety of the battle arena is going to become one-on-one fights, or group battles, for people to enlist in," Ryker said. Rapidly he filled in rooms with those walls, placing them in varying sizes and shapes, then adding in furniture, landscapes, or simple obstacles.

"Dear? What are you doing?" Marybelle asked inside his mind.

"Building. Changing the battle arena," he sent back to her.

"Oh, alright. They're starting to watch as you work. That's all," she said.

"Got it. I'll make it quick. Were you working on something?"

"Nothing important, dear. I was just adding in some detail work to make things pretty," Marybelle said, her tone changing near the end into something else entirely. *"Are you hungry? Would you like me to put together a simple lunch for us and join you?"*

"Actually, that'd be great. Do you mind?"

"Not at all. I'll make some for Shirley as well. See you soon, dear," Marybelle said.

She's awfully attentive. More so as time goes on.

Nodding his head as he finished the rooms, Ryker then went to the entrance and put up a sign, explaining the dueling arena rules.

They were just like the cube, but they had no monsters. Everyone would be fighting each other. People could fight for a lot of wealth if they chose. Fight to the death with their fellow soldiers.

Or fight for only a little bit of coin, to first blood. There was also a middle ground, first disabled, with a bonus if they killed their opponent.

Then Ryker took hold of the entirety of the field around the battle arena and dropped a massive working spell pattern onto it. No one in the field could be identified by their face any longer. Everyone would suddenly be wearing a hood. They couldn't pull it off, and it wouldn't come off for any reason.

He'd made the entire thing anonymous. If someone wanted to go fight, they could. They just had to make sure they didn't speak, or wear anything identifiable.

But that was on them.

Ryker had done what he could.

Easing back from the construct, he smiled. People were already starting to wander over to the sign out in front.

Only after trying to pull the hoods off their heads, of course. Several people immediately recognized what had changed and darted into the walled-off battle arena.

Good. Now we just put it in so the activations are the same as the dueling arena. Rooms with occupants get a green for waiting for opponent, red for in combat, and black for empty.

I wonder how long it'll be before the first fight starts.

Done with the work there, Ryker continued on his way to the dungeon. The church of light had begun sending in people at first light this morning. They were obeying the dungeon rules as well so far.

They did try to blow a hole in the wall last night, though, and ended up losing a hundred people for their troubles. Maybe they realized the only way through is through the dungeon.

Settling over the top of Robyn's temple, he arrived just in time to see her get stabbed through the chest with a sword.

Collapsing to the ground, Robyn began to breathe her last. It was unfortunately part of the rules of the dungeon. She could only act within a certain amount of potential lethality toward the group that came in. If they brought enough force to match the listed danger level, they could probably win.

The number of those groups were in the minority though. For every one that got through, two or three perished outright.

Stabbing forward, the soldier skewered Robyn again, even as she died.

Irrationally, Ryker was angry.

It was rude and uncalled for to do that to Robyn. She would suffer for no reason because the man was bloodthirsty. She had already been down and dying.

Channeling his fury before he could rein it in, Ryker acted.

All that anger went into the man's sword as he withdrew it from Robyn. Ryker wanted it to explode.

And it did so happily. Bursting apart, the soldier's arm up to his shoulder became a shredded lump of meat and blood.

"Sorry!" shouted a second soldier, lifting up a placating hand above his head. "That was uncalled for! We'll leave!"

Huh?

Frowning, and glaring down at the squad of men as they pulled their companion away, Ryker didn't know what to make of it.

The golden glow of Robyn that had attached itself to his dungeon sense seemingly permanently spun around once and then settled back down. As if stretching itself to make sure it was in every part of Ryker's being.

So locked to him was Robyn that Ryker couldn't even dispel his sense anymore. It was up constantly now. Even in his sleep.

"Ryker? What'd you do?" Wynne asked, her voice coming through the dungeon sense to him.

"Sorry... did something stupid. Someone stabbed Robyn even as she lay there dying. I blew up a sword," Ryker admitted.

"Oh. He didn't die?" Wynne asked.

"No. His friends are pulling him out now. They apologized... and are just leaving," Ryker said.

"To be fair, the entire dungeon growled," Wynne said.

"Growled? Like... a wolf growl?" Ryker asked, confused. There were small worries in the back of his head that maybe the soulless dungeon crystal had picked up another soul somehow.

"No. Like an angry wizard growling," Wynne corrected.

Oh. Got it.

Sighing, Ryker moved on, going to the trap hallway. He'd already spent an entire hour simply watching people attempt to get across. It'd been a grab-bag of horrible ways to die along with people doing their best to get through to the other side.

Now, however, he was disappointed to find that the vast majority of groups were treating it more like a gambling game. They picked a line, got in order, and ran to the other side. There was no fighting the hallway, surviving the traps, or preparing for it.

They were minimizing their risk and sprinting to the other side.

Though as far as Ryker could tell, it wasn't working half as well as they would have liked. For every five groups that ran in of five members, only twelve or so people made it through.

"Doesn't seem as chaotic," Meino said, watching the display.

"No. It really doesn't," Ryker said. "Oh well. It was fun watching. Now it's more like a comedy. Especially if they hit a gas trap of some type. It'd wipe out the whole party and that'd be the end of it. If they really wanted to get through, every group would have a rogue in the lead, and they'd walk."

"It'd take an hour or two, but they could do it."

"I don't think they're allowed to take their time," Meino said.

"Yeah… whatever." Ryker turned and looked to the caves.

Sadly, they were exactly what Wynne had predicted. People were very lost, wandering around endlessly. They weren't dying, though, as it was only the first day. People were moving in pairs, and doing their best to map it. Everyone had paper out and was writing down everything they felt they needed.

"Great, so… I'll be changing that every night, practically. That or adding some things to make it lethal. I hadn't wanted to, but… yeah, not turning out the way I wanted," Ryker said.

"You've said before plans get fucked up," Meino said. "Why are you surprised now?"

"Good… point. Yeah. Alright. Lethal it is. More traps like before, but much more targeted and direct ones. That way they can't just wander however they like.

"Add a lot of magical turnabouts and nasty things. This'll also be a good opportunity to let the blades loose. Give them the ability to see exits and entrances keyed only to those who've earned a token. Let them come and go as they please and earn more counters," Ryker said.

Shirley shuddered and came back to herself, immediately pressing a hand to her stomach.

"Ugh. Why do they always go for my chest or stomach? That's the third time I've been eviscerated tonight," she grumbled.

"Because of that reason," Ryker said, then killed the feed to his table. "How'd it go?"

"I got four. Two groups of two. The lightning worked much better. I tried to get fancy with number five and use fire. He killed me even though he was clearly burned to nothing," Shirley complained.

"Lightning stops the heart. Burns just hurt unless you can get their face quick. The eyes, really," Ryker said.

"Ah, yes. That makes perfect sense. I'm going to go again, ok?" Shirley asked.

Chuckling, Ryker nodded.

"Alright. Don't have to ask me for permission though, remember? I'll be right here. Though I might go see Lauren. Want me to say hi to your cousin for you?" Ryker asked.

Shirley opened her mouth, then closed it. Turning to him, she looked unsure.

"Should I?" she asked. "Does she… hate me?"

"Pretty sure she doesn't. Otherwise she would have said to kill you. I think she's just happy more of her family is alive and supporting her. So… is that a yes?" Ryker asked.

"Uhm. Yes, please. Tell her hello… and that the doll she gave me was still in my room last I saw. Before I left home," Shirley said, then closed her eyes and dove back into a new avatar.

Interesting. Must be a code or a secret.

"Have fun," Meino said, then moved away from him.

Sighing, Ryker got himself comfortable. Trips to Lauren took a while.

***

An Imp he didn't know stepped out in front of him as he finished moving himself into the avatar. Apparently it was very obvious when he was traveling this way.

On top of that, he seemed to have come out in an antechamber directly before the queen's bedroom.

"Welcome, my lord king. I'll let the queen know you've arrived," said the Elven Imp. She bowed her head to him and left quickly. He was now standing amongst two other Imps. One was a human, and the other looked like some type of half-giant.

"Shit, have to take a running leap at you to kiss that pretty face," Ryker said, looking up at the seven-foot woman.

"You can try, or I can pick you up," said the woman in a deep tone.

"Eh... maybe another time. I'm on a fit and lean diet right now, so to speak," Ryker said, and looked back to the door the Elf had gone into.

"She'll see you immediately, my lord king," said the human. "She's been waiting for you."

Ryker ended up waiting for what felt like only a minute or two before the Elf came back.

"Please follow me, my lord king," the Elf said, gesturing as she walked back into the room she'd come from.

When Ryker walked in, he was immediately overwhelmed with opulence and an absolute display of wealth. There was enough gold inlay in the furniture to fund an army.

"Don't judge me," Lauren said from deeper inside. "I know you are. I had nothing to do with any of this. My family bought it all long before I was born."

Ryker snickered to himself and shook his head. Following the location of the voice, he found Lauren seated in bed. A book in her lap, and a candelabra sitting beside her lighting the nearby space. She was dressed in a white nightgown and seemed to be ready for bed.

"Good evening," she said, even as the Elf exited the room and closed the doors. "They've taken over as my personal guards. I must admit I judged them wrongly at first glance. Immaculate soldiers, and able to deal with anything. My own house guard is guarding the palace now, which makes me feel more at ease all the way around."

"Ah, you're welcome then," Ryker said. Grabbing a chair, he pulled it over to the side of her bed and sat down in it. "Good to see you, Lauren."

Lauren smiled at him and turned her head to one side, eying him.

"You seem to be on your best behavior around me as of late," she said, lifting her book up and tapping her chin with it.

"Best? I dunno about that. Maybe I'm trying to be a bit nicer to you. Feel like you need some nice in your life lately," Ryker said. "Oh. Shirley says hi, and that doll you gave her was still in her bedroom when she left."

"Really?" Lauren asked, a small smile spreading across her face. "Hm. Tell her I said hello in return, and that I'm glad she enjoyed it."

"Sure, sure. Figured you'd say that," Ryker said, then sniffed.

Lauren's cinnamon smell was everywhere here in her bedroom.

"Even smells like you in here," Ryker said, glancing around for some type of flowers or spice hidden away.

"I smell?" Lauren asked, her brows creasing.

"Like cinnamon. Well, I think so at least," Ryker said.

Laughing softly at that, Lauren raised her eyebrows. "I smell like cinnamon to you?"

"Yeah. Why?" Ryker asked.

"Just... never mind. With you, every conversation is an experience all on its own. What do I owe the pleasure of the visit to?" Lauren asked.

"Checking in. Dark church soldiers broke through. I'm sure you knew that, though," Ryker said.

"Indeed. I knew as soon as they made it to the other side, but thank you for confirming it. It puts my mind at ease," Lauren said.

"Adelonians died to the last when Trevail and the church of light turned on them," Ryker said. "Now I'm playing wave-breaker and holding them all up and out of the Queensland."

"I thank you for your noble and valiant service, husband-to-be," Lauren said. "I'll be very gracious once this is all over."

"I mean… we could try now if you like. Candelabra's right there," Ryker said, nodding at it.

"No… I'll pass on that. Though I'm tempted to try right now without it," Lauren said, giving him an arched smile. "It's been a very rough couple days lately. We've lost several battles due to treachery. I could use a change of pace."

Ryker didn't know how to respond to either one of those statements.

"Going… badly?" he asked.

Lauren gave him a small, sad smile and nodded her head.

"Very bad. Those church soldiers will help. But I don't think I can stop them from advancing their own agendas once they arrive," Lauren said. "I fear my time on the throne is coming to an end.

"Now… how about that change of pace. Would you… whisk me away to that little space of yours, lock the door and… help me forget things?"

Not what I was expecting, but… fun. Let's go see if the queen is anything like her cousins.

Chapter 18 - Breaker -

Ryker built out the spell pattern in front of himself and Shirley. He filled it in slowly and let it grow at a speed Shirley would surely be able to follow.

"I built this on the fly to knock that champion into the sky like a kite," Ryker said. "The whole thing is a construct meant to cup, propel, and leach magic as it goes. That's it. And because of that, it doesn't cost much mana. You don't seem to have the same problem I do, so the efficiencies I use don't really need to apply obviously."

"Maybe so, but I see no reason to not benefit from your methods and research," Shirley said, one hand raised to follow the pattern with a finger as he drew it out for her. "I'm your apprentice, after all. I should learn from you."

That felt weird to Ryker, but she wasn't wrong. It hit a spot inside him that had withered to the point of being dead. To him, it felt like light shining into a very dark place and finding there was something there.

"Uhm, alright. Then one of the biggest tricks to writing patterns I can tell you is to keep it all tight. Tight, simple, and use as many amplifiers as you can. It'll be infinitely harder at the start, but the more you work like that, the easier it'll come to you later," Ryker said.

"That makes sense," Shirley said, then pointed to a point in the pattern. "What's that?"

"Hm? Oh. That's just how I tied it off. You're looking at the gate that switches on to off, then back off to on as it loops around. Rather than tying it closed with the leaching effect, I tied the end to the beginning. The spell will exist in perpetuity as long as it's fed, rather until the pattern fades," Ryker said. "Which means if that champion never got off the cup, he'd be feeding it as long as he lived."

"Could you do this for anything? Make it self-leaching?" Shirley asked.

"Of course, but it isn't a question of *could* you, it's *should* you. I would never attach this to a fire spell, obviously, as it would… well, I wouldn't even want to imagine what it would do. Lightning wouldn't be as bad, since it would fade out as soon as it lost people to jump to."

"Could I use a jumping, leaching, self-filling spell on the army?" Shirley asked.

"You sure could, but it would be rather indiscriminate. And there's no guarantee it would stop with the army. If it had enough power, it could theoretically start leaping from tree to tree till it found a new city," Ryker said.

Shirley shook her head, letting her hands fall to her sides.

"This seems like a bit too much power for any one person to have," she said.

"Well, to be fair, most people can't do what we're talking about. The amount of control required to coil a pattern this tight is… unique to me so far," Ryker said.

"What? Then why teach me at all?" Shirley asked, looking at him.

"Because I think you can do it. You're very smart, Shirley. And you're determined, and willing to put in the time so far. I bet you could make this very spell if you tried," Ryker said. "In fact, use it on the next one who shows up. Let's see if we can't pin him to a wall."

With a dismissive hand gesture, the pattern faded from the air and left Ryker standing alone with Shirley at the end of the tunnel.

They were acting as guards for the end while Marybelle and Wynne rapidly constructed as many Death Dungeon wings as they could. It was going to be a series of increasing and escalating battles and fights. Going upwards in a massive tower that stretched to the sky. Only to come back down the other way in more fights, all the way back to the ground.

The tower was going to be an ungodly and horrifying mess of brutality. But unfortunately, until it was done, Ryker had to play goalkeeper.

Pushing hard and fast, the church of light was doing everything they could to get through the Death Dungeon quickly.

Well, not so much the church. They're mostly pushing those poor little Trevalians out in front of them.

"Ah, here we go," Shirley said, getting down behind the boulder.

Ryker slunk down beside her. They had created the boulder to give themselves time to prep for whoever was coming. It looked like another turn in the cave system, but it was actually just a large boulder with the top half see-through on one side.

Shirley was holding her hands up in front of her, trying to reconstruct the pattern Ryker had showed her.

He knew it was going to be difficult for her. It was one thing for a pattern to be displayed; it was another to recreate it by yourself. An old teacher of his had compared it once to drawing. Everyone would have their own art style in the end.

Flickering, the pattern failed and fell in on itself.

Shirley shook her head and tried again.

Slowly, the enemy squad kept walking in their direction. To Ryker it looked like a group of four soldiers and an officer.

She's got another try before I have to intervene. Give or take. Let's give her as much time as we can afford. Practice under duress is the best thing in the world for her.

Once again, Shirley's pattern collapsed on itself. Grimacing, she bared her teeth and started to try it again.

He could remember having felt the same way under his father's guidance. The rigid lines, hard turns, and perfect squares and rectangles that made up Ryker's style weren't his own.

They had only become his own because his father had forced them on him. Ryker could remember wanting to make them all squiggly lines just to get his father angry.

"Try making it your own," Ryker said, reaching out to push his hand through her pattern. "Don't copy mine exactly this time. Do what I did, but how 'Shirley's mind' would see it done."

"I… ok," Shirley said, starting again from the rune center. This time, instead of the exact, perfectly straight, and extremely controlled lines of Ryker's doing, long flowing curves created themselves.

It looked exactly like Ryker's pattern. But where his were all squares and rectangles, hers were now all circles and ovals.

And it was impressive. They had all the same control and efficiency of his own, just with much less rigidity of the mind required.

Smirking to himself, Ryker felt pride in the woman. She didn't fight anything he taught her. She threw herself fully into everything with absolute trust.

She'd scrapped everything she'd been doing in an instant and tried something she'd had no idea would even work.

Ryker realized she was going to run out of time before she finished her pattern, as he'd been afraid of. Standing up, he put together a force construct that was like a web.

Building his spell with his father's style made him wonder what would happen if he tried it differently later.

Something to test.

The squad walked past him and Shirley. Ryker released the spell with an upraised palm.

As quiet as a breath, the spell smashed into the group of five and pinned them to the wall. He'd done his best to make the spell quiet, and he'd put a silencing spell into it as well.

Those trapped on the wall would make no noise, and everything would happen without a sound. He didn't want to disturb Shirley in what she was doing.

Shirley finished her spell and stood up to look down the tunnel. Then she turned to the right and found the target already pinned.

"Oh," she said dejectedly. "I was late."

"Yes, but that's alright. Cast it on me," Ryker said, walking to the wall. "Let's see how fast I can cut or counter it."

"Are you sure…?" Shirley asked.

"Yep. No sense in wasting such a beautiful pattern," Ryker said, indicating the swirling pattern in her hands.

Shirley nodded, then cast it at Ryker.

Seeing it coming at him, his first instinct was to immediately punch out the central rune. But that wouldn't help Shirley's confidence, nor would it help her learn.

Letting it hit him, Ryker grimaced as it immediately began siphoning mana out of him.

"That's rather good," Ryker said, looking at the much-expanded pattern now that it was activated. "Look how the energy flows. It's not quite as good as the one I demonstrated, but it's very close. For a first-time casting, this is amazing."

Shirley came over and stood in front of him, looking between him and the pattern.

"Is it... that good?" she asked.

"Very. This would hold any mage up to a master level easily," Ryker said.

"What about you? Can you get out?" Shirley asked. There was an odd tone in her question he couldn't identify.

"Yes. Would you like to see me do so?" he asked. "Might be a good lesson for you."

Shirley nodded.

Ryker smiled, then punched out the rune with a single tap of mana. The spell immediately disintegrated to nothing.

"How... how'd you do that?" she asked incredulously.

"If I know the rune you're using — at the center, that is — I can just... punch it out by inverting the same rune atop it," Ryker said. "A good battle mage, or battle wizard if you prefer, will obscure the rune, hide it. Make it look like something else. Most mages aren't battle mages, though. They rarely consider such things.

"Now, would you please go take care of those bugs over there? I want to check in with Marybelle."

"Ok. I'll practice some spells on them," Shirley said, turning and walking back to the pinned soldiers.

She's as cold and ruthless as me now.

Ryker paused to smile ferally at Shirley's back.

She's amazing.

"How you doing?" Ryker sent to Marybelle's fluttering dungeon sense. She and Wynne were working in concert to construct the tower.

"Almost done. You can probably stop now. The Death Dungeon will be done momentarily," she sent back.

"We're done after this," Ryker said aloud, looking to Shirley.

She was holding a hand up in front of a soldier's head, and a small, dense cloud of acid was melting his face as he screamed soundlessly.

"Okay," she said, turning her head to look at him. She gave him a small smile. "Is it weird that I can do this to people without caring about them at all?"

"A little," Ryker said, coming over to stand next to her. "But then again, most people will tell you that a mage loses that part of them first. My father had me killing convicts by the time I was six. I didn't feel anything after the first one."

Though that doesn't seem to apply if you kill someone with something other than magic.

To this day, Ryker still felt a strange sense of regret for Gavin and Nikki.

Shirley nodded and looked back to her victim. His head was gone.

"Acid is too slow," she said.

"It's good for a defensive barrier if they have to walk through it. But as an attack, it is indeed too slow," Ryker said.

"Unless you get their eyes, right?" Shirley asked, moving to the next soldier.

"Right."

"Let's try suffocation next," she said, then held up her hand in front of the man's head.

Ryker watched with interest, standing at Shirley's shoulder.

Twenty minutes later and they were done. The bodies absorbed by the dungeon, the souls filled into the massive bank of cores the Dark Lord of the North had provided.

"What are you doing for dinner tonight?" Shirley asked.

"I imagine the normal, I suppose. Why, thinking of making an appearance in town?" Ryker asked.

"Actually… no. Maybe we could have dinner together? Just us?" Shirley asked, facing him head on.

What…? I don't even… oh. Oh!

Huh.

"Sure. We could do that. Would you mind if it's in my farm house? All my cooking things are still there, and I can't do a damn thing without them," Ryker said with a shrug.

"You'll cook me dinner?" Shirley asked, her eyebrows rising.

"I mean, you asked me out to dinner; I'm saying yes, but I'd like to do the cooking if you don't mind. I'm not bad at it, thank you. I had to survive on my own for years," Ryker said.

"I… no, that's… that sounds great," Shirley said, giving him a small smile. It fit her demeanor. "Tonight then? Come get me when it's time to head up?"

"You got it," Ryker said.

Then Shirley's avatar winked out, leaving him alone in the tunnels.

That was rather brave of her. I never would have expected it, either.

"Ryker," Robyn said, pushing hard at his dungeon sense. "*I need you.*"

Ryker instantly canceled his avatar and went to Robyn, who now lived inside his own dungeon sense.

She wore him like a coat.

"*What's wrong? How can I help?*" Ryker asked.

"*Nothing is wrong. I just need you,*" said the once-paladin.

Sighing mentally, Ryker tried to pat the golden being inside of his own dungeon sense on the head.

It didn't quite turn out, but he managed something that seemed reassuring.

"*I see. I'm here. Can I help?*" Ryker said.

"*No. Yes! Yes. I need another core. Just like the one I'm in. Then I need you to split me in half so I'm in both,*" Robyn said. "*I'm tired of only being in one place at a time with my mind. I think with two, I can have two avatars and split my attention better.*"

"*Wynne, is that possible?*" Ryker sent to Wynne.

Except there was no response. She was busy.

"*It's possible, and it'd work,*" Marybelle said. "*I'm having a core brought up to you from below. And sorry, dear, I didn't mean to eavesdrop. The strength of her desire for you to come to her immediately was strong enough that it bled through to our own bond.*"

Ryker's paranoia immediately cooled. Marybelle seemed to understand him far better than even Wynne ever had.

Then again, Marybelle was in his head.

"*Done,*" Ryker said. "*I'll split you in half as soon as you're ready.*"

He felt a strange warm tingly sensation from Robyn at his words. It took Ryker several seconds to realize she was blushing.

Err… right.

***

Walking into the chapel Robyn had put up in the heart of Dungeon, Ryker felt strange.

It looked almost exactly like the temple she'd constructed in the dungeon. This one, though, had considerably more ornamentation and was clearly built to house the faithful in worship.

The one in the dungeon was a shadow of this, and was clearly primed to be fought inside of.

"You came!" Robyn said, standing just inside the doors. She was dressed in robes that went well with her skin and hair color but made her look like a sack.

"Yeah. I said I would," Ryker said, smiling at the paladin.

"Good, good," she said. "I'm so glad. Would you go sit in the chair I put next to the pulpit? It's for you."

"Yep," Ryker said, nodding. He headed over to the indicated chair, dropped into it, and started playing with spell patterns.

Shirley had inspired him to try and find his own style. He wouldn't be upset, though, if he found his style was indeed his father's.

His father had been a very accomplished wizard. Thrice considered to be an arch-mage, and he had declined every time. He hadn't wanted to become a target.

That and they'd have probably dug into his secrets. Secrets he didn't want anyone to know. Heh.

Experimenting, Ryker tried his hand at the same curves and swirls Shirley had done.

And immediately hated it. It flowed and swished around. Having tried it, he instantly knew for a fact that it wouldn't fit him. He could see the merits in the style, and he thought it'd do well for Shirley. Though he now had a few minor concerns about her ability to utilize his own methods of control with such a style.

Pulling his spell pattern apart, he started again. This time with squiggly lines, as his childlike self had once wanted to do.

"We'll be starting momentarily," Robyn said, breaking Ryker out of his spell-play as he started to test the squiggles.

"Oh, yes, sorry," Ryker said, focusing his concentration on the paladin standing next to him now.

"Thank you for coming," Robyn said, staring at him. "I'm grateful. Do not fear, Ryker. I will save you, as you saved me."

O… k. That's weird.

"Consider me yours to save," Ryker said, not really sure how to respond.

"I will. As I said, don't fear. I'll be with you," Robyn said, giving him another one of her beautiful smiles. Then she turned her head forward.

Looking out, Ryker was shocked.

The pews were full. Full, and looking like she was going to need to expand her chapel to accommodate more people.

I suppose that's to be expected. They've had no spirituality for a while now. There's no temples here after the church of light went crazy on them.

A sea of faces all turned to Robyn, curious, and looking like they needed direction. Direction from a spiritual source, and not at all from a material one such as a count, a queen, or a mayor.

"Thank you one and all for coming," Robyn said. "I'll not bore you with a sermon. I'll not speak of donations or contributions. Nor will I speak to you of fear and punishment.

"My goal isn't to scare you into obedience, frighten you into listening, or wrangle you into giving of yourself."

Turning her head as she spoke, Robyn did her best to make eye contact with a good portion of the people in the audience.

"I only wish to speak to you of the words of my deity. I know not their name, but it isn't needed. For their tenets are simple, and honest. They require no deeper understanding to believe, but an infinite amount of time to comprehend and commit to," Robyn said. "For this first meeting, I will give you their words and then bless you all in their name. You're welcome to remain after that, but it will be spent in quiet contemplation of their words, and seeking resolution."

Interesting take on it.

Pretty sure this is usually where they ask for money or other things, or tell them how they have to listen or suffer.

Ryker was listening, however. The purity of her words had him honestly considering them.

"You must approach the world with a patient heart, one that can weather the storms that come, and not debase yourself in your anger at the world.

"Give to those who are injured and suffering as you would to those whom you care for. You may not know them today, but that doesn't mean you'll not know them tomorrow.

"Treat them with warmth and kindness as they deserve it until the very moment they do not.

- 101 -

"And when they prove themselves unworthy of your attention, of your warmth and care, of your tenderness, you must give them a smile and then shut them out.

"You need not worry for them, for they will worry for themselves. It is not for you to save them, only to have given them the chance to receive and give back to you."

As she spoke, there was a slow building of energy in the chapel. A strange and heavy aura that seemed to be growing as if from the very words. That they were the truth of a heavenly portfolio, calling upon another's presence.

"For in your actions, you might plant a tiny seed in them. And in turn, they may eventually come to see the error of their actions and redeem themselves. Because ultimately, everyone can be redeemed and forgiven," Robyn said. "For the words of my deity are that they were once debased. They were once anger and fury. Hatred and evil. Rather than be destroyed, they were given the chance to be redeemed, and so it has been done.

"And that is all I have for you today."

Robyn closed her eyes, bowed her head, and made a strange motion with her hand toward the congregation.

In that act, that single hand gesture, Ryker felt the swelling energy rise and burst.

A golden and pure warmth fell over everything in the chapel, along with gentle sky-blue sparkles.

And in that glow, Ryker glimpsed the face of Robyn's deity.

Dazzling sapphire-blue eyes that looked as if they'd gone down a long road. Across a terrible landscape and back up out of it, for redemption.

As well as forgiveness.

It burned Ryker inside and out. Burned him, hurt him, and raked him over coals till it felt like his skin was a giant blister.

He hadn't forgiven anyone.

He felt regret for the deaths of Gavin and Nikki, but not entirely for the act of snuffing out their lives. In his heart of hearts, he regretted also that he hadn't felt joy in their deaths.

That he'd happily butcher Rob if given the opportunity.

Ryker had forgiven nothing, and this god was anathema to him.

As if sensing his pain, the deity drew away from him, but it didn't leave. It watched him. A willing and patient sentiment.

Waiting for him to come to it.

Chapter 19 - Firsts -

Shirley sat down at the table and smiled to the server. "Thank you very much."

"Of course, Lady Claire," said the server, bowing to Shirley.

"Please, just call me Lady Ryker, or Lady Dungeon," Shirley said with a bright smile. "Or Mrs. Ryker, if you like."

"Of course, Lady Ryker," said the server, bowing her head again. Ryker was all but forgotten.

And he liked it that way. The more frequently Shirley interacted with the public, the better off everyone was.

Especially since Shirley had decided they should have dinner in the common room of the inn itself.

"What can I get for you today, Lady Ryker?" asked the server.

"We'll both have whatever the special is for the day, same for our drinks," Shirley said.

As if remembering him, the server turned to Ryker, looking rather nervous all of a sudden. After nodding her head at Shirley, she scurried off.

Laughing softly to herself, Shirley looked to Ryker.

"They're all still terrified of you," she said.

Ryker shrugged, not knowing what to say.

"Not something I can really fix. They all suspect I'm the dungeon. Or so in league with it that it's not even a thought anymore," Ryker said.

"Well, we'll just have to work on that," Shirley said, adjusting herself in her chair. She looked around the room with a small smile.

To Ryker, it was strange. She was wearing just enough hair product and a touch of makeup, and she looked so much like Claire it was disturbing.

Except it wasn't Claire. Claire didn't smile and make eye contact with people she wasn't concerned with.

"You know, I owe this to you," Shirley said, her eyes drifting back to Ryker. "You've been telling everyone so often that I'm not the same person anymore, that I can more or less do as I please.

"A number of local women are just attributing it to me being happily married. They invited me to one of their odd little quilting parties."

"Heh, good. No sense in making you take up the mask and wear it. Easier to just have the mask become you, rather than you the mask."

"Yes, well, thank you. It's interesting to be her, without being her," Shirley said. "You're looking at me oddly. Almost as if—oh. Yes, that's not very fair, is it?"

Shirley looked down at herself, then to Ryker. With a wink, she held her hand off to one side, below the table and near the wall. A small blue ribbon that matched her clothes appeared. Reaching back with it, she tied her hair up behind her head.

In an instant, Claire vanished, and Shirley was there in front of him.

"Better?" she asked.

"Yes, actually. Thank you," Ryker said, smiling.

"Of course. It's only a minor thing, and I know it all makes you uncomfortable," Shirley said with a wave of her hand.

"It hasn't been that long, but you're honestly taking all this a lot better than I ever expected," Ryker said. "In fact, you seem happy."

Shirley gave him a strange smile that almost looked like a frown. Lifting her chin, she peered down at him, her smile only growing wider.

"Why... Mr. Ryker, are you actually curious about me? How I feel?" Shirley asked.

"Course I am," Ryker said, shaking his head with a chuckle. "I often ask how you're doing."

"Yes, but you actually mean it," Shirley said. Then she blew out a breath, laying her hands on the table. "I'm good. I'm... actually happy. I thought for sure I would end up as little better than a forced concubine and left to rot in a room.

"And… none of that happened. Not even a little bit. You just… leave me to my own devices and expect me to do what I said I would," Shirley said, smiling at him, her fingers interlaced on the wood. "And you've even been training me to become a mage on top of that. You're teaching me how to fight, defend myself, kill—and do it efficiently. It wasn't just empty words."

"I mean… yeah?" Ryker said, not really sure where she was going with all this. "I don't really understand."

Shirley's smile grew at that, watching him all the while.

"I know. And that's partly why I'm happy," Shirley said. Then she reached across the table and laid her hand on the back of his. "Yes, I'm happy. I'm doing quite well, thank you for asking."

The server came back at that moment and began laying out food and drinks.

Shirley didn't pull her hand back, but instead watched the server with that same smile from earlier.

"Will there be anything else for you, Lady Ryker?" she asked.

"No, my husband and I are quite well. Thank you for your assistance," Shirley said.

"Of course, Lady Ryker," said the server, and ran off almost just as quickly as last time.

"Hm. Be careful, Lady Ryker, or I'll think you're actually interested in me," Ryker said, turning his hand over and catching hers in it.

Narrowing her eyes, Shirley pointed at him with the carrot she'd picked up with her fingers.

"I'm not going to respond to that, just to antagonize you," Shirley said, then put the carrot to her lips and slid it into her mouth slowly with a smile for him. Then she flashed her teeth and bit down on it savagely.

"Feel free to visit me at night and test your luck, though," she said while chewing at him. Then she gave his hand a squeeze and took her hand back.

I wonder if this is how Lauren feels with how I act toward her.

Nodding, and biting his tongue with a grin, Ryker chuckled.

"For what it's worth, I think this current you is rather interesting and fun. I wonder where the mousy little girl I caught on the battlefield went," Ryker said. "You're somewhere between Adele and Lauren in personality."

"Oh? Good. They're both quite nice. I'd be happy to be like them.

"As to who I was… gone. Long gone, and good riddance. I'm Lady Claire Ryker now, a woman of decent power and position who's already able to kill all on her own. No one will take advantage of me in any way or shape again," Shirley said. "Now, eat your dinner, husband. I want to go hunting after this, and you promised me you'd go with me next time. Next time is tonight.

"I also want to bring Robyn along. She's a nice girl and I think she fancies you. It'll be fun to watch you have to deal with her. I do so enjoy making your life problematic in fun little ways."

"Uh huh. One day I'll get even with you, wife. Then we'll see what you think about all your little games," Ryker said.

"Oh, I'm sure I'll think they're exactly the same. Little diversions to make your life fun, and humorous to me," Shirley said, picking up a chunk of beef and simply biting into it.

She'd clearly figured out the normal etiquette for eating here in the inn, and she wasn't about to deviate away from it.

"Fine. As you like, I'll be happy to join you in an outing tonight. It'll be interesting to fight next to my apprentice. I'm curious to see what you've been playing with for patterns," Ryker said, and tucked into his food.

***

Ryker slumped into his bed and lay there unmoving. He'd spent the last two hours killing as many soldiers as possible with Shirley and Robyn at his side.

Shirley's aptitude was very good, and her talent was far above average. She was growing exponentially as a wizard.

She'd have done well in his family. Her abilities weren't quite at his own level, but she also had a far-more-normal mana pool than he did. If not even slightly bigger than normal.

Technically… she doesn't have my talent or ability, but her pool is much bigger. Much, much bigger. Realistically, father would have chosen her over me.

Great.

In the end, Robyn had almost been as tiring as casting that many spells, though. She doted on him, gave him way too much attention, and generally spoiled him while they were in the field.

Much to the delight of Shirley, who seemed to encourage it constantly. Even going so far as to make outright suggestions to Robyn that the paladin happily obliged.

Closing his eyes, Ryker groaned into his pillow.

"That bad?"

When he lifted his head, he looked over and found Wynne standing there. She was dressed in a thin black nightie that seemed just barely able to cover her. It looked like it was a single movement away from ripping free from her shoulder.

"I like her," Ryker said. "She's a very nice girl. Talented. It wasn't that being with her was bad. I'm just tired. My avatar has more mana than I'd ever think possible to dream of. But after that much casting, my brain is just done."

"If it makes you feel better, Shirley passed out on her floor," Wynne said, easing the covers back from the bed. "I had Arria get her taken care of."

"Thank you, my queen. You're ever my partner," Ryker said, turning his face back into the bed. "This would be impossible without you. I'm glad I didn't kill you and eat you when we met."

Wynne laughed at that. Ryker felt her hands on his back, her fingers gently pushing at him as if to roll him over.

"I honestly thought you might kill me that day. Didn't think you'd eat me though," Wynne murmured.

Ryker complied with her hands and rolled over onto his back, moving more towards the center of the bed.

"I've eaten Fairies before. My father threw me into a dungeon that was empty except for things like rabbits and Fairies. He wanted me to toughen up. To kill and eat what I could," Ryker said. "I think I was seven."

"Well, I'm not any ordinary Fairy," Wynne said, smiling down at him. She began to carefully slip the buttons back through their holes. "Then again, I'm not sure there's ever been a Fairy that was fully the size of a human woman. I'm taller than some of them, in fact."

"Yeah, you're kinda amazing," Ryker said, closing his eyes as Wynne worked. "Like I said, without you this wouldn't be possible."

"Thank you. I love you, too, Ryker," Wynne said, pulling the sides of his tunic open. Then her hands came to his shoulder, and she started to help him slide it off.

"I find it amusing that you swore up and down that Fairies didn't feel such things, and yet here you are," Ryker said, lifting his shoulders up as she pulled away the tunic. "You, Marybelle, Tris, and Charlotte. All apparently in love with me."

"Consider it a pleasant surprise on my part. Though I truly dislike the jealousy I feel when you're with anyone else. It's very vexing," Wynne said, starting to work at his belt. "Now, I wanted to also talk to you about our dungeon."

"Do we have to? I'd really rather talk about that nightie you're wearing," Ryker said.

"I'm glad you like it. I wore it specifically for you to view me in it. But yes, the dungeon. The enemy has only made it through the first two floors of the tower. They're making progress, though," Wynne said. "And I'm starting to get a bit nervous about it all. I think we've fundamentally forgotten what a dungeon is, and what it's supposed to do."

"What's that?" Ryker asked, shifting toward Wynne, giving her a better angle at his belt.

"To empower those who survive," Wynne said, pulling the tongue free of his belt and then pushing the buckle to one side. "Already those who have made it deeper are getting stronger. They're also not leaving the dungeon. They're coming in with enough supplies and simply remaining. That started after Robyn killed two groups that came back the other way."

"Mm, that's definitely a concern. I honestly did forget that, I suppose. I was treating it as something that couldn't be beaten if we did it right," Ryker said.

"No matter how hard we make it, there has to be a chance to win. And they're finding them," Wynne said. She began pulling his belt out of its loops, then went down to his feet and started in on his boots.

"Great. What do you suggest, my beautiful and attentive queen?" Ryker asked.

"Nothing. There isn't much more we can do. You already weaponized the tunnels and increased the number of people allowed in there. After that, we really can't do much. The Death Dungeon pushes the boundaries already," she said, pulling his boots and then socks off. "Slide over this way so I can get your pants."

"Yes, my queen," Ryker said, then did as she had requested. "Ok, well, can we do anything else? Can we make the dungeon spit them back out near the start point? Does it have to be an exit to where they want to go?"

"Unfortunately, yes. They have to reach the exit they intended from entering the dungeon. I think we're going to end up killing a good number of our foes, but empowering those who survive," Wynne said, pulling his pants down. Taking his boxers at the same time. "Oh. I didn't think that'd be like that."

Ryker knew she was talking about the fact that he was extremely aware of her nightie, and that he was giving her a full salute with his privates.

"Yeah, sorry, you look really good in that nightie," Ryker said. "Next time don't pull the boxers off."

"But how am I supposed to convince you to make love to me tonight without pulling them off?" Wynne asked, patting his thigh. "I want to try tonight. I'm nervous… and a little scared… but I want to try."

Lifting his head up, Ryker rested on his elbows and looked at the giant dungeon Fairy.

"Now… tell me what to do so I can make love to you, Ryker. My silly king. You've been patient with me so far, I ask for more patience of you. And that you pardon me if I seem utterly clueless and far too excited," Wynne said, giving him a strange grin. "I never thought I'd be Queen of the Fairies and Imps. Or have a human husband. And… well… have sex."

Definitely a month of firsts.

Ryker didn't feel as tired anymore.

***

When he woke up the next morning, Ryker didn't open his eyes. In fact, he didn't want to move. Wynne was naked, warm, and cuddled all over him. Her head wedged up under his chin.

They'd spent the better part of the night exploring what Wynne liked and didn't like when it came to sex.

He'd also been forced to test out stamina potions. Surprisingly, they'd worked exactly as intended.

And they could be used multiple times. For which he was infinitely grateful.

Before and after, they'd talked more about the dungeon. About what Wynne was afraid would ultimately happen.

Ryker had been forced to agree with her in the end. It was far more likely that they'd eventually start breaking out of the dungeon and reaching the other side.

In fact, it was more of a when than an if. She was absolutely right.

It meant he had to start planning for how to handle that, and what he could do about it.

It meant that with the dungeon, the best he could do was thin out their numbers. Just as he'd done previously, although he'd felt like a failure for doing only that.

How do I get around it this time, then? Shirley seems more than happy to go out and kill as many as she can every night. But that'll only work until they start responding immediately with overwhelming force.

I can have archers just dump on them for the entire time, but that's the same problem in the end. The enemy will just respond with overwhelming force.

Frowning, Ryker curled his arm around Wynne's bare shoulders and opened his eyes. Staring up at the interior of his room, he couldn't think of anything he could do that would prevent the enemy from getting through.

Which meant he had to have plans for that eventuality, rather than trying to prevent it.

Get the blades ready. Tell them that dog-tags can be turned in for points, and no questions will be asked. Church of light, dark, Trevail, or Adelonia tags will be exchangeable.

Then let slip that it's likely they'll start breaking through out of the dungeon and appearing on the other side. Alone.

Without food, water, or help.

The blades might be able to kill them all outright. If the enemy can't forage for food or water without overwhelming numbers, that's attrition in and of itself, is it not?

Ryker nodded slightly as he thought about it, feeling like that'd be a good first step.

Let's also… poison all the water sources nearby. Chase off all the game, and get rid of anything usable for fire.

It'll be rather awful to destroy our own lands, but… the alternative is to let them have an easy foothold. Just need to make sure our people know we're doing it.

"Don't forget, we can always summon up an army of avatars and have them block the entry. They'll get ground down eventually, and we obviously lose mana if they die or are injured before returning, but it should significantly thin their numbers," Marybelle said in his mind. "We could probably start that today if you wanted. We have a large number of Imps looking to prove themselves."

"Marybelle…" Ryker sent to her. "How often are you just… sitting there, reading my thoughts?"

"Honestly? Always. It's ok, though. I love you. Just think of me as your personal assistant in your mind. By the way… I really want to try that position you did with Wynne."

"Where you grabbed her hair and bent her backward till she was looking up at you?"

"Marybelle… we're going to talk about this. Deeply. And we're going to set rules. Do you understand?"

"Unfortunately."

Chapter 20 - Footstools and Love -

Rolling along the road towards them was the current shipment of resources for the church of light.

Food, water, alcohol, weapons, armor, shields—anything and everything they might need to continue their siege of Dungeon.

It'd been two weeks since Ryker had taken Shirley under his wing as an apprentice. She'd come further in that period than most pupils did in years. She was already at a level where anything he could teach her was already beneath her ability.

The basics and methods were entirely within her grasp. She'd technically graduated her apprenticeship, though she refused to call herself anything but his apprentice.

Now it was mostly distilling everything he knew into reasonable lessons and giving them to her. She soaked them up readily, made them her own, and then utilized them in her nightly attacks on the church.

"Much larger than the last one, isn't it?" Shirley said.

"It is. Though I do have to wonder why they haven't expected us to raid the supplies before. I mean... we've done it before," Ryker said. "Why wouldn't they expect us to do it again? It's not as if we wouldn't expect them to resupply."

"Arrogance, if I had to guess," Shirley said. "The vicar and Claire are both arrogant in their ways and seem to assume everyone is far beneath them in intelligence."

"Mm, fair enough. I certainly can't argue that after having met both," Ryker said. "How do you want to play this one out?"

"Uhm, who's doing what again?" Shirley asked.

She didn't have a head for tactics. Strategy and planning, certainly, but not the day-to-day stuff.

"Charlotte's going to hit the west, Tris the east, and Robyn is behind them," Ryker said. "They're mostly going to be keeping people moving toward us, rather than attacking. The goal is to kill or capture the guards and take their supplies. Not blow everything up."

"I don't know," Shirley said after a beat. "I was just going to use lightning and kill as many as I could."

Ryker chuckled at that and reached over to put an arm around Shirley's shoulders. He'd gotten brave with her, and he'd started making deliberate efforts to touch her.

Shirley didn't lash out at him, though, just stood there with his arm over her shoulders.

"I ever tell you that I think you're pretty interesting, Shirley? I like you, in fact. I should marry you," Ryker said. "Wait... I'm already married to you."

"You're an idiot," Shirley said. "Don't make me tell Charlotte that you've been sleeping with Tris lately. She's left you alone for a while because she thinks Tris isn't moving on you either."

"You wouldn't," Ryker said, pulling Shirley closer to his side.

"You're welcome to test me, husband," Shirley said, giving him a look and a quirked brow, a smirk on her lips.

That seemed to be her catch phrase lately. That he was welcome to test her. It was always said with an ominous tone as well.

"One of these days, I might just come tapping on your door, you know. It's not like I have any shame," Ryker said.

"You're welcome to test me, husband. Come and find out," Shirley said.

"Ugh, fine," Ryker said, but he didn't move his arm. Bending his elbow, he lightly patted her head. "You're a fun lady, Shirley. That brain of yours is incredible. Kinda wish Lauren had sent you instead of Claire—then you'd actually be my wife already."

Shirley made a soft humming noise but didn't respond to his statement.

"So, lightning?" she asked.

"Yeah. Lightning. Mind if I we try something new? I want to build a pattern with you. I've never done it, and it requires a good deal of understanding of the other person," Ryker said.

"I'd rather not. That's something married mages do, isn't it?" Shirley said. "I've always heard it ends up becoming a permanent thing."

"It does often, and yes, but that's just because of how easy it is with two. We don't have to if you don't want to," Ryker said.

"Oh, fine. You'll just be hurt about it for days if I say no," Shirley grumbled. "You're such a sensitive man inside that gruff exterior. I have no idea how any of your other women haven't figured this out."

"Really? Great. I'll build the core, the chain, and the build-up of energy. You work the exterior? The lightning, trigger, and loop?" Ryker asked.

"That'll be fine," Shirley said.

Lifting his left arm, Ryker held it out and began building the spell. It took a fraction of a second for him to do it.

Before he could admire his own work, Shirley had looked over his pattern and added hers to it.

Evaluating the result, Ryker found that they fit perfectly. They didn't look like it, one being a very formal and rigid—a literal square—while the other was all loops and swoops. But one perfectly encompassed the other, giving it a strong core and a fluid exterior.

Shirley activated the spell and sent it out toward the lead guard elements.

A massive bolt of lightning crashed out from her hand and obliterated the two guards in front, then careened into the horses and went up into the sky when it had no one left to jump to.

A bit… more power than intended, but… ok.

Building another spell pattern, this one a dense fog meant to sit atop the wagons, Ryker called it up in front of Shirley.

Who instantly finished it and dropped it on the wagons. It was a perfect cube that blotted everything out. No light shone from within, and nothing could be seen either.

"That was… almost too easy," Shirley muttered.

"Yeah, it was. Sure you don't want to be my wife? We could be a pretty nasty mage duo," Ryker said.

"Shut up, never marry you," Shirley said. "Give me some more patterns to work with. Just pull them up and I'll pick the spell. With your control you can hold like six or seven up, right?"

"Yeah, yeah," Ryker said, then began building out multiple patterns. Lightning, fire, acid, confusion, poison, and a fairly debilitating stun.

Shirley took a step closer to him, her shoulder wedged up into his armpit now. Her eyes rapidly jumped through all his constructs.

She added bits and pieces to each and every one, forming the spell into something much larger, but she didn't launch any of them.

"Two more, please," she said. "A wind spell and some raw force."

Holding up all the spells she'd already asked for, Ryker was actually feeling taxed. He did as she asked, though, and managed to draw up two more patterns, holding the eight of them aloft.

"You are far too strong, husband. I don't think I could do half of these," Shirley said, quickly building onto the two new ones. "Your control is amazing."

"Didn't you just tell me you weren't going to marry me?" Ryker said.

"Changed my mind. Let's go conquer the continent. You can be my servant and spell holder. I'll let you love me tenderly when I desire and be my footstool when I don't," Shirley said. Then she started modifying the spells again, and rearranging their placement. "Put them together in this order from now on. Ok?"

"A footstool? Fine, one second," Ryker said, struggling to memorize the placements while holding up the spells at the same time.

People starting coming forward out of the fog, all the while shouts were going up from all throughout it. They were all armed and looking at Ryker and Shirley.

"You'd be my footstool? I'm flattered," Shirley said, then tripped off the fire spell. Except it clearly wasn't fire anymore. She'd added earth to the thing, and a stream of molten lava came out like a bolt from a crossbow. It smashed into the two guards in the front and literally covered them completely. "I promise to treat you well."

"No, I said fine to memorizing the pattern. As to being your footstool, never. I'm already a footstool to Lauren and Diane. I don't need to be a third one for someone else," Ryker said, then pulled up the same spell Shirley had detonated with a duplicate.

She instantly reformed it while firing off the wind spell. Which she'd also added earth to. A hail of small slivers of stone tore through the three soldiers in front.

"What if I loved you better than them? Would you run away with me? Leave it all behind?" Shirley asked.

"Maybe. Once I secure the queen on her throne again… well, maybe. I kinda do love the others, you know, even if you're amazing," Ryker said, rebuilding the wind spell again.

Shirley's left arm came up around his middle and hung around his waist, her right arm held out in front of her. "Woo me later. Let's focus for now."

The soldiers were charging forward at them now.

Ryker added more power to the force construct, then started to launch it. But he was late. The second he powered it, Shirley had already activated it and spun it in a half-sphere around them faster than he could have.

Grabbing the lightning spell, she started to feed it into the shield.

When he realized what she was doing, Ryker chained the end of it to a looping pattern and finished it right as Shirley completed her task.

Lightning began arcing out around their shield in every direction. Hitting and lighting up soldiers like candles, turning them into screaming torches.

Without being asked, Ryker called up replacement spells, and Shirley continued to activate and add to them.

Five minutes later, no soldiers stood around them. They'd been killed to a man. Just in time too, as the lightning shield faltered and then faded.

A single man was running toward them now from the fog. He'd apparently been waiting for the shield to drop. His right hand was pulsing with a faint white light. In his left hand was a spear.

Shirley touched off all the combat spells Ryker had already rebuilt for her. They smashed into the man, alternating between fire, wind, lightning, acid, and pure force.

Then they deflected off him and went spinning off into the sky, only to detonate elsewhere.

"Mage-killer — use indirect stuff," Ryker said, pulling up the spells again.

"A what?" Shirley asked. Pulling on the earth spell, she caused a massive boulder to rip from the ground and go hurling at the man, rather than a spelled boulder conjured from mana.

Dodging to one side, the mage-killer hit the ground and tumbled away.

"He can deflect or block magic. They're called mage-killers for that reason," Ryker said. *Damnit. I don't want to build another avatar.*

A giant glowing ball of fire smashed down into the man from the sky, followed by an angry-looking Robyn, her golden wings extended.

She shone brightly and looked like a deathly angel of retribution.

Her weapon swung down and slashed at the man before he could take two steps away from her.

Robyn pulled her sword back, and the man collapsed to his knees. Holding her left hand up beside his head, Robyn waited a moment. As if to receive his last words.

The man said nothing, glared at Robyn instead.

Without a hint of emotion, she took his head from his shoulders with a lazy slash of her weapon.

"Wynne, how much mana does it cost for us to use those abilities?" Ryker asked.

"None," Marybelle sent back instead. *"Wynne's busy. The church is trying something different. Can explain it later. Robyn isn't pulling in mana. She's using faith. It's… being directed to her from a deity."*

Oh. I'm not sure if that's better or worse.

"Ok. You can woo me now," Shirley said, patting Ryker's stomach with her right hand. "You were just telling me you'd let me steal you away to be my personal footstool, despite loving your other women."

Rolling his eyes, Ryker let the spells fade away.

"Kinda missing that mousy little woman I found with a bolt in her chest," Ryker groused.

"No you're not," Shirley said, her fingers caressing his stomach. She hadn't moved away from him.

***

Sitting down in his throne, Ryker leaned his head back with a sigh. Shirley was next to him, holding his left hand in her right. He hadn't gone into his avatar like that, which meant she had taken his hand after he'd departed.

Things are getting weird between us. I think I need a break from her.

Not really wanting to be here when she came back to herself, Ryker closed his eyes and tossed himself into his dungeon sense.

Settling into it, he started to make a plan to go see Marybelle and ask about what was going on.

Robyn overwhelmed him before he could do anything, however. Overwhelmed him, and drowned him with her golden dungeon sense. The essence of what she was.

To the point that Ryker couldn't even think or react.

He was submerged into Robyn's own essence and inundated with a pure and savage amount of attention and affection. Robyn mauled him, stuffing his essence back into hers and then blending the two.

When he finally got a handle back on himself, the world wasn't the same. There was no clear point where Robyn started or he ended.

"Oh, that was heavenly," Robyn said triumphantly in his mind. It wasn't in the dungeon sense or the spot Marybelle inhabited. It was somewhere else entirely.

"Robyn, what'd you do?" Ryker asked, feeling panicked.

"We blended ourselves. You were very needy and took quite a bit from me. It was surprising. We're linked now, for a time.

"When you took me from my body, I had no idea what to do. You gave me a path back, and a way to right my wrongs. And I want to share myself with you forever going forward," Robyn said, her tone taking on a strange reverence. *"Don't fear, beloved Ryker. I'm... going to go lie down for a spell and just enjoy this. Sorry, I'll ask next time, but I really wanted to be in you and have you in me."*

He felt it when Robyn left him, the space strange and empty once she was gone.

Feeling extremely panicked and altogether unsure of what to do, Ryker grabbed Wynne and Marybelle both and threw them into his mind, joining them.

Wynne and Marybelle both looked shocked at the treatment, turning to each other and then him.

"Ryker... what are you doing?" Wynne asked. "This isn't... this is inside of you. You shouldn't bring anyone here. Ever."

"Robyn just did something and I need you two to look at it," Ryker said with a real sense of urgency.

"Huh?" Marybelle asked. "Oh. Yes. That. Looks like she's merged your soul with hers. It won't last, of course. Maybe a day or so."

"Don't be concerned about it. Her soul is rather buoyant and very... good. Yours isn't. It'll bring her down and lift you up. You might even feel pretty good when you go back to your body," Wynne added.

"You're acting like this is nothing," Ryker said, unsure now but no longer panicking.

"Because it is. It's... well, she basically just made your souls have sex. From the looks of it, yours is benefiting greatly," Wynne said, her gaze somewhere in the middle distance. "Hers is looking a little pale and worn out, though. Try not to let her do it too often. It's not going to help her much."

"But... it helps me?" Ryker asked, confused.

"Yes. She's feeding you parts of her soul, in a way. She took some of yours, you took some of hers," Marybelle said. "You're much more evil than she is. She'll be fine in a few days, but for a time she might feel a little sick."

Frowning, Ryker really had no idea what to make of this whole thing.

"I really don't understand," he said.

"Don't worry about it; nothing is wrong. Just don't let her do it too often, even if it does feel good," Wynne said. "Now, we should probably talk about the dungeon. There's been some changes."

Marybelle had already made herself at home in his mind. Immediately calling up furniture, a display table, and changing the temperature and time of day.

As if she knew everything inside out.

In fact, Wynne was now watching Marybelle as she began calling up snacks and drinks like it was the easiest thing in the world.

Even though they would do nothing here.

Ryker turned and started to watch as well.

Since their last talk, Marybelle hadn't intruded on his thoughts in any way, shape or form. But that apparently didn't mean she wasn't there. At least he assumed she was, based on how easily she was using his own memories and thoughts to craft what was essentially the interior of his own mind.

She had never left; she was just a silent witness to everything he did.

As if realizing she was being watched, Marybelle paused, looking at the two of them.

"Is something the matter?" she asked.

"No," Wynne said after a second, a small furrow in her brows. Then she looked back to Ryker. "The church is attempting to destroy the dungeon core. They keep going through the old dungeon wings now. Those who can't get into the Death Dungeon, that is. They're running the old dungeon."

"They can try all they like, since that's not a real core," Ryker said with a shrug. "Sounds like a good way for them to waste time."

"I'd normally agree with you, but they already figured out it's a fake. They clearly have some artifact or spell that's guiding them. Because they stop right under the spot where the core actually is, beneath your home. It's in the outskirts of the old city wing. Off to one side. They always go there and look around," Wynne said. "The most recent group started to look up, and they even tried digging for a time with an earth spell."

Great.

"To me that definitely sounds like they know where the core is and really want to get to it," Ryker said. "Do we need to do anything or alter our plans?"

"Not yet, but it's worth knowing and keeping an eye on. All it'd take is someone realizing the core is beneath your basement," Wynne said. "Then going and breaking into your farm. To everyone else it looks like a ruin, much like the rest of dungeon, teeming with fatal magic. But if a champion really wanted to see inside, they could probably manage it."

"Okay… can we put up some type of trapdoor, so the core would fall from the basement and land somewhere much further down in the dungeon if someone came?" Ryker asked.

"Easily," Marybelle said, then lifted a hand and flicked her fingers. "And done. It'll now fall quite a ways into a small pool of water. It's some four hundred feet below the lowest point of the dungeon, but it would still cover ninety percent of the total area that it is today."

Wynne looked far more annoyed now than she had previously. Her fingers were slowly curling into her palms.

"Great, thank you Marybelle," Ryker said, smiling at the Hob. "I suppose that settles that for now. Wynne, would you stick around for a minute? I wanted to run something by you."

Getting the hint, Marybelle walked over, gave him a tender kiss, and smiled at him.

"See you later, dear," she said, then winked out of existence.

Chapter 21 - Adaptations -

Ryker held up his hands toward Wynne.

"What's up?" he asked. "You looked like you were… not very happy. Not very happy and angry, actually."

Wynne shook her head, her lips pressed together in a thin line. Her brows were drawn low over her eyes.

After several seconds, Wynne's shoulders slumped, and then she nodded.

"I don't know what to do with… all this," she said, patting her hands to her chest.

"Your chest? Yes, it's rather massive. I'd be happy to explore it for you and tell you what to do with them," Ryker said.

Wynne's face screwed up for a second. Then she let out a breath and laughed softly.

Then she started to cry, walking over to Ryker and pressing herself to him, her face wedged into his shoulder.

"Oh come now, I was only teasing," Ryker said, holding her and patting her back gently.

"There's so much going on in my head," Wynne said, sobbing softly. "I want to… I want to hurt Marybelle because—because she knows so much about you. Because she knows what you want. Because she's close to you.

"But then I realize what I'm thinking, and I'm shocked at myself. I don't know what to do."

Ryker held on to Wynne, petting the back of her head and shoulders.

"Wynne. Charlotte, Tris, and Marybelle have all said similar things, but with much less… extremes," Ryker said cautiously. "They all had similar feelings at some point, in one way or another. But they're over it, as far as I can tell. Or at least to the point that it doesn't bother them anymore."

"Really?" Wynne asked, her face still pressed to him.

"Really. Now… it wasn't that I did or said anything for them. Just that I told them it was normal, and that their emotions weren't… wrong. Certainly not wrong to have, at least," Ryker said. "If we did a simple comparison of you versus them, the only real difference is you're not filtering everything through an avatar."

Wynne nodded, her fingers pulling at his clothes.

"You've said before that Fairies don't have jealousy, or things of that nature. I would argue that… Fairies also don't get as big as humans, or have sex," Ryker said. "And that maybe it's time you looked into making an avatar. Even if it's just a complete recreation of your own self, but in a normal sentient race."

"You think so?" Wynne asked, not moving an inch.

"I do. I'm not positive, but… it seems logical to me. Doesn't it?" Ryker asked.

"Yeah," Wynne said. "But… could we still… have sex while I'm in my normal body? I don't want to feel it through an avatar."

"We could do that, sure. Whatever you want. You don't have to use an avatar at all if you don't want to. I'm just suggesting what I think would help. I could easily be wrong," Ryker said.

"I don't think you are. I think you're right," Wynne said, calming down significantly. "Because it's all… right. Marybelle, Charlotte, Tris all told me the same thing. That they were feeling. That they were nervous about not feeling at home in their real bodies anymore. That's not normal. But they're all dealing with it. And much better than I am."

Ryker kissed the top of Wynne's head.

"Whatever you decide, I'll go with it and help as best as I'm able," Ryker said.

"I know. Thank you… dear," Wynne said, rubbing her face back and forth on his shirt. "I'm… going to go to work now. I'll be back later. I may be quiet for a time, however. I'm not ignoring you, just… processing."

"I understand. I'm going to go work on the Death Dungeon. I think I have a better idea than the tunnels," Ryker said.

"Ok, uhm, can... can you help me make an avatar tonight?" Wynne said, taking a step away and looking up at him through tear-stained eyelashes.

"Yeah... not a problem, Wynne. I can do that," Ryker said. "After all... you're my partner. My dungeon queen. The one who started this road with me, right?" Ryker said, reaching out and ruffling her hair with a grin.

Smiling while looking sulky, she grabbed his hand and then kissed the palm. "Love you. See you later."

Then she vanished.

And instantly was replaced with Marybelle.

"My word, I had no idea she was so jealous of us," Marybelle said, walking over to him and patting his shoulder. "You handled that very well, darling."

"Marybelle," Ryker started.

"I can't. I'm sorry. When you pulled me in the first time, I attached myself quite firmly. There is no going back from this," Marybelle said with a shrug of her shoulders. "I'll never intrude on your thoughts again without you calling to me. But I felt we should talk about this and get it in the open. Because it is what it is now. You pulled me in, bound me to you in a way I wasn't expecting, and I reciprocated. You can't replace me, and no one can share that space with me. It's like... it's how a dungeon core would normally interact with a Fairy."

Sighing, Ryker pressed a hand to his brow.

"Ok, but... you'll promise you won't intrude? You won't just read my thoughts and memories?" he asked.

"Well... I promise I won't intrude or read your thoughts. But your memories are fair game. How else am I supposed to help keep your mind clear?" Marybelle said. "Have you not noticed how clear and clean your thoughts are since you brought me in here? That you are literally thinking faster, and you're much more clearheaded?"

Frowning, Ryker stopped and thought hard on that. He really had been performing beyond what he normally did. Far and above.

"Ok... but... I pulled Wynne into a similar bond and space before. She never said anything about this," Ryker said.

"Because she's bound to the dungeon core. It's quite brain dead, so for her, it might as well be an empty room. I doubt she spends any time there," Marybelle said. "I suppose... I suppose it could be said I'm your personal Fairy. Oh! I'm a housewife for your mind. I take care of the little things, clean up bits of loose trash fluttering about, and generally keep things moving smoothly.

"You would not believe how often I have to balance the chemistry in your mind."

Raising his eyebrows at that, Ryker didn't know what to say. There really was no denying that he generally felt better as well.

"And before you start fretting over it—your mental changes, asking for forgiveness, and your general mood were all already on the mend before I set up home in your mind and soul," Marybelle said, waving a hand at him. She sat herself down lightly in a couch, then changed the color with a touch of her finger. "I'm not in control of anything you do, think or say. I can only make sure any distractions you might have are very limited."

"And if I wanted to lock you in my mind, imprison you, and torture you till your body died?" Ryker said.

"You could indeed do that," Marybelle said, looking up at him with a smile. "But you won't. You wouldn't even think it. As much as you hate the idea of me being your Fairy, you also love the idea of having someone always there for you. Always willing to listen, share in your darkest thoughts, and give you love for them. Because that's the simple reality here. I love you, Ryker. I promise to never intrude without you asking, nor read your thoughts.

"Now. You said you wanted to change the tunnel system. Shall we get to work? I'd personally really rather have some fun with my bonded, but I don't think you're really interested right now."

Stuffing all his thoughts and emotions about the matter down deep, he sighed, then dropped down on the couch next to her.

"You really won't?" Ryker asked, looking at her.

Smiling, she leaned over and kissed him tenderly, then patted his cheek.

"I really won't. Now, come on. Talk to me about the tunnel. Or are you actually feeling like fooling around?" Marybelle asked with a slowly raised eyebrow.

He grinned at her, then looked away. He didn't really want to right now, but he knew he would later.

"After. Uhm, for the tunnel—wait, you're not doing anything at all?" Ryker asked.

"No. I'm not. All I do is make sure your beautiful mind is running at its full capacity and capability. That's it. I may collect a stray memory here and there that I really like and store it away for myself, but that's it," Marybelle said.

Ryker shook his head, determined to move on.

"The tunnel. It isn't working at all. So much so that I'd rather be rid of it," Ryker said.

"Yes, it certainly isn't doing much other than becoming a checkpoint for the church to regather themselves," Marybelle agreed.

"Right? Ok, so, what if I just... replaced the whole thing. Completely. But what I want to replace it with is a one-on-one thing. I realized when I watched the trap hallway that the more they can band together, the better off they are," Ryker said.

"Hm. I can only draw from my personal experience, but everything you said does line up with my small viewpoint and what I can check it against," Marybelle said, her right hand coming to rest on his thigh and beginning to lightly stroke it. She never looked past a chance to touch him.

"Here's my thought. I want to just... get rid of the tunnel system entirely and replace it with one-on-one dueling requirements. Where if they want to proceed to the next section, they have to individually complete a number of duels," Ryker said, turning partially to face Marybelle. "If they want to move fast, then they have to take a much riskier duel. If they want to move slow, they can take on a larger number of duels. It becomes a choose-your-risk type of gamble, which means it should be perfectly valid.

"On top of that, I would personally think that I can have as many duels as it takes to reach the same amount of effort it would take for an individual to get to the end of the tunnels by themselves, today."

Marybelle looked thoughtful, her eyes losing focus as she dug into the idea. He was fairly confident she'd agree. Everything was set up as a choice, with a pre-set risk.

Those who took the slow and easy route would spend a lot of time moving forward. So much so that he figured they'd run out of stamina, time, or patience. It would catch up to them in the end. And if they wanted to move backward, they'd have to duel again.

Then there'd be those who would overestimate themselves and die to the challenge.

As far as Ryker figured, it was perfect. Far better than his tunnel idea, or so he thought.

"It'd work," Marybelle said, coming back to herself with a blink. "It'd also fit with all the rules, as far as I can determine. I'd normally check with Wynne, but... I think she wants to be left alone."

"Yeah, no, leave her be," Ryker muttered. "Alright, so, ten by ten-foot squares from one side to the other. Each one being a dueling tile where people have to pick the difficulty. Every duel being to the death, of course."

"Not a problem," Marybelle said, and then a viewing table appeared before them. It had a two-dimensional view of a space in front of them on it.

Marybelle had finished the request instantly. There was a checkerboard pattern that extended significantly into the distance.

She started to fill in each row with patterns, the far left being the least difficult and the far right "nearly lethal" as far as Ryker counted it.

Then as if she weren't blowing through things that would take Ryker quite a while to do, she carved off massive sections of each path and fiddled with the number of squares in each.

Till it looked something like a sliding scale of squares, where the far left had many while the far right had only ten.

"There. I think that fits everything you just described, darling," Marybelle said. "I already added signs to the front as well that explain the whole thing."

"Oh... that's... really well done," Ryker said. He'd wanted to try building it himself, but he wasn't about to complain about Marybelle saving him a massive amount of time.

"Thank you," she said. "Sorry, I'm motivated to get this done quickly. I really do want to see if I can't talk you into coming and seeing me in my home after this. Your little Hob woman would like some attention."

Ryker snorted at that, but he wasn't against the idea. "Yeah, I'm down for that. Alright, put that big ol' mess in place, and let's move the tunnel out."

"Already done," Marybelle said. "I simply pushed half of the people in the tunnel to the start of the dueling squares, and half past it. That way it's fair to both sides."

"Huh. Good show then," Ryker said. "You really are a bit... willing... right now, aren't you?"

"You have no idea, darling," Marybelle said patting his leg. "Come quickly."

She vanished with a soft puff-like noise.

Leaving Ryker alone in his bond space.

I feel like... I'm spending more time navigating emotions than anything else at this point.

Is that good or bad, I wonder.

***

Ryker appeared at the exit point, same as he always did.

Benni was on him in an instant.

"Evening, my lord king. Lauren left instructions for you to simply join her as soon as you arrived," said the Imp. "I have an avatar prepared for you specifically for the current time and location."

"Oh?" Ryker asked, smiling at Benni. "Good work. Alright. Point the way."

Rather than pointing it out, Benni grabbed hold of his sense and hurled him into a pattern.

Suddenly finding himself in a duplicate avatar of his real body, Ryker took two steps forward and looked around.

It looked like an antechamber.

Or a closet.

Interesting. I wonder if that could work out. Have a bunch of closets with avatars in them, and just hop from avatar to avatar.

Moving forward, Ryker opened the door and peeked inside.

Lauren, Diane, and Adele were seated at a table, eating what looked like a very late dinner.

"Hello," Ryker said, not wanting to move any further without them knowing he was there. He still felt bad for eavesdropping the first time he'd come.

"Ryker?" Lauren asked, smiling at him.

Adele bounced out of her seat, Diane a single second behind the first. Both women came over to him and gave him a hug.

"It's good to see you, husband," Diane said, hooking her arm into his and leading him to the table.

"Good timing," Adele added. "Having a bit of a strategy meeting and I'm at a damn loss. Maybe you can add something."

"Strategy meeting?" Ryker asked, looking at Lauren.

"Yes. The war isn't going as poorly as it was in our last meeting," Lauren said. Then her cheeks flushed a faint red, apparently going to the same memory Ryker had of their last meeting. Lauren had been very curious about many things.

Many, many things.

"But it isn't going much fucking better," Adele said. Then she grabbed her chair and slammed it down next to where Diane was sitting. There was now a third chair between their seats. "The damn church of dark keeps pulling back when we need them, and won't even commit to a fight anymore."

"It's like they won't get involved unless Lauren makes concessions every time."

"I can't imagine that going well long term either," Ryker said as Diane guided him to sit in the chair that was next to her own.

"Quite right," Diane said, patting Ryker on the shoulder and then taking her seat with the delicate grace she always seemed to have.

Looking over, he found Adele scratching just under her breasts with one hand. She frowned when she noticed him watching and put her hand down, looking nervous.

"My boobs sweat," she said. "And this bra makes me itch like crazy."

"Oh, ok," Ryker said, then turned to Lauren. "Can I do anything?"

Lauren smiled and shook her head. "I'm afraid not. It's… really just a question of how long we can rely on the church to be neutral before they just attack us."

"It's more or less what I've feared from the very start," Diane said. "Mother frittered away the stability of the entire nation, all for an ambition that would never come to pass because of what she did to get it."

"Uh… I'm sorry, but this feels a lot like you're saying that… the end is nigh?" Ryker said, feeling an odd sense of defeat in the room.

"I suppose… I suppose that's what we're saying," Lauren agreed, then sighed, patting the table in front of her. "That's what we were talking about just before you walked in. It's more or less over. It's a question of how we maneuver out of this, protect our people, perhaps save our army, and keep up the fight."

Now that he thought about it, the fact that Lauren had been leading from the capital was bad. It meant that her army wasn't leaving the city, or at best was within a day's ride of the capital.

"Maybe it's time to retreat to Dungeon?" Ryker asked, looking around. "It'd be a fairly defensible location to fight out of."

Diane smiled and reached over to pat Ryker's hand.

"That was both Adele's and my suggestion. Lauren is resistant to give up her capital, though— not that I blame her. It'd be hard to fight her way back," Diane said.

"Better than dead," Ryker said, putting a bit more heat in his words than he wanted. "Do I need to throw you over my shoulder and abduct you, Lauren?"

Looking nonplussed at the question, Lauren drummed her fingers against the table.

"You wouldn't—"

"I would," Ryker said, interrupting her. "Because I'd rather you be mad at me for saving your life and sacrificing your capital city than having to bury your pretty ass."

Lauren sighed, leaning back in her chair.

"Fine. We'll… start making plans to get out, if things continue to go poorly," Lauren said, shaking her head. "I can't believe I'm going to lose my family's throne."

"And you'll live, so you can fight to get it back," Ryker countered.

Making a soft humming noise, Lauren chuckled darkly.

"Maybe it doesn't matter anyways. You may not have heard it yet, Ryker," Lauren said. "But apparently the Dark Lord of the North landed an army on the continent. They spread out around Norman's Point and rapidly deployed. There's a massive military encampment there now."

"I… I see," Ryker said. That was dark news indeed.

Chapter 22 - Running Ahead -

Ryker was inhabiting an avatar he never thought he'd be.

A bird.

He was literally flying over the black tents of the Dark Lord of the North's army. Guiding himself into a slow circle, Ryker glided around again for another pass.

It wasn't as if it mattered, though. He'd already passed back and forth several times. The sea of black tents seemed to have no end and stretched from one side of the plain to the other.

Everywhere he looked, he could see soldiers moving about. In black leather armor, black plate mail, or black chain mail. Black and red everywhere.

On top of that, even Ryker could see the strict discipline being enforced. Nothing was out of place, every soldier seemed to have a duty or job, and everyone was moving.

Ryker couldn't even question the efficiency or cohesion. Even though he could see every possible race under the sun, there was a unity in their efforts.

I'd thought for a minute that perhaps we didn't have to worry about them. I was wrong.

Terribly wrong. Whatever deal I made previously, no matter how nice she seemed, this is indeed an invasion.

Moving out past the tents again, Ryker slowly hovered over what was clearly no-man's land in between the camp and enemy soldiers.

The mainland factions weren't waiting for action to be taken by the Dark Lord. They were already working to attack and push back the enemy. A collective force of thousands upon thousands were already banded together, more arriving by the day. They were digging in, building defenses, and generally working to hem in the opposing force before they'd even moved.

For all of that, the forces of the Dark Lord seemed uninterested. Unconcerned.

Whatever the enemy put up, it apparently wasn't going to sway them in the least from their current task.

Which means they either have a way around it, or it won't take them any effort to go through it.

Ryker mentally sighed and realized there was nothing more he could do for or about this. He'd confirmed everything Lauren had said and found there wasn't a darn thing he could do.

"*I've taken the liberty of relaying the information to Benni,*" Marybelle said in his mind. He'd asked her to come with him on the trip. She was flying nearby in an avatar very similar to his own.

Birds were often used by his people in one way or another to scout out enemy forces. Even Benni did the same thing for Lauren and her troops.

"*Thanks. It's… this is all a mess. Everything. How are we supposed to fight a civil war, a religious war, and fight off the Dark Lord at the same time?*" Ryker sent over to Marybelle.

"*I don't think we're supposed to be able to, dear. Maybe this is the end. At least for some things,*" Marybelle sent back. "*Maybe it's time we just… hunkered down in the dungeon. Or… ran away.*"

"*We could always just… ditch the dungeon and run away together. You, me, Wynne, Charlotte, Tris, Shirley, Adele, Diane, and Lauren. Find a quiet place and live on our own.*"

"*I actually wouldn't be opposed to that. At all. In fact, I'd love to run a farm,*" Ryker said, laughing. "*Become a farmer. Get a real stupid simple name like Steve or something. Just grow things and not worry about the world. But I don't think Lauren would ever go in for that.*"

"*She wouldn't,*" Marybelle said with a sad sigh. "*Shall we cut the avatars and head home?*"

"*Yeah, I'm done here. You are, too?*"

"*Yes. I'm afraid I've had my fill of bad tidings.*"

Ryker cut the avatar free and found himself lying in his bed. Standing next to him was Charlotte. She had one hand in his hair, the other on his stomach.

"Welcome back," she said, then smiled at him.

"Hello," Ryker said, grinning up at her. "What, is it your turn? Pretty sure I saw you last night. And a lot of you. Then again, it'd be nice to see more of you all over again. You wanna be bent over again, or on your back this time?"

Charlotte grinned at him and shook her head at the same time.

"If I didn't know you actually loved me, I'd probably hurt you," Charlotte said. Then she leaned over and kissed him warmly.

Taking the opportunity, Ryker fondled her openly, then yanked her into the bed and rolled her onto her back.

"Ryker, stop it," Charlotte said, laughing, but she didn't resist at all. Even when he started working at the buttons on her blouse. "Ryker... really... I'm flattered, but I came to talk to you about the defenses for Dungeon, the city."

Nodding his head but not stopping at all in his quest to undress her, Ryker smiled.

"Ok, and? You can talk all you want about it. I'm just going to unwrap this lovely present that was hand delivered to my bed," Ryker said, finishing with the buttons. After pushing the tunic off her shoulders and pulling her arms out, he flicked the tunic to one side.

Charlotte smiled up at him and then lay still under him, resting her arms above her head.

"Fine, I could use the stress relief. Undress me while I talk. Fair warning, though—I'm going to take charge this time and get what I want out of you," Charlotte said.

"Warning received. I could use some direction. Feel free," Ryker said, smiling at her.

"Dungeon is at risk," she said. "We need to start talking about how to protect it in case of an actual invasion. The enemy got their first troops out this morning. Ten of them.

"The blades were able to kill half, but then the enemy changed tactics. The exit of the dungeon is becoming fortified."

Ryker had unbuckled Charlotte's belt and dropped it to one side by this point. Frowning, he thought on what she'd said. His hands didn't stop, but they were only slowly working at unbuttoning her pants now.

"More are making it out. They're all rather strong," Charlotte said. "The blades will be able to pick some off and prevent them from leaving their camp, but that's about it. Thankfully all the precautions we took to limit their ability to forage and find water are done."

Nodding, Ryker chewed at his lower lip. At the same time, he shifted gears and went down to Charlotte's feet to start pulling off her boots.

"In other words, they're doing exactly what we expected. A little bit quicker, but more or less where we thought they'd be," Ryker summarized, pulling Charlotte's second boot off.

"More or less. The problem is they sent out their first foraging team. That team found the main road to Dungeon and immediately tracked it back. They discovered almost instantly that from this side, Dungeon appears almost normal," Charlotte said, watching Ryker with a small smile. It was clear to him that she was actually looking forward to him getting her undressed, even if the subject they were discussing was unpleasant.

"Ah. I see. And you think it's going to go sideways pretty quick," Ryker said, starting to pull Charlotte's pants down.

"Mmhmm. We'll need to do something about it, but I'm not really sure. Alright, enough of all that," Charlotte said as Ryker got her pants off. "Time for you to do what I tell you. Come over here."

Ryker immediately, and happily, obeyed.

***

"They're pushing harder," Marybelle said, looking out at the enemy forces arrayed against them. Unfortunately, it seemed the rate at which they were losing soldiers hadn't stopped them in the least.

Nor had the fact that their own people were killing one another in the dueling squares.

It was chaos, death, and madness. And yet the church and its ally still pushed on. There was no stopping them, it seemed.

News of the Dark Lord wasn't helping either, Ryker assumed. It seemed like the vicar wanted to get behind the walls of Dungeon all the faster, if only to put them between himself and the Dark Lord of the North.

"Yeah, it definitely feels that way, doesn't it?" Ryker muttered. Standing beside him were Robyn and Marybelle, the three of them viewing the battlefield in a shared bond space.

Robyn had joined them when Ryker hadn't locked the space against others. She'd also forced their souls together again the moment they'd started to separate in different directions.

Ryker got the impression Robyn wasn't going to let them separate again. And if she did, she'd rectify it as soon as possible, regardless of what it did to her.

"To be fair, they have the numerical advantage," Robyn said. "They will pass through us eventually. It isn't a question of if, but when."

"So I've come to realize," Ryker muttered. "At least we'll remove as many as possible. Give Lauren a chance."

Shaking his head, he realized that was almost a pointless endeavor. Even if he did limit the numbers of soldiers going through, from what he'd heard from Lauren, it might not matter at all.

"All we can do is persevere and try," Robyn said with a firm nod of her head. "We'll do the best we can and all that is possible for Queen Lauren. Beyond that, we must concern ourselves with our city and our dungeon."

"Too true. Even if not for Lauren, this isn't a chance we can let past us," Marybelle said. "All of these souls and deaths are only empowering us further and further. The sheer number of cores we hold of people's memories and skills is staggering. I've tasked a number of Imps to sort and clear those with no useful abilities."

"Yeah, I mean, it sounds awful, but we do need to keep room, don't we?" Ryker said.

"Oh, that reminds me of something I need to take care of in person. I'll return later," Marybelle said, then faded away out of existence.

"Who are you kidding, you're still there," Ryker said to her.

"Oh, I am. I'm always with you, dear. But Robyn doesn't know that," Marybelle sent back. *"And it's only polite. Don't think of me unless you need me. Otherwise I won't be listening."*

"Yes, dear," Ryker sent back in a patronizing tone.

"...njoy my sermon?" Robyn asked.

"Hm? Oh, yes, I did. Though... I must confess, your deity was a bit much for me," Ryker said, being honest with the paladin. She was too close to him right now on a couple different levels for him to risk lying.

"Yes, they mentioned that you were... especially... difficult to them," Robyn said, leaning in closer to Ryker. She constantly invaded his space now. To the point that it was somewhat frustrating.

The big knightly woman wasn't unfortunate looking, and she'd only grown in attractiveness since her rebirth. Many of her small flaws had been vanishing as she constantly recreated her own avatar.

It only added to his problem of dealing with her, however. She was more or less forcing their souls to have sex while she practically stood on his feet and eye-fucked him.

Ryker would have to be blind, dumb, and deaf to not know what Robyn wanted. Except he wasn't going to do that. Not under any circumstance. He wasn't about to risk Adele, Diane, and Lauren.

Then again, isn't there a strangeness building with Shirley, too?

Robyn put her hands on his shoulders, her grip rather relaxed given how often she underestimated her strength with him.

"Don't worry. Our souls will never part, and you'll be accepted, as we're one," Robyn said in that strange devoted tone she used with him. It was creepy, in a way. "I look forward to escaping my core and splitting my soul back into a human host. My deity has already sworn it to be possible, and that I'd even live for all time as long as part of me dwells in your cores and dungeon."

"I told them I wasn't ready yet, though. That I wouldn't be ready until I knew we were one, and you were healed."

"Ah... Robyn... about that," Ryker said, deciding to risk it and bring it up.

"I'm aware we cannot couple until I speak with your wives," Robyn said, then leaned in and kissed him before he could respond. It was warm, tender, and cautious, but it was also not what he was expecting. Pulling back from him, she smiled down at him. "Fear not. I'll get their approval. I'm tempted to consider violating the spirit of their wish, though, as this place is not a physical realm. And it would—"

Robyn's head snapped up, and her eyes seemed to stare into nothing.

"Ryker!" Wynne said in his mind. "There's a group of soldiers who defeated the dungeon and are moving to attack the Dungeon city gate guards!"

Damn it, I should have listened to Charlotte's warning rather than bed her.

Robyn vanished outright.

Casting his dungeon sense out to Dungeon, Ryker looked down from on high to see what was going on.

A group of twenty or so soldiers were charging toward the gate of Dungeon. It was obvious they had murder in mind. Their swords were out, spells being prepped, and archers looking for targets.

Robyn appeared at the edge of the city of Dungeon. Glowing white wings appeared from her back and began to spread themselves out behind her. Her simple armor rapidly became the glowing steel she'd had on last time he'd seen the wings. A burning silver sword with yellow flames licking off it appeared in her hand, and her helmet vanished.

Several soldiers ran up to her and attempted to engage her.

Their weapons struck something solid in the air. As if they'd hit a wall.

Robyn began to speak to the soldiers. Ryker was too far away to hear her and zipped in closer.

"…is subject to the protection I can give it. This includes all its rightful pilgrims on the road to or from here," Robyn said. "This is your one and only warning. You shall now get thee hence from where you came, or I will end you.

"Choose your course of action, and I'll provide you with the result."

"We already killed her once, let's do it again," said one of the men who had attacked her. "We can use all our strength to do it this time, too. Doesn't even have to be a group."

As if agreeing with him, everyone else focused on Robyn and attacked.

She lifted a hand and batted several spells out of the air with it, striking them directly.

Using her sword, she deflected the swords of two men and skewered the third.

Her left wing snapped out in front of her, and a number of arrows slammed into the feathers. As she shook out the wing, the arrows dropped to the ground. None had passed through at all.

Stepping forward, Robyn whipped her sword around, cleaving the head off a man who got too close to her. Pausing for a moment, she knocked away a rather large fireball and sent it straight into the air, where it detonated harmlessly.

Crafting an avatar, Ryker appeared off to Robyn's left side. In the same instant, Shirley dropped into the spot directly in front of him.

She pressed in close to him, then lifted her right hand up while wrapping her left arm around his waist.

Recognizing what she wanted, Ryker crafted all the patterns she had asked for last time and arrayed them out in her requested spaces. At the same time, he wrapped his right arm around her shoulders and his left arm became his focus.

Shirley touched off several spells even as she modified them, and missile-borne spells began streaking out from her.

Not waiting, Ryker replenished her stock and then built a shield spell that would envelope them with a basic force shield, setting it off to one side in front of Shirley

Adding to that shield, Shirley activated it with a glance and went back on the offense.

Robyn was engaging everything that came close enough to her. Shirley and Ryker worked on the archers and casters who were further away.

Now every time a spell came for Robyn, Shirley deflected it or punched the rune out of it.

Several of those passes happened before Shirley just started punching the runes out of them outright without trying to deflect them anymore.

Smirking to himself, Ryker felt immense pride in his apprentice. She was already above and beyond some "masters" who had never learned combat applications of their magic.

In the space of half a minute, the battle ended. Robyn stood triumphant amongst the corpses of everyone who had stepped up to her. The enemy back line was just as devastated by Shirley and Ryker's work.

Shirley let her arm fall, and then Ryker did a second behind her, dismissing all the spell forms he'd already brought up for her.

It didn't even take him any effort to do it. Everything felt entirely natural. Almost too natural.

Taking in a sharp breath, Robyn let it out just as quickly.

"In her name, I dedicate this field in her honor," Robyn said, her wings lifting above her head and spreading out behind her.

Her silver sword burst in a clear white light and then faded, Robyn returning to a far more normal appearance.

Standing beside her, right at the gates of Dungeon, was a statue. It bore three people in miniature upon the plinth.

Robyn, Ryker, and Shirley. Ryker and Shirley were in an embrace, much as they stood even now, and Robyn had been placed a scant half inch to Ryker's right.

"Hm," Shirley murmured, her arm tightening around Ryker's middle. "Suppose I can't be your apprentice anymore, if I'm your mage-wife."

"You haven't been my apprentice for a while, Shirley," Ryker said, patting her gently with his arm around her. "You're far too good at being a wizard to be an apprentice."

Robyn turned and came over to them, giving them both a wide smile.

"We have joined battle together and defeated a vastly superior foe," she said. "We should fight as a unit going forward."

Shirley sighed, then shrugged with the shoulder that wasn't wedged in Ryker's side.

"Why not? My husband and I will join you as we're able," Shirley said.

"What, I don't get a say in this?" Ryker asked with a smirk.

"Of course not; you're my loving footstool. I make our decisions. And speaking of, I want a foot rub tonight," Shirley said, turning to look at him up.

"I'm just supposed to agree?" Ryker asked, grinning now.

"Yes, it's part of your husbandly duties. So shut up and put out," Shirley said, the hand on his back petting him in a very loving and different way from how she was speaking to him.

Such a strange change in her.

"Yes, dinner and foot rubs," Robyn said, looking at Ryker. "I'll provide dinner, you shall rub our feet. It is decided."

"See? It's decided," Shirley said, then turned to Robyn. "Your wings are lovely, by the way. Can you summon them at will?"

"Why yes! I can, would you like—"

Ryker tuned them out and closed his eyes.

Then shrugged and gave up.

Things could be worse than having to rub the feet of two pretty women.

Chapter 23 - Testing -

Ryker laid a hand on Meino's head as she studiously groomed his shoulder.

"Meino, what would you do if I said I wanted to run away from it all?" Ryker said.

Making a deep humming noise, Meino paused, her tongue trailing up from his shoulder.

"Follow you, of course," she said, and immediately resumed her grooming.

"That's it? You'd just pick up and go? You wouldn't have to, you realize. You could go live your own life," Ryker said.

"No, I'd follow you. I love you in my own way," Meino said, her lips nibbling at his shoulder. Apparently having found something she couldn't get loose with her tongue.

"So if I said… I wanted to become a farmer again, hook up a harness and plow to you, and let you be my work-Minotaur, you'd say thanks where do I sign?" Ryker asked.

Meino bobbed her head, not pausing as she worked up toward his neck. "Yes. As I said, I love you. I would follow. The others would too. Are we done here in Dungeon?"

Ryker tugged gently on one of Meino's horns, making her head shift to one side.

"Maybe," he said as she moved her head back in toward his neck. She ignored it when he played with her horns. "It sounds like Lauren is going to lose, and we're not exactly winning here either."

"No, we're not," Meino said, licking at his throat. "More are getting through every day. I've killed some of them with an avatar. It helps me test myself."

"Ugh, every time you do my throat, it tickles," Ryker said, turning his head to one side and grimacing.

"I can do your privates again if you like," Meino said, her tongue working its way higher.

The unspoken end of that statement was "or you can be quiet and let me do this."

"Err… maybe next time," Ryker said. Fighting Meino when she decided it was time for grooming didn't work anymore. It just made her angry, and she ended up taking longer to groom him the next time. She also deliberately paid more attention to his nether regions.

He'd been trained to not resist her anymore.

Meino paused, lifting her head up to peer into his face, her pale blue eyes nervous.

"If I died, would you bring me back to life?" she asked.

"Of course I would," Ryker said, then grabbed hold of her horns and pulled her head to one side. "What kind of stupid question is that?"

"Ow," Meino said, not resisting him in the least. "Ow, ow."

Ryker pulled at her until he'd wrestled her to the ground, her head twisted to one side.

"Seriously, that's annoying. What kind of stupid question is that, Meino?" Ryker asked, sitting down on her chest.

"I'm just a guard," she said, her hands resting on his hips. "There's a severe mana shortage right now, isn't there? I cost a lot of mana to keep going. I'm expensive."

"And you're my personal guard. The only one I have. Of course you'll come back. Stupid," Ryker said. "Just for that stupid question, our grooming session is done for today. You can think on how dumb that was and how important you actually are to me."

"I am?" Meino asked.

"Yes, dumb-ass. Do you think I just spend so much time with you for no reason? I have lots of things I could be doing instead of sitting, chatting, and letting you groom me," Ryker said, tweaking her head in the other direction. "Use that brain of yours. I know you have one. You're damn smart when you wanna be."

"Ow… stop it," Meino said, but she didn't fight him off.

"No, say you're important and I will," Ryker said, slowly bending her head further.

"Ow! Ok, I'm important, you'd bring me back," Meino said. "Stop!"

Ryker let go of her horns and made harrumph noise.

"Good," Ryker said. Reaching down, he patted her cheek. "You really are cute like a puppy sometimes. I'm going to—"

"*Dear, the church is rushing the dungeon!*" Marybelle said.

"*The church is overloading the dungeon! What should we do, my love?*" Wynne asked.

Freezing, Ryker frowned. He and Meino were locked away in a private room no one could access. It was so people would stop trying to peek at him being groomed.

Casting his mind into the dungeon sense, Ryker immediately flew over to the entrance of the dungeon.

Robyn was battling a mass of soldiers. They were all crowding her, trying to beat her down in her spirit-of-vengeance form. Most of her retainers were down already.

Ryker immediately constructed his wizard avatar in the far corner. They'd have to go through him to get out.

Popping into existence, he threw out his hand and a wall appeared between Robyn and her enemies. Cutting her off from their attacks.

Robyn pumped her wings, darting away from the mad scrum she'd been in and arriving at his side. Her wounds were rapidly closing as she stood there.

"Ah, my savior," Robyn said, her tone heavy with feeling. "I didn't think you'd let me fall like that without showing up."

With a soft pop, Shirley appeared out of the air in front of him. She immediately snuggled in close to him, her arm wrapping around his waist. She lifted her other hand up and looked to the wall.

Ryker constructed all the spells he knew Shirley would ask for and put them in their order.

"You're a good footstool, and you took care of my feet so kindly, but you're a better partner," Shirley said.

"Yes, he is," Robyn said, her wings flexing behind her back.

The wall cracked and then shattered.

Robyn didn't move forward. She stood to Ryker's right, holding her half of the hallway. Shirley moved in closer to Ryker, her head resting against his shoulder. Then she began firing off spells almost as fast as Ryker could put them back up.

Charlotte and Tris appeared, followed by Marybelle and then, most surprisingly, Wynne.

They formed a small band and took the space between Robyn and Ryker.

Holding tight to Shirley, Ryker ignored everything but what his partner was doing. Time ticked by.

Slowly, it became a crushing ache on his mind as they battled.

"Ryker, I—" Shirley started to say. She hadn't said a word since they'd started.

He saw what Shirley needed before she asked. There was a knot of enemies who were preparing to rush them from an angle.

He modified a shield spell into a physical wedge and dropped it down in front of her as she spoke.

Shirley added an element he didn't catch and launched it into the enemy mass. Unfortunately, Ryker could see Tris was going to be overwhelmed shortly out of the corner of his eye. He could also feel that Shirley needed a mental break as much as he did now.

They were making progress, but the enemy was still sending in more people.

Ryker reached the ceiling above them and built a massive wall spell.

Shirley quickly modified it and dropped it down.

With a crash, a massive load of rocks simply materialized next to the ceiling and smashed down.

Having noticed where Ryker's attention was a moment before, Shirley snapped off a lightning spell and flung it toward the Fairies.

It curved out and away from their side of the fight after hitting the soldiers, and it began cycling from person to person. Freeing Tris from being drowned in swords and shields.

"Thanks," Ryker muttered. He couldn't even begin to describe how easy it really was to have two wizards working in concert.

Shirley nodded her head against his shoulder.

"I hate this," she said, her pattern quickly closing around one of his and touching off a cone of fire from her hand. It torched the last few people who were standing on their side of the rubble. They'd bought themselves a break. "It's too easy. Too simple. And I can't be bothered to work magic without wanting you there anymore."

Now that he thought about it, he'd had similar experiences. It was annoying now when Shirley wasn't around and he used magic.

There was another part of it, though. One that he didn't share aloud with her and wasn't sure if he should.

For him, there was actual pleasure involved when they were like this, casting with one another. To Ryker, it felt like a scalp massage.

On top of that, it also normally felt like foreplay. The exciting build-up before a roll in bed that made his stomach tighten and his skin prickle.

It was unnerving when he'd gotten a hard-on after the first few spells.

"If it makes you feel better, I feel the same way," Ryker said, letting his raised hand drop to his side. "I get mad when you're not there and I have to build the whole spell."

"Do you get a weird… building… pressure in your stomach?" Shirley asked. "It's… it's right above my privates."

Ok. That's not something I expected her to say. Then again, if she has no sexual experience, she probably doesn't know what that is.

Ryker cleared his throat and hoped some enemies would show up.

"Do you?" Shirley asked. "It's not unpleasant, it's just a touch distracting after a while."

"It's uh… yes, I get the same feeling. It's similar to how I feel when I engage in foreplay," Ryker said directly.

"Oh," Shirley said. Then she groaned, her arm dropping to her side. "You were supposed to be awful. Be my jailer, make my life wretched. I was going to kill you and escape, be a free woman."

"Why do I have to find myself thinking of you late at night? That we're engaging in magical foreplay. That I get mad at you when you're fucking your Fairies," Shirley said, the strength of her displeasure at the end of her sentence causing a half-formed spell in front of her to detonate and go spinning away.

"Sorry," she muttered. "You were supposed to be awful, not amazing."

"You're pretty amazing yourself," Ryker said. "You frustrate me. Constantly. You annoy me and make me mad and I want to pull your hair out sometimes.

"But you're funny, and witty, and you make me laugh. You're… you're great. And I kinda care for you."

"This is so the worst time for this," Shirley said. "We're literally standing next to three men I cooked the faces off of."

"You started it," Ryker said, chuckling.

"Shut up, footstool," Shirley said.

Laughing at their conversation and the entire situation, Ryker felt like everything was wrong. And all he could do was laugh about it.

"Maybe I should come knock on your door tonight, Shirley," Ryker said, his arm tightening around her shoulders.

"You're welcome to try, husband. Come and find out," Shirley said, her tone sounding the same as ever.

"I'll rub your feet, before or after," Ryker said.

"My back, too," Shirley muttered. "If I let you in."

"I can do that," Ryker said. He didn't mind.

Grumbling under her breath, Shirley waited.

"They've given up," Wynne said, walking over to stand beside him.

Slowly, the rest of his comrades in arms came over as well.

"They sent in over a hundred of them," Marybelle said, shaking her head. "I was spent. I don't think I could have held up much more than that."

"Nor I," Tris said, leaning heavily to one side. "My avatar is on the verge of death."

Now that he looked, he realized Charlotte was missing outright.

- 125 -

"She died in that last wave," Tris said, having noticed his look and slowly collapsed to her knees. "She took a sword-master down."

"This a problem," Robyn said, her wings settling over her back. "If they push as strong, or more, we'll lose the temple. I'll spawn in to simply be slaughtered."

"Yes, they're not playing by the rules," Wynne said. "And we don't have enough mana to push back in equal numbers for a sustained period."

"In other words, we're being pushed to the brink," Ryker said.

"That would be... accurate, dear," Marybelle said with a sigh. "I'm going to go see where I can make some efficiencies. I'm sure I can find some things to clean up or clear."

"Yes, I'll do the same," Wynne said, sounding equally as forlorn as Marybelle. "I'll work on the old wings, you do the new stuff?"

"Yes, that's fine," Marybelle said. Then both Fairies vanished.

"I'm going to go challenge people to duels. Each kill will give us mana," Tris said, nodding her head. Then she vanished as well.

It left him alone with Shirley, who was cuddled up to his front, and Robyn, who looked annoyed and joyful at the same time.

"Do not fear, beloved," Robyn said. "Regardless of the situation, we shall survive and persevere in Dungeon. My goddess protects it, as it's the birthplace of her religion. I must go, as I fear the enemy will return soon."

Robyn winked out of existence, returning her avatar to the greater mana pool.

"I guess that means we'll probably end up doing this a few times," Shirley said. "Defending the tunnel from a mass invasion like that. You know that won't stop them. The simple fact that we had to block the pass will only encourage them. Especially if that shit-fit of a sister of mine has anything to do with it."

Ryker took in a slow breath, then let it out.

Once again, he was coming to the same end he'd experienced with the church of dark. There were simply too many people trying to get through him, and he didn't have enough resources to stop them.

If their goal was to eliminate Dungeon, that'd be different. It'd be easy.

There'd almost be no question of how he'd handle it.

But trying to keep multiple armies out wasn't going to be doable.

I need to put in something that will limit their ability to move a mass amount of people through.

A non-lethal narrow rope-bridge that just loops around almost endlessly and can only support one person. Follow the rules, no issue at all.

I could shut down the entire old dungeon for a bit to do it.

Switch out the traps in the tunnel for gas and explosives. Traps that are more likely to wipe out multiple people, rather than individuals.

Ryker felt like those changes would be likely to help limit the ability of the army to move through the dungeon. He might not be able to prevent them from overloading the dungeon, but if he limited their ability to rush through, he could make it that much harder for them.

Robyn could easily appear, kill several, and fight over and over as mana becomes available. Chipping away at them as they try to push through as quickly as possible.

In fact, we could put those stupid one-way one-person rope bridges between every area. Use some type of portal magic between floors in the tower.

Limit and slow over and over and over.

"Ryker," Shirley said, her voice snapping through his attention like a lightning bolt.

"Yeah?" he asked, looking down at her. She was leaning against him now, her arm still around his waist but her hand now in his pocket.

"You care about me," Shirley said.

"Yup," Ryker agreed.

"We haven't known each other long enough for that," Shirley said, her tone strange.

"Not really, no. We haven't," Ryker agreed.

"Is it a shared enemy? A shared and forced perspective? That you trusted me implicitly, and I you?" Shirley asked.

"I really don't know. Up until this year I didn't even consider the possibility of having a normal relationship, let alone being married," Ryker said, being completely honest. "I was just a crazy little farmer with dreams of revenge and wanting to murder people."

"Mm," Shirley said, lifting her head up and then thumping the back of it against Ryker's chest. She repeated this several more times. "I'm going to come knock on your door tonight."

"You're welcome to try, wife. Come and—"

"I'm going to come knock on your door," Shirley said again, thumping the back of her head to his chest again. "And you're going to open it, invite me in, feed me, rub my feet, rub my back, and we're going to formally consummate our marriage. You're going to put out, and like it. Do you understand me, husband?"

What about Lauren, Adele, and Diane? I can't. It wouldn't work.

"I guarantee your other wives will not fight this," Shirley said. "I would bet they expected it when they named me wife."

Ryker thought on that. He didn't want to hurt his wives. But he also really didn't know how to handle Shirley.

Mentally sighing, he resolved himself to the fact that he'd fucked up. He'd let Shirley get close when he shouldn't have. Now he'd have to throw himself to his wives in an apology.

He did honestly believe they had expected him to make a move on Shirley, though. They were very bright women, after all.

"I understand," Ryker said with a small smile as Shirley squirmed in his arms. It was obvious she was uncomfortable, but forcing herself. She was extremely honest when she decided on something.

It was one reason he treasured her personality, and when it came right down to it, why he was willing to see out a relationship with her.

When he really thought about it, all the women in his life were critically honest with him. There was no side-stepping from any of them.

"I'm going to go now," Shirley said. "I find that I suddenly want to freshen up and... maybe find something nice to wear for tonight."

"And that means you should do so as well. Shave, too. Maybe a haircut if you can get time for it."

"I understand," Ryker said, grinning now. Shirley tended to get a bit bossy with him.

"Ok... uhm... I'll see you tonight... then," Shirley mumbled, then faded to nothing.

Out of curiosity, he followed her back to where her body was. More often than not, she sat in the throne room in her chair.

He found her sitting in her room, standing in the middle of it, screaming into her hands. Eventually she stopped, took a deep breath, and started screaming into her hands again.

Alright. I'm just going to assume that's her... blowing off steam... maybe?

Shirley then started to spin in place, stamping her feet as she screamed.

"*She's... excited and frightened by what she said to you,*" Marybelle offered. "*Or at least, that's my interpretation of this. I'm fairly confident, though.*"

"*And I do agree with her. I imagine Lauren and the others expected this outcome.*"

Shirley collapsed into her bed, staring up at the ceiling. Rather than get caught peeping on her, as she could indeed check the dungeon sense and find him right there, Ryker fled back to his own body.

"*Won't deny I'm rather surprised at it all. I didn't think she actually cared. I thought she was just being obnoxious and flirty at the same time,*" Ryker sent back to Marybelle.

"*Yes, well, she apparently does indeed care. Oh, goodness. I don't think anyone expected that. I'm... ah... I'm going to go work... on the dungeon. Good luck,*" Marybelle said.

Good luck?

Ryker stopped just outside of his own body. He wanted to think, make some plans, and move a few things around in the dungeon. At least before he returned to his body.

This small area where Meino forced her grooming sessions on him was private, off limits to everyone. Even the dungeon sense couldn't penetrate here.

The only person who could see anything here was Marybelle due to her bond with him.

And he was incredibly grateful in this moment.

Meino was still laid out underneath him. But she'd resumed grooming him, and the only available spot to her was what had been in front of her.

Except at some point it had transitioned from grooming to something else entirely.

Awkwardly, Ryker ignored what Meino was doing to him and focused on the dungeon. With any luck she'd stop at some point, and he could jump back and pretend nothing had happened.

Hopefully.

Chapter 24 - Cut Loose -

Ryker watched as the enemy milled about outside the boundaries of the dungeon.

They'd retreated after their initial push had failed the previous day. They hadn't returned yet, but it was obvious they would eventually. If they weren't going to attack, they had no reason to be here.

Sighing, he watched as they continued to gather into rigid grid formations. They were ordering themselves according to something he couldn't deduce.

"It won't work. Putting in all those single-file passages would overload the dungeon," Marybelle said in his mind. *"It's just too much. If it weren't a fatal flaw, it'd be fine."*

"If it's not a fatal flaw it's —"

"Pointless, I know," Marybelle responded before he could. *"I agree with you. It would be pointless, but in the same breath, we can't do what you wanted. I'm sorry, dear. I wish I could give you a better answer."*

"It's alright. You did all that you could and gave me the best possible alternative," Ryker sent her way.

"I'm glad you recognize that. Because I'm going to need some attention today at some point. And if I don't get it today, I want double tomorrow."

"I'm feeling needy and lonely. You've visited Charlotte and Tris more than me, and I'm a little jealous," Marybelle said.

"Got it. I'll sneak over at some point and make sure you know you're loved," Ryker sent back to her.

"I might want to try something different, as well," Marybelle said, her voice becoming coy.

"How different are we talking? I'm up for some adventure. Tris has certainly pushed my boundaries at times, but I'm not looking for changes."

"I think… I think I want you to have sex with me in my real body," Marybelle said finally. *"And I'm not sure if I want to be in it, or just watch… watch you do it."*

That's… different. Must be something going on again in that head of hers about not being herself.

Let's just play it cool for now.

"Oh, alright. That's fine. Anyways. Anything else for me? I'm just watching them assemble out there. Looks like a massive formation. I get the impression they're just going to rush us and push straight through," Ryker said.

"It does… seem that way, I'm afraid. Best we can do is fill the hallway Robyn's temple is next to with avatars and just grind them to a pulp. Then have other avatar checkpoints that do the same thing," Marybelle offered. *"All the while, constantly unloading into their numbers from the dungeon and the monsters. I've already shut down everything that cost mana in the old dungeon. It's just accumulating now."*

"Yeah, that's… that's going to be it, I guess. This really sucks. Dungeons aren't meant to be a defensive line. We take territory, we grind them down, and we take lives. We don't keep things out – we want them in," Ryker complained.

He got the impression Marybelle agreed with him.

Sighing, he looked back out at the army.

There was a distinct possibility this was the fault of the Dark Lord of the North. His troop landing at Norman's Point seemed to be stirring everyone to action.

"I think when it comes down to it," Ryker started. *"I think we're going to have to just… bring out every single Fairy and Imp, and commit to a last stand. Just beyond Robyn's temple. Assemble the true vanguard."*

"Honestly, that does seem to be about right," Marybelle sent back to him. *"As you said. We're not supposed to stop an army dead. We're supposed to slowly grind it, chew it up, and kill it over a long period of time. What we're doing is… just not the expectation."*

"Yeah. Anyways. I guess that's all we can do. I'm going to move on then," Ryker said.

"As you like, dear. Oh, how'd it go with Meino? Looked like she was pretty into it. I mean it was all the way in her thr —"

"Don't talk about that ever again," Ryker sent back to her quickly. *"It didn't happen. Figment of your overactive imagination."*

"As you like, dear, though I'm ever so curious. I'm always very eager to please you, but even I can't help but gag on it," Marybelle offered sweetly.

"Marybelle?"

"Yes, dear?"

"Not going to visit you if you continue."

"Oh, that's a pity. But I'd understand. Well, you could always go see Meino. I'm sure she would be happy to try again?"

Ryker didn't respond to that. He didn't want to, and he wasn't going to. Instead he backed away from the army and went back into his own body.

Sitting up in his throne, he looked around. Meino was in the corner, looking subdued and troubled.

She hadn't stopped in the administration of her forced blow-job until he'd finally gotten back into his body and put an end to it.

Immediately.

Now she was just acting like a child who'd been caught being naughty around him.

Sitting next to him in her throne, and holding tight to his hand, was Shirley.

True to her word, she'd shown up the night previous. Taken a foot rub, a back rub, a bath, and then him. In that order.

It'd been strange to share a bed with a woman who looked so much like Claire yet demonstrated a clear and vibrant desire to be with him.

"Going to stare at me the whole time?" Shirley asked.

"Maybe. Was thinking of picking you up and carrying you off to the bedroom while you were 'out' as it were," Ryker said, grinning. "Would you mind terribly?"

"Not really," Shirley said, opening her eyes and turning her head toward him. "So long as you're willing to part with your privates afterward when I feed them to some pigs."

"Ah, oh well. Was worth a shot," Ryker said, grinning at her.

"You do realize I'll be calling on you again tonight," Shirley said archly. "I expect you to perform your husbandly duties. Just wait till then."

She sounded confident. Looked it. Reeked of it.

But he knew better.

He'd seen the young woman who had been screaming into her hands just after saying something similar. She was soft hearted, but she wanted to be in charge at the same time.

"As you like, wife. I'll make myself available at your disposal," Ryker said. Then he leaned forward and kissed her before she could pull away.

Shirley leaned closer to him, coming partway out of her chair.

When he broke the kiss, he patted her cheek with a smile.

"Love you," he said.

Looking much like a small rodent caught in a trap, Shirley's eyes were wide, her cheeks flushed, and her lips parted.

After a few seconds, she shook her head and pouted.

"Not fair. Not fair at all," she hissed. "You can't be loving when I'm trying to be imperious. You're supposed to agree, then let me collapse into you later and give me control."

"Hush, you like it. And you can be as imperious as you like. I enjoy it to a degree," Ryker said, then sighed. "I'm going to go visit Lauren and give her an update. She needs to know to expect this army. We're not going to be able to hold them back either."

"To be fair, no one ever actually expected you to," Shirley said. "Those armies were already running rampant all over the area long before you got the dungeon involved. Being completely honest, you already gave Lauren more of a chance than she probably deserved."

Frowning, Ryker wanted to argue that. All of it.

Except he couldn't. She wasn't wrong, really. It was all pretty much exactly as she'd stated it.

"Trust me, Ryker," Shirley said, not pulling away from him. "We've been ruthlessly honest with each other, haven't we? Listen to me. As your actual wife, as someone who cares for you and thinks you should run away with her to live alone away from everyone else, you've done more for Lauren than she deserves and accomplished more than could ever be asked. If she hasn't told you that by this point, she's a fool.

"Oh, and do tell her I'm only a little sorry for seducing her husband. A little. I didn't want to hurt her, but… well… things happened."

Nodding once at her own comment, Shirley frowned and looked away.

"And if she can't forgive you or doesn't know what you're worth, she's a fool. A fool who doesn't deserve you. Run away with me—be my loving footstool. You'll never want for anything," Shirley said, raising her eyes back up to his own.

Chuckling at the single-mindedness behind Shirley's words, he opened his mouth to respond. And stopped.

He realized in that instant, she wasn't kidding. She was actually asking him to run away with her.

Sighing, he pressed his forehead to hers.

"If everything else fails, yeah. We'll run away together," Ryker muttered. "I might take a few others with me, though. Would you be okay with that?"

"Uhm… maybe. I don't mind Marybelle, or Wynne. Charlotte seems ok… Tris doesn't talk to me much," Shirley said, looking annoyed. "Go see Lauren. You're making me flustered."

"Yes, dear," Ryker said in a meek voice, then sat back in his throne and cast himself out towards Lauren.

"Can I chat with you, Shirley?" asked Meino as Ryker fled away from the scene.

Sometime later, Ryker appeared inside his normal wizard avatar, Benni having apparently shunted him into it as soon as he arrived.

He even appeared inside a small room where Diane, Adele, and Lauren were having lunch.

I swear I always seem to land either when they're eating, having a meeting, or going to sleep.

All three women were watching him even before he looked around.

"Oh, there he is," Adele said, getting up out of her chair. "Benni was right. She's always so on target."

Walking over to him, Adele snatched him up in a bear hug, practically hanging off him.

"I missed you," she whispered in his ear, her arms tightening around him even more.

"I… I missed you too, Adele," Ryker said, hugging her back. It was a very strange greeting for her. Then again, she'd been getting slowly more and more emotionally honest with him.

That or things are much worse up here than I thought.

Then Diane was there, hugging him before Adele had even moved away. She latched on to him with a tenacity equal to Adele's.

"I missed you as well, husband," Diane said, burying her face in his neck. Adele was still glued to his other side.

Looking over to Lauren, Ryker raised his eyebrows.

Slowly, Lauren shook her head, giving him a sad and forlorn smile. Then she leaned forward, put her elbow on the table, and rested her chin in her hand. The sad smile on her face didn't leave, but it was obvious to him she wanted to join Diane and Adele.

"Alright, alright. Yes, hello, I missed you both as well. And I love you both as well," Ryker said. "Though I must confess to you all at the same time, Shirley made a move on me, and I didn't say no. I slept with her."

Diane nodded her head against him.

"We know. We figured you would as soon as we saw she looked like Claire. We couldn't decide if it would be healthy or worse for you having her so close," Diane said. "But we already expected it."

"Oh. Got it. That… that's incredibly intelligent, I guess," Ryker said. "Shirley said she felt bad for seducing me, but it just happened."

"I wouldn't feel bad if I were her. And it's not that that intelligent on our part, not really, we just know you," Adele said, then thumped him with her fist. "Still annoys me, though. Why can't you be here instead? Asshole."

Ryker began to deliberately walk forward. He dragged Diane and Adele with him. He wasn't going to make Lauren wait longer than he had to, and if he had to force her into a four-way hug, then so be it.

Before he made it to Lauren, Adele and Diane separated from him and started to leave.

"No, stay," Lauren said. "We're... all in this together. You two threw your lot in with me and you deserve to be here when I talk about it."

Not waiting for her, Ryker reached down, picked Lauren up, and bodily hugged her against himself.

"Lauren, I missed you," Ryker said into her ear just as Adele had done for him. It had brightened his heart, and he knew it would do the same for the queen.

Groaning against the force of his hug, Lauren hugged him back.

"Oooof, Ryker, you hug me too hard," Lauren said when he finally relaxed his grip on her. She lifted one hand and stroked the back of his neck, her other hand locked around his shoulder. "And I missed you, too."

"If you think that's too rough, wait till I get a chance to finally pull your clothes off," Ryker said.

Laughing, Lauren shook her head and looked up at him.

"I've lost the war," she said. "My army is in shambles, my generals are requesting to surrender, and I have nothing to hurl back my enemies with.

"I've had your people secure my treasury, my heirlooms, and anything I can't stand to see looted or destroyed. Everything has been locked deep away below ground."

Ryker nodded. That was a sensible thing to do. It also signified that Lauren would return for all of it at some point.

"All that's left is holding out and waiting," Lauren said, her voice catching. "There's still the possibility of winning this thing. All we need is one good victory at this point."

Lauren took in a shuddering breath, smiling up at him. Ryker immediately saw the tears welling up in the corners of her eyes.

She might be saying they had a chance, but she genuinely believed it was all over.

Laying a hand to the back of her head, Ryker guided her face into his neck and then started patting her back.

"It's alright," he said. "We'll get you three back to Dungeon, and we'll start up a new campaign and win back your crown and throne. It isn't a question of if, just when."

Lauren made a humming noise at that. After a short time, it was followed by a sniffle. Then several more.

Till it finally turned into low-toned and muted sobbing.

Holding her, Ryker continued to gently pat her back. Stroking her shoulders and neck tenderly.

The unending sobbing continued unabated, even when Ryker sat down in a chair and pulled the queen up into his lap.

Diane and Adele made polite conversation, which Ryker dutifully ignored. He was comforting his queen while she still was one, for perhaps the last time. She deserved all his attention.

Thirty minutes after it began, it came to a shoulder-shuddering end. She continued to shake and let out soft whimpers on occasion.

"I'm going to lose my family's throne," Lauren said as she looked up at him, her cheek resting against his chest.

"Well, first off, you're really ugly when you cry. Crying is a no-no for your complexion. Your whole face, actually," Ryker said, smiling at her. "It's a damn good thing I'm in love with you. You as a person, not what you are."

Lauren stared up at him with wide eyes. Then she laughed nervously.

"You're awful," she said. "You're... truly awful."

"I am," Ryker said, nodding. "And I truly do love you. For who you are — not what you are, what you were, or what you might become."

Lauren let out a shuddering breath and closed her eyes.

"I suppose, then... that's pretty good for you and who you are," Lauren said, her left hand patting him on the chest. "And I love you, too. As awful as you are."

Ryker grinned and nodded.

"Well, my awful Count Ryker, the one man who stood beside me and ran to my aid as everything came crashing down, what brings you here tonight?" Lauren asked.

"Oh. Not much actually, I just came to see you," Ryker lied. "Fighting the church of light, killing lots and lots of their soldiers, nothing out of the ordinary."

"Uh huh," Lauren said, peering at him. Of everyone he'd encountered, Lauren had the most natural ability to see right through him. "I don't believe you."

"I felt guilty for sleeping with Shirley," Ryker said, shrugging. It was the actual truth. It just wasn't the reason he'd come. "It happened last night."

"Mm, that feels far more likely. I appreciate your guilt, and thank you for rushing to tell us," Lauren said. "I think I agree with Adele, though… it's still annoying. I mean… if I'm not going to be Queen much longer, it could have been fun to be, ahem, deflowered in the royal bed?"

Having already given Lauren a solid round in the bond space, Ryker had no doubt in his mind that she'd be up for the task in reality.

A sudden and heavy weight slammed down on Ryker's senses. It was as if a massive wall flattened him, his guts being squeezed out through his mouth.

Crumpling in the chair and lashing out with his dungeon sense, his body, and his magic, he struggled in vain to find a hold against whatever was happening to him.

Slowly, Ryker came back to himself. He was still sitting in the chair, but Lauren was looking at him with a worried expression. Clearly something had happened to him and she'd seen it.

"Ryker? Are you well? What was that?" she asked.

Ryker shook his head. He had no idea. Except when he moved his head, he had a strange mirrored-image type of sensation.

He tried to move his head again, only to find it moved two seconds later than he wanted.

"I don't know," Ryker said.

Or tried to say.

"Duuuuhnoooo," Ryker slurred, feeling awful from top to bottom.

Slowly, it felt like the disconnect between his brain and his body started to fade away. Things were speeding up and his thoughts were becoming clearer, his body's response much quicker.

"Ryker?" Lauren asked, sitting up in his lap.

"M'okay," Ryker said. Feeling considerably more human. "Dunno 'at 'appen."

Exiting his avatar and into his dungeon sense, Ryker immediately saw the problem. And felt his soul shriek at him when comprehension dawned.

The way back to Dungeon was gone. The path back to his body was severed. There was nothing for his soul to fly back to.

Between him and where his body was, something had fallen. Something massive, powerful, and unable to be moved. It was as if the hand of an angry god had smashed down and literally severed Ryker's soul from its body.

And now he was attached to the avatar through a thin, wispy bit of his soul. He could see it was binding more closely by the second, but it was a slow process.

It explained why his body wasn't responding.

"I 'ink I died," Ryker mumbled. "'Y body died."

"Your body… died?" Lauren asked.

A beautiful, full-bodied, and perfectly put-together Orc woman with long black hair, short tusks, and big eyes walked in the room.

"Queen Lauren, the castle itself is under attack by church of the dark troops. They're already in the garden, and preventing an escape.

"We've been betrayed. We have to go immediately," said the Orc. "And we… my lord king? What… what's going on. You're here. Actually here. Not just in an avatar."

"'Es," Ryker said, nodding at the Orc.

I think that's Benni.

"Soul 'ut free, stu' here," Ryker said.

The Orc's eyes widened.

"We need to flee, now. The castle is falling, and you're here. If you die, you're dead. Your soul can barely hold to your avatar as is," the Orc said, shaking her head. Turning in place, she lifted her hand and whistled sharply in a signal Ryker didn't know. "We're leaving. Now."

The fall of Dale had apparently begun.

Chapter 25 - Watcher -

The Orc Ryker assumed was Benni grabbed him up, and threw him over her shoulder. Her hand slapped to his ass and held him against her.

"Damn," Benni grumbled, then shook her head. "I think… I think everyone just died."

Turning her head, the Orc looked at Lauren. "All of my people are dead. We need to hide. The only place in your castle not on a map and not known to anyone else is the spawning vault."

"But that's in the throne room," Lauren said.

"Yes," Benni said. "It is. I'll shut it. You all must hide there for a time, and then get out. My people are hiding in their cores. They can't return to their bodies.

"I'll… do the same when the end comes."

"Benni, you're going to need to cut your avatar or kill yourself," Lauren said, following Benni as she walked off. "You know… you know what they'll do."

"I do. And I will, have no fear of that," Benni said and then chuckled, slapping Ryker on the ass. "I'm determined to have my first time with this one. I can't let someone else have it."

Adele, Lauren, and Diane were behind Benni now, everyone walking along rapidly toward what Ryker assumed was the throne room.

Ryker was taken into a large, empty, open room. It had massive vaulted ceilings, stained-glass windows, and it was impressive. That was the only word that fit Ryker's mind when he looked around.

"It looks much bigger when it isn't full," Lauren said, apparently having noticed Ryker's look.

"I didn't even get to show him the garden," Adele said.

"That would have been nice," Diane said, her dress held in both hands as she followed along. Lauren was in a similar situation, the fabric clutched tightly to her sides.

"Here," Benni said, and bodily shoved Ryker onto Adele's shoulder. There was a creaking pop, followed by a grinding noise. "Alright, everyone in. Use the peephole, look for an opportunity, escape. Get my king home."

"Is that all you care about?" Adele asked, one of her hands on Ryker's rear end.

"Honestly, yes. He is. He ordered me to protect all of you, and I'd die for you. But he's still my king," Benni said.

Adele moved forward and Ryker lifted his head up.

He could see Benni standing in the arch of a darkened doorway. She had one hand on the wall, and the other held a hand axe. She pulled her waist pack off and tossed it into the room. It slid to a stop somewhere behind Ryker.

"Take my core home. Give me another chance," Benni said. Then her arm flexed, and the heavy stone door began closing. By the time it closed, Adele had dropped Ryker into a darkened corner.

There was a thump as the heavy stone frame settled into place. Locking them in.

Sitting there, Ryker had no idea what to do with himself. From what he could tell, he'd lost contact with his body. His soul had been cut free, and it had lodged itself in the avatar rather than float away and become… whatever it was souls did.

He could still faintly feel his contracts with Wynne, Marybelle, Charlotte, and Tris. What remained of Robyn's last soul joining was all he felt of her, however. And the dungeon was beyond him. It might as well not even exist.

But the fact that Wynne still lived told him the problem wasn't the dungeon, or anything in Dungeon.

Diane was not far from him, pressed up into a curious stone box. It had a space for her to stand up, but seemed like it was meant to keep light from going inside the box.

In fact, now that he looked around, he saw light coming from a back area, and where he was right now was almost entirely darkened.

"Benni's just standing there," Diane whispered softly.

Adele and Lauren were standing not far away, holding hands.

"To be fair, not sure what she can do till they show up," Adele muttered. "Braver than I. I think... I think I'd hide or kill myself."

Lauren nodded.

Ryker didn't have much he could do right now, so he focused inward. Focused on his dungeon sense spell-work, and what he could feel within himself.

His soul was hanging by a few frayed tendrils to the avatar. It was clearly moving towards firming itself up within the body, but it also looked a long way off.

To Ryker, it almost looked like his soul had been ejected from the avatar but had somehow clung in there by a filament. One particular section.

Getting in close with his very diminished dungeon sense, Ryker could see it. It was Robyn. Or to be more precise, a small fraction of a piece of Robyn that had been left behind.

It desperately clung to the avatar the same way Robyn had attached herself to him.

No more making fun of her. Ever.

Smiling to himself, Ryker began to stuff his soul deeper into his avatar, tying it into place. The pattern that was his avatar shifted and changed each time he did it. The mana that powered the pattern was being replaced with his soul instead. He was filling it up and becoming one with the avatar.

Letting out a slow breath, Ryker opened his eyes, taking a break from his work. He felt infinitely better.

Infinitely better and like he was in control of his own body.

"I can't watch," Diane said, stepping out of what Ryker assumed was the peephole Benni had mentioned.

Frowning, Ryker pushed back into his dungeon sense and eased through the wall that separated them from the throne room.

Benni was down on the ground, stripped naked. She was being held there by five separate men. Not far away was the vicar of the church of dark, working at his belt buckle.

Beyond him were a number of dead, dying and wounded soldiers. Benni had taken them with her.

There was a small shell of force around Benni that seemed to prevent her from severing her own avatar. She was stuck in her body.

I'll need to remember that for the next time Shirley goes out to kill people.

A thread of her soul connected her to her core, which was behind Ryker somewhere.

Yeah, no. That's not... no.

Ryker gathered himself and attacked the shell that surrounded Benni. Pushing his mana into the spell through the dungeon sense.

And nothing happened.

No, no, no. NO.

Diane was standing with Lauren and Adele. She was crying softly.

Panicking, and with nothing available to work with, Ryker thought hard on his situation.

Then he thought of his soul and how it was powering the pattern of his avatar. Reaching into himself, he snapped off a bit of his soul.

Building a pattern in the dungeon-sense again, he concentrated wholly on it.

It was a spear of absolute force, built from inside a place people couldn't see. He was confident no one would even see the spell when it hit.

Slowly, Ryker fed the piece of his soul into the pattern. It lit up and practically burned with power.

Shifting around behind the vicar, Ryker took aim.

Robyn's goddess. I don't know your name, and I'm sorry for that.

I'm not worthy of any attention from you, but... if you're listening, I could use a hand here.

The church of the dark vicar deserves no redemption, and no second chance. Benni doesn't deserve what's about to be done to her.

As soon as the vicar dropped his pants to the ground, Ryker triggered the spell.

With a resounding boom, the spear became a brightly glowing white light. Holy light that didn't just add to the spell, but took it over.

Streaking with energy, it plowed through the vicar and his wards as if they weren't even there. Then it went through Benni, cracking right through the shell around her.

The Vicar's chest blew outward and became a red and purple splatter of organs and blood. Benni was split in half from her crotch to her head, becoming two separate pieces.

There was a soft tinkling of bells throughout the throne room. It felt like righteous anger to Ryker, even as Robyn's deity turned her attention on him.

Sapphire eyes saw his very soul.

And burned him, inside and out. It brought forth an unending torrent of the suffering he'd wrought on others out of revenge. Out of pettiness.

Out of anger.

Ryker took it, and accepted it. He felt it was owed to this goddess for helping him save Benni from her fate.

Standing in that deity's judgment, Ryker was found absolutely wanting.

Except there was no sentence passed. In fact, the deity seemed to pity him, and it forgave him in that moment.

It promised him redemption. A redemption that would be incredibly painful, and long. But a redemption.

As if realizing he was willing but not ready, the deity vanished. Ryker slowly came back to himself. His body and soul intact.

He noticed her then. Fluttering there in the throne room was Benni's spirit. It was lost, and confused.

Slipping a tendril of himself into her spirit, Ryker guided the soul into the room he was in and back to the core behind him. The one he knew that was hers.

All the other cores were filled with the souls of those who had come with her and were already dead.

Benni's soul resisted him putting her in the core. It seemed more as if she wanted to remain with him in the dungeon sense. But that wasn't possible. She had nowhere to retreat to if something were to happen.

After several seconds, she relented and joined the core. Her soul settling into it.

Coming back to his body, Ryker lifted his head up.

Adele was standing in the peephole now, her body quivering. Stepping out of the box, she looked to Diane and Lauren.

"He's dead!" Adele hissed. "His entire chest is missing, and Benni's dead, too. It's like something just… exploded out of the vicar."

"I killed them both," Ryker said, his voice sounding rusty in his ears. "I had to do it through the dungeon sense to not give the game away. I built it, powered it up, and then… hit them. Benni is back in her core now."

Ryker closed his eyes and rested his head against the stone wall behind him. He felt tired, but far more put together now.

A warm pair of arms wrapped around his shoulders and pulled him to one side.

"Thank you, husband. Benni was my friend," Diane said. "She and I spent many days simply talking. Thank you."

"Yup," Ryker said, then promptly passed out.

***

For the last two days, they'd hidden inside the alcove. Everyone was beyond hungry by this point, but Ryker could at least summon water with a simple spell.

That and it was incredibly awkward for everyone to be going to the bathroom in full view of everyone else.

The space was just too cramped for anything other than practically living in each other's laps.

Everyone had huddled together into one corner and slept pressed in tight. The stone floors and walls had been incredibly cold at night and sapped the heat from them.

Lauren was on peephole duty right now. Watching and listening to what was going on in the throne room.

Diane and Adele sat side by side nearby in a quiet conversation.

Ryker was sitting next to Lauren, watching the throne through his dungeon sense.

The minor contracts he'd made with all three of them had expired after his body had been cut from him. None of them could access the dungeon sense right now but him.

"The new vicar is a dickhead," Ryker said.

"Yes, well, the old one wasn't much better," Lauren said. "It still warms my angry little heart that you murdered him, though."

Ryker slipped his right hand into Lauren's dress and began to stroke up and down her calf.

"Don't worry, my beloved queen," Ryker said. "I'll get you your throne back eventually. It'll just take time."

Lauren's hand settled atop Ryker's head, and she began to comb his hair back with her fingertips.

"Thank you. I know you will," Lauren said. "You know... this sounds awful, but I'm very thankful to be able to spend so much time with you.

"This is the first time we've been with one another for longer than just a few hours."

"I love you, too," Ryker said, his hand moving from her calf and gliding up the inside of her thigh.

Lauren didn't move or swat his hand away.

Instead, she sighed.

"I wish we had a bed, a bath, and some privacy," she said. "If I'm a queen on the run, I might as well be a queen on the run who's enjoying her husband."

Raising his eyebrows at that comment, Ryker snickered to himself.

"No condoms available, you realize. Other than that, I'd be in. You've always been the fun one, it seems like," Ryker said, his fingers playing across the expanse of her skin from her inner knee up to where it met her underwear.

"I know there aren't any, and I didn't mention one. And thank you. I do try. When it comes to you, at least. I have to keep you on the hook somehow since I haven't been able to do much with you," Lauren said. "Oh, what's this? A messenger."

Lauren shifted her weight from foot to foot and seemed to deliberately spread her legs further apart.

Heh. Maybe sleeping in next to me for two nights is making her just as pent up as I am.

Focusing on the messenger while moving his hand just a bit higher, Ryker looked in through his dungeon sense.

A man in the colors of the dark church ran up and handed off a letter to the vicar, a woman in black robes that looked like she was approaching old age faster and faster the longer she was the vicar, even though she'd looked only forty when they'd first seen her two days ago.

"Damn," said the woman, flinging the letter back at the man. "I've sat my throne for only two days, and already a new challenger."

"Her throne, ha. Her throne, my ass," Lauren hissed.

Shrugging, Ryker reached up, took a handful of Lauren's rear end and gave it a squeeze.

Lauren became as still as a stone, then chuckled under her breath.

"Move it down and keep it there. Adele might be watching. She gets hurt easily when you pay me or Diane too much attention," Lauren said. "We'd need to make sure to keep things quiet if we did do something. I don't want to hurt her. Or Diane, for that matter."

He couldn't fault her that. And honestly, he didn't want to hurt the others either. Lauren seemed the most prepared for a bad marriage. Diane as well, or at least almost as much.

Adele seemed fine with the idea of Ryker being with the others, but she didn't handle any type of physical representation of that where she could see it.

Ryker deliberately squeezed Lauren's bottom one more time, then let his hand fall back down between her legs, his fingers tickling back and forth lightly.

"That's almost worse, but… at least it's less visible," Lauren grumbled, not telling him to stop.

"…able church of light. How'd they get through Dungeon? I thought that shit hole was done, and that we killed the count. Didn't we have people there to take control of things?" asked the vicar.

"No, we never did," responded someone that looked to be one of the hangers-on that kept close to the vicar. "We had a minor deal with Claire, but… she joined the church of light instead."

Unsurprising.

"So, the church is coming along with some Adelonians. The queen's troops won't do anything for us, and the entire Queendom is still in open rebellion against us," the vicar said. "Fine. Crush everyone. Make examples. Execute anyone who doesn't listen."

"Can you kill her?" Lauren asked.

Ryker frowned and looked at his soul, wedged in his avatar.

Everything seemed to be bonding together very well. There was only a small portion of his soul that was fluttering about, and it was slowly joining the rest.

The small corner where he'd broken a piece of his soul off seemed to be regrowing as well. Though very slowly.

"Yeah, but it'd be messy. It'd make them worry about what's going on. It'd possibly give us away. So why?" Ryker asked.

"Kill her for me. Right now," Lauren said.

Ryker shrugged, then built the pattern in the dungeon sense and dropped in a piece of his soul.

"…ill their families. Then their friends, and—"

A massive bolt of force slammed out from nowhere and splattered the vicar all over the throne. Turning her into a gooey paste from the waist up. The spell struck the throne and simply washed into it without harming it.

Everyone ran away shrieking and screaming, in a panicked mad dash to get away from the throne room.

"Good. Thank you," Lauren said. "I'm… thank you. You've done so much for me, Ryker."

Sliding down from the viewing box, she sat down next to him and then pushed his hand under her dress to rest on her thigh.

"Uhm, keep… keep touching me. I like the feel of your hands," Lauren said. Then she cleared her throat. "You really have done far too much for me. Far more than I deserved. For a woman who forced you into this, took you to marriage without your consent and brought you to ruin.

"You did more with what little you had, and gave me more than anyone else did or even could, all for the sake of loving me."

Lauren sighed and then laid her head on his shoulder.

"Even if I never become Queen again, I'll be happy just to call you husband, Ryker. Just… be patient with me when it comes to farming. I think I'll have a lot to learn."

Snorting, Ryker started to pet and stroke Lauren's thigh.

"You could always just be a housewife. No need to farm," Ryker said.

"I could, couldn't I? Just stay home, keep pushing out children, and keep the house clean," Lauren said. It sounded like that idea was the better one to her.

"We need to escape tonight," Ryker said, his stomach rumbling loudly. "If we don't leave tonight, I'm not sure we'll have the strength to get anywhere or get anything done."

"Yes… you're right," Lauren said, then closed her eyes. "Let's… ask the others and see what they think, but I believe they'll agree. After that, we should turn in, get some sleep.

"I'd rather make our break for it in the dead of night."

"How exactly are we… getting out of here? I never asked," Ryker said.

"Unfortunately, the answer to that question is the same way we came in," Lauren said, indicating the stone door. "With any luck, you killing the vicar will keep them out. From there… we can hopefully escape out into my garden. I can't imagine they know where my escape tunnel is, and after that… we get out into the city itself. Then… I don't know."

"Then we go to Dungeon and settle in to take it all back," Ryker said. That was the plan.

Chapter 26 - Flight -

"There's no one there," Diane said, her head in the viewing box.

"We can't really wait any longer, can we?" Adele asked.

"Not really," Ryker grumbled. "I'm glad that water isn't an issue, but I'm starving here."

"Agreed," Lauren said. "Our first goal is to make it to my garden. Thankfully we can get to it from an adjoining room. There's no reason to go into the royal apartments."

"Should… should we go then?" Adele asked, looking annoyed. "I mean, the longer we wait, the less time before sunrise. We need time to get into the city, get disguises, or just escape."

"Disguises," Ryker said immediately. "Even if we escape, we need disguises, or just a way to blend in. Our first order of business is hacking all your hair off or dying it."

"That means scissors and putting something in it, or a shawl."

"What?" Lauren said, her hands immediately going to her long hair.

Diane pulled her head out of the viewing box, her hands touching her long braid. Then she nodded. "Yes. That'd be wise. I assume we'll need to get clothes from the peasantry as well."

"Yup," Ryker said. "What'd Benni throw in here again?'

"Ten gold, five silver, and some basic things. Flint, steel, a knife," Adele said.

"That's more than enough for us to get everything we need, but we'll need to change the gold to much lower forms of currency," Ryker said, then walked over to the stone door. Not waiting for approval, he disengaged the locking mechanism and shoved the door open.

Torch light and fresh air washed over them as soon as they did it.

The stink of piss, unwashed bodies, and a cramped space immediately became noticeable at the same time.

Ryker had apparently gotten used to the smell, right up until he got hit with a normal scent.

"Ugh, I stink like piss," Adele said.

"Good news then," Ryker said, peeking out from the door. The throne room was empty. "Smelling like piss will help us blend in where we're going."

"Poor quarter," Adele muttered.

"Yup, ok. Let's go. Lauren, you lead the way, but I'm going to be walking on your ankles," Ryker said.

"Wish I had a damn sword," Adele said. "Anything with an edge, really."

Wait, can I still work the dungeon…? I have cores with me. They're all in my bag.

Casting his dungeon sense spell for a second, Ryker saw he had a small space to work with, that could function as a dungeon. Perhaps twenty feet around Benni's core in a sphere.

Benni's core was the same as a dungeon core, just with her as the spirit inside rather than a soul. A captaincy core.

Ryker couldn't do much right now other than summon a monster, though, and that wouldn't be useful.

Unless…

Building a pattern for an animated object, a longsword, Ryker called it forth. Being an animated sword meant it would respond to Adele even as she used it.

It cost all the mana he had in his body, and there was nothing left. It'd take him time to fully recharge his pools.

Except… I'm not crippled in this body. This is easily forty times the ability I previously had in mana. And speaking of… where's Tar?

Flipping it over, he gave it to Adele as they followed Lauren through the throne room.

"Ryker, I'm going to make you whimper in pleasure later," Adele said, taking the sword from him eagerly.

Ryker grinned and looked to Diane.

"Where's Tar? He left with you and I never saw him again," Ryker said.

"I haven't seen him in a while, actually," Diane said, looking confused. "Now that I think about it, it's been days. I thought he'd gone back to you, to be perfectly honest."

What? Huh. I wonder where he went. I'll have to make a spell to track him down. Especially since... well, he's probably not my familiar anymore. Is he?

Is my body dead?

Lauren marched them through a hallway and paused in front of a door. She looked to Ryker, clearly unsure of what to do.

Getting the hint without it being said, Ryker walked up to the door, and pushed his dungeon sense through it to the other side. With almost no mana, it was difficult to say the least.

The room was empty.

"It's clear. No one's in it," Ryker said, looking at Lauren.

Rather than respond, she opened the door and rushed in, Diane right behind her.

Moving through the room, Ryker found it was full of gardening tools. Lauren was waiting at the next door, eyes on him.

"I got nothing in me. Sorry," Ryker said.

Lauren grimaced and turned to the door.

"Adele, please be ready," Lauren said to her cousin.

Holding her sword in front of her, Adele sidled up next to Lauren, who opened the door for her.

"Hey, wha—"

Adele darted forward, her sword extended. There was a whoosh of air, and then a groan. Moving out the door, Adele disappeared into the dark night.

"Clear," she said after several seconds.

Marching out, Lauren, Diane, and Ryker moved into the gardens.

Ryker immediately went to the dying man. He was doubled over, Adele's sword having caught him in heart. Sparing the man, Ryker kicked him upside the head. With a pop, the man's head whipped back and his body stiffened up. With any luck, he'd die before he woke up.

Then Ryker went through the man's pockets and satchel, and stole his sword and sword-belt.

"Here, take this and the belt; I'll eat that sword for mana," Ryker said, holding it out to Adele.

"But I like this sword," Adele said, taking the sword-belt from him. She flicked the guard's sword out and dropped it to one side. Strapping the belt around her hips, she slipped her sword into the sheath. It fit for the most part. A half-inch of the blade stuck out the top. "I'll fix that later with some leather."

Grumbling, Ryker stuffed the coins from the dead man in his pockets and pulled the wedding ring off his hand.

"Did you take his ring?" Diane asked.

"Yes—he doesn't need it. And we can sell it for some coins," Ryker said. "In fact, if you're wearing any jewelry, be prepared to part with it. Selling it for coin would be best. Throwing it away as a last resort. It'll just attract unwanted attention."

"I suppose it's a good thing I'm only wearing things that were pretty, with no sentimentality," Lauren said, looking at her necklace and rings.

Diane nodded, but she was looking sadly at the ring on her left hand. It was her wedding ring to Ryker.

Adele looked similarly upset, her right hand covering the left.

"If you don't want to toss them or sell them, just... hide them. Make sure they can't be seen," Ryker said, relenting.

Grabbing the man by his belt buckle, Ryker dragged him over to a bush and stuffed him into it. It'd help a little.

"Where do we go now, Lauren?" Diane asked, looking to the other woman.

"Ah... we have to get to that big tree there. There's a boulder on the other side in a small depression. From there we go straight to the wall. There's a hidden door there, just like the throne room," she said, looking around.

"Is it somewhere we could hide in for a day or two?" Ryker asked. "If I can hit the city without you three, I can probably get supplies and disguises."

"Maybe?" Lauren said cautiously. "I'm not sure. It's meant to just be a way to get out of the castle for the royal family."

"Alright," Ryker said. "Lead on."

Lauren nodded and set off for the big tree. It was hard to miss, really.

Reaching it, Lauren immediately scurried around it to the other side. When she found her boulder, she started straight for the wall.

Ryker had no idea how she knew where she was going in this utter darkness. It was as if she'd done it many times before.

Then again, maybe she has. She just never opened the door.

Up above them, Ryker could see movement on the wall. There wasn't much to be said or done about it, though. He could only hope they'd never think to look inside of the garden, that they would be entirely concerned with looking outward.

Lauren reached the wall, and her hands began moving over the stones there. Looking for something.

Ryker nervously stood behind Adele and Diane.

"I can't find it," Lauren hissed.

Mentally spent and feeling like he wanted to throw up from a lack of mana Ryker tried to call up his dungeon sense.

Staring into the stones, Ryker looked for anything out of the ordinary.

Then his dungeon sense started to fail and fall away as he ran out of mana.

"This one," Ryker croaked, pointing to a stone. It was much lower to the ground than Lauren was looking. Tilting slowly to one side, Ryker stumbled, then righted himself before he fell over.

He hadn't felt mana sickness this extreme in a long time. Not since he'd worked magic without a dungeon.

I miss Shirley.

"What? Oh. Oh!" Lauren said, bending down and pushing on the stone. At the same time, she pushed on a different stone three feet away.

With a pop and a clank, part of the stone wall slid out. Grabbing the edge, Lauren heaved it open.

"Go, go," she said.

Everyone went inside quickly, Lauren coming in last and closing the door behind them. Immediately, they were cast into impenetrable darkness.

Ryker took a step forward and practically ran someone over.

"Oww," Diane said. After that, a pair of arms wrapped around Ryker's middle and hugged him tight.

Holding on to what he assumed was Diane, Ryker tried to crab-walk to one side, getting out of the way.

Diane didn't let go, clutching to him.

"Is everyone here?" Lauren asked.

"Yes," Ryker said.

"Uh-huh," Adele said, the sound of something rustling accompanying her voice.

"Here," Diane said from directly in front of Ryker.

Then a hand came up and touched his face, guiding it down. Soft, warm lips pressed to his. Diane broke the kiss after several seconds, her hand patting his cheek. Then she stepped away from him, her presence vanishing in the dark.

"Got it. Uh… is there a torch or something in here? Something for me to light? I found the flint and steel Benni left us," Adele said.

"Yes. It should be…" Lauren's voice trailed off, and Ryker heard the sound of scrabbling fingers and hands. "Got it. Where are you?"

"Here," Adele said. The light click of what sounded like steel on flint began tapping repeatedly.

"Oh, there we are," Lauren said, apparently orienting on the noise.

"Hey, hands off," Adele said.

"Sorry. Here's the torch," Lauren replied.

"Hold it up. I'll try to strike right on it."

There was a pop, and a flutter of sparks. In that brief moment, Ryker could see Lauren and Adele staring down at a torch between them.

Several strikes later, the torch caught. Apparently it had been soaked with something that would last on the wood and remain combustible.

Lauren held the torch out and up, casting light on the room.

It was empty of anything useful. There was nothing here that would be valuable to them. Off to one side was a stairwell.

"There, we go down that. At the bottom is… well, I don't know, honestly. I always practiced how to get to the door, but never went in. That seems like a mistake now," Lauren said. Walking over to the stairs, she began going down them, the torch held aloft.

Diane immediately followed her.

Adele was still putting things in her pouch as the light started to fade away down the stairs.

"Come on," Ryker said, laying a hand against Adele's back and guiding her along. "We need to keep going."

"Yeah, yeah, I know. You just want to touch me," Adele said, letting him guide her as she put her things away.

"Kinda, yeah," Ryker said, then deliberately moved his hand back and forth across her back. "That a problem?"

"No, not really," Adele said, then closed the flap to her satchel and started down the stairs. "It's just annoying cause I wanna do more than just touching. I'm kinda horny."

Ryker blinked at that admission.

Adele's head turned around as she walked. He couldn't see her face, but he got the impression she was grinning.

"What? I'm human. It's not like women don't feel the same things men do.

"Although I'm glad I still surprise you," she said, then took the steps faster to catch up to the others.

And then some.

Reaching the bottom, Lauren looked at the torch and seemed unsure what to do with it.

When Ryker got off the stairs, he realized why. The room was already lit with enchanted items set evenly throughout.

Taking the torch from her, Ryker set it on the ground, put his boot on it, and rolled it slowly back and forth.

After several passes, the torch was smothered and smoke began to drift up from it.

The smoke traveled upward, and Ryker watched it. With any luck, it wouldn't go back up the stairs but rather show him if this room had an appropriate chimney or other way for the smoke to escape.

It drifted up to the stones above, then seeped through them and vanished.

Huh. I wonder where that goes. Strange.

Looking back around the room, he found the three women were going through the boxes set throughout.

"Most of it is… hm, unusable," Diane said. "It seems the intent was for this to be maintained regularly."

"Yes, that does seem to be the case," Lauren said with a sigh. "I blame my mother. I don't think she ever recovered from my sister's passing. She didn't do much to prepare me."

"From what I personally know of fashion, and because my grandmother wore a pattern like this, I would agree," Diane said, holding up a very destroyed blouse.

Ryker moved to a corner and dropped down heavily. He needed to sit and do nothing but recover his mana.

"I suppose that answers that question," Lauren said with a sigh.

"Yeah," Ryker said, closing his eyes for several seconds. "Where does this come out exactly? Are we beyond the wall? Are we close to the city?"

Lauren gestured to a hallway that led off into darkness. "That way will go on for quite a while. I don't know exactly where it ends, but it's supposed to come out into some old ruins.

"They were scoured publicly and opened to the public, then flattened till they were little more than a foundation. My family made it so open, so barren, that no one ever bothered with it."

"Oh, that's well done," Diane said, making a pile of rotten and destroyed clothes in one corner. "We'll need to make sure we take precautions to have all this repaired, replaced, and retained once we come back. Our children will need to know of it."

Lauren smiled crookedly at that, then frowned.

"Mm. That does… raise some interesting inheritance questions down the line," she said. "Your children will simply retain your familial titles. Mine the Queendom. Adele…"

Diane and Lauren both looked at Adele.

She was busy working on her sheath and looked up for a second, then shrugged and went back to her work.

"My family serves yours, Lauren. We've never really had titles," Adele said.

"What are Shirley's kids going to get?" Ryker asked.

Diane, Lauren, and Adele looked shocked for a moment. They'd apparently forgotten he was sleeping with her.

"Shirley is taking her family's titles and lands, since the only other person alive is Claire," Lauren said. "Their lands were actually rather… extensive and plentiful. We'll reinstate them once it's over."

"Then Adele is Countess of Dungeon," Ryker said. "And our kids inherit my count titles."

"Oh, that works out rather well," Diane said with a smile. "Everyone will end up reporting to Lauren and her children, and it maintains the Queendom."

Ryker wasn't sure why they all suddenly felt the need to discuss this, but he chalked it up to coping.

In making plans for families, and how inheritance would go down, they were forced to focus on the future. To look beyond the current moment at what they'd do when it was all over.

Pulling the bag at his side to his front, he opened the flap and looked inside. The cores of all the fallen Imps and Fairies were here. Safe and secure, filled with their souls.

Nodding, he closed the flap again and then pulled the bag off and set it to one side. When he went into the city for things, he didn't want to take them with him. Just in case something happened.

They'd at least have a chance even if he didn't.

"…ed out to the city with Ryker," Adele said, looking down at herself. "Honestly, I'm a little dressed up, but the dirt, filth, and stink will help me blend in. You two just aren't wearing anything that could pass."

Diane and Lauren looked at one another, then Ryker.

"What? She's not wrong," Ryker said. You two look out of place in those dresses, even if they're filthy. Adele is out of place, but not as badly. She looks like an adventurer who lost a sponsor recently."

"Sponsor?" Diane asked curiously.

"Adventurers can be sponsored by others and have their equipment upkeep paid for, or other things. They get back a percentage of anything the adventurer brings back," Ryker said, closing his eyes. "Some of the best adventurers have sponsors. The houses like it because it gives them a chance to get special items cheaply. Most adventurers just end up on a payroll and going 'dungeon diving' for specific things."

"Huh," Adele said. "I think I missed my calling. Especially after Wynne gave me that core with all those sword-master skills."

Ryker let his mind wander, taking a moment to just rest and relax.

And fell asleep.

Chapter 27 - Conquered -

Ryker dreamed. Dreamed terribly, of things that woke him with an actual start.

Of Marybelle and Wynne beating on a wall trying to get to him. Of his body dying back in Dungeon. Of Shirley standing over his corpse and left with no idea about what to do next.

Robyn attempting to hold the gate as an unending stream of soldiers attacked and killed her over and over.

And through all that, an army of the church of light bearing down on Dungeon and ransacking it, razing it to the ground, where no two stones stood upon each other.

And when he woke from all that, he had the distinct impression that some of it was quite real.

That what he was dreaming was actually happening.

Groaning, Ryker ran a hand over his face. Everything was so wrong right now that he didn't even know how to get through the day. The world felt absolutely hopeless at the moment.

His stomach took that moment to remind him he hadn't eaten in days. That the overwhelming weakness he still felt wasn't going to go away.

Clambering up, Ryker got his feet under him and shook his head.

"You woke up. You ready then?" Adele asked, sitting not far from where he'd been sleeping.

Diane and Lauren were fast asleep on a pile of worthless moth-eaten clothes. It was probably the best thing they'd slept on since they'd hidden away.

"Ready as I'm going to be, I suppose," Ryker mumbled. "First thing on the list is some soup. Something to put in the stomach and sit there for a bit. We'll have to get some in canteens and bring it back for them, too."

"Soup?" Adele asked.

"Soup. Something light and easy. We need simple things to eat first. Berries might be alright. Some of the softer fruits and the like," Ryker said. "There's always the possibility of finding yourself stuck in a dungeon. One of my old teachers harped on what you should do when you get out."

"Okay," Adele said, getting to her feet. "I already scouted the hall. It goes on for a ways, but the door to exit looks simple. Dunno about getting back in."

"Did your sword vanish when you got far enough away?" Ryker asked, starting to head down the hall.

"No. Was it supposed to?"

Technically, yes. But I suppose… this isn't a normal situation anymore.

It took the better part of an hour to get to the end of the hallway. Adele had taken one of the enchanted light devices with them. It didn't exactly make everything visible, but it was enough to walk by.

"I can smell food," Adele muttered, looking at the open doorway in front of them. The light was intense. Ryker could only describe it as blinding.

They'd been living mostly in the dark for four days now.

"Yeah. I wonder how far from the city we are," Ryker said.

"If it's the ruins I'm thinking of, not far from the part that's outside the main walls," Adele said.

"Good. That'll make it easier to slip out when the time comes. Alright, let's… figure out our cover story," Ryker said.

"Husband and wife, fucked up a contract, looking to get back into the swing of things after losing all our gear," Adele said immediately. "I'm a swordsman, you're the wizard, we work in tandem. Talked it out with Diane and Lauren after you passed out."

"Oh, right. What names are we using?" Ryker asked.

"I'm going to be Jane, and you're Alex," Adele said.

"Alex? Alexander, you mean? Great," Ryker said, his mouth a flat line. "Always wanted to be a pretentious prick."

That settled, the two of them walked out the doorway from the lowest part of the ruins and started making their way toward the town.

***

Adele and Ryker were huddled behind a shed. They weren't about to walk in without knowing what to expect.

On top of that, Ryker's dungeon sense wasn't going to go very far without the cores. It barely went five feet beyond him in any direction.

Which left them only with the option of simply watching.

"Soldiers are damned everywhere," Adele muttered.

"And then some," Ryker agreed. "Going to need to cut your hair and change your clothes before we do anything else."

Adele clicked her tongue. "I was just starting to let my hair grow out, too. Probably should have done it before we left the ruins."

"Harder to think without food. And your hair will grow back. Besides, you're beautiful regardless. You want a hand?" Ryker asked.

"Yeah, just hack it off into something short enough for a ponytail. I'll dump my jacket and cut some strips off to bind my sleeves and hair," Adele said with a sigh. "Really liked this jacket."

"Could be worse—could be Diane," Ryker said. "That's a lot of hair she's going to have to cut."

"Hah, yeah. That sucks," Adele said, pulling her jacket off. "Lauren's not going to be happy about that either."

Adele pulled out the knife Benni had stowed for her and set to her task. When she finished with the jacket, she handed it to Ryker.

"Try not to make me look too wretched," Adele said with a sigh.

Ryker snorted at that. "As if I could ever make you look wretched."

Adele squatted down in front of him, glaring up.

Managing to not make a comment about the position, Ryker began to carefully trim away Adele's hair. It fell away cleanly, littering her shoulders and back as he worked.

Taking hold of her chin, Ryker lifted her face up. He peered at her one way and then the other, and he felt like he'd managed to not mess it up. At least not too badly. It was definitely adventurer short now.

"So?" Adele asked.

"Beautiful as ever. Alright, tie your hair up. We need to go get clothes, supplies, packs, and horses if we can manage it," Ryker said. "First on that list is a place to break those gold coins into smaller currencies."

"Huh?" Adele asked.

"We can't go around showing off gold. Won't work out. At all," Ryker said. "Which means something you'd have to pay a gold for, that an adventurer would need after falling on hard times. A horse or a wagon sounds like a good idea. A good blade for you. I'm leaning towards wagon personally. What's your preference?"

"Wagon," Adele said with a nod. Then she took up a tie and tied her hair back. "Are we… going in now?"

"Yeah. Just keep thinking of us as poor adventurers down on our luck," Ryker said.

Suitably prepared, smelling of piss, looking like they'd rolled around in dirt and muck, Adele and Ryker walked out from around the shed. And right into a guard patrol from the church of the dark.

The men eyed Adele with equal parts lust and disgust.

I cannot imagine the occupation of the country is going to do anyone any good.

Ryker didn't make eye contact with the guards, and Adele somehow didn't lash out at them. As they walked along the street trying to figure out where they could find a stable or a wagon shop to buy a wagon, they saw more and more soldiers acting as guards.

Hanged from posts and from pillars were the soldiers of Dale. The vast majority were dead, either previously or from the hanging.

Some were alive but had been gutted, their intestines hanging out.

"I... I don't think... I don't think we should let my cousin enter a city," Adele whispered as they walked by a man groaning on a post, his intestines coiled on the ground in front of him.

"Yeah, no. Remind me to do my best to eradicate these guys completely when this is over," Ryker said.

Falling silent, Adele and Ryker marched on. Finally, they found a livery stable that was open and even seemed to be conducting business.

When they bought the wagon after some haggling, Ryker and Adele felt somewhat better. Their coins had been exchanged into lesser currencies, and they weren't on foot anymore.

That feeling fled immediately when the wagon was searched as soon as they got on the road.

Then again by the next patrol, and the next.

And then the next.

The wagon was subjected to a search by every single soldier who saw it. They were all looking for Lauren, and the vast majority of them had a likeness of her in hand.

A few cast strange looks at Adele, then moved on once they checked her face against Lauren's.

The most recent soldier was now walking away down the road, having searched the very empty wagon and even gone so far as to look underneath it.

Ryker had expected them to get handsy with Adele as well, but it seemed no one wanted to risk her sword, or her filth.

He was rather thankful for that. He wasn't sure he could handle the idea of someone touching her like that.

"I think I'm going to skip the bath till we're clear of the city," she grumbled. "I keep getting eye-fucked. And it doesn't stop. A few of those assholes made a beeline for me. Didn't slow until they finally got up close—got a good whiff and a look at me."

"Yeah, probably a really good idea," Ryker said. "I don't think it'd go very well if I had to start killing people.

"I can make water for a bath anyways. Let's just... get the supplies, head back, and make our plans."

Adele nodded, suddenly looking far more nervous than he originally thought. Then again, he knew her pretty well by now.

By all outward appearances, she was projecting strength and a lethal confidence in the weapon at her side.

As they led the wagon to a general store at the edge of the poor section of town where it met the middle class, they were stopped over and over.

Ryker waited nervously with the wagon while Adele did the haggling and bartering. There was no doubt in his mind she'd end up paying more than she had to. Especially with the state of the city.

Despite that, he certainly couldn't leave the wagon by itself, nor Adele by herself with the wagon. That would be inviting trouble.

His thoughts were only confirmed with the obvious stamp of panic and terror on every face he saw.

If he didn't miss his guess, a good part of the city had already fled. Especially anyone who had wives or daughters, as there was no question what an army soldier of the dark church was likely to do.

An hour later, Adele had already come back out once with a chest and loaded it onto the wagon. Apparently it had been full of clothes.

"You—what're you waiting for?" said a man to Ryker's left. Around him were two other soldiers, standing in the space between the shop and the wagon.

"My wife. She's buying supplies for our next dungeon dive. We're going to head out of country," Ryker said. The number of times he'd been stopped and questioned had given him a frequently-asked-questions checklist he now had prepared.

"I saw her. She looked... fun. I think we'll take her out for some questioning," said the lead soldier. "You don't mind, do you?"

Ryker gave the man a flat stare. Ever since he'd seen the soldiers moving about as they had, Ryker had expected something like this.

"Do you?" said the soldier.

Ryker didn't respond. Instead, he began to construct a half sphere of force. It was wide, and the lip was low. He sharpened the edges of it so it would dig into the ground. Over the top of the pattern, he covered it with an illusionary stone latticework.

Finally, he attached a large mass of mana to it to act like a battery.

"What, going to do something stupid? Don't worry, we won't hurt her. It'll just be a few minutes each," said the man, removing any and all doubt from Ryker's mind about the necessity for them to die.

Activating the spell, Ryker jammed it down into the ground with as much force as he could will into it.

With a sickening crunch, the three men were smashed into the stones. Multiple pops and cracks sounded as their bones were pulverized by the spell crushing them like bugs into the ground.

Ryker looked around, as if he were looking for the sound. Everyone around him did the same; no one could identify the source of it.

No one could see the spell that had just turned three soldiers into jam. It'd dug fairly deep into the ground. People would probably trip over the lip of it or lose their balance, but there wasn't much else Ryker could do.

When he checked the battery, it seemed to be spending itself rather slowly.

Sniffling, Ryker rubbed a thumb across his nose. The smell of blood and meat was pervasive. Overwhelming, in fact.

The horses danced in their leads, getting panicked by the smell of it.

Shit. I didn't even think of that.

Adele came out of the shop, paused, and then hurried over to the rear of the wagon. Her boot caught the invisible disk, and she almost sent her large trunk flying. She put it down next to one she'd put in earlier.

"This is everything—let's go," Adele said, clambering into the back. "I have no idea what you did, but holy shit does it reek of blood."

"Doesn't look like you got much," Ryker said, glancing back at the single big chest.

"Not much to buy, and what they had was expensive as hell. We'll be better off trading with people on the road, or bothering farmers," Adele said, trying to get herself seated even as Ryker drove the wagon along. "So… what happened back there?"

"If I don't miss my guess, a prelude of what's to come for all of what was once the Queensland. Might as well not even call it Dale ever again, because it won't be the same after this," Ryker said. Glancing back into the wagon, he saw Adele glaring at him. That apparently wasn't answer enough. "Three men wanted me to agree to letting them rape you. I turned them into paste instead."

Adele blinked several times and frowned. "I see. I don't think we should be visiting any other cities on our way back to Dungeon, unless they're unoccupied."

"Would agree with you," Ryker said. "But the bigger problem is there's a church of light army, a church of the dark army, and probably a whole lot of bandits and ne'er-do-wells running around."

Adele sighed and pressed a hand to her brow. "Let's just… get back to the others and eat. I'm starving, and this is all just depressing.

Rather bland understatement there.

As the wagon rolled along down the street, they managed to only get searched twice more. Both times they got off with the soldiers losing interest as soon as they got a whiff of either Ryker or Adele.

Just as they were leaving the city, Ryker saw two soldiers moving past in the opposite direction. One had a box with him that was filled with nails and a hammer, and the other with an armful of what looked like fliers.

Turning in his seat, Ryker watched as the two men started putting up posters against the side of someone's house.

As if they cared little for anything other than their job, they started hammering the paper directly into the side boards.

In short order, three posters were put up.

They were bounties, one each for Lauren, Diane, and Adele. Each one had a pretty good likeness as well.

Looking ahead, Ryker clicked the reins on the horses and got them moving faster. The sooner they got back to the ruins and hidden away for a while, the better.

Shit keeps getting worse. And when that spell fades and they find the squished soldiers… I don't even know what that'll kick off.

Fuck.

***

Lauren was shaking her head slowly back and forth. Ryker had managed to squirrel away the wagon after grabbing the cores of his people and creating a temporary dungeon space around it. The cores being loaded into the wagon to keep it hidden.

Everything else was brought into the escape tunnel. They planned to hunker down for several days further now that they had some supplies and food. It'd give the soldiers time to assume Lauren and company had moved out of the area.

If they didn't think they were nearby, they hopefully wouldn't look as hard.

And if it really comes down to it… could I summon a dungeon pig… kill it… and eat it? It's no different than what we did at the inn, is it?

I'm kind of operating as a dungeon… without a dungeon core.

I don't even want to think about how badly this is going to piss off Wynne.

Or the horse, I guess. But then the wagon is pointless.

At the thought of the queen of his dungeon, his partner, he reached out with his soul to the bond he shared with her.

It was there. It was still active. Just mostly inert. As if he were watching someone shout from across a valley, but not hearing them.

"It sounds… like you're hiding a lot from me," Lauren said, looking at Ryker, her eyes tired but clear. Food had done wonders for everyone.

Ryker shrugged.

"Maybe I am, maybe I'm not. You're certainly not going to find out, and you're damned sure as hell not going anywhere near that city," Ryker said. "So it's a moot conversation."

"And… what should we do then? We've agreed to wait a few days, but… at what point do we start moving? We can't stay here forever," Diane said.

"I might be able to solve the food thing now that we have some more space to work in. Plus wood from those trees outside," Ryker said. "So we might be able to stick around for a while if we really wanted to."

Lauren sighed and lifted her hand to her mouth, her fingers drumming against her lips.

"I propose we do as we said. Wait several days, escape during the night, and travel southwest. Away from Dungeon and the armies. We take backroads and wheel along as if we're just a group of people escaping everything that's going on," she said. "What do you three think? I'm not the queen anymore, just a refugee like the rest of you."

Sighing, Ryker leaned back against the wall behind him.

"I've got a whole lot of nothing, I'm afraid," he said. "It's half a dozen of one, six of the other. No matter what we do, we're going to hit patrols. Adele and I should be able to make short work of them providing they're not too numerous."

"I suddenly wish I had learned to use spells, my fists, or a weapon," Diane murmured.

"Whatever," Adele said, scratching underneath her left breast. "Doesn't matter. We could just as easily ditch the wagon now and travel overland and through the brush on foot. It almost might be easier."

Not a terrible idea. The wagon won't really do us much good if everyone is patrolling and using the roads.

"I like that," Lauren said, nodding. "I don't think I'll hold up very well, but I like the idea. Much more than traveling on a road that's likely to be very, very watched. It's a good thing you bought packs for each of us.

"Yes, I like that idea. Good work, Adele."

Adele shrugged, yawned, and then slowly tilted sideways, her head landing with a soft puff on Ryker's shoulder.

"Great, going to sleep, my belly is warm and full of food, do whatever you want," Adele said as she closed her eyes.

Snorting at her dismissal of everyone and everything, Ryker laid an arm around her shoulders.

Lauren and Diane gave Adele a look, then turned their eyes to Ryker.

"What?" he asked. "If it's about the plan, she's not wrong. It's probably the smarter idea. I'm just not much of a woodsman."

Lauren only nodded at that.

Sounds like we're bushwhacking.

Chapter 28 - Hitchhiker -

Ryker shook his head.

He was at a loss. There was no possible way for them to cross the river, even with him at full mana and rested. It was simply too wide.

It didn't help at all that he wasn't skilled at constructive conjuration. Nor did it do them any favors that his ability with illusion and enchanting was pitiful.

For all intents and purposes, Ryker was a weapon. A very strong one, but only a weapon.

"And we're going to just... walk in there?" Adele asked, staring at the small river city in front of them. It was a major crossing point and the only one they could reach without running out of supplies.

"I'm open to other ideas," Lauren said, her face an unhappy frown.

"Well... shit... I mean... we already discussed everything, and we didn't come up with anything else," Adele grumbled.

"Hence why we're doing this," Diane concluded. "It isn't ideal, or even very bright, but it's our best option given our resources."

They weren't even three days away from the capital on foot, and already they'd fallen prey to a number of problems.

A lack of camping gear was one of the foremost. Ryker could carve out a rough shelter for them using his dungeon sense spell-work if they stopped early enough.

But it cost them time.

At this rate, it was going to take them a little over three weeks to make it to Dungeon. And that was a fairly "fast" version of the trip. If they played it conservatively and dodged everyone they could, it could take longer.

It wasn't that Dungeon was that overly far. It was that the Queensland was swarming with soldiers, refugees, bandits, and all sorts of other dangerous elements. The land was in utter turmoil and chaos.

"We could swim the damn river," Adele said. Not for the first time, either. It was her fallback for the whole situation.

"Current would pull us right back into the city, remember?" Diane said. "Come on. We'll get through this. You're our swordswoman, and Ryker is our wizard. What soldiers could really stand up to you two?" Diane said. "We just have to get through, and quickly. And if it goes really well, we stop for supplies so we don't have to rely on Ryker exploding small animals."

Rolling his eyes, Ryker didn't respond.

He wasn't a hunter. He could find animals they could eat easily enough, even larger ones. But he had no idea how to butcher or skin an animal. Hell, he didn't even know how to kill an animal without extreme violence.

Adele groaned, her hands opening and closing at her sides.

He didn't blame her. He'd seen how all the soldiers had eyed her in the capital. It was unlikely this little city would be much better, except that perhaps it might not have as many soldiers in it.

"Okay. Let's... let's go. We'll get in, get out, be on our way," Adele said.

Lauren nodded her head and stood up, Diane a moment behind her.

They'd both cut their hair as short as Adele's. They'd dressed in peasantry garb and looked appropriately dirty as well.

He knew they were both suffering blisters on their feet and heels, but they didn't complain. Ryker did insist on frequent breaks, though, to check their feet. It would be easier to take a rest and let them get some aid than to make it infinitely worse and take longer to heal.

Leading the way into the city, Adele had her hand on her sword hilt long before they'd even come in view of the guards at the city entrance.

They immediately gave the three women a once-over, both soldiers pausing to eye Adele's sword. Then they both noticed Ryker at the rear of the group.

The flat stare he gave them invited them to their deaths. Once more, he had to thank his instructors back at the academy. They'd taught him that sometimes the quickest way to avoid a fight was to be willing to go straight in for a kill rather than an escalation.

And the promise of that sure and fatal exchange would often deter people.

"Err... that'll be... uhm," the man said, still locked in a death stare with Ryker.

"Don't cause any trouble," finished the man lamely, breaking his eyes from Ryker's.

Adele started forward again, Diane and Lauren walking along behind her. They kept their faces turned down and huddled in their cloaks. They looked like every other refuge out there right now.

Ryker began to scan in every direction as they walked along the main road into the city. All around them were men and women crowding together everywhere. They were huddled in almost any open space they could find that kept them out of the street and out of people's way.

This was going to be the part Ryker had been dreading. He knew Lauren was a good queen, and that while she perhaps didn't understand the plights of her peasants, she did care for them. She had tried to do right by them.

Several small patrols of soldiers gave them a once-over as they went past, but Ryker stared each one of them down. Begging them to come over and try something so he could snuff out their lives.

Halfway along the street, Ryker was starting to feel like maybe they had half a chance instead of no chance at all. He'd been expecting to have to start up a fight right here in the street when someone thought they could take one of his wives.

Yet it didn't happen.

At least, not to his group.

Up ahead, a group of soldiers had surrounded a young woman and a young man. It was clear they were a husband and wife simply passing through, the same as their group.

It seemed they didn't have enough strength or speed between the two of them to dodge the patrols.

"We should do something," Lauren said, her head turned and facing Ryker.

"Do what? Get killed? Sorry. It's a shitty situation but realistically, we can't do anything about this," Ryker said. "Not without risking ourselves. And honestly, your life is worth a bit more."

Lauren scowled at him and traded places with Diane. Putting herself directly in front of Ryker now, and Diane behind Adele.

"Ryker, I want this to happen," Lauren said. "And I want you to make it happen for me. Can you do it?"

Grimacing, Ryker glanced over to the man and the woman. They were resisting the guards, but it was obvious the guards weren't going to take no for an answer. They seemed determined to make the woman leave with them.

"Yeah... but it'll cost me to do it," Ryker said.

"Can you do it without getting caught?" Lauren asked.

"Probably."

"Then please do it," Lauren said. "I'll help you pay the cost somehow."

"I don't really think you can, but alright, I'll do this. For you," Ryker said, shaking his head with a sigh.

Building his dungeon sense up, he slipped into it even as he walked along.

Lauren was talking to him, but he was ignoring her.

To work a spell in the dungeon sense in this situation, Ryker would have to snip a piece of his soul off again.

Thankfully, it seemed to be healing itself all on its own over time. He just hoped he'd be able to let it put itself back together after this.

Building six spears of force, Ryker dropped tiny fragments of his soul into each.

They were about to hit the edge of his range, and there was no telling if they'd simply force the woman out behind a building at any moment.

So Ryker activated the spells.

With an explosion of force and power, the six soldiers detonated as the spears blew threw them.

Body parts, blood, meat, and organs sprayed in every direction.

Suddenly weakened, Ryker almost stumbled, his entire body feeling incredibly heavy.

"Ryker?" Lauren asked, one of her hands immediately coming up to steady him as they walked. "Are you ok?"

"No," Ryker said, grimacing. "I have to burn bits of my soul to make that happen. Adds up, I guess. I feel sick."

"Your soul!?" Lauren hissed at him, her face turning different colors rapidly. "We're... we're going to talk about this, but—"

People screamed, shouted, sprinted by. Everything had become complete chaos now.

"What the hell just happened?" Adele asked, glaring back at Ryker. He wasn't sure if she knew he'd done something, but clearly she was blaming him. "Fuck, that's... ok, we're going. Now. Fast."

Adele started jogging away from the whole thing, Diane following her immediately. Lauren grabbed Ryker's hand and started pulling at him, and they ran after Diane.

They made it to the city walls, where several guards were refusing to let anyone through. They didn't know what was happening behind them, but they seemed unlikely to let anyone go by until they did know.

A small boy with bright blond hair and green eyes walked up to Ryker and stared at him.

"You're different. I can see it," said the boy.

Looking down at the child, Ryker didn't know what to say. He looked like he could be five or six years old.

"Yeah, I'm different alright," Ryker mumbled. Adele was slowly forcing their group to the front. She didn't want to stay here any longer than she had to, and that was obvious. He walked forward, keeping pace with Lauren.

"You're not normal at all. You've got bits of broken things in you. I can see them. Were you born like that?" asked the child.

"What? I mean... we're all born the way we are, aren't we?" Ryker asked. He was getting very confused by the boy and didn't feel like he was keeping up in the conversation.

"For some of us. You're not normal, though. It's like... someone opened a jar and emptied it, then poured the contents of a different jar into the first one. And that's you. You fit, you belong, but you don't," said the child, staring at him intently now.

What the fuck? Did he just tell me my soul doesn't belong in this body?

The guards were arguing with Adele now. They seemed hell-bent on keeping everyone in the city till they could determine what had happened.

Looking around, Ryker felt unsure on how to proceed. Then he spotted the man and the woman who had been the start of all this. They were pressed into the group trying to escape now.

At least Lauren got her wish. But she's going to need to fucking fix that stupid 'save everyone' attitude of hers or she's going to get us killed.

Turning his eyes to Lauren, he saw she looked pained, frightened, and angry. Probably all relating to what she'd had Ryker do.

"Oh. A champion is coming," said the boy, looking back the way they'd come and partially to the sky.

Snapping his eyes to where the boy was looking, Ryker could see a small dot approaching against the blue horizon.

Apparently this one could fly, too.

Shit.

Stepping up to the soldier closest to himself, Ryker wrapped him up in a cocoon of force, then contracted it.

With a wet squish, the man's head tore off from his shoulders at the neck. Immediately after that, his guts sprayed out from him like a sausage being squeezed from its casing.

Before the second or third guard could react, Ryker smashed them flat with a large circle of force from above. Though Ryker did take a moment to angle the disc slightly.

- 154 -

Popping and crunching, the men were smashed flat. Blood and guts burst out and rushed in the direction Ryker had angled the disc.

The spells hadn't cost him too terribly, and his mana still felt quite full.

It's nice not being a cripple.

Adele, Lauren, and Diane wasted no time. They sprinted out of the city, Ryker being dragged along by Lauren.

"That was messy!" shouted the child, following along behind Ryker. "I've never seen spells like that before. It was impressive. Daddy likes to use projectiles instead."

Unable to respond, Ryker was pulled along off the road and into the fields outside of the city.

So much for supplies.

Way to go, Lauren.

***

They finally came to a stop, having run with the river deeper into the wilds. Further from civilization and the road that was sure to be filled with soldiers.

Lauren and Diane collapsed on the grass, lying on their backs and taking in giant gasping breaths.

Adele looked slightly winded, but unconcerned.

Ryker felt the same way, and he'd been feeling better by the minute.

Using my soul as fuel is a bad idea. Especially when my it isn't completely fit to this avatar.

Need to stop doing that.

Sighing, Ryker looked back the way they'd come. Hoping that at some point the child had headed back home.

And found the boy right in front of him.

"You all run fast," said the child. "I couldn't run that fast. I used a spell and I was able to keep up."

Ryker frowned. He hadn't even felt, heard, or sensed a spell being used. Which meant it was infinitesimal in power and scale, or the kid had deliberately built in a mass of dampeners around it.

"Dampeners," the child said, as if reading his mind. "Daddy taught me how to build them into everything to hide my power."

"Okay, but it doesn't really work very well to hide it if you're telling me you did it. Does it?" Ryker asked.

"Oh. You're right," the child said, looking annoyed. He nodded, then looked at Ryker with a smile. "You're smart."

"I mean, I try," Ryker said, then looked to Lauren, Diane, and Adele. The three women were watching him talk with the boy. With varying degrees of disbelief.

"Ryker… who's that?" Diane asked, sitting upright.

"Hi, call me Rick!" said the boy.

"Hello, Rick," Lauren said, managing to get herself into a sitting position.

"Hi," Rick said.

"What's your last name?" Lauren asked.

"Oh. Uhm, Daddy said I shouldn't tell people if I don't know them. I'm sorry," Rick said.

"No, that's… very good advice, honestly," Lauren said, smiling at the child. "How'd you end up in that city? Is that your home back there?"

"No. I used a spell I watched Momma Fox use. I didn't do it right, though, and ended up here. I don't know how to get back, and the spell won't work," Rick said, nodding his head.

"Momma Fox?" Ryker asked.

"Yes, she's very pretty and nice. We like to sit and watch things from her balcony," Rick said with a big smile.

"Rick, can you get home from here?" Lauren asked.

"No," the boy said simply, smiling at Lauren.

"Do you have any family around?" Diane asked.

"No," he said, looking at Diane. "You're pretty."

Diane smiled at the compliment.

"Thank you, Rick. I'm sure all the ladies will find you quite handsome when you grow up," Diane said.

The boy looked to Ryker again, his eyes peering into him as if he could see his very soul.

"You're broken," Rick said. "But it looks like you're being fixed. You used some interesting spells. Can you teach me?"

Ryker raised his eyebrows. He wasn't quite sure what to say.

"Rick, you said you can't get home, and you have no family. How long were you in that city?" Lauren asked.

"Two days. Someone dropped some bread in the mud. I ate that," Rick said. Then he sighed and put a hand to his stomach. "But I'm hungry again. Can I have some food, please?"

Great. Another mouth to feed.

Ryker had no doubt that Diane and Lauren were going to drag the child along until they could figure out what to do with him.

Adele knelt down in front of the child, holding out some jerky to him.

"Here, I'm Adele," said the booger-picking, armpit-scratching princess.

"You're pretty, too," Rick said, smiling at her. Then he took the jerky from her. "Thank you very much."

Adele beamed at the kid, then turned the big grin on Ryker that made him worry for his future. Then she looked back to Rick as the child chewed methodically.

"We're going to take you with us for now," Adele said, not asking anyone else for their opinion. "We'll figure out how to get you home, alright?"

"Okay! Can I stay close to you?" Rick asked, looking to Ryker.

"Uh, sure. Why... not. I'm Ryker," he said.

"Ryker! Okay. Good. Where are we going?" Rick asked.

"Dungeon. It's home. We'll be traveling through the woods and trees, and staying off the beaten path," Ryker said. "So it's going to be unpleasant. Okay?"

"Okay, I understand. I've gone on trips before. Sometimes we walk, sometimes we ride, sometimes we use magic," Rick said. Then he looked at Adele. "Your sword is very strange. It shouldn't exist. And it's alive."

Grimacing, Ryker moved off to one side and sat down, putting his back to a tree. He didn't need to hear what he already knew about Adele's sword. For whatever reason, it was dungeon summoned, but it didn't disappear when removed from the dungeon.

Which was the sphere around Benni.

Closing his eyes, Ryker took in a slow breath and looked inward to his soul.

It was frayed and had a few chunks taken out of it, but it looked intact. It was still binding itself to his avatar as well. Nothing seemed to have changed. His soul just had a few holes in it.

"You used your soul?" Lauren asked, her voice coming from directly to his right.

"I have to, to use a spell inside of the dungeon sense. Not enough power otherwise," Ryker said. "And you seemed determined to save them, so... I did what I had to do."

"I want you to not listen to me next time," Lauren said. "I almost got us all... all caught because I couldn't prioritize myself."

"Uh huh," Ryker said, not opening his eyes. "That's accurate."

"And if I want to help my country, I have to get to Dungeon and rally my forces. Then take back everything," Lauren said.

"And you can't do that if you're dead or captured," Ryker said, finishing the thought.

"Exactly. So... don't... listen to me in the future," Lauren said.

Ryker felt Lauren press her lips to his, her breath washing over his face as she did so. Then she pulled away.

"But… thank you… for doing what I told you to. I appreciate your loyalty and dedication to me, Ryker. I don't deserve you," Lauren whispered softly. "I'll be sure to make up for it as soon as I can."

Delightful.

Chapter 29 - Respite -

Ryker was walking about the town with Rick. No one paid them any attention at all.

A man with his son out for a walk had to appear fairly mundane, or so the townsfolk seemed to think.

Whenever they spoke to anyone, asked a question, or interacted with the town, most people seemed to immediately look at Rick with a smile.

All around town, though, they saw posters of Lauren, Adele, and Diane. They were practically wallpapered to some homes. If they hadn't taken the time to change their hair and dress, they would have been picked out instantly.

Even now, Ryker had the uncomfortable feeling that despite the changes they'd made, people would still recognize them. Then it'd be a question of whether they were loyal to Lauren, Veronica, or the churches.

With so many possibilities, there was no telling which way they'd go.

"They really want to find them," Rick said, his eyes tracking from poster to poster.

"Yes, well, it's pretty much what I told you," Ryker said with a shrug.

"I know, it's just surprising. This town isn't on the main path, nor is it anywhere near any major cities," Rick said.

Ryker looked to the child and raised his eyebrows. That kind of talk and context was surprising for a little kid.

At least it was to Ryker.

"I said something I shouldn't have, didn't I?" Rick asked.

"I mean, only for a kid," Ryker said. "As far as what you said, it was intelligent and accurate. What you pointed out demonstrates an insane need on their part to find the girls."

"Hm. Is there anything else I've said that a child wouldn't?" Rick asked.

"Well, that right there is one. Makes it sound like you're not actually a child. What are you?" Ryker asked. Looking up, he saw there was a patrol of soldiers on a street corner. They were inspecting every person walking by.

Really looking for them. Rick is absolutely right.

All it's going to take is someone to wonder what they'd look like in peasant clothes and cut hair.

"I'm a child, of course," Rick said.

"Uh huh, and I'm your fucking fairy godmother," Ryker said, looking down at the kid.

"You shouldn't curse," Rick said.

"And your name isn't Rick, and you aren't a child. So, little asshole, what are you?" Ryker said. They'd walked through the street once already and were now heading back to the girls. They'd gotten the information they needed to know.

Rick sighed expressively and folded his arms across his chest.

"I am a child," Rick said, his voice rising as he spoke. "And I'm five years old. I'll be six in a few months. You shouldn't curse at me."

Ryker suddenly felt like he was getting too many looks from everyone around him. Rick's outburst was getting attention from people.

"Right—sorry, Rick. I'll be sure to be polite. You're a child, got it," Ryker said, not wanting to press the subject. He suddenly realized how much he was at the kid's mercy if he suddenly decided he really didn't like what Ryker was talking about.

"Good. Thank you, Ryker," Rick said, nodding his head firmly.

"Uh huh. So, any other stunning observations from the child who isn't a child who is?" Ryker asked.

Rick looked at him and blinked slowly.

"Only that I can understand now how your wives seem to constantly hit you, get frustrated with you, and tell you to be quiet," Rick said. "You can be insufferable. Even my daddy doesn't make people as angry as you do. And he seems to try."

Ryker nodded. He had nothing to argue with in that statement. It was absolutely true, after all.

"Yeah, I'm an assh… jerk," Ryker said.

Rick laughed at that.

Exiting the town without a problem, Rick and Ryker walked along like they had somewhere to be and were merely passing through for something.

When they turned the corner on the path that put them out of view of the town, they both turned toward the woods to one side.

As they wandered through the growth of bushes and grass, Ryker made sure to go first. It'd give Rick a chance to walk in the trampled path.

"Can you hold me?" Rick asked.

"Uh… yeah, sure, fine," Ryker said. Turning around, he picked up Rick and held him awkwardly. After moving the child around for a few seconds, Ryker finally found a spot that worked.

"Thanks. Those bushes hurt," Rick said, one arm clutched around Ryker's shoulders.

"Uh huh," Ryker mumbled, walking forward again.

He could see the clearing they'd camped out in before he saw the girls.

"Hey, it's us," Ryker said aloud, making sure they knew it wasn't someone who didn't belong. "Coming in."

When Ryker stepped into the clearing, he was surprised to find something had changed.

A corpse was off to one side, and Adele stood in the middle of the clearing. Off to the other side, Diane and Lauren were getting to their feet. They had been huddled together in the brush.

"We had a visitor?" Ryker asked, indicating the corpse. Then he put Rick down and tapped him on the back of the head with a few fingers.

Rick tended to spend his time with Adele when he could. They got along famously.

"Bandit," Adele said, glancing down at Rick, who walked up to her and then hugged her at the middle. "Was alone, I took care of it."

"Nicely done. I don't think I've said recently how appreciative I am of your sword work."

"So, do we think he was scouting or just really alone?" Ryker asked, walking over to the corpse.

"Dunno. Betting on just alone, though. He didn't try to run away, escape, or call out. He just… died," Adele said, patting Rick on the head. "How'd your trip into town go?"

"They're looking for you!" Rick said. "Pictures of you three are everywhere. Everywhere! It doesn't really look that much like you, but it kinda does, too."

"Yes, I've seen them," Adele murmured. "Suppose that makes it impossible for us to wander into town, doesn't it?"

"Not without murdering all the soldiers first," Ryker said, searching the dead man for coins, valuables, or anything of use.

Adele didn't seem to have a head for checking corpses for loot. She could take a life easily enough, but robbing them seemed to be crossing a line for her.

Sure enough, Ryker found a small bag with a good many coins in it. Two daggers, and a few bits and ends of things. There was no pack, though, nor a horse.

Either he ditched it, left it with others, or had been robbed himself before this and hadn't replaced it yet.

"Could we do that?" Diane asked. Her tone sounded curious.

"What, kill them all?" Ryker asked. "Probably. The problem becomes whether we can get them all before they escape, run, or call for help.

"And if we do, how do we guarantee the residents won't go running for help? The citizens could be just as much a problem as the soldiers, really. Especially for the bounty."

Sighing, Ryker gave up on finding anything else that might be useful on the body. He stood up and walked over to Lauren and Diane. Adele was talking quietly with Rick, a smile on her face.

"Ryker—the soldiers, do they go back to their garrison house at night?" Lauren asked. "My soldiers often complained about having to go back into their garrisons at night due to the populace being questionable. I would often hear about it when discussing housing."

"Huh, now that I think about it, I didn't ask. Probably?" Ryker said. "They'd be just as nervous about the citizens as we would, really. If not more. They probably do all gather in their garrison house at night."

"Did you see their garrison?" Diane asked.

Frowning, Ryker had to think on it. He was also mildly annoyed.

Diane and Lauren worked too well together. They often seemed to build on one another's questions, concerns, and thoughts. Till it led to a larger one that they shared. It was frustrating at times to get it from both of them.

"Hey, Rick, did we see the garrison house?" Ryker asked.

"Yes, we did. It was at the end of the street and outside of town, technically. It looked like a stable that was converted," Rick said, turning partially away from Adele.

"There ya go," Ryker said, hooking a thumb toward Rick. "The child, not-child has the answer."

Lauren quirked a brow at that, but she didn't respond. Clearly she had the same reservations he did.

Diane merely gave him a smile, which meant that not only did Lauren share his reservations, she'd already talked to Diane about it.

"You two need to... not... be the same person. You're not sleeping together, are you?" Ryker asked.

Diane's eyebrows shot up at that, and Lauren looked shocked.

"What. You two are like... the gruesome twosome now. You're practically joined at the hip and you seem to be more like sisters," Ryker said, making a flippant hand gesture at them.

"Hm," Diane said, looking at Lauren, who in turn was looking at her. Then they both turned to Ryker at the same.

"And?" they said in unison.

"Anyways," Ryker said, feeling his mood turning sour. "Why? What about their garrison?"

"Could you kill them all? Make it look like an accident?" Diane asked.

"Without using that previous resource we discussed. I don't want that to ever be used again," Lauren added quickly.

Diane looked lost for a brief second.

Didn't share that with her, huh? Odd.

"Maybe? I dunno. Really depends on the garrison, I guess, and what I can make happen," Ryker said, frowning, lost in thought. "Tell you what, let's sleep for the rest of the day, then go take a look at the stable-garrison-thing tonight. Alright?"

Lauren thought on that, then nodded her head with a smile.

"Prudent. We'll do that, and go from there," she said.

Diane seemed pleased with the choice as well.

"In other news, Rick wasn't kidding. They really are looking pretty hard for you three. There were enough posters I could have made a house out of them," Ryker said. "And as Rick pointed out to me, that's surprising. Considering how far out of the way this place is."

"Yes, that's... concerning. It also makes me wary that we're perhaps being tracked as well," Diane said. "All we can do is what we have been, though. And that's... it."

It was true. Whether they'd been tracked or not, it wasn't as if it would change their destination, mode of travel, or choices.

Except maybe 'run faster' I guess.

***

The five of them were hiding in a low and short gully nearby the garrison.

"They all rode in, and... went to sleep," Adele said. "I don't see anyone on guard duty... watch, or... or anything."

Listening to Adele speak was interesting as of late. She often paused when she considered what to say around Rick. She was actively curbing her vocabulary of curse words.

It was amazing to see.

She'd even stopped picking her nose. Or at least when Rick was around.

Ryker was looking up at the chimney of the place. Smoke was coming out of it, and it looked as if it was in full use.

"I could probably drop an air-tight shield around the house, then stuff the chimney shut on airflow," Ryker said. "If it doesn't burn as well, it should suffocate them. Would probably look like an accident. Would need to go in and see if I can't damage the chimney afterward, though. Might help."

Turning his attention to Lauren, he waited.

"How… do you know this?" she asked, her tone curious but with a hint of accusation.

"Because lighting a fire in a dungeon can be a death sentence if it's too enclosed, doesn't have enough oxygen to burn correctly, or if the smoke doesn't have somewhere to go," Ryker said. "Being a dungeon diver is a career. There were many lessons taught, and I took them all in my course study."

Shrugging, Ryker looked back to the stable. "It didn't do me much good, but it's all still there.

"Actually, I take that back. It's been helpful in killing people."

Lauren blew out a breath.

"Do it then. Let's see if we can get them in one swoop. Maybe I can have a bath and a hot meal tomorrow morning. And if we're real lucky, beds," Lauren said. "I'm not opposed to continuing as we have been, but I wouldn't say no to some simple luxuries."

Diane nodded her head the entire time Lauren talked. Not that it was surprising to Ryker. He figured those two would have a rougher time than him or Adele.

Shrugging, Ryker built a large pattern of air. He solidified it, dumped a mana feeder on it, and then hardened the whole thing.

Stopping once he'd built the base of the pattern, Ryker held it out in front of him. Several seconds passed before he realized he was literally waiting for Shirley to finish it off and activate it.

Damn.

Grimacing, Ryker began filling in the activator for the pattern. He had it at the exact height of the chimney.

They'd suffocate due to a lack of air, or the fire not burning right. Either way, they'd be dead with similar symptoms.

"Why'd you stop in the middle?" Rick asked once Ryker had activated the spell.

"What?" Ryker asked, ignoring the question.

"You stopped. You made half the pattern and stopped," Rick said.

"You can see his spells?" Diane asked.

"Yes. They're very good. Precise, made in squares, and very efficient. Daddy would be a little jealous, I think," Rick said. "But he stopped. Right in the middle, and waited."

Ryker didn't answer him. He really didn't want to explain he was in a mage-duo with Shirley.

"Oh! You have a mage-partner," Rick said, as if reading his mind. "Who is it?"

"Mage-partner?" Adele asked.

"Yes, a mage-partner. He's bound himself to another with their magic. He sacrificed some of his power and casting time when he's not with them, but when he is, everything is much more powerful and very quick," Rick said.

"And how do you know all that, hm? Child that isn't a child?" Ryker asked.

"Daddy taught me," Rick said.

"Is it Shirley?" Diane asked.

"Yeah," Ryker said, not wanting to lie to her. "It just… happened."

"Before or after the coupling?" Lauren asked him.

Off to the side, Ryker could see Adele looking uncomfortable.

"Before," Ryker said, then got up and walked to the stables. He wasn't going to be able to tell if they were dead from here.

And he really didn't like talking about the strange pit in his stomach he felt without Shirley.

Mage-partner, huh? I mean… it does explain a few things.

I wonder if she's missing me, too.

***

When dawn came, Ryker led everyone into town and straight to the inn. They'd gone early enough that no one was on the street, but the innkeeper was open and ready for travelers.

"Hello," said the older man behind the counter. "You stayin' the night or just here for a meal?"

"Staying the night, but also meals, baths, soap, and a laundry tub," Lauren said. There would be no compromising with her this time.

To be fair, Ryker was looking forward to it as well.

Lauren and the innkeeper haggled briefly on a price. Ryker watched the clientele carefully for any clues about who and what they were.

Inns were great places for spies to gather information. The simple reality was most people needed to stay somewhere. And if you didn't live in the town, you ended up at the inn.

The soft clink of coins being exchanged for a key brought Ryker's head around again.

"Up the stairs, last on the left," said the man. "Bath is the one at the end on the right. Water will be up shortly. Tubs for washing your clothes and breakfast as well."

"Thank you kindly," Lauren said with a bright smile.

Everyone gathered themselves again and began tramping up the stairs and then down the hall.

Lauren handed a key off to Adele as she passed, Rick in tow. Diane followed Adele without a word. Lauren looked at the door she was in front of, put the key in and turned the lock.

She walked inside and then turned, holding the door open for him.

Hm.

Walking in, he looked around the room. There was only a single bed instead of two.

Lauren shut the door behind him.

"As you can see, I have designs on you this evening," Lauren said, one hand pressing to the middle of Ryker's back and guiding him into the room. "If the worst happens on our trip... I'm going to at least make sure I meet that end having known my husband."

"I see," Ryker said, looking at her with a grin. They'd already had a go in the bond space, but apparently she didn't think that one counted. "Still need a condom here, you realize."

"I do. And I don't care. I'll leave it to the fates. And that other time was only practice. Tonight, it's time for the real thing. Well, after we bathe and eat," Lauren said. "There's no way I'm dirtying our bed right now. We're filthy and we reek. After we've taken care of ourselves and our clothes, then you can... well... get me dirty again."

Hm. Can't argue with the logic, so why bother?

"And tomorrow morning, we'll buy more supplies and get out of town with the sun. It'll be unfortunate to head right back into the wilds and get dirty all over again, but... it'll still be nice to be clean for half a day," Lauren said. "Now, how about we go investigate that bath. You'll be taking one with me, and we'll be washing one another."

Lauren looked excited, and Ryker suddenly felt that way too.

It was hard not to.

- 162 -

Chapter 30 - Rabbit -

Ryker closed the door behind him and looked around the interior. Lauren, Adele, and Diane were all sitting on the two beds. Rick was in the corner playing with something by himself.

Surprisingly, even his and Lauren's packs were off to one side.

I wonder when she got those.

He briefly considered where to sit rather than let the paranoid thought take root. In the end, simple numbers and symmetry decided for him.

Walking over, he sat next to Diane since she was sitting alone.

"Sleep well?" she asked, giving him a small smile. Her eyes picked over him quickly as if ensuring that he was well, then returned to his face.

Glancing over to Adele and Lauren, Ryker found them engaged in a quiet conversation that seemed full of smiles.

"I did, it was very entertaining. Thank you for making it happen, Diane," Ryker said. As subtly as he could, he moved in for a quick kiss. "Remind me to show my appreciation to you later. I'm sure that was more your idea than anyone else's."

"It was. And of course, I'll always support you," Diane said, watching him, her smile growing wider. "What kind of wife would I be if I didn't make sure to keep everyone's fences mended?"

"Considering how messed up our marriage is, probably a normal one," Ryker muttered. "I mean, I can't imagine this was what you really wanted."

"It's not so bad, considering all the options I could have been forced to pick from," Diane said with a shooing motion of her left hand. "It's enjoyable having Lauren and Adele around and on my team, so to speak. I also quite enjoyed talking with Marybelle. Now, let's turn this over to the real discussion at hand. Shall we?"

Diane turned her eyes from him and looked toward Adele and Lauren.

As if sensing the other woman had decided it was time to begin talking, Lauren ended her discussion with Adele and looked at Diane.

Way, way, way too close between those two.

"I had several supplies and things arranged for us last night," Diane said by way of starting the conversation. "Our packs will be quite full, but I'm afraid our coin is spent."

"Ah, that's fine. So long as we can get to Dungeon, all will be well," Lauren said, nodding. "Did you happen to hear anything? Did they say anything?"

"Actually, it was almost harder for them to not talk about it," Diane said, her face turning a bit sour at her own words. "The rightful queen and her ladies in waiting are on the run, supposedly straight toward the count of Dungeon, her last faithful retainer and husband."

Everyone seemed rather amused by that description.

"First and foremost, the Dark Lord of the North hasn't done anything. His armies grow and grow, and skirmishes continue, but no true battle has happened. Or so everyone is saying. There's no telling what's changed since news made it through Dungeon last," Diane said.

It was true. News would be much slower now that it all had to travel through Dungeon. The walls would do a significant job of funneling everything.

That does leave a sea landing open, though. I suppose ferrying troops in the end might be easier than trying to run Dungeon.

Need to keep that in mind.

"The Church of Light apparently has landed a force on this side of Dungeon as well, though greatly reduced. Their Trevalian allies also seemed to have gotten a force across.

"The dark church, though suffering a loss of leadership, has moved out to engage the church of light," Diane continued. "Everyone is moving toward Dungeon for what might very well be the final battle between the churches for the Queensland of Dale."

Lauren took in a quick breath, then let it out slowly.

"Okay, that's nothing unexpected, I suppose. I wonder what their numbers are," Lauren mused. "In the end, the dark church only had about sixty thousand soldiers ready for combat. My own troops numbered only thirty thousand. Veronica was also lacking in troops, though. It was the church who destroyed me in the end, and Veronica had nothing to do with it. I can't imagine she's having a much better go of it then I am."

Diane sighed, looking tired and emotionally drained.

"I do love my mother, because she's my mother," she said. "I can only wonder where she is and what she's doing because there's been no word of her. At all. I fear the worst may have befallen my family. Which means I may have to scoop together what I can of them when this is over."

"We'll do that together," Lauren said, waving a hand at the other woman.

"I know. I know," Diane said, then looked to Ryker. "Any idea on the numbers of the enemy?"

Ryker shrugged at the question. "The church of light were losing about eight out of every ten to the dungeon. If they made it through with any numbers, it'd be by sacrificing a massive portion of their force.

"Even if they followed through with rushing the dungeon, Robyn, Shirley, Marybelle, Tris, Charlotte, and Wynne were ready for it. They were going to grind them to absolute bits for every inch of ground they wanted."

"That was before you ended up here, though," Lauren said. "Would they continue to fight as hard with you... essentially... dead?"

Frowning, Ryker thought on that. He could still feel Wynne, Marybelle, Tris, and Charlotte with his soul. It was muted and still, but he could feel them. He was sure they could feel him in the same way.

"It's hard to explain, but my connection to the Fairies is on a level that isn't physical," Ryker said. "I can still feel them right now. And I'm sure they can feel me. So they're aware I'm alive, just not where I am or what's going on."

The three women around him nodded, though Adele had a frown on her pretty face.

"Then we'll assume they carried on as they were. Although," Lauren said, pausing mid-sentence.

"It doesn't solve the problem that everyone is rushing toward Dungeon," Diane finished. "The question becomes... how do we get through? And if we're not there before the armies arrive, how long could we end up having to wait? Hiding?"

"Yes, exactly," Lauren said.

"If we can get to Dungeon's wall, any of it, we might be able to contact Tris or Charlotte," Ryker said. "If they're monitoring it. They might have pulled in all the spawns and contact points to conserve mana to hit the church."

"That could work," Lauren said. She looked thoughtful, as if considering something related to that.

"Though it'd also be the quickest way to get caught," Diane said. "There'd be little to no room to maneuver if we were pressed up to a wall."

"That's very true," Ryker said. "I suppose the simple answer is I go on foot to the wall when we get close enough and test it. That way it's just me if there's a problem."

"I don't like that," Adele said, her arms folded across her chest.

There was a commotion from downstairs, and also in the room next door. The room Lauren and Ryker had stayed in. There was a crash, followed by stomping boots.

Ryker immediately got up and shoved a dresser in front of the door. Moving quickly to the window, he looked outside. There was no one out behind the inn.

With any luck, they'd have a few minutes.

"Come on, out the window, quick. I'll catch everyone," Ryker said.

Grabbing two packs, he opened the window and then stepped out onto the roof. Moving to the edge, he walked right off, cushioning his fall with a pattern of thickened air.

When he reached the bottom, he dropped the packs to one side and looked back up to the roof.

Adele was carrying a pack and hopped down from the roof, not hesitating in the least.

Shifting the pattern over, Ryker caught her easily. Scooting off the invisible pad, Adele stumbled to one side and then grabbed the two packs. She started off at a jog, headed for the trees out behind the inn.

Diane came next with a pack on her shoulder. She looked off the edge of the roof, then at Ryker, and then hopped off. Her eyes were closed tight, her face screwed up in fear.

But she apparently believed in Ryker enough to jump.

Catching her easily, Ryker tilted the pad a bit to help her slide off.

"Follow Adele," he said, looking back up.

Lauren stepped to the edge of the roof. Perched on her hip was Rick. Her eyes found Ryker and then she walked straight toward him off the roof.

After catching her with the pattern, Ryker didn't wait for her to get off. Instead he slipped some of the pattern around her waist and held her tight to it. Then he set off at a quick pace to catch up to Diane and Adele.

They all ducked into the bushes and squatted down low. Canceling the pattern, Lauren landed on her feet, Rick still in her arms.

"How'd they find us?" Lauren asked. "I was so sure no one recognized us."

Ryker didn't know, nor did he want to guess. He had no way of knowing one way or the other.

"They have a magical tracker who uses a spell he made with them," Rick said. "He's following Lauren. Since her army never formally surrendered, her nation never capitulated, and there are retainers who still support her, she's the lawful queen."

Uh huh. And how do you know all that, child who isn't a child?

"We split up then," Ryker said, turning to the others. "Adele, Rick, and Diane, you're going to go off by yourselves. I think between the three of you, you should be able to make it back to Dungeon without a problem.

"I'll take Lauren, and we'll do the same but take a longer path. Going to run them through the wilds and see if they can keep up."

"Got it. I don't like it, but if you're sure," Adele said, leaving the end of it hanging.

"I'm sure we don't have much in the way of choices," Ryker said. "But I'm open to any other ideas in the next… ten seconds."

Everyone looked at Ryker, looked around, and then looked at the ground.

No one wanted to say they didn't have another idea. Nor did they want to split up and leave Lauren to her fate with Ryker.

"Alright, get going. We're going to go back the way we came and loop around the far side of the village," Ryker said.

Grabbing the two packs he'd taken earlier, he tossed them at Lauren. Two packs were left for Adele, Diane, and Rick.

"Ooh! What are—" Lauren started.

Ryker enfolded her in a pattern of thick air, restrained her and the packs with it, and then started off at a sprint.

His body—his magically created avatar body—was fit. Very fit.

It was far and above what he'd been athletically able to do previously. Not to mention his mana well was massive in comparison.

This body was, for all intents and purposes, a perfect version of himself.

Need to thank Benni.

This all meant carrying Lauren with a spell would be faster than waiting on her.

Sprinting through the brush and trees, Ryker pushed himself.

He stopped beside the road for several seconds and looked to one side, then the other. Seeing no one, he sprinted across the road bed.

"Ryker, I don't like this," Lauren said. She had gotten as comfortable as she could on the tethered mattress of air that followed him.

"Yeah, well, too bad," Ryker hissed. "I'm not about to lose you now just because I wasn't willing to spend some effort to get you out of harm's way."

"Ryker... I could easily just go turn m—"

"You're an idiot, Lauren. And if you finish that sentence, or try to, there will be hell to pay," Ryker growled. Dodging low under a tree branch, he took them into the woods. Most of the Queensland of Dale was forested. Plains had to be carved out rather than simply existing.

"Hell, hm?" Lauren asked.

"Yeah, like not sleeping with you for months," Ryker said.

"Oh. That's a credible threat," Lauren mused. "Last night was delightful and messy at the same time. You even let me lead and humored some of my... curiosities."

"Idiot. Shut up, don't distract me," Ryker grumbled, hopping over a small ditch.

"I love you," Lauren murmured softly. He wasn't sure if he was meant to hear it, but he had.

***

Ryker was stooped low to the ground. His hands were on his knees, and he was sucking in heaving breaths.

His legs trembled every now and then, but he didn't feel terrible either.

Best of all, he felt no mana exhaustion. Decent food, lots of water, and rest had given him the maximum amount of mana possible for his pool.

Kinda wish I had found Tar. Then I'd be even stronger.

I hope... he's ok.

"Are you alright?" Lauren asked.

Looking over to her, he gave her a smile. She was crouched low in the mattress of air. Small bits of foliage stuck to her, but she didn't seem concerned about it.

He knew he'd dragged her through some large ugly swaths of nature, but she'd said not a word about it.

"Yeah, just tired. We'll get moving again shortly," Ryker said, then stood up.

"You've been running for hours, Ryker," Lauren said. Then she reached behind herself as if to push off the mattress.

Disconnecting the bit of the pattern that held her down, Ryker watched as she slithered out of the spell.

Brushing herself off quickly, she came over to him. She laid a cool hand to his brow and the back of his neck.

"Goodness. You're drenched in sweat. Can I get you some water? Something to snack on?" Lauren asked. She pulled a handkerchief from a pocket and began dabbing at his brow and temples with it.

She's a tender thing when she isn't acting the queenly part.

"You did well, you know," Ryker said.

"Mmm?" Lauren hummed, concentrating on her task of tending to him.

"You did well. You were dealing with an ally who had more soldiers than you did, an enemy who wanted to see you crushed, and a religious war kicking off in your front yard," Ryker said. "All throughout, the populace supported you. You did well, all things considered."

"I was incompetent; I needed to be saved," Lauren said, her tone dry. Reaching up, she undid several of the buttons on Ryker's tunic and continued to wipe him down.

"You needed to be saved, sure. But you weren't incompetent. Not at all. You just had more problems than you could reasonably handle, given your circumstances," Ryker said. "Only a fool would call you such a thing."

Lauren didn't respond. Instead she went to the packs. Pulling out a small canteen and dried jerky, she came back to him.

"Eat. If you're going to continue to carry me like this, the least I can do is make sure you're taking care of yourself," Lauren said.

"Going housewife on me already?" Ryker asked with a smirk, taking the proffered items. "Thank you."

"I think I'd be a good housewife, thank you," Lauren said, laying one hand in another.

"Uh huh. Do you even know how to wash clothes?" Ryker asked. Unstopping the canteen, he quickly began to take gulps from it.

"I… suppose I don't at that. I can't cook, I can't clean, I can't mend clothes or sew. I don't know how to use a spinning wheel or a loom. Now that I think about it, I'm not sure what I could actually do as a housewife," Lauren said, frowning. "Incompe—"

Ryker lifted his head up as she started saying that word again, and he made an uncomfortable amount of eye contact. So much that she stopped talking.

"Right. Well, I was good at… that… last night," Lauren said, a small smile on her lips as she lifted her chin up.

Nodding his head, Ryker couldn't disagree.

"Wouldn't worry much about the rest of it. I learned how to be a farmer in no time at all just by doing it," Ryker said. "Anything can be learned. It just takes time."

"Then I thank you in advance for being patient with me," Lauren said, taking the canteen from him after he re-stoppered it.

"Honestly, I wouldn't worry about it. I plan on putting you back on your throne soon enough," Ryker said. "It'll be sad to see you move back to the capital when I'm done, though. It's been rather nice spending so much time with you."

"Likewise. I honestly feel like… well it'll sound strange saying it aloud, but you're not just my husband and lover. You're somewhat my best friend," Lauren said, packing away the canteen again. "I feel like we can talk about anything. Do anything. It wouldn't matter."

"I mean, I really don't want to see you picking your nose like Adele, but I wouldn't kick you out of bed for doing it either. Little would honestly bother me after those days in the throne room," Ryker said. Finishing off the jerky, he sighed and stretched out his back. "We need to keep going, I think. I have no idea how far back they are, how good at tracking they are, or if they'll even stop for the night."

"Yes, those are all fair concerns. And who knows… maybe I want to test how dirty I can get before you do kick me out of bed," Lauren said. Moving over to where the packs floated in midair, she reached out for the mattress.

Stretching one way and then the other, Ryker got ready to start running again. His goal was to get through these woods and up to a ridge ahead of them. It would mean a point he could wait at the top of once they climbed it.

It would take several hours to do so, if not more. But once he did, he could wait there and see if anyone was behind them.

It was a chance to confirm whether they were still being chased. With any luck, Ryker was hoping his extreme flight and speed had broken the trail outright.

Add him some magical traps, spells, and roadblocks, and they might spend a day or two climbing the ridge. Or just maybe die.

That'd be great. If they just died. I think I'd prefer that, actually.

"I'm ready," Lauren said, scooting around on the air spell. "This is rather comfortable. Is there any possibility of sleeping on it tonight?"

"Definitely," Ryker said. Grabbing the pattern, he locked it around her hips and shoulders again.

After a final check, and getting a tired smile from Lauren, Ryker set off at a run again.

Hours later, just as the sun began to set, they'd cleared the ridge. From that point on, Ryker had been staring down the side of the cliff toward where their trail went up.

If someone was following them, they'd have to start right there.

And with the number of traps and tricks I left behind, there's no way they'll be getting past them without some work. Magical or otherwise.

"Come' on, Ryker," Lauren said from behind him. "I managed to actually get a fire going, and I even cooked some of that meat Diane bought. I think I did a fair job of it; it isn't too blackened."

Too blackened? Oh heavens.

Laughing to himself, Ryker turned away from the cliff side. No one would get through there without setting off magical traps. And each one of those was tied to an alert that would notify Ryker.

Lauren was leaning over her cook fire, meat skewers coming away. Turning, she offered him one with a smile.

Looking at the meat, he found it wasn't blackened at all. In fact, it looked rather well-cooked.

"You're a funny girl, huh?" Ryker asked.

"As I said before, I have to keep you coming back for more somehow," Lauren said. "Do be a dear and make sure that air mattress is visible tonight. I'd hate for us to roll off of it right in the middle."

In the middle?

Oh. In the middle.

Yes.

Chapter 31 - Can't Stop Won't Stop -

Ryker sat bolt upright in the air mattress spell. Looking around himself, he tried to figure out what time it was. Best he could figure, it was early in the morning. Pre-dawn, in fact, with just a bare tinge of light in the distance.

What had brought him from his sleep was a magical thread attached to his mana pool.

It'd been snapped.

One of his spells had just triggered that he'd set up in the ridge.

Which meant the enemy had been moving perhaps the entire night. They hadn't stopped for anything.

How the fuck did they manage that?

With a groan, Lauren's hand fumbled at Ryker's middle. It'd been on his chest moments before. Pulling her arm away from him, Lauren curled into herself, clearly not wanting to wake up just yet.

They'd been up a bit later then he'd expected. Talking mostly, followed by intense coupling, and only then going to sleep.

Kinda glad we got dressed and made everything ready after our fun. Just in case.

Grabbing her by the shoulder, Ryker gave her a firm shake until she opened her eyes. He put a hand in front of his mouth, a single finger raised in front of his lips. Then he slid off the mattress and went over to the edge of the ridge.

He wasn't sure where they were, but he was hoping it was the start of their group and not the back end of it. Otherwise his traps and spells had failed him utterly.

He knew the spell that had activated had been on the first turn up the ridge. He'd buried the thing behind a boulder. It wasn't directly in the path and would only activate if someone touched it.

Considering that both he and Lauren had practically been forced to hump it to get around it, he'd figured it'd be a great spot for a lethal spell.

Getting down on his stomach to decrease the amount of weight he had at the edge, Ryker eased himself forward until he could peek over.

Far below, he could see blue magical swirls zipping and swirling about. Ryker couldn't be sure at this distance, but it looked a lot like priest magic.

"They must be trying to save whoever it is. That's a lot of magic for one person, though," Lauren said. She'd apparently snuck up into the spot beside him and was now looking down at the same thing he was.

"Might be the tracker," Ryker said. "That'd be lovely. Wouldn't it?"

"Why can't we hear anything?" Lauren asked.

"Dunno. Sound travels oddly," Ryker said. "I've spent too much time playing with echoes and small lightning bolts.

"Anyways, there we are. We're being followed."

Ryker tried to do a head count and ended up failing. They were too close to one another, and the light too poor. Not to mention the wild spray of magic in every direction was making it all the more difficult.

"Time to go," Lauren said, scooting away from the edge.

Time to go indeed, but where? How do I shake a magical tracker that's locked on Lauren? No matter where I go, they'll follow.

Or is that the answer?

No matter where I go, they will follow.

With a nod of his head, Ryker had come up with a plan. It'd work for now. He knew where the enemy was going, knew where they had to be. Which meant he controlled the battlefield.

Ryker started to get up, and hesitated.

Lifting his hand up, he began building a massive pattern out above the ridge. One of fire. Fire with a self-filling element.

Something he'd warned Shirley not to do.

Taking a single precaution, Ryker set a timer into the pattern. Instead of eternally looping, the pattern lost a counter each time it looped. He had no idea how long each loop would take, but he set it for six hundred loops.

Activating it, he wiggled away from the edge of the ridge.

A massive curtain of fire appeared in the air, then dropped away down the ridge. The roar and crackle of the magically fed fire was loud in his ears.

I sincerely hope that works. That I didn't just create a permanent ridge of fire.

Getting to his feet, Ryker jogged over to Lauren.

The queen of Dale shoved their belongings up onto the air mattress, and then she got up into it herself.

"Come here, hon," Lauren said, waving a hand at him.

Frowning at the sudden nickname, Ryker came over to her instead of simply yanking the mattress along. Locking Lauren against the mattress, he came to a stop in front of her.

"Here," Lauren said, pressing a roll of bread that'd been stuffed with cheese and jerky into his hand. "Eat that either as you go or right now. I have your canteen out and ready, so if you get thirsty, just drop back and I'll take care of it. Alright?"

Grinning, Ryker raised his brows at the queen.

"What? It's something I can do to help," she said. "So I'm going to do it. Also, you should try to time it so there's a period where I walk on my own and you recharge your mana."

Leaning in, Ryker kissed the serious-looking queen. Several seconds passed before he pulled away.

"Thank you. All things considered, you're doing very well," Ryker said.

Lauren gave him a crooked grin and patted his shoulder.

"As I've said before, I have to do what I can. Not only to keep you on the hook, but because you're keeping me safe," Lauren said. She spun him around and then slapped him on the ass. "Now get going, hon, or start eating."

Chuckling, and forgetting the stress they were under, Ryker set off at a jog. Behind him, the mattress of air floated along with Lauren playing the role of their storage keeper.

After eating quickly, Ryker kept his eyes open.

The land changed around them after some time passed as they slowly transitioned out of the lightly wooded area that had been atop the ridge.

When they came out onto a plain, Ryker stopped and looked around.

"I have no idea where we are anymore," he said. "I know we generally need to head southeast, but that's about it."

"Here," Lauren said, the pattern of air coming to rest beside him.

He looked over and found a canteen in her hands. Taking it eagerly, he began to drink.

"As far as where to go, as you said, southeast. There isn't much more that can be said about it. I know Diane and Adele will likely head eastward, then south. With Rick in their party, and me not with them, they're far more likely to escape notice," Lauren said. "They'll just stay out of the cities and towns while moving during the night, probably, and still beat us there. They can take a straighter path."

Hm. Wish we could do that. It feels like it's getting harder rather than easier the further we get from the capital.

Blowing out a breath as he stopped drinking, Ryker stoppered the canteen.

Before he could even try to hand it back, Lauren had smoothly taken it from his hands and tucked it away. She replaced it with a small handful of what looked like blueberries.

"I found those last night. I thought they'd make a nice snack at your first break," she said. "You've been running for a few hours already, hon."

I have? And she's really pushing the nickname.

Ryker frowned, and thought back. It didn't feel like that long, but if he tracked it back in his mind, it probably had been.

Ryker took the berries from her hand and literally stuffed them all in his mouth.

Lauren wrinkled her nose at that but gave him a smile as well. "Can I get you anything else?"

"No," Ryker said, chewing. He was suddenly infinitely grateful to her. The berries were delicious and honestly, just what he needed. "Going to try and lay traps as we go, so we might slow down a bit."

From where they were, he could see what looked like a sunken forest off to one side that led into lowlands. With any luck, he could set up some kill points there.

"I want to head over into that," Ryker said, pointing.

"Ah... I take it this is where we're going to drag them into and force them through some traps?" Lauren asked.

"Yeah, something like that."

"So in other words, treat it like a dungeon. They have to get to the end — me. So we litter the path with problems they have to engage in if they want the reward," Lauren said.

Ryker blinked, unable to disagree with that. It was accurate. He nodded at Lauren.

"That's about right, sweetie," Ryker said, hitting the word hard with a smile.

Grinning, Lauren shook her head and then patted her thighs.

"Let me down then, hon," she said. "I'll walk for a time while you lay traps. Is there any way you can attach the air spell to me instead?"

Ryker couldn't argue her point. He disconnected the harness around her and then tied it to her instead.

Turning, he started moving across the plain quickly. This was an open bit of land they'd be spotted in and he wanted to get out of it fast.

Glancing over his shoulder, he made sure to keep a pace it seemed Lauren could match. She'd never say a word even if she couldn't keep up, her ankles fell apart, and her lungs exploded.

Which meant he had to watch her carefully. Watch her and plan for her inevitable collapse because she wasn't taking care to pace herself.

There was no way she was going to be able to match him in this avatar body. It was the pinnacle of health in almost every way. Benni had spent a lot of time on it for him and had clearly invested many hours in the body.

Lauren gave him a fleeting smile when his eyes met hers, but she looked to be doing fine.

Moving a little faster, Ryker decided he wanted to get ahead and figure out if he could put in a trap just before they entered the sunken wood. They'd expect it on entering the wood, not just before it.

When he reached a drop-off point that led into what was indeed a much lower ravine filled with trees, Ryker searched the area for a way down.

By the time Lauren caught up with him, he'd figured out the best location to put something in as well as get down.

Panting hard, Lauren walked up to him.

"I need to — exercise more," Lauren said between gasps.

"Queens shouldn't have to," Ryker muttered. Turning, he scooped up Lauren in his arms and stepped off the drop. Lauren squeaked, her arms locking up tight around him.

Falling six feet, he landed on a cushion of air and stepped off it.

"Warn me next time," Lauren said, smacking his shoulder lightly. "Treat your wife with more kindness. Or I'll not treat you with kindness tonight."

Snickering, Ryker kissed her once and then set her down.

"Sorry, I needed to get down quick and get us out of sight. Go ahead and move a bit away — and pick a narrow path for the one you take. They're tracking you, not me," Ryker said, turning around. Moving to the jump-off point, he saw exactly where others would land.

Ryker scooped away the earth for ten feet all around the drop point. Even if someone climbed down, they'd still hit the same pit.

With a soft pop, the ground vanished. He had no idea where he sent it, and he didn't even want to consider it right now.

Looking down into the pit, Ryker began fashioning solid stone spears that came up from the bottom. Using a lesson from Marybelle, he got the pattern right and then duplicated it, then duplicated the two of them, and then the four.

In under thirty seconds, the pit was filled with spikes.

As finely as he could manage, he covered the entirety of the pit with thread-thin snippets of air spells. He tied them off as short as he could to prevent someone from noticing them. As minutely as possible, he also put in a single trip-wire spell on the air spells. If any of them broke, it'd break his trip-wire.

Thickening them slightly, he began to grab leaves with a spell of force from behind him.

He dumped leaves all over the air spells and watched as the whole pit was covered easily. There was no way to see it from above.

Judging it as good, Ryker left it like that. He didn't have more time to spend on it.

He found Lauren not far away, standing between two large tree trunks. It was a game trail, and everywhere around it looked to be thick, dense bush.

Perfect.

"You're a beautiful and smart woman, Lauren," Ryker said, running up to her.

"Not now, hon. Flatter me later when I can show you that flattery works on me," Lauren said, then started moving down the path. She moved twenty feet in, stopped, and turned. She clearly knew what he was doing without needing to be told.

In front of the spot they'd be forced to enter rather than the narrow gap itself, Ryker buried small balls of mana in a thin shell. He disguised the whole thing as just earth magic meant to obscure a trail, and he set them all over.

Anyone who touched one would definitely lose most of their leg or die outright. He couldn't tell. Mana mines tended to have variable force.

After putting them on a hair trigger, Ryker started moving toward Lauren again.

She waited patiently for him and started moving again as soon as he got close enough.

"Would it help if you got on the air spell? Could you float by and make spells if I led it along?" Lauren asked.

"Uh, yeah, that'd work. Good thinking," Ryker said, then hopped up onto it.

Lying flat on his stomach, he looked at the path behind them, leaving the way they were going to Lauren. At the moment, he was feeling immensely appreciative of her.

Ryker began embedding explosive spells, mana mines, trip-wires, and some simple spells wherever he could behind them.

They were all built to only last for three days at most, then fade from existence after that. All the spells were made to be one-off use with a limited time frame.

Time passed as they moved through the dense growth of the game trail. There were several times where Lauren dragged them through a mass of growth, seemingly unwilling to deviate from their southeastern direction.

After what felt like a few hours, she came to a stop.

Turning around, Ryker looked at her and found her bent over at the waist. She was huffing and puffing, her face a red mask of sweat and exertion.

While she hadn't jogged the whole way through, she'd never stopped. Even if it was just at a walk, she'd kept them going.

Looking beyond the spent queen, Ryker saw a massive cliff face rising up above them.

Yep, nope. Not going to be able to get up that without a solid spell-working.

"Come over here, sweetie," Ryker said, patting the invisible air mattress.

"Flattered," Lauren said, waving her hand at him. "Too tired."

She stood up and stumbled over to him, panting the whole time.

Laughing softly at her comment, Ryker moved the packs around.

"Come on, my valiant queen, come take a lie down. I'll get us up the cliff then take over, alright?" Ryker asked.

"Sure thing, hon," Lauren said, then collapsed into the air spell. Lying there unmoving, she huffed and puffed. Her eyes were open, though. She was watching him.

Reaching over, he gently moved her hair back out of her eyes.

"Very impressive, sweetie," Ryker said. "I'll never doubt you in anything."

"Better not," Lauren grumbled.

After strapping the exhausted queen into the spell, Ryker put a new spell of air behind the mattress and angled it low. Activating it, he shot them straight up into the air with a single blast of magic.

They soared through the air, going up and up. When they passed the cliff face, Ryker cut the feed to the spell and shot a gentle puff of air backward.

After moving over the edge of the cliff, they slowly came back down to the ground overlooking the sunken forest.

Feeling like he had more mana to spare than stamina right now, Ryker reactivated the spell that simply pushed out air behind them and leveled it off for the most part.

The air mattress shot forward across the empty field.

It took Ryker a full three minutes to figure out how to steer the damn thing, and another two to feel comfortable enough that he wasn't going to make them crash.

"I'm really not sure what to say about this, but I get the impression we're more or less… flying," Lauren said, her eyes wide, staring in the direction they were going.

"I guess?" Ryker said. "It's more like a boat. But in the air. Airboat."

"Could make a big one? A big air… ship? One that could carry troops or ferry people around?" Lauren asked.

"Uh, probably? It'd take a lot more time and work than I have the ability for right now. Would probably need the dungeon itself for the amount of mana a spell like that would take. Even this is draining me pretty quickly, but we're moving. Moving fast," Ryker said.

They were long past the "sprinting speed" stage and moving more like a horse at a full-on dash now. If not faster.

"This is a little unnerving," Lauren said. "And it makes my eyes water."

With a ping, Ryker felt his pitfall trip activate. Their pursuers had just entered the sunken forest. Which meant they were actually catching up.

"Well, as unnerving as it is, it's better than running, and a lot faster," Ryker said. "On top of that, they just hit the pitfall. I felt the spell give way."

"Oh. Then, yes. This is much preferable to moving on foot. We were perhaps half a day ahead of them, and now it feels like only a few hours," Lauren said.

"They're definitely moving with speed," Ryker muttered. "Rather annoying, to be perfectly honest."

"Do you think they're burning magic to catch up with us?" Lauren asked.

"I would be. So that's not really a question, I suppose. I'm just hopeful this lovely plain continues for a bit longer. The longer we can burn across it, the better," Ryker said. "And the closer to Dungeon we get."

Lauren nodded, then snuggled in close to Ryker and closed her eyes. Her fingers were tight in his tunic. She wasn't hiding her fear at this situation at all.

"I can't watch. It's a bit too much for me," Lauren said.

He couldn't blame her. They were still gaining speed with every second. He'd have to think about how they were going to stop soon enough. Because he really didn't know how to do that.

Chapter 32 - Mercy -

A spell detonated behind them. The sound of the magic ripping through the thin shell that held it together was loud and ominous.

"That's the one you put down thirty minutes ago?" Lauren asked, hustling after Ryker as they ducked and dodged through trees.

"Yeah," Ryker said, not wanting to think on the fact that the trackers had closed in on them this much. It'd only been a single day since they'd climbed out of the sunken forest.

"What do we do?" Lauren asked. She sounded out of breath.

I have no idea how she's carrying on as she is. We've only stopped for a single four-hour rest period.

She can't... continue on like this.

This is the turning point.

Turning around, Ryker helped Lauren up over a massive log that was lodged in the path they were taking.

She stumbled when he put her back down and collapsed on her hands and knees.

"I'm sorry, honey," Lauren muttered, shaking her head. She was taking great heaving breaths. Lifting her head up, she gave him a tired and weary smile. Her eyes were ringed with shadows, and they looked slightly glazed over. "I wish I could do more, but I think I'm spent."

"Yeah, you're done," Ryker grumbled, looking back the way they'd come. Ryker was still Ryker. He'd been somewhat domesticated lately, but his time with Shirley had only reinforced for him how different he and she were compared to most others. Shirley was more like him than he'd ever thought possible.

Then again, that's how wizards regard the world as a whole. Isn't it?

Something to test, experiment with, and then exert control over.

Sighing, Ryker shook out his hands and then pushed one against his neck. It popped satisfyingly.

"Keep going, sweetie," he said, then patted her on the rear end. "I'll catch up with you when I can. No need to rush, but don't lag behind either."

"No, I don't want to. I want to stay and stand with you," Lauren said.

"And die? Get in my way? Become a hostage?" Ryker asked and then sighed. "Lauren, I love you, but you're not useful in this situation. You're far more a nuisance than a help."

"While I can't apologize for saying what I did, I can at least apologize for the hurt I'm sure it's causing."

Sighing, Lauren got to her feet and teetered to one side for a moment.

"At least you recognize it," she said. Then she came over to him and gave him a lingering kiss. After several seconds, she pulled away and patted his shoulder.

That done, she started to walk determinedly away from him.

"We can figure out how to punish you for your words after you catch up. I'm going to keep going and look for a campsite. I'm done," Lauren muttered. "I need sleep."

Ryker smirked at the way she was handling this.

It was a simple reality, though. If Ryker failed in his task, it didn't matter how far Lauren got from here. The mattress of air glided along behind her, their packs floating in midair.

Giving himself a quick check, Ryker found he still had two health potions and his water.

Damn shame that I don't have anything to restore my mana or stamina. We could have gone a lot farther and faster if I had.

Sighing, Ryker looked at the log in the path. It'd be a perfect place to launch an ambush.

Dropping a rather large mana mine right before the log and then a quick pit-spike trap after it, Ryker moved off into the brush on the side of the path. He hunkered down low next to the trunk of a tree while he considered how to do this.

They're moving fast. They might not even see the mana mine or the pit. And if they do, that'd be when to attack.

When they're trying to solve them.

Nodding at his own thoughts, Ryker began to quietly build small spell patterns. They were all simple constructs designed to kill and little else. A simple projectile in almost every element he had access to.

He didn't even bother to disguise the runes. They'd be launched cold. If the mage was good enough to punch a rune out in that little time, Ryker was in a lot more trouble than he'd thought.

Building a chain-lightning spell, Ryker began to sink some extra time and power in it. If he did it right, he might be able to catch whoever came first over the log after the pit was solved, someone on the log, and maybe whoever was behind them.

Ryker didn't think he'd have long to wait. The enemy had been closing their distance on them all day.

Twenty minutes from the point he laid the traps, he could see people jogging quickly down the track toward him.

It was six people, four of whom looked like they were there to assist either the fifth or the sixth.

The fifth was clearly a mage who was using some type of modified spell designed to track.

And the last was a robed individual who could only be their priest.

Are you the reason there's six of you still? Healing everyone even as they're wounded by my traps? You must be exhausted.

Unless you're living potion to potion – then I'm just fucked.

Holding out a hand in front of himself, the mage simply detonated the mana mine. He didn't bother with it at all, really.

No sooner was it gone than one of the soldiers grabbed the log and leapt over the top of it.

Only to fall straight into the pit-spike trap.

The soldier screamed at the top of his lungs from the bottom of the pit.

Scrambling up over the top, two more soldiers dropped down to either side of the log and then began working to get their comrade out of the pit.

The last soldier, the priest, and the mage waited. Apparently, they were so confident they didn't see the need to rush.

Then again, they were constantly closing on us, so… maybe they have the right to be that confident.

Once they'd gotten their fellow out of the pit, the priest stepped up to the top of the log. Ryker saw his chance.

Dropping a chunk of extra mana into the chain-lightning spell, Ryker targeted the closest soldier and flung the spell.

It smashed into the man's chest, zipped to the second, then popped up over the log into the priest and down into the soldier behind them.

Collapsing in a heap, the two soldiers out front lay on the ground twitching and shivering. The man who'd fallen in the spike trap had somehow managed to not get hit by the lightning.

Falling backward, the priest vanished behind the log.

Ryker targeted the three men in front of the log, smashing together his air spell, water spell, and acid spell and dumping them right on top of his enemies. He also put an obscurer over the rune, just to make it harder for the mage to punch it out if he tried.

A dense cloud of green mist immediately dropped over the whole area. Screams and shrieks immediately pierced through it.

Ryker didn't move to further engage, though. He wasn't sure what the enemy would do, and he didn't want to tip his hand further if he didn't have to. So far, it was unlikely they even knew where he was.

If he was really lucky, they might not even know if he was there or if these were traps.

Crouched low and unwilling to act, Ryker waited.

The screaming eventually stopped, and the cloud began to dissipate all on its own. It didn't seem as if the mage had the power to counter the spell, or he simply didn't wish to.

In either case, Ryker was going to hope he'd managed to kill some of them.

Finally, the fog more or less lifted and Ryker could see what was going on.

There were three lumps of little more than meat on the ground in front of the log. Flesh bubbled and oozed off of them, and they seemed more like candles than people. They were also quite clearly dead.

Ryker couldn't see anyone beyond the log anymore, though. And there wasn't a way for them to get off the path. Which meant they were probably hiding in the brush just off to the sides.

It's what I'd do… so… the question becomes… how far do I go?

I could set the whole fucking thing on fire, but… that'd just end up bringing it back to me in the end, wouldn't it?

Or worse.

Frowning, Ryker decided the best course of action was to wait. The narrow path that led through this dense, nasty wooded area was the only way through. He and Lauren had chosen it for that reason to begin with.

It made it so much easier to force their trackers to go through trapped areas if they couldn't go around them.

With as little mana as he could, Ryker set the several spells he had called up in front of him to drain their power from the ambient mana rather than from him. He didn't know how long he'd be sitting here waiting, and he didn't want to slowly bleed out his mana well.

Changing his position, Ryker got into something a bit more comfortable.

I need to make a school that teaches all this shit in Dungeon. Not like the university for wizards, but the dungeon stuff.

It seems like almost all of it is useful for combat rather than just dungeoneering.

Or maybe that's just me.

Smirking to himself, Ryker finally felt like he wasn't stressing out. He'd met his foe and killed some of them. They'd been driven to ground and were even now trying to figure out what to do about him.

He had the high ground, he had time, and he had awareness.

And with any luck, Lauren is resting right now.

Time passed. Seconds became minutes.

Eventually, Ryker was starting to wonder if they were going to just sit there all day.

Then, slowly, a head began to rise from behind the log.

It was the helmeted head of the last of the soldiers, who had apparently been ordered to take a look.

Slowly, the soldier peeked up over the top of the log, seeming poised to duck back down at a moment's notice if it saw anything it didn't like. Wide eyes were visible behind the full helmet, eyes that seemed to be trying to see everything possible.

Slowly, the helmet turned one way and then the other. Inspecting the entirety of the path ahead and the brush to each side.

Ryker remained absolutely still. He knew he was actually fairly well hidden, and that any type of movement would draw the eye toward him.

So… they're just hiding behind the log right now. Perhaps with a shield, if they survived the acid cloud.

Hm. I could kill him with a pretty easy-to-hit ice bolt. Or something similar, I guess.

But… I think letting him live for the moment is the better option.

The head vanished back down behind the log after being satisfied with whatever it had seen.

Or hadn't seen.

Several minutes went by with no new developments.

Once more, the soldier's head came back over the top of the log. Then they stood up.

Ryker did nothing still. He wasn't concerned with the soldier. He was primarily interested in the mage and the priest. Those two could give him problems.

A single soldier wasn't going to be anything that could trouble Ryker.

Crawling over the log, the man cautiously scooted to one side to avoid the pit trap, then slid over to Ryker's side of the barrier.

After looking around as if expecting to be immediately attacked, the soldier waited.

Watching, Ryker did nothing. He was entirely content to sit and watch, waiting for his real targets.

Moving to the three corpses, the single soldier went to each one of them. Seemingly hoping to find one of them still alive.

Ryker was ignoring the man at this point and staring at the log. He was hoping the mage would pop up next. If he could take him out quickly and efficiently, everything else would fall into place without much effort at all.

A priest was no match for a wizard, nor was a soldier.

Ryker felt a strange tingling sensation building in the air. Tilting his head to one side, he tried to follow the mana currents and determine what was happening. With how small of a magical well he'd had, Ryker had trained himself to be sensitive to mana.

The current in the air was changing. It was moving behind him, further down the path.

Frowning, Ryker dipped his chin down slowly and then turned his head, doing his best to limit his movement but gain some vision.

He was starting to greatly regret that all the Imps and Fairies had ended up in either Adele or Diane's pack. Having such a limited dungeon sense without a core nearby was starting to really annoy him.

There.

Ryker could see the where the mana was pooling together. It was all congealing in one area. There was no pattern to see, which meant it was more of an end state than a starting point.

Looking back at the log, Ryker began to study it as closely as he could.

Can he perhaps see from somewhere I can't? Could he be looking at a spot he thinks I'm at?

Beyond that… could I track the flow back to him?

Closing his eyes, Ryker focused on the spot where the spell was building behind him and began trying to work it backward. He knew he could do it with his dungeon sense, so why not without?

Slowly, he began to follow what felt to him like a slightly thicker concentration of mana. It weaved its way through the trees around Ryker, through the brush, over the log, and then sharply to one side.

He's right there then?

Opening his eyes, Ryker looked at the spot where the mana terminated. Vaguely, he could just barely make out what might be a small gap between the log and the ground. Small enough that if one were desperate, he might see through.

Let's… just… try.

Forming a slim disc of super-condensed air and sharpening the edge, so to speak, Ryker wedged it into the hole. Then he activated the spell before the man could react.

With a detonation, the log exploded out in every direction.

There was a scream, followed by a massive outlay of mana in every direction.

Targeting the single soldier—who was now sitting on his rear end staring at where the log had been—Ryker flung a rod of ice at the man.

It speared him through the middle of his spine and blew out through his chest.

There was a gory mess around the man now as he slumped to one side and fell over unmoving.

Slowly, the unending waves of mana ended and everything went silent and still.

Building a shield in front of himself, Ryker reinforced it several times and then began walking over to see what he could.

As he passed by the quickly cooling corpses of the four soldiers, Ryker felt his heart hammering in his chest.

Reaching the remains of the massive log, Ryker looked into the mess on the other side.

The mage was there, and very dead. Half of his head had been crushed inward by a chunk of wood.

Lifting his eyes, Ryker looked for the priest.

He wasn't far away, laid out on his side near the edge of the road. His chest was rising and falling, and he appeared to be recovering from the lightning bolt.

One more to go, I guess.

Stepping over the mess of wood and the very dead mage, Ryker kept his shield up as he got closer to the priest.

Getting close enough, Ryker kicked the priest in the ass just to see if he was doing anything at all.

The priest grunted and rolled further away from Ryker.

Huh. Let's get some answers, then.

Detaching the shield and turning it into a bowl-like shape, Ryker set it over the priest and began to press it down.

Shrieking, the priest flipped over and the hood over his face fell away.

It was a priestess, not a priest.

Staring into her visage, Ryker felt a strange sense of familiarity. She had dark eyes, black hair pulled back, and a darker complexion than was completely normal here.

"Oh," he said after a few seconds. He finally recognized her. It was the same agent he'd let out of Dungeon. She'd been running information back to Lauren, and he'd gotten her out by pretending she was his personal whore. "Looks like I saved your life only to take it later."

"Count?" asked the woman through chattering teeth. The shield was pressing her down into the dirt rather roughly, not to mention that she was recovering from the lightning blast.

"Yep. Tell me what's going on, quickly," Ryker said, pushing on the shield for a moment.

As she groaned under the pressure of the shield, the woman's face paled and her eyes widened. She nodded her head rapidly.

"He was a bishop," the woman said. "The mage, he was a bishop, he was running the spell. A champion recruited all of us to hunt down the queen. I didn't have a choice in it. After my last run-in with a champion back in Dungeon, I joined the clergy. I didn't want to be here. I didn't want to be in the church anymore. But I couldn't leave."

"Tough shit," Ryker said, then pushed on the shield again, crushing the woman into the dirt.

Moaning, turning her head sideways, and looking like her whole body was being flattened, the woman squeezed her eyes shut.

"Are more coming? Was this the only team? How'd they track us?" Ryker asked once he'd eased up on the pressure.

Whimpering, the woman shuddered uncontrollably.

"There's another team; we were both sent out to track the queen. They followed a different path with the champion than we did, but we realized later that they followed it backwards. The wrong way," said the priestess. "They're probably two days behind us! That's it! We were following the queen by magic. That's it. It's just a spell. The champion cast it and taught the bishop how to cast it."

"Hm. Suppose I need to prepare for another team then," Ryker mused aloud.

"They're a bigger team. They thought they had the right path. There's twenty of them," offered the priestess.

"Oh? Huh. Thanks for that. I'll make this quick for you," Ryker said.

Lifting his hand, he rapidly built up an ice spear pattern.

The priestess turned her head to the side again and began to sob softly.

With a grimace, Ryker hesitated for a moment.

In the back of his mind, he saw a blue-eyed deity. One that had judged him but had given him a second chance, even though he hadn't deserved one.

"You wanted out?" Ryker asked.

"Yes," murmured the woman.

"Renounce your god and m—"

"I renounce Rannulf and all that he is!" shouted the woman. "I curse him and spit upon his very name. He's brought nothing but pain and death to everyone around me."

There was a pop, and the necklace the woman wore cracked in half and fell away from her.

"Huh," Ryker said. Canceling his spells, he sighed. "I'm sparing you. Because many people deserve a second chance, so you're going to get one. You can thank the deity of Dungeon for this. And Robyn. Fucking goodie-goodie that she is."

"What…? You're letting me live?" asked the woman, staring up at Ryker.

"Yeah, I am. Don't make me regret it," Ryker said, then started walking away. He needed to find Lauren.

Chapter 33 - Crazy -

Walking down the path, Ryker felt exhausted. After having run for so long carrying Lauren on the air spell, and then ambushing the trackers, there wasn't much left in the tank, so to speak.

Looking at the ground, he could easily see Lauren's boot prints as they stumbled and weaved their way down the path.

I have no idea how she made it this far from the capital, other than with sheer determination.

Following the trail, Ryker watched as it veered off the path toward a small trail that led off into the brush.

Must be looking for a camp site.

Walking along, Ryker was surprised when he found a sudden clearing. It was tucked away to one side, and quite hidden. Unless someone was looking for it or following a pair of boot prints, it'd be completely missed.

Wondering how she'd found it, Ryker looked around the clearing. It was small, but not too small. It was ideal for two people, a campfire, and their air mattress.

"Oh, thank goodness it's you," Lauren said from behind him.

Turning his head, Ryker found Lauren stepping out from a cluster of brush beside the path. A big rock was in her hand.

Damn, she could have brained me if she wanted.

Smart girl.

"I took care of that group. There's a larger group coming up behind that, though. Supposedly they're a day or two behind," Ryker said.

"Does that mean we get to sleep?" Lauren asked. Dropping the rock, she started to move back into the clearing. Her gait was wide, her steps uneven.

"Yeah, we get to sleep. I backtracked a ways and put in some trip-wire spells to notify me if people are on the path. We'll have about an hour's warning, give or take," Ryker said.

"You talked to one of them?" Lauren asked.

"Yeah. There was a mage, a priest, and four soldiers. I killed everyone but the priest. Priestess, that is," Ryker said. "Was actually the agent who came through Dungeon with information for you."

"Erin," Lauren said easily. Turning where she stood, she looked at Ryker. "Her name was Erin. She's dead?"

"Uh, no. I let her live. She told me everything she knew, and I don't believe she was lying at any level. Then she renounced her god," Ryker said. "So... I let her go. I didn't see the need to kill her and she'd already told me everything she knew."

"Huh, well, thank you for that. She wasn't a bad person, just one who worshiped the wrong god," Lauren said.

"Whatever, time for bed. I'm pretty tired," Ryker said.

"Great thinking. Come on then, time to sleep, hon. Wish I had the energy for sex," Lauren said, turning back to the floating bed. Without another word, she collapsed into the condensed air spell that she spent most of her time on. Before he even made it to the mattress, she was already snoring.

Smiling to himself, Ryker ran a hand through Lauren's hair. He could only hope he'd handle a situation as well as she did if the roles were reversed. Climbing into the spell next to her, he draped an arm around her shoulders and closed his eyes.

***

Two days after Ryker's ambush of the first group, they were practically back in the same situation again.

The team tracking them was moving faster than Ryker felt was possible. Or even fair, really. The distance had been brought down to within six hours of catching up to them.

"I swear," Lauren said. "I swear I'm going to start exercising every day. Practice running for hours at a time."

Ryker blew out a breath, jogging along the path. They'd moved so far south in their attempt to break contact and move further away that they'd ended up running up to the wall of Dungeon.

A path ran along next to it, leading all the way back home. But it also made them very obvious, if anyone cared to look in that direction.

He still couldn't feel anyone beyond the same muted and dull sensation. It was as if something had literally enclosed all of Dungeon.

"To be honest, if you have to do this type of thing regularly, we're really going to need to reconsider your Queendom," Ryker said. He was trying to conserve mana right now, so the option of utilizing the air-propelled mattress like a horse was out of the question.

He'd gotten lucky last time with his ambush; the simple reality was that the enemy had been rushing. They hadn't been paying attention or even thinking that Ryker might double back and attack them outright.

I doubt very much that this second group would commit the same mistake. I'm sure they're moving fast, but they're also probably screening for an actual ambush.

"...a very fair point, I suppose," Lauren said. "I should just move the capital to Dungeon. It'd be safer for me in the long run. That or you put a dungeon down right on the capital itself."

Put a dungeon on the capital...?

That's actually possible. I just have to make a bunch of cores and hand them out. Like Benni. Then just set up shop and make an active dungeon.

But the same thing could happen, couldn't it? Getting cut off like this and being unable to communicate with anyone.

Trudging along, Ryker's eyes kept being drawn to the wall next to him.

It looked colossal from the ground. Rising up far above him, it clearly wasn't going to be conquered by anyone anytime soon. It would take a massive amount of troops to do anything at all to it.

He'd even tried to get to the top of it with several blasts of air, but in the end he just hadn't been able to generate enough force to propel him that high.

And all it took to make the wall, keep it secure, and make it impossible to break, was to keep it connected.

A sudden thought blasted through his mind.

Could I do that with dungeons? Could I make a line of dungeons from Dungeon to Queensrest?

Ryker frowned, his thoughts rapidly spiraling out of control.

"What if I turned all of your domain into a dungeon?" Ryker asked. "Every inch of it."

"Could you actually do that?" Lauren asked.

"Probably. I'd need a lot of cores, but yes. I could. At least, I'm pretty sure I could," Ryker said.

"Then I'd tell you to do it immediately. If my domain was secured by my husband through one massive dungeon, I'd say I could easily hold even against the Dark Lord of the North," Lauren said.

Ryker winced at the mention of the black and red army that was even now growing larger and larger.

"I'll see what I can do," Ryker said. "And... what the fuck is that?"

Looking ahead, he could see what looked like a camp of some sort. It was fairly distant at this point, but there was no way to miss it. It looked like it could easily hold at least a hundred people, and it was entirely made out of tents.

"Looks like an outpost," Lauren said. "Church of light, maybe?" she asked. "They'd be the far more likely force to be down this way. Wouldn't they?"

"Yeah, they would," Ryker grumbled. He was now faced with an ugly choice. One that he was fairly certain didn't have a good answer either way.

"Do we continue to run from the wolf, or head straight into the lion's den?" Lauren said, voicing the problem for them. "And do we wait for nightfall, or do we rush in during daylight hours? Can we even wait for nightfall?"

"I'm not sure," Ryker said. "They're pretty close. I'd almost rather spend some mana and creep through their camp. If we're real lucky, it'll break the trail away from their tracker. Unless they're willing to go through the camp."

"That's... a good point. If they're following me, my exact trail, and it goes into that camp, what will they do?" Lauren asked

"If it were me, I'd loop around to the other side to try and pick up the trail again. I'd assume that you weren't caught but had moved through it," Ryker said after a moment of thought.

"Alright, do we go around it then?" Lauren asked.

"Honestly, I think going around would take just as long. Let's... go now. During the day," Ryker said. "And we'll just stay as close to the wall as we can? We could try an air burst as far as possible. See if we can't make it all the more difficult for them to find the trail."

"I don't have a better plan, and yours is workable and likely to succeed," Lauren said. "Your mind is a treasure and a wonder, hon."

Ryker slowed down to a walk and began building an air spell that would bend all light around them.

Before he finished it, he dropped a massive non-lethal mana mine. It was just a loud explosive noise. The fact that it was non-lethal would help obscure the ability for any mage to actually see it.

Then he activated the air spell.

Almost instantly, Ryker couldn't see.

"What'd you do?" Lauren asked. "I'm blind."

"Uh, sorry. Apparently light is required to see. One second, just... stay on the mattress," Ryker said.

Slowly, Ryker created a small porthole in the front of the spell and began to slowly let light in.

"Oh, I can see now. Somewhat," Lauren said.

Ryker could just barely see what was in front of them. It wasn't great, but it was enough to see where they were going. He started to jog again, feeling relatively sure there was no way they'd be seen now.

"Good work," Lauren said. "Your talent at wizardry is ever impressive."

"Lot of compliments from you. Did you do something wrong?" Ryker asked.

"No... no. Just trying to make sure I vocalize my appreciation. You're a good man, Ryker. I value you as... well, as my best friend as well as my lover, and husband, and confidant, and... I guess everything," Lauren said, her voice growing soft. "You're amazing. You've lived your life by your own rules, and you just push on."

"You going soft on me?" Ryker asked. They were getting closer and closer to the camp now. He was fairly certain they'd get through it easily, but he was still nervous.

"Maybe a little. Don't fault me for it... there've been few people I could unload everything to," Lauren said.

"Totally going to fault you for it. Your punishment will be carried out later tonight on your back," Ryker said, watching the camp.

"Oh. Consider me a villain then. A truly evil woman. Punish me a few times," Lauren said. "As much as I enjoy our banter, I think we should be silent now."

Agreeing on both accounts, Ryker fell silent.

Slowly, they ended up entering the camp. It was much larger than he'd originally thought. It went from the path to the plain beyond, and all the way to the wall.

It was a camp that was far larger than his expectation.

It wasn't until they passed the picket lines that he understood why it was so large. Or at least, why he assumed it was so large.

To him it looked like a secondary headquarters or fallback position for the leadership of the army. A secure position to work from if the front line fell away.

There were a number of elite soldiers here, a resource dump, and even some prisoners. Large tents that no regular soldier would ever have, and embroidery on the flaps that marked general ranks and priest's symbols.

Ryker frowned. He wanted to take this opportunity and make moves against the church of light. But he was leading the queen back to safety.

Anything he did here and now would endanger her. Which meant there was nothing he could do that would work out.

There was nothing he could do for anyone held prisoner—no soldiers, generals or priority targets he could kill.

No resources he could poison, set fire to, or spoil.

He had his job, quest, and duty—and it was Lauren. Everything else was secondary.

Moving through the tents as quietly as he could, Ryker was thankful that the vast majority of the enemy soldiers were out drilling in a yard. There were few people in his way. If he'd been forced to dodge and weave through tents, it would have been infinitely harder.

"…Claire. I'm Claire. I'm Claire. I'm Claire," said a voice from a larger tent as they passed. There was an edge to it. One that made the hair on the back of Ryker's neck stand on end.

He also immediately recognized the voice. A voice he hadn't heard in a while, but there was no way he'd forget it.

In that moment, he felt his heart lurch sideways in his chest. It was exactly who the person claimed to be.

Claire. His one-time wife who had tried to murder him and who'd been pregnant the last he'd heard.

Ryker would never admit it to anyone, but he couldn't deny to himself that he'd been somewhat infatuated with the woman. More even than he'd originally been with Diane or Adele.

So much that Wynne had often made fun of him for watching Claire whenever she was around. Like a dog on point, she'd called it.

Forcing himself to ignore Claire, Ryker kept going. He didn't want anything to do with her right now. Her parting gift to him had been a blade in his side with the intent to kill him.

"I'm Claire. She's not. I'm Claire. She's not. I'm Claire. She's not. She's not. She's not," Claire said, over and over. "I'm Claire. I'm his wife. I'm having his child. I'm Claire. I'm Claire. I'm Claire."

Chewing at his lower lip, Ryker slowly drew out of hearing distance. To his ear, it sounded like Claire was having a break from reality. A break from reality about who and what she was.

And more than likely, that was because he'd turned Shirley into her. Turned her into Claire, and gave Claire's identity from top to bottom. Even going so far as to claim Claire was an actual impostor.

Giving her Claire's life and stealing it all away from her. As if it had never been hers.

There was nowhere for Claire to go now. Veronica was likely in hiding just as Lauren was now, working to re-establish herself in whatever capacity she could.

The dark church was in charge of the country, and the church of light wanted to fight them for the Queendom.

Claire was little more than a once-useful piece that had outlived its usefulness. She was without significance or value now.

Moving out of the camp, Ryker started toward the wall. It didn't take long for them to get to the edge of the camp. Moving ahead, Ryker stopped at the point someone could get to where they'd be seen easily from inside the camp.

Getting down to one knee, Ryker began to build air spells that would blast force out behind them. Behind them and down at the same time.

He put them together in stages so that when one failed, the next would activate. And the next. And the next.

He kept working until his entire mana pool was almost spent. At that point, he built a spell that would slow them down. A massive column of air that was thickened and would slow them back down.

Then he was out of mana entirely. There was not a drop left in his well.

Turning, he reached out almost blindly. He couldn't really see where Lauren was.

"Oh! What… I don't think this is the time or place, hon, but I'm flattered," Lauren said when Ryker found her. He had found her chest first. "Well… maybe I'm a little interested. I'm curious to see what else you have in that mind of yours. Later though."

"Don't be a tease, sweetie," Ryker said. He was determined to hit her with his own nickname every time she used hers. His hands moved to her hips and took hold of her. "Grab the packs. We're going for an ugly ride."

"I'm not teasing. And I'm already wearing them," Lauren replied. "I wasn't sure what would happen, so I'm ready to run."

"Hold on then," Ryker said, dismissing the air mattress. Lauren dropped down in front of him and wrapped him up in a tight hug. "In three… two… one."

Ryker activated the first spell. With a sickening thump, Ryker and Lauren shot up into the air and forward at the same time.

I really hope the slow-down spells work. Really, really hope.

I can't afford to break a leg right now.

Pressing her face to his neck, Lauren clung to him. A small frightened squeak was all the noise she made.

With another thump, Ryker and Lauren went higher and much further through the air.

Then a third as the next spell activated. They continued to activate in order.

Reaching the ninth activation, Ryker knew they'd be on the way down now. There were no more.

Lauren's hands and fingers dug in tight to him as they started to fall. Faster and faster toward the ground.

A column of air came into being as the last spell activated. Ryker and Lauren crashed into it, hung there in the air, and began to slide down the middle of it.

The air felt disgusting to breathe, almost like he was breathing in something solid. It made his lungs hurt.

Except he wasn't willing to do anything to cancel or alter the spell. Not till they reached the ground. The moment they did, though, he cut the spell all the way down to a mattress of air again.

He rebound the spell in the same way the previous one had been, and then tied it to Lauren.

They were on the ground now, with no spells and no mana.

Ryker felt his knees wobble for a second.

"I've got you, hon," Lauren said, her arms locking tight to his middle. She was holding him upright. "I've got you. Let's just get you up into our bed, and I'll keep going. You rest."

He wanted to argue, but he knew she was right. Even he couldn't fight the fact that he was absolutely spent for the moment.

"Thank you, love you," Ryker muttered as Lauren wrestled him onto the bed.

Dropping him atop it, she let out a breath and then put her hands on her hips.

"I love you too," she said, then nodded her head at him. "You rest. I'll take the lead for now."

Turning on her heel, Lauren began marching away. Slowly, she built up to a very slow jog.

Ryker slumped into the air spell and stared at the sky up above him.

His mind slowly turned to Claire.

He hadn't seen her, but based on what he'd heard, she wasn't doing very well.

The mother of his unborn child sounded like a crazy person.

Fucking great.

Ryker sighed and put his hands over his face.

A minute later, he fell asleep without meaning to.

Chapter 34 - Family -

Jerking awake, Ryker looked up at the purple sky above him. It was full night. Which meant he'd slept all the way through the afternoon and evening.

When he lowered his gaze, he found Lauren ahead of him. She was trudging along at a determined and steady pace.

Her mentality is way too strong. If she were someone other than a queen, like a warrior, I think there would be few who could fight her without losing something of themselves.

Shaking his head, Ryker got off the mattress of air and moved up to Lauren.

Before she could react, he scooped her up off her feet and turned around to the air spell.

"Wha—? Ryker? What are you doing?" Lauren asked tonelessly. She sounded beyond exhausted to him.

"Giving you a chance to sleep," Ryker said, then dropped her onto the air mattress. "Now sleep. Is there anything I need to know before you drop off?"

"Out of water," Lauren said, her eyes sliding shut. "Was a giant boom back the way we came earlier. Made my ears ring. Maybe two hours ago."

"How long have you been walking?" Ryker asked.

Except there would be no response coming. Lauren was already asleep. Her mind had shut down almost as soon as her eyes had closed.

Damn. Okay, so… that boom must have been the spell I laid in the ground.

Which means they could still be behind us.

Really depends on whether that camp was able to catch them or not.

Then again, they might have been strong enough to beat the camp.

Muttering under his breath, Ryker took up where Lauren had left off and started walking along.

Searching along the wall for any hint of his Fairies or Imps, Ryker found nothing.

It was a dead wall with absolutely nothing there. Nothing there, and a whole lot of mana rushing off toward Dungeon.

Which meant things were still happening, but the city was probably closed up tight.

And here I am, walking along while being chased down like a worm.

Doesn't matter how strong a wizard I am if I can't plan and prepare. Doesn't matter that I run a dungeon if I can't build anything.

Grinding his teeth back and forth, Ryker could only blame himself. He'd gotten overconfident and believed he was untouchable.

Unassailable.

That so long as he remained in his dungeon and used avatars, no one would be able to touch him.

Shaking his head, Ryker focused all that anger into his steps and the slightly chilled night air.

Hours later, as the sun began to crest the horizon to the east, Ryker got more answers than he'd ever wanted to have.

At some point, perhaps after the camp they'd passed, they'd moved into enemy lines. Well and truly behind them, in fact.

Off ahead and to the left, Ryker could see the actual front line of the church of light. They were already set up for the day, staring out across a field at an equally set-up and ready army of the dark church.

To the right, he could see where Dungeon would be. Out in front of it was a secondary force. It was arrayed out facing Dungeon and the dungeon exit.

Whatever his people were doing, it had the church of light on edge and ready to defend at a moment's notice.

It also meant that Dungeon was technically under siege.

Thank heavens for the dungeon, then; otherwise it'd be unlikely the people could hold out.

"Where are we?" Lauren murmured from behind him.

"Oh... not far from Dungeon. The problem is there are two armies right over there, both looking for you, and a smaller army between us and our destination. Also probably looking for you," Ryker said, nodding his head. "I currently have us mostly hidden, but that won't do for much more than where we are.

"There are random clouds of magic popping up all over, both to spy and kill. They're quickly being countered by the light church, but they're still happening."

"My poor country," Lauren said softly. She sounded pained. "I can only begin to imagine how this will impact my citizenry."

"More so when you begin to consider that Dungeon is acting as a stranglehold for both armies. They'll not receive supplies they can't get in country," Ryker said. "We'll have to figure out how we supply the citizens and your soldiers who have remained loyal out there without adding resources to the enemy."

"Oh heavens, and... and shit. Shit, fuck. Shit, fuck, cock, balls, asshole," Lauren said, her voice growing heated and angry.

"Wow, I think that's more than Diane knows," Ryker said, glancing over his shoulder. "I'd love to hear you say other things, though. Maybe tonight?"

Lauren was propped up on the mattress, her mouth pursed in a frown and her face a scowl. It wasn't directed at him.

When she looked at him, her brows drew down.

"Ok, that's funny and tempting, but right now I'm just a bit more angry than eager for you," Lauren said.

"What if I promised to get curious with you?" Ryker asked. "There's a whole lot of things I could do with you. Or to you."

After having experienced Adele, Diane, and Shirley, he had a fair idea that the females of the nobility had more than a passing interest in sex and what one could do.

Lauren's face turned a faint red. Then she broke down and laughed softly. Pressing a hand to her eyes, she shook her head.

"I hate you so much. Alright, so... what's our plan then? You always have a plan," Lauren said, not removing her hand from her face.

"Honestly... I don't have one," Ryker said, looking back ahead of himself. "We've got... a lot of bad-lands to cross. And the moment we're spotted, you better believe they're going to collapse on us."

"Yeah... yeah, they will," Lauren said.

"So... yeah, I don't know. I mean, we could just sit here and wait for things to happen. I have more than enough mana to keep us tucked away to one side and invisible. Out of harm's way," Ryker said. "Wait for something to happen that we can work with."

"That sounds like the best option so far," Lauren said. "And you can manage it without having to do anything extraordinary?"

"Yep," Ryker said. "There's just one problem with that, though. I'm pretty sure those trackers are still back there."

"What? They are? How?" Lauren asked. "Can you be sure?"

Sighing, Ryker turned and looked back the way they'd come from. Throughout the night, he'd dropped small trip-wire mines that had done absolutely nothing. Other than alert him that they were broken, disabled, or failed.

They'd begun going away fairly steadily, and with an increasing speed throughout the night and morning.

"Same as ever. Warning spells that let me know how far off they are," Ryker said. "I think they're about an hour out, but I guess we'll find out soon enough."

"Which means we really only have about an hour before we're forced to make a choice."

"An hour," Lauren said.

"An hour," Ryker agreed. "Except what probably woke you up was a horn. A horn that I'm almost positive was the 'prepare to charge' horn."

"To charge?" Lauren asked.

"Yeah, to charge. Like that the church of—"

There was a short blast of a horn, and the church of the dark began marching forward. The light church responded with two quick blasts of a horn, but they didn't move to engage their foes.

An inexorable sense of dread and death began to spread over the entirety of the surrounding areas.

No one actually wanted to fight, least of all the soldiers who would be doing the dying.

But everything was well beyond that point now. There were no other options left, since the Queendom was now defunct as a country.

"What do we do, Ryker?" Lauren asked.

"We wait, as long as we can. Then we move forward, I guess," Ryker said. He didn't have another plan. He still couldn't feel anything of the dungeon. Not a bit of it. Which meant that until he was in the dungeon itself, he was unlikely to contact anyone.

"If we wait too long, couldn't our trackers catch us?" Lauren asked.

"Yeah," Ryker agreed with a sigh. "Yeah, they would. Suppose we should start forward now. We'll just… creep along the edge and—"

"Ryker, I see them," Lauren said, interrupting him.

Turning his head, Ryker looked at Lauren. She was looking back the way they'd come.

In the distance, he could see a group of people, perhaps ten strong, sprinting forward straight at them.

Damn.

"Fucking great," Ryker muttered, then looked ahead again.

The two churches were engaged in combat now. Both lines fighting one another, and both sides dying. Except the church of light was being pushed back. Their line wasn't buckling or breaking, but definitely moving.

Right into the path that Ryker would have to take to reach Dungeon.

Shit, damn, fuck.

Moving at a jog, Ryker started heading straight into the fray of battle. It was now or never. With any luck, he could keep the invisibility spell working. At least enough that people wouldn't pay them any mind.

And if they could lose the trackers in the press of battle, all the better.

Play one against the other, just like we always have. Play it like the dungeon. Lead them into risk and reward, and leave it to them.

"Ryker!" Lauren hissed.

"I'm getting you home, one way or another," Ryker said, and then he ran them straight at the church of light line.

Heading right for the point where the lines met at the extreme flank, Ryker skirted around them. They were close enough that he could actually feel the spray of small bits of things bouncing off him.

It was unnerving.

He couldn't tell if it was dirt, armor, blood, or something else. He just knew they were way too close, yet he probably should get them even closer. Close enough that he could slap one of the soldiers on the shoulder.

Gritting his teeth, Ryker kept them as close as he dared while he ran down along the flank of the army.

He dodged to one side as a woman in full plate armor collapsed in front of him, and he nearly tripped over her.

Damn, this is fucking risky. Why the shit am I doing this?
I should just be trying to kill Rob or something.
Shouldn't I?

Finally, he made it past the mass of combat and began turning around the back end of it. Running up along the rear of the church of light's forces. He needed to stay close and in their lineup. It'd make it almost impossible for the trackers he hoped.

It'd also probably help disguise him from anyone looking. Either side might view him as some sort of scout or something.

Or so he hoped.

Running along, he constantly had to shift to the right as the line was forced further and further from the front.

What the hell is going on up there that they're getting shoved this hard? Shouldn't they be more evenly matched on a soldier-to-soldier basis?

Ryker had to practically dive to one side to avoid a massive soldier tumbling backward. An arrow had somehow managed to slip between the cracks in his armor and found a home in the space between his helmet and breastplate.

He wasn't quite quick enough, and Ryker ended up having the man's elbow smash into the top of his foot.

There was an ugly crunch, and pain traveled up his leg. Forcing Ryker to practically hobble along instead of run.

Hopping on one foot away from the battle, Ryker fit a band of force around his foot to lock it in place.

It wasn't going to solve the problem, but it might give him enough time to get Lauren squared away. That was his most fervent hope right now.

Not bothering to check it since it didn't matter, Ryker put his weight back down on the foot and started running again.

He heard a single grinding noise from his foot, and then he was able to run on it again. It didn't feel right and it hurt like nothing else, but he could move.

Giving up on being so close, Ryker turned toward the backfield in earnest now. He headed straight for the large force arrayed out between him and Dungeon itself.

His first task would be getting through the support group that was working between the two forces. It was full of magic users, priests, and all sorts of other things he wanted nothing to do with in any way, shape or form.

All of them would happily murder him and take Lauren for themselves. She'd become little more than a puppet or a piece on the board.

Or a corpse.

Moving as quickly as he was able, Ryker started to skirt wide around the group, but not far enough away that it looked like he was completely avoiding them.

Mostly so it looked like he wasn't about to have a head-on collision with them.

And that was if anyone even saw him or was paying him any attention at all.

It wasn't until he practically overtook them that something changed.

There was a mad clatter and racket from behind him. It sounded almost like spells detonating, or at the very least being activated.

Glancing over his shoulder, Ryker found that the entire tracking group was bearing down on them. They'd be on him in minutes. They were being chased by people from the church of light, and the casting group was directing fire their way.

Except that the wizard in their group was clearly punching out runes as fast as they were heading their way. It was very clear to Ryker this person had an extreme amount of experience.

Looking ahead, Ryker could see now that the group in front of Dungeon was turning his way. There was no possibility of getting through now without being seen.

Their options had just dwindled to nothing.

Turning, Ryker faced Lauren, and the air spell practically delivered her into his lap.

"Ryker, I'm so sorry," Lauren said, floating in close to him on the spell. "I'm so... so sorry. I love you."

Ryker smiled at her and then gave her a kiss. He'd come to a decision.

It was just a pity he couldn't join her. There was simply no way he could build the spell he wanted without being outside of the construct itself.

At the same time, he built a large spherical spell that would encircle her. Around that he built a cushion of air that would activate itself once she was airborne. Then he put one on the inside of the sphere so she wouldn't end up getting flung about.

Creating a sizable chunk of mana, Ryker attached it to the large spell that was filling in around Lauren.

Atop it all he dropped an obfuscation rune that'd prevent the rune from being punched out easily, or at all.

Pulling away from the kiss, he sighed.

"I love you, too," Ryker said. "Think fondly of me if I fuck this up and don't make it home tonight."

"What? I don't under—"

Judging the distance and angle along with how much force he'd normally put behind an earth attack, Ryker felt like he'd gotten everything right.

Lauren's voice was cut off as Ryker smashed a force construct to the back of the spell and launched Lauren like a damn stone toward Dungeon.

He heard her shriek fade into the distance as the glowing sphere that was Lauren arced over everything toward Dungeon.

Spinning and tumbling, she soared through the air.

The sphere started to lose altitude and slowly tumbled back down toward the ground.

With a strange bounce, the sphere hit the ground thirty feet shy of the entrance to Dungeon. Then it bounced back up into the air, still heading for the gates.

Amusingly, it came to a rolling stop just as it passed through. Lauren had made it to Dungeon.

Sighing, Ryker canceled his partial invisibility spell and looked to the support group nearby.

He was about to do something he'd been cautioned against, warned of, and physically threatened to be beaten by his father if he ever did it—but Ryker felt like he had no choice.

His mana was low. Low and not going to refill on its own. Not to any extent that he could fight his way free with.

Targeting the closest six people who looked to be using mana-based magic, Ryker built up a small spell that would leach away their mana. Leach it away and feed it back to Ryker.

The problem was that the spell was obvious. If the opponent could get ahold of it and overpower the original caster, it would be very easy for them to reverse the flow.

It would go from a drain to a feed. The spell also heavily favored the target, since they had the pattern right there in front of them.

But Ryker truly believed he had no choice.

Activating six copies of the spell, Ryker hoped against hope. It was the best way for him to refill his pool and give him a fighting chance, if not an edge.

The casters were so engrossed with the tracking team heading their way that they didn't even seem to notice their mana spilling away.

Not wanting to waste the opportunity, Ryker began to build up an arsenal of spells in front of him. It was similar to the way he'd supported Shirley, but this was entirely put together for himself.

He began to modify, add, and build the patterns, adding mana at a slower rate than he was receiving it. If he did it just right, he'd drain the six completely while wasting no mana at all.

Suddenly, the casters began to drop to the ground as their wells emptied.

When the sixth hit the ground, Ryker let out a breath and looked to the tracking team. They were only twenty feet away now, though they didn't seem as hellbent on reaching him.

Not that he could blame them; the queen was gone. Their losses were for naught, and all that greeted them was a wizard behind enemy territory.

Taking the initiative, Ryker slapped his lightning bolt spell and sent it zipping toward the enemy.

It crackled as it struck the wizard in the hooded robe in the front of the group and leapt from him to the soldiers all around them.

With a shriek and a cry, half of the riders around the wizard fell to the ground, twitching and shivering.

He parted it. He parted it?
Was it a shield? A spell? Did he partially knock out one of the runes?
Damn. I didn't even see them move.

The remaining soldiers broke away from the robed and covered wizard to rush the support group. In seconds, both sides were locked in a struggle to the death, both forgetting Ryker and this other wizard.

"Well then, come on," Ryker said, standing there. "A wizard duel it is."

"Boy, you have no idea what kind of trouble you've given me," said an older man.

Ryker felt the breath rush out of him.

He knew that voice.

Knew it with a certainty. There was no need for the man to reveal his face.

"I'm going to kill you, son," said the man. "Then I'm going to torch your city and knock it to the ground. Say hello to your mother for me when you cross over."

Tight, perfectly formed squares began to form in front of the other wizard. Perfectly built patterns that looked identical to Ryker's in every way.

Except there was no way it could be his dad.

He was dead. Very dead.

Dead and long since gone.

Then the lightning spell crackled to life and zipped across toward Ryker.

And suddenly every memory of being punished came roaring back to the front of his mind.

Chapter 35 - Waits for No One -

With little more than a stray thought, Ryker punched out the rune without even looking for it.

He knew the spell. Knew it and could trace it with a single finger while underwater and blind. It was the same spell he often used himself. It wasn't his own creation.

Wasn't even his father's creation.

The spell was snuffed out as if it'd never been there.

"Look at you," said his father. "You didn't even take the time to break the whole spell. You just hit the rune. That's sloppy. Sloppy and incomplete. It's like training you all over again."

Growling, Ryker threw together a molten comet of iron built off a rune for fire rather than earth or metal. Bringing it all together into a small neat package, he slapped it back toward his dad.

"Oh?" said the robed wizard. His head tilted to one side as the ball of death sped his way.

The entire spell winked out two seconds later as if it had never existed. Apparently the black cowl did nothing to hinder his sight.

"You see? That's how I taught you to do it," said Ryker Senior. "It leaves no room for it to be rebuilt upon."

Fuck.

The exact same spell he'd just used was now coming back at Ryker. Except the rune center was obstructed. He couldn't see it no matter which way he looked at the pattern.

Diving back into lessons he'd long since deliberately forgotten, Ryker tried to peel back the whole pattern.

What Ryker called punching out the rune was the last step in his father's process of canceling a spell. It provided the actual result that was being looked for, but it didn't actually get rid of the spell.

If someone were quick enough and close enough, or just powerful enough, they could recover the spell and rebuild it. That meant it was more or less a moot issue because no one could rebuild a spell further than ten feet out. Ryker's simplification of the whole thing down to punching out the rune had made it quicker and easier.

Peeling the pattern back itself took considerably longer, and Ryker hadn't ever truly had the patience for it.

Seconds before the screaming ball of molten iron goo struck him, Ryker broke the pattern apart completely. Just as his father had done.

"Hmph. Well done," said his father. It was probably the first time he'd ever heard the man give him any type of praise before. "Time to die, son."

Spells began to fly towards Ryker now, one after another.

Fireballs, lightning bolts, arrows made of acid, ice spears.

Anything and everything he'd ever heard of as a combat caster, and quite a bit he'd never thought of.

Working furiously, Ryker peeled back patterns as fast as he could. If the rune wasn't obscured, he wasn't above just punching it out either.

A fireball slipped through his guard and zipped past his shoulder, missing him by a scant inch.

Struggling to break down all the spells, Ryker managed to barely fashion a functioning shield in front of himself at the same time.

While this was all happening, his father remained utterly still. The people who had made it this far with him hadn't been idle either. They'd been singlehandedly butchering the support group as if it didn't exist. These people were experts in their fields.

Grimacing, Ryker knew he needed to take up a different tact. The spells kept creeping closer to him, and he wasn't getting rid of them any faster.

Think, think, think!

Yes, father taught me a lot, but not everything, right?

Thinking back to his time under his instructors, Ryker couldn't think of any way to actually counter the spells.

But he did think of a possibility to redirect them.

Using a force construct of mana, Ryker batted three spells away with a swipe and sent them hurtling toward his father's minions.

A woman in leather armor was struck with a ball of molten iron and went down shrieking, and another person was hit with the other two spells.

Ha! Two down, and it worked.

Holding tight to the mana construct, Ryker began to bat the incoming spells away in between picking them apart.

Ryker wasn't his father. His father had far more patience, experience, and control to rip the spells out from their roots.

Soon enough, the dark church elites were forced to pull back behind Ryker Senior. The spells heading their way were simply too many for them to not keep taking losses.

Suddenly the assault stopped, leaving Ryker in the lurch of waiting for the next attack.

Almost immediately, the spells started up again, except from different angles and directions, and never one after the other.

Now they came erratically. Randomly.

There was no pattern to any of it.

It left Ryker scrambling to knock the spells away, punch out runes, or rip out the patterns completely.

More and more, they began to slip past his defenses and detonate on his shield, or the ground around him.

Then the spells stopped again.

Panting, Ryker stood there, blood dripping down into his left eye. At some point, something had hit him in the brow. He'd thought nothing of it, but now it made sense that he couldn't see as well as he thought he should.

Across from him, his father stood untouched. He looked quite statuesque right now. An imperious figure staring down at a bug.

All around them were the forces from the church of light. They didn't seem like they wanted to interfere any further in the fight, but they were also clearly building up their numbers to attack both wizards.

Pulling a potion out of his belt pouch, Ryker Senior reached up and pushed the cowl back from his head.

Most of the flesh on his face looked waxy. Waxy and stretched tight over his skull, without a single bit of hair on his head.

Upending the potion into his mouth, the man who had once been his father smiled at Ryker. The way his lips pulled apart on that twisted face looked far more like a grimace.

"Cute," Ryker Senior said. "I'm growing tired of this, though."

Flicking the empty vial to one side, Ryker Senior pulled the cowl back down over his head. At the same time, the remains of his elites started moving toward Ryker.

Glaring at them as they moved toward him, Ryker wasn't sure what to do.

Fuck me.

Fuck him.

Fuck that lady.

Fuck her especially, damn. Fuck her a few times. She's pretty as I've ever seen. Maybe I could capture her and —

A man in chain mail armor and a sword leapt forward at Ryker, his sword tip pointed forward.

Ryker let out a small air spell that knocked the blade to one side with his left hand; with his right, he punched an earth spell shaped as a dagger into the man's guts.

Before Ryker could finish the man or attack him again, a woman was advancing on him with a short spear.

Ryker took a step back and pushed his left hand out, a cone of fire leaping out of his hand for the woman's face. No sooner had she started screaming than Ryker dodged to the right and slashed out with his right hand, a sharpened spell of air slicing through the flaming torch that was her head.

A fireball smashed into Ryker's shield and sent him tumbling backward head over heels.

Getting to his feet, Ryker had just enough time to register that a man with daggers was in front of him before he was forced to act.

Detonating the mana-construct spell he'd been holding on to in front of the newest attack, Ryker was launched backward again.

Groaning, and feeling like his head was ringing, Ryker struggled up to his feet again.

The incredibly beautiful woman was coming toward him now. She had a long sword in hand and was advancing rapidly on him.

Feeling petty and stupid, Ryker clapped a ball of mana-locked force around her, then slammed the spell into the ground. She was instantly buried as if she had never existed at all. The earth swallowed her whole.

Not wanting her to suffocate before he could come back, he pushed a small air circulation spell into the sphere and then had the whole thing feed off the mana in the earth around her.

When he looked back to his foes, he realized he was about to pay for his stupidity.

A massive ball of lightning crashed into his shield and sprayed out in every direction, making the world crackle and hiss.

Ryker once more went spinning and rolling across the ground.

Not bothering to get up, Ryker just lifted his head and then his right hand.

Spears of ice shot out as he rapidly cast spell after spell at the elite soldiers heading his way.

They began crumpling to the ground as the mana-propelled projectiles simply passed through their bodies.

In a single breath, they were all dead and gone. Leaving Ryker with his father once again.

"You're not such a failure after all," Ryker Senior called distantly. He was much farther away now. Ryker had been knocked much farther than he thought he had.

"And you're not dead for some reason," Ryker muttered, getting to his feet slowly.

"Yes. I am dead," Ryker Senior said, apparently somehow having heard him. "I was brought back by my glorious lord Rannulf."

Wouldn't that mean you worshiped him to begin with?

Fuck.

Having made it to his feet, Ryker stood there, panting, bleeding, and feeling like he'd been kicked around by a giant.

"That all ya got, old man?" Ryker asked. "I remember you being a lot scarier when I was a kid.

"Or maybe that's all you're actually scary to. A kid."

Snorting at his own words, Ryker coughed, then hacked up a glob of something that didn't look like spit to one side.

Don't look at it. It's fine.

Wiping at his brow, Ryker only managed to clear his vision. He blinked several times and looked around.

The church of light soldiers were still piling up. Getting ever deeper. They were all waiting for a chance to simply attack.

Even if I survive dear old Dad, how do I get out of this?

Spells began to come at Ryker again. Spells that were overly complex to the point that Ryker couldn't even begin to break them down or apart.

Instead he formed a mana-force construct again, and readied it.

Then he began to bat the incoming spells to one side or another. Ryker didn't even try to read the runes. They were too much for him right now in his current state.

He wasn't just weakened, he was broken. Broken, bleeding, and falling apart.

Massive explosions of mana and elemental magic washed over Ryker from either side as the spells hit everywhere around him. The entire area became little more than a magical smoking crater in no time at all.

So much so that Ryker was forced to back up further. Lest he end up falling into a hole.

Smashing away a rather large ball of what looked fiery lightning, Ryker felt like his mana was draining faster than he really wished.

He wasn't even casting spells, but the sheer force of the spells being sent his way was immense. It was forcing him to actually reinforce the spell he was using as a club so it didn't break apart.

Much like previously, the spells cut away suddenly. As if they'd never been used at all.

Smoke and steam drifted away from the ground around him. There was even a lodged earthen mound off to one side that was smoldering.

Walking toward Ryker slowly was his father. It seemed like Ryker Senior were just out for a stroll and nothing was the matter at all.

When he got within ten feet, he stopped and began to build a pattern in front of himself. Ryker only knew that because there was an obfuscation screen up. It prevented him from seeing beyond it.

I don't think I could counter, block, or break something from that close. Neither could he though, right?

Snapping together a lightning spell, an ice spear, and a fireball, Ryker flung them at his father from three different angles.

Ryker Senior lifted his left hand and a shield appeared in front of him, which simply ate the lightning bolt.

The ice spear, however, came in from the side and simply passed through the man.

Unfortunately, the aim on Ryker's fireball was off. It clipped his father's shoulder and went spinning off into the distance.

It… went through him. It went through him?

His father seemed to be considering him and how to respond, while the spell acting as his screen was still being built.

As if they'd been waiting for this moment, the hordes of the church of light rushed in on them.

To be fair, even Ryker thought the timing was ideal. Two wizards only feet from each other and ignoring everyone around them as if they didn't exist in the least.

Panicking, Ryker clapped his hands together and a shield of solid force came to life around him in a sphere. There wasn't much in his mind that he could do other than this, simply because he didn't have enough time.

A crush of bodies slammed into him and his shield. It was more than enough to actually shift the entire spell construct to one side.

Then the other side was hit by the same wave of angry church soldiers.

The incredible amount of force being pressed against the shield was overwhelming. Ryker could feel his shield already starting to buckle.

Attaching a leaching spell to the shield, he had it begin feeding on everyone it was in contact with.

Soldiers dropped as what little mana they had in their bodies was whisked away. Everyone had mana in themselves—most just had a very marginal amount. Just enough to live and function. It wasn't enough to do anything with, and the effort it would take to drain it from someone would cost more mana than it would gain.

But working it like this, it was buying Ryker time. Time he desperately needed, and a slow trickle of mana that was outpacing his expenditure.

Swords flashed, daggers blurred, skills, abilities, and spells were used. A multitude of attacks came to try and break Ryker's shield.

I need to do something. I need to act. I can't just sit here and wait. I can't just let this keep going.
I need to act.
But how? I need more mana.
I need more mana.

Holding it for all he was worth, Ryker began to slightly alter his mana-leach spell. To drain away mana from people nearby, not just those touching the shield.

Once he fleshed out the pattern, he locked it into place and began feeding more mana into the shield.

He felt better, more secure. His well was filling up. It was slow, but it was filling.

Unfortunately, there was still no way out. No way out, and even if he did beat back this force of soldiers, what was to prevent the dark church from doing the same?

Nothing.

Nothing would prevent them. I'm a rock in an ocean.

Ryker briefly considered building some series of air spells that would propel him out. Just like he'd used near the wall to get over the camp.

Except he couldn't risk it. If he put together a spell like that and activated it with his father still there, he could easily knock the runes out.

And Ryker would come crashing back down to earth like a rock thrown into the sky.

Testing that theory, Ryker made a large chunk of earth magic, slapped an air spell on it, and hurled it toward Dungeon.

Before it had even gained enough altitude to clear the mass of soldiers, the spell was cut clean off it.

Ok, Father is still there. And watching. He's not knocking out my spell now cause he can't see it through the bodies.

What... else can I do then?

Ryker began to build another addition to his spell pattern. This time it would receive the strikes, blows, and spells used against the shield, and channel it into mana. All of that was redirected back into the shield, in effect, charging itself from the attacks against it.

I'm... ok. I guess.

Glancing down at himself, Ryker did a physical once-over.

His right foot was very clearly broken and looked rather bad.

Ryker's left leg had a deep gash that didn't seem to be actively bleeding, but his leg was coated in blood.

There was an arrow in his stomach, from when and where he didn't know, but it didn't seem to be killing him right this moment.

Holding up his hands, he looked over the rest of himself and then felt at his face. Everything seemed to be alright other than a very large cut in his brow that was still trickling blood.

Directed bolts of elemental water magic began coming down from above into his shield. They were indirect attacks, however. The force they struck his shield with wasn't actually magic. Nor did the water have any type of magic inherent to it.

Each attack drained more off of his well than he gained.

Time's up.

It's now or never.

Chapter 36 - Fire and Fury -

What do I have to work with? A full mana well and… that's it.

I don't even have a weapon. Hah.

No familiar. No friends.

Nothing.

I hope Lauren made it.

I hope Diane, Adele, and Rick beat the army here or are somewhere safe.

I hope Tar is okay and just went off to find a mate or something.

Closing his eyes, Ryker let his chin drop.

I wish I wasn't here.

Letting out a short chuff of breath, Ryker shook himself out a little. Trying to beat his brain around into the right mind-set. Unfortunately, that just reminded him of the arrow in his guts.

Ryker opened up his dungeon sense and started to build a lightning spell. The pattern he laid out was massive. It took up the entire space of his dungeon sense. It was a densely coiled and perfectly structured cube divided into four, rather than a flat plane.

Each surface of the cube had its own spell components. Triggers and functions that the spell would perform based on what it encountered and bounced to.

Winding in a deep and ugly leaching spell, one that would drain a mage in seconds if they didn't counter it quickly enough, Ryker tied it into the central part of the spell. He made it the rune that everything was based off of, because this thing had a job to do.

It needed to wipe out two armies. Wipe them out and somehow take out an undead master mage.

Coiling the pattern tighter, Ryker gave it an air element to help it get through the spaces between jumps.

He stuck the start to the end and gave it an on/off gate so it would cycle endlessly as long as it had mana to draw from.

Looking at himself, he saw that his soul had attached itself completely to his avatar body. It was as if it were his real body now.

On top of that, the bits he'd removed to fuel and empower his spells were healing. Clearly regenerating themselves and becoming whole again.

Let's… give this the best chance it has to deal with dear old Dad.

Breaking off a chunk of his soul, Ryker dropped it into the pattern and activated it.

With a massive crackling boom, the spell erupted out from Ryker's shield. Rapidly spiraling around him from soldier to soldier, the bright red and white bolt of lightning killed.

And killed violently. The spell actually exploded every time it hit someone, and more often than not whatever part of the body the spell entered in and exited from was turned to hamburger. Hamburger and bits of bone that went everywhere.

The spell was growing louder with each jump. The booms became deafening after the twentieth hop.

Covering his ears, Ryker realized he was on his knees. He felt sick to his stomach, and his world had a strange black-and-white shift to it at the edges.

Think I pulled too much soul out.

Maybe.

A woman in chain mail scrambled against Ryker's shield, as if she could get through it to safety. She looked panicked, her eyes wide.

Then the lightning spell hit her, and her entire body became chunks and a spray of blood.

Holy fuck. What'd I do?

Blood, bone, and meat were being thrown about as if they were nothing more than leaves in the wind.

The ground began to shudder with the impacts of the spell. Small craters were forming around the people hit now.

Soon, there was a large clear space around the shield. All that remained were bits of bodies and corpses.

Like a candle being snuffed, the noise, the spell, and lightning all stopped.

Lifting his head, Ryker looked around.

Not far off, he could feel a building pressure. Mana being pooled and spent faster and faster.

Slowly, he got to his feet and began shuffling forward. He was hoping it wasn't his father building a spell to crush him.

If it was, there was little Ryker could do right now. His mind felt like mush, his body was failing, and his soul felt injured.

On top of all that, his mana pool was severely depleted.

Ryker finally saw what was going on.

The lightning bolt spell had pinned his father to the ground and was draining him. Draining him faster and faster, even as Ryker Senior fought against it.

His mana well must be massive. Truly and frighteningly massive.

Having grown to the size of a Troll, the spell looked as if it might be large enough to blow up a city now. It had started as little more than a spark about the size of Ryker's pinky nail.

Fuck.

Growling, making electrical crackling noises, and sounding alive, the spell seemed hell bent on destroying Ryker Senior.

As if it were aware of itself.

Angry.

Screaming at the top of his lungs, Ryker Senior managed to push the spell away from himself with his mind and spell control.

Except there was nowhere for the spell to go now, except back to Ryker.

Damn. I didn't put in a safety at all, did I? That thing's goi –

With a boom that made Ryker Senior's body bounce against the ground and turned his chest and legs into meat, the spell screamed toward Ryker himself.

Shit oh shit oh fuck.

Scrambling, Ryker punched at the rune in the center of the spell.

And nothing happened. It was just too strong. The rune didn't budge, the spell didn't stop, and it smashed into Ryker.

Screaming as the lightning arced through him, Ryker felt like his body was going to come apart at the seams. Like his arms and legs would simply come out and go flying off in different directions.

There was a presence in the spell. An angry and hungry one.

Grabbing at it, at the part that had once been part of his soul, Ryker jammed it back into place. Pushing the spell's core into the spot the soul energy had come from.

With a roaring sound, the spell fought him for a millisecond and then slammed itself home into the place it clearly felt it belonged. Ryker felt a sense of completeness from the entity that had become the spell, and then it vanished as it reincorporated into his body.

But now there were mountains of mana ripping through Ryker's well with nowhere to go. Stolen from the dead and Ryker Senior.

The pattern hadn't faded at all. It still had all the mana it'd collected, and it still wanted to complete its purpose.

To jump, kill, feed, and jump again.

Feeling like his skin was on fire, Ryker needed to get rid of the mana immediately.

Now.

Before he went full magical burnout and became little more than a torch.

Building a pattern for an air burst under his feet, Ryker pushed off and shot upwards.

He streaked into the sky like a flaming comet as he worked to build a new extension to the existing lightning pattern. An add-on that would hopefully let him out of his own trap.

Soaring higher and higher, Ryker clenched his teeth together. His jaws ached from the pressure of it.

He felt like his skin was starting to crisp up as the mana overwhelmed him. Running free of his well and breaking it at the same time.

When he reached the peak of his flight, the point where he'd start falling back down, Ryker checked the pattern he'd been building.

It was a splitting spell. Several patterns that would provide a single function.

To take all the mana collected in the lightning bolt and redirect it into multiple targets all around him and a number of newer, smaller spells. To send it into the nearby soldiers and start all over again.

Though this time without the soul element that seemed to have put it into another category altogether. That piece of his soul that had gone out for a bite to eat would be staying with him.

Then he activated the spell.

With a monstrous boom, spells shot out from Ryker. The flames around him grew brighter even as he hung there in the sky. Multiple lightning patterns flew out in the air in every direction.

Screaming with the pain of the sudden outpouring and barely holding on to all the patterns at the same time, Ryker felt like his entire body would crumble before he could get all the mana out.

Then he was spent. With barely enough mana in his well to keep him conscious, the fire around Ryker went out and the lightning spells coursed toward fresh targets.

Letting out a shuddering breath, Ryker began to fall back toward the ground. Red and white streaks of magical bleed-off trailed behind him as he fell.

Scrounging up the mana somehow, somewhere, Ryker put together a tiny mattress of air beneath him and landed into it.

The spell gave out from under him as soon as it took the full impact from him, and then Ryker hit the ground from only a few inches up.

Groaning, Ryker lay there for several seconds. Then he remembered he needed to get up.

Get up and make sure his dad was dead.

Struggling to his feet for what he hoped was the last time today, Ryker groaned and trembled. When he looked down, only half the arrow in him remained. At some point, a large portion of it had broken away.

Grimacing, Ryker hunched over himself and then reached down to pick up a sword. There were plenty of them around him, and he had his pick of them all.

Ryker stumbled toward his father's body. He knew he needed to make sure the man was dead. He was practically a champion of Rannulf and needed to be returned to death.

Looking around as he got closer, Ryker could see the lightning bolts whipping around, jumping from target to target. Soldiers were dying by the score every second. Both those in the church of light and dark.

The lightning had no favorites to play, nor allies. Everyone was a target.

Grunting and then coughing several times, Ryker stopped in front of his father's body.

Turning his head to one side, Ryker suddenly threw up a considerable amount of blood. Followed by another fit of coughing.

I think I'm dying?

Yeah. I'm dying.

Fun.

When he turned his eyes back to his father, he saw no life there. The spell had caved in the man's chest when it went for Ryker. The man looked like someone had taken a giant spoon to him and pushed down in the middle.

Sucking on his teeth, Ryker lifted the sword and then hacked his father's head from his shoulders with three chops.

He flung the sword down to one side, then collapsed to his knees next to his father's corpse.

Reaching into a belt pouch, Ryker started looking for anything that might help him. Like a healing potion, really.

That was the one thing he desperately wanted to find right now.

I've been stabbed, shot with an arrow, knocked around, blown up, electrocuted, and set on fire.
I think I'm done playing hero.

"Ah," Ryker said, his somewhat limp fingers closing around several glass vials in the pouch.

Ryker pulled them out and looked at them with his one good eye. The other kept having blood run into it, so he was just keeping it closed at this point.

"I don't… fuck it, whatever," Ryker mumbled. He couldn't tell the potions apart. Their contents were all clear, and there were no labels.

Pulling the top off each one, he downed them all in succession. One after the other. After dropping the glass vials, Ryker sat down on his ankles and looked around.

His spells were getting really big again. They'd clearly been gorging themselves on the lives of the enemy.

Thankfully, he sensed no presence in any of them. That had been part and parcel to the piece of his soul he'd put into the spell, apparently.

Thinking about it, Ryker turned his thoughts inward while he waited for the potions to do something.

In his soul, he watched a change occurring. The fragment he'd put back in his attempt to survive the spell had fit in perfectly. It looked no different in its shape and size.

The color of it was a bright white, though. It also seemed to crackle with electricity. There was a slow spreading of that elemental energy throughout his soul.

It was moving slowly from one corner into the whole of everything. There was nothing Ryker could do about it, either. There was nothing he could feel there, nothing he could affect, and it was spreading so quickly that this would be done in a minute at most.

Watching it happen and wondering what it would do to him, Ryker waited.

When the elemental energy filled his soul, nothing happened.

There was no physical change, Ryker didn't die, and his mana well didn't explode.

Which had been a serious concern. His mana well had been terribly abused today. He didn't even want to look at it, because he knew he'd find it a fractured and tattered thing. It would take some time to get it to rebuild itself.

If it could rebuild at all.

Sighing, Ryker opened his eyes and looked back at his surroundings and the real world.

He sat amongst corpses, chunks of corpses, arms, and armor. Nothing had changed.

His lightning spells were storming to and fro, devouring people whole now.

Damn. I hope they don't escape this area. If they make it out into the world… that'll be a lot of dead.

As if in direct response to his thoughts, several bolts of lightning broke away from the army in a mad dash.

Heading straight for Ryker.

They were approximately the size of a house. Each one of them. And they were all filled to the brim with power.

Really?

Ryker hung his head and waited.

The lightning spells crashed into him, one after another, and the world went dark.

***

Opening his eyes, Ryker felt groggy. Groggy and insanely tired.

And in a lot of pain. So much pain that his eyes swam and he felt like he wanted to retch.

Pain is good, though. Wanting to puke is good.

Feeling like someone worked me over with a bat is good.

I'm alive!

Laughing softly to himself, Ryker tried to focus on his surroundings to figure out where he was.

When he lifted his head slightly, he realized he was looking up into the blue sky. But it was moving. Everything was moving.

He leaned his head to one side and saw a number of beautiful women, all of varying races. Looking the other way, he saw another group of them.

Fairies and Imps.

Looking down at himself, he could see where the broken arrow shaft was still sticking out. He was being carried on a tarp held between six pairs of hands. It looked like they were rushing him away from the field of battle.

There were no bolts of lightning rushing around anymore, and there were no soldiers visible.

Walking at a quick jog behind him was Shirley. There was a whirling vortex of angry spells circling her, and she looked like she would attack anyone that approached.

Her head was on a swivel, looking in every direction around herself.

She's protecting our butts.

"He's awake," someone said.

Shirley's head jerked toward him, her eyes seeking his out.

Then she gave him a brilliant and warm smile, her eyes crinkling. She shook her head once, as if to clear her thoughts, and looked back to everything around her.

"Put him back under," said a second Fairy. "We need to keep him moving. It's going to hurt him."

"I can feel him already," said a third. "The dungeon is waking up again."

The dungeon wasn't awake? What does that even mean?

The faint tap and pat of booted feet on dirt was replaced with stone.

Ryker was taken over the border of Dungeon, and the entry point of the dungeon's proclaimed territory as well.

A massive maelstrom of sound and magical power blew out from everywhere.

It was as if a giant stirred and had taken a deep breath. Mana rushed in a single direction, and the world went gray as the very life of everything was pulled at.

Like the Fairy or Imp had said. Something waking up from a deep and deadly sleep.

Then the sensation went away. There was a sense of renewal and growth. Like he'd slept on his arm, and he'd lost the feeling in it. Now the blood was rushing back in, and everything tingled terribly and actually hurt.

And Ryker felt it, the dungeon itself.

He also felt them. Felt them as they began to dash over and crowd around him in the dungeon sense.

His Fairies, his Imps.

His people.

Marybelle simply appeared in his mind, the woman's presence immediately filling his thoughts. He could feel her setting to work at doing things there. Doing what exactly, he didn't know, but he felt better immediately.

Wynne's presence fluttered over him and wrestled him into the dungeon sense. All the bindings and bonds he had through one and everyone were immediately reaffirmed by her. Reaffirmed, reinforced, and bolted down tightly. Wynne apparently wasn't taking any chances.

Then Robyn forcefully injected herself into his dungeon sense. Spreading herself out and around him as if it were the most normal thing in the world. She didn't blend his soul with hers, however, for which he was grateful.

There was a jumble of communication between everyone and everything. It felt like someone had pulled a blindfold off that Ryker hadn't even been aware he was wearing.

Closing his eyes, Ryker slipped back into unconsciousness and a dreamless sleep.

Epilogue

Opening his eyes, Ryker found himself looking up at the interior of his room.

Closing his eyes, he lifted his hands up and pressed them to his face.

"You're awake," murmured a soft voice next to him.

"I think so?" Ryker said aloud. His throat felt dry, his voice raspy.

"Here, take a drink, honey," Lauren said. "It's been about a day since the battle. It's morning."

That answered the first question Ryker wanted an answer to and was also the first request he had to give.

A hand pressed to the back of his head and lifted it up partially. What felt like the mouth of a canteen was pressed to his lips.

Drinking slowly, Ryker didn't feel quite ready enough to gorge himself.

"Before you ask, both armies retreated away from Dungeon after you... well, after you destroyed their front lines. The church of light has retreated to the west, the dark church back to Queensrest," Lauren said. "Though both are greatly diminished. There are no armies in the front of Dungeon, and for all intents and purposes, we're safe."

Ryker grunted even as he took another sip.

"Adele, Diane, and Rick all came in right behind you. They weren't far away but on the other side of the encampment. Once your spells... once they went away, they made a run for it," Lauren said.

Thank fucking goodness.

Or maybe thank Robyn's goddess.

You listening, Robyn's goddess? If that was your doing, thank you.

"...as if the dungeon went dormant the moment after you were cut from your body. Which... died... by the way. Wynne sealed it in a tomb as soon as it happened, but it rotted from the inside out. Without your soul to sustain it... it just turned to little better than dust."

Figures.

Ryker made a grunting noise, and Lauren let his head slide back down to the pillow.

"Nothing is going on here in Dungeon," Lauren said. "After you fell, Shirley and Wynne took over. They ran both Dungeon and the dungeon by what they felt you'd want.

"Everyone knew you lived, much in the same way you could feel them. Just not where you were. Apparently it was the intervention of a god. More of a divine curse, apparently."

"A curse?" Ryker mumbled, closing his eyes. "That seems... oddly specific."

"I spoke with Wynne about it, told her what we saw from our side. Benni confirmed it as well," Lauren said. "It was a curse, and it had been designed solely to separate your soul from your body. The goal was rather simple. Kill you."

"Well, no need to look for suspects. Church of light or dark, or both," Ryker muttered. "That's fine. We'll kill 'em all anyways and put your ass back on your throne."

A gentle touch to his brow was accompanied by a deep chuckle.

"I love you, hon. I appreciate your steadfastness for my crown. But... maybe we shou—"

"Put your sexy ass back on the throne," Ryker said.

"Yes, I hear you. But, please listen. It wouldn't be that b—"

"Bad to put your lovely rear back on the throne," Ryker said.

"You're not listening," Lauren said, her tone getting cross.

"If you want me to listen, you'll need to be my queen," Ryker said.

Scoffing, Lauren didn't immediately reply. Her fingers slid across his brow and then lightly began to caress his hairline.

"Okay... put me back on my throne, Ryker, Count of Dungeon. Though that'll make you the prince, or prince consort," Lauren said. "You're my husband, after all."

"I could argue I'm not," Ryker said, his mouth quirking up at the corners.

"Mmm, you could. You won't. You love me," Lauren said. "And it would hurt me terribly if you even hinted at not being my husband. You don't want to hurt me, do you?"

His smirk died on his face, and Ryker blew out a sigh.

"Obviously not if I sent your ass flying through the air like a damn bird to get you out of harm's way. Fine, wife, whatever," Ryker said. "Though with our luck, you're already pregnant. Didn't use protection, remember? Have fun fighting a war to get your throne back while full with child."

"Do you want her to be?" Marybelle asked in his mind. *"We could probably make it so that she would be. We couldn't prevent a pregnancy from happening, just make one happen."*

"Hello, good to hear from you; I missed you," Ryker said, ignoring her topic choice. *"I love you."*

There was a strange fluttering sensation inside his mind. Obviously he'd had an impact on the Hobgoblin with those words.

"I love you too. I missed you. Horribly. We were all terribly worried and frightened. We'll catch up later. You're missing the conversation with your wife.

"Do you want her pregnant or not?" Marybelle asked.

"Let it happen naturally or not at all," Ryker said, deciding.

"Good, because she's already pregnant," Marybelle said.

Ryker wasn't altogether surprised. Sex typically resulted in pregnancies.

"...wouldn't know what to do at that point," Lauren said with a sigh. "Though it'd be exciting to have a child. Claim my throne back, have an heir, and settle... everything."

"S'ok, sweetie," Ryker said. "I'll be happy to try every night till you catch a child just for the added challenge. Or the candelabra, if you prefer it."

"Hmph. You're back to being your normal self," Lauren muttered. Then a soft lingering kiss was pressed to his lips. "And I'm glad to see it. As for tonight, you're welcome to try, but I think you have a number of women all waiting to garner your favor, and I'll not be their roadblock.

"I'll have to begin negotiations with the other queen in your life, Wynne."

Ugh. That's not a good thing, is it?

Two queens...

"I've only talked to her a few times since we arrived," Lauren said.

Ryker cleared his throat.

She can probably hear you... Maybe you –

"And so far, she seems quite reasonable and lovely to deal with," Lauren said, ignoring Ryker when he cleared his throat. "She's already stated she only wishes to hold her sovereignty over the dungeon itself. Not the walls, or any other land it would move to further.

"Apparently her key focus is just making a useful dungeon, being with you, and ruling over the Fairies and the Imps."

Oh. Well... that's good.

"They get along quite well," Marybelle said. *"It was rather sweet. They were both terribly nervous to be alone with the other. They worked out pretty quickly that neither wanted any of the other's possessions and that... that was that, really."*

"Why is all this shit working out so well? I feel like it should all be blowing up in my face?" Ryker sent back to her.

"Because we're all talking? I mean, come on, my silly love. We all want this to work. And that happens by talking. Misunderstandings don't exist if both sides care enough to talk, dear," Marybelle said. *"And no, she has no idea Wynne can hear her. And Wynne is very much eavesdropping right now.*

"Oh, and by the way. It was Shirley who got to you first. On the battlefield. She rushed out and fought her way through before the lightning spells had even finished."

"...the surprise of my life. I had no idea she'd gotten so big. She was such a cute thing the first time I saw her. She's rather beautiful now," Lauren said, then sighed. "I'm so plain looking in comparison to them all."

"Uh huh. Can I... get up? Am I bedridden? Am I dying? Paralyzed? Am I going to pee blood?" Ryker asked.

"Huh? Oh! Oh. No. Everything is fine. You're probably just going to be weak for a while.

"The lovely Hob woman, Marybelle, took care of you with Robyn. They worked in conjunction. You're perfectly fit," Lauren said.

"Great. I need to take a shit," Ryker said. "You can keep talking to me as I do it, or you can wait for me."

"Uhm... well, I guess that doesn't matter much anymore, does it?" Lauren said. "It's not as if we didn't talk while we were going to the bathroom out in the wilds or in the room, is it?"

"Not really. You share something like that with something and the mystery kind of goes away. Was really surprising how much gas you have, though," Ryker said, pulling back the sheets. "And I never want to feed you another rabbit. That was awful and rancid every time."

Lauren laughed softly, then kissed him again.

"Yes, it really was, wasn't it?" she murmured.

***

Walking into his throne room, Ryker looked around. It was completely empty. No one was waiting to ambush him, and everyone seemed to be letting him get his bearings slowly.

He could feel Meino very close by, though. Perhaps waiting in her alcove.

Through his interactions with Marybelle, he got the impression there really was a number of people all wanting some of his time.

Easing himself into his chair, Ryker sighed and leaned back into it.

He heard the soft tread of a heavy foot heading his way.

"Hi, Meino," Ryker said, not bothering to look.

"Hello," said the Minotaur. She came to stand next to his throne, then slowly got down on her knees next to him. Her large eyes were at his level. "I missed you. I want to talk to you about what happened before you left, and how it made me feel. You can grab my chest while I talk if it helps make you less mad."

Turning his head, Ryker looked at the big Minotaur's face.

Grabbing her by a horn, he pulled her in close and kissed her. Pushing her head away afterward, he settled back into his chair.

It was weird kissing a Minotaur, but in the end, it wasn't terrible.

"Don't care. Talk to my wives. No more doing what you did, grooming, or playing with your chest till then. Anything else?" Ryker asked. After having come close to death so many times recently, his patience was extremely thin.

"Uhm, no. No questions. You're not... mad?" Meino asked.

"No. It was flattering. Well, a little weird, too. But no, not mad. Get outta here and send in my first visitor. I'm sure someone is waiting," Ryker said.

"Ok. I'm... I'm going to go talk to Lauren," Meino said, getting to her feet. Her heavy plodding steps carried her out the front door, past Robyn, and into the hall.

Stepping into the throne room, the slightly cracked paladin came walking toward him.

"Robyn," Ryker said with a smile. "The only reason I'm here is that part of your soul was still with me. It clung to this body even as my soul fled the field. I'm here only because of you."

Frowning at first, Robyn walked straight up to him. Getting down on her knees in front of his throne, she put her hands on his knees and stared into his face.

"Truly?" she asked.

"Yep. So, next time you want to blend our souls, just let me know and I'll help or... make it better... or... whatever. Ugh, weird conversation," Ryker said, grimacing at Robyn.

She snorted at that and smiled at him in return.

"Now?" she asked.

"What? I mean... sure. Why not. I'm not quite the same, though. My soul looks a bit... lightning-y," Ryker said.

"I noticed. It's fine. Now..." Robyn said, her soul moving toward his.

Before she could force it on him, though, Ryker grabbed her soul with his own and mashed them together.

It felt amazing, and it made his soul feel incredibly bright and warm. It was nothing like last time.

Then he did it again, and again, and again. He did it repeatedly until there was absolutely nothing left of her own soul, or his.

There was just them, in the middle.

"I... I need to rest," Robyn said, her cheeks flushed. "That was... far more intense. It didn't hurt this time either. It tingled and felt good, and... I need to rest. My heart is racing."

Robyn pressed a hand to her chest, taking deep breaths.

"I'm holding a service tonight. I'd like you to be there. My goddess asked for you as well," Robyn said, her voice soft.

"I'm sure she did," Ryker said. "I owe her a favor. I'll be there."

"Good. Be on time. Rike likes punctuality," Robyn said breathlessly. Then she simply vanished. Canceling her avatar.

Rike, huh? Alright.

"That was in poor form. You mauled the poor girl," Marybelle said.

"You're next when I catch you alone. I plan on visiting you today or tomorrow. Would you prefer it in your Fairy avatar or your real body?" Ryker asked, deliberately calling her Hobgoblin self her real body.

"Uhm. Ah... maybe... maybe in my Fairy... Fairy avatar, and then my real body?" Marybelle asked, her tone nervous.

"Ok. Anyways, I'm sure I have another visitor, so..." Ryker said, tuning her out.

"Next!" Ryker yelled.

The door swung open slightly, and Shirley peeked her head in.

Grinning, Ryker levered himself out of his seat.

He wasn't about to forget who had apparently rushed out into the battle to find him.

Shirley stepped into the throne room, looking very subdued. Her hands were clasped behind her back and she was slowly walking over to him.

Not making her take the entire initiative, Ryker started walking to her as well.

Shirley smiled at his approach and shook her head.

"Ooh? Getting up to meet me halfway?" she asked. "Feeling guilty about leaving your blushing bride behind?

"Trying her out in bed and then—"

Ryker shushed her by kissing her, wrapping his arms tightly around her. Pulling her in close to him, he tried to push her into his own body. Kissing her all the while.

Shirley melted into him, her hands clutching at his tunic.

Breaking the kiss much later, Ryker sighed and held her.

Without meaning to, he opened up his mana well and shoved it at her, almost at the same time she did the exact same thing.

Magic and mana spilled all over in every direction as their magical link was restored. There was a strange wholeness to himself in that moment.

"I hate using magic without you. You awful wretch. What'd you do to me?" Shirley said. "You're not allowed to ever leave again. It makes me sick to use magic without you."

"Likewise. It really fucking sucks. A lot," Ryker said.

Shirley nodded her head, then shoved at his chest.

"I'm going to go sit in my throne. You can get on your hands and knees and be my footstool," Shirley groused, pushing at him again.

"Oh, stop it," Ryker said with a chuckle. Then he sobered quickly. "I saw Claire. Well, I didn't see her; I heard her.

"I think... I think she lost her mind. I think the fact that you took her life and her name broke her."

"Oh?" Shirley asked, peering up at him. "Good. I hope she chokes on it. And if I get the chance, I'm going to steal away your child from her and raise it as my own. I'll take everything from her that she threw away."

- 204 -

That's... different.

Before he could ask more on that, the door opened again, and Adele, Diane, and Rick walked in. Shirley darted to one side, moving away from Ryker.

Adele and Diane were both all smiles as they headed toward him.

Rick looked bored.

"We've already met," Diane said before Ryker could even think to introduce Shirley. "And we've all already bonded as well. Forgive me for saying it with you right there, Shirley, but she's so much better than her sister in every way, Ryker."

"I know, and I agree," Ryker said, smiling at Diane. "It's good to see you."

Adele walked right up to him and hugged him tightly, pulling his head down into her shoulder.

"I missed you," she said, squeezing him tightly.

"Missed you too. Good to see you," Ryker said, hugging her back.

"Ryker! That spell you used. What was it?" Rick asked.

"Which one?" Ryker asked in return as Adele released him.

"When you became a giant ball of fire and shot lightning out," Adele said. "It was like something out of a book. Like a phoenix rising."

"...looked to be a soul construct and—"

"It was very impressive," Diane said, talking over Rick.

"...begin to understand it. What'd you do, Ryker? Was it—"

"I was able to follow some of what you did, but not the patterns," Shirley said with a sigh. "You'll have to show me what you did later."

"...built it so tight that it could do it. Ryker? What'd—"

"I could do that," Ryker said. He felt good.

Everything was coming together in Dungeon. His wives, his people, his friends were all here. *I need to find Tar, though.*

"UNCLE RYKER!" Rick shouted at the top of his lungs.

Turning his head, Ryker looked down at the red-faced kid.

"Sorry, Rick, didn't mean to ignore you. No, it wasn't a soul construct, it was a regular spell. But I did feed it part of my soul to power it," Ryker said.

The women in the room looked shocked at that.

He hadn't told Adele or Diane what he'd done. Only Lauren.

"Oh. Ok. Thank you, Uncle," Rick said, nodding.

"I ain't your uncle, kid," Ryker said.

"Sure you are, Uncle. And call me Al," Rick said, nodding his head still. "I like that better than Rick. Al."

Rolling his eyes, Ryker blew out a short breath.

"Right. Al," Ryker growled out. "Still pretending to be a kid?"

"For now, Uncle. For now," Al said.

Thank you, dear reader!

I'm hopeful you enjoyed reading Dungeon Deposed. Please consider leaving a review, commentary, or messages. Feedback is imperative to an author's growth.

Oh, and of course, positive reviews never hurt. So do be a friend and go add a review.

Feel free to drop me a line at: WilliamDArand@gmail.com

Join my mailing list for book updates: William D. Arand Newsletter

Keep up to date—Facebook: https://www.facebook.com/WilliamDArand
Patreon: https://www.patreon.com/WilliamDArand
Blog: http://williamdarand.blogspot.com/
My Personal Group: https://www.facebook.com/groups/WilliamDArand
Harem Lit Group: https://www.facebook.com/groups/haremlit/

If you enjoyed this book, try out the books of some of my close friends. I can heartily recommend them.

Blaise Corvin- A close and dear friend of mine. He's been there for me since I was nothing but a rookie with a single book to my name. He told me from the start that it was clear I had talent and had to keep writing. His background in European martial arts creates an accurate and detail driven action segments as well as his world building.
https://www.amazon.com/Blaise-Corvin/e/B01LYK8VG5

John Van Stry- John was an author I read, and re-read, and re-read again, before I was an author. In a world of books written for everything except harems, I found that not only did I truly enjoy his writing, but his concepts as well.
In discovering he was an indie author, I realized that there was nothing separating me from being just like him. I attribute him as an influence in my own work.
He now has two pen names, and both are great.
https://www.amazon.com/John-Van-Stry/e/B004U7JY8I
Jan Stryvant-
https://www.amazon.com/Jan-Stryvant/e/B06ZY7L62L

Daniel Schinhofen- Daniel was another one of those early adopters of my work who encouraged and pushed me along. He's almost as introverted as I am, so we get along famously. He recently released a new book, and by all accounts including mine, is a well written author with interesting storylines.

Runner is coming.

Made in the USA
Lexington, KY
14 March 2019